Kirby Manga Mania

VOLUME 2

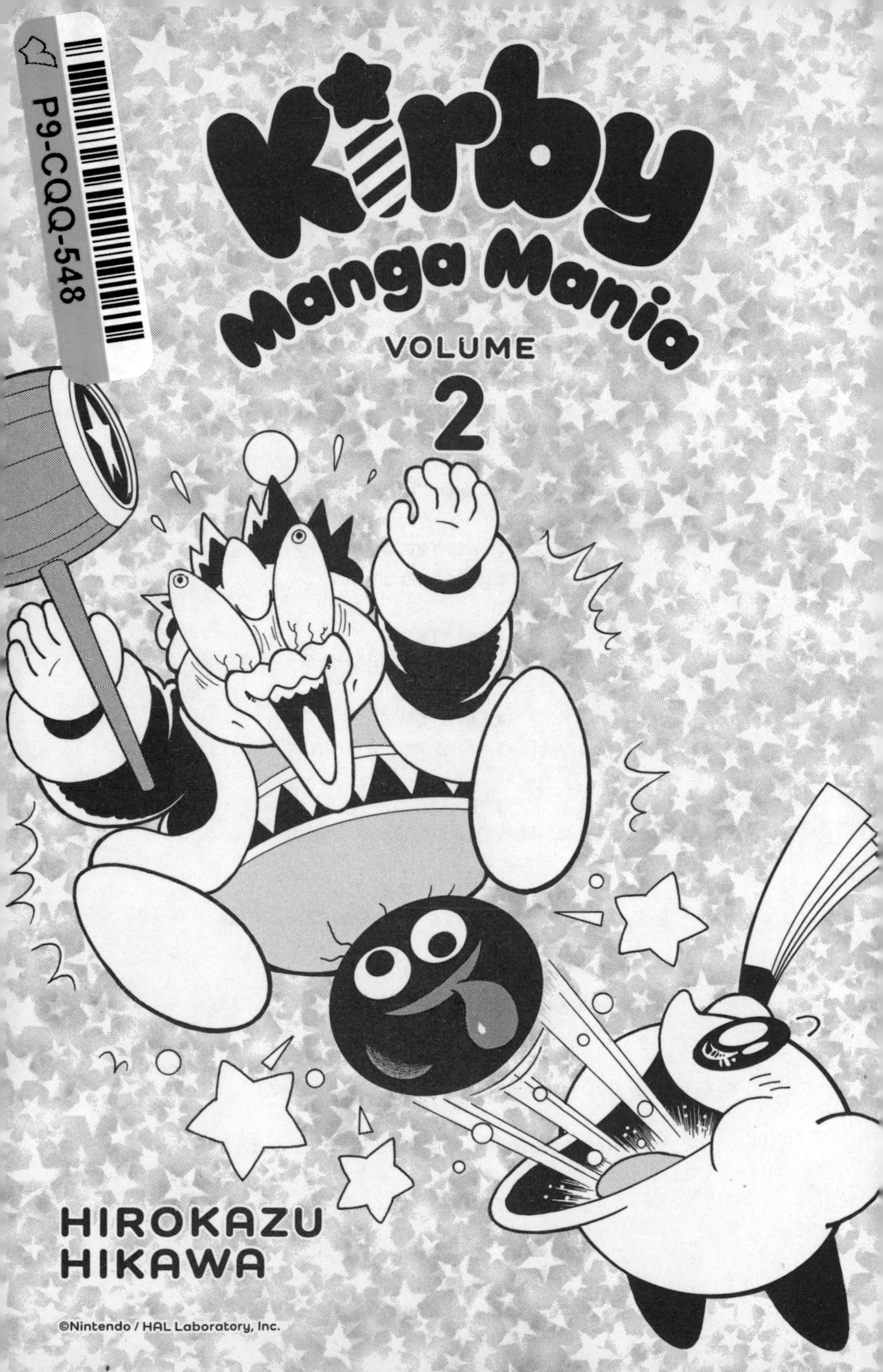

HIROKAZU HIKAWA

CONTENTS

CHAPTER 1
Everybody Wants to Be the King of Dream Land? 3

CHAPTER 2
Kirby Becomes a Walking Weapon?! 19

CHAPTER 3
Kirby, Volunteer Thief?! 35

CHAPTER 4
Hero Kirby Appears! 51

CHAPTER 5
Operation Kirby Secret Agents! 67

CHAPTER 6
Kirby Joins the Self-Control Dojo?! 83

CHAPTER 7
Go for the Gold! The Dream Land Olympics 99

CHAPTER 8
A Full Course of Table Manners?! 114

CHAPTER 9
The Start of the Eraser Shock?! 132

CHAPTER 10
Eye in the Sky Kracko Cracks Down on Kirby! 148

BONUS COMICS! 34, 50, 82, 98, 131

AUTHOR NOTE 157

CHAPTER 1: EVERYBODY WANTS TO BE THE KING OF DREAM LAND?!

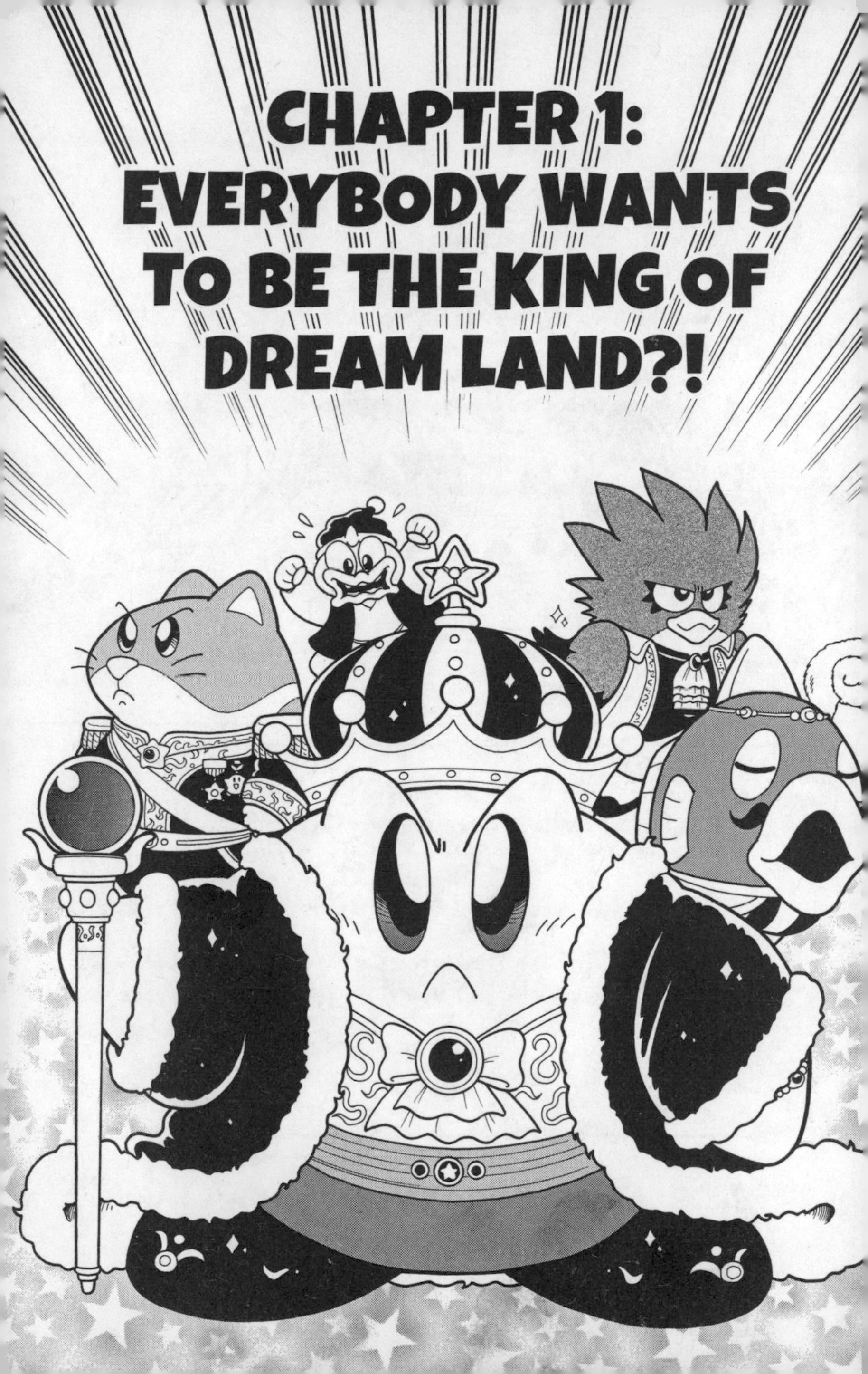

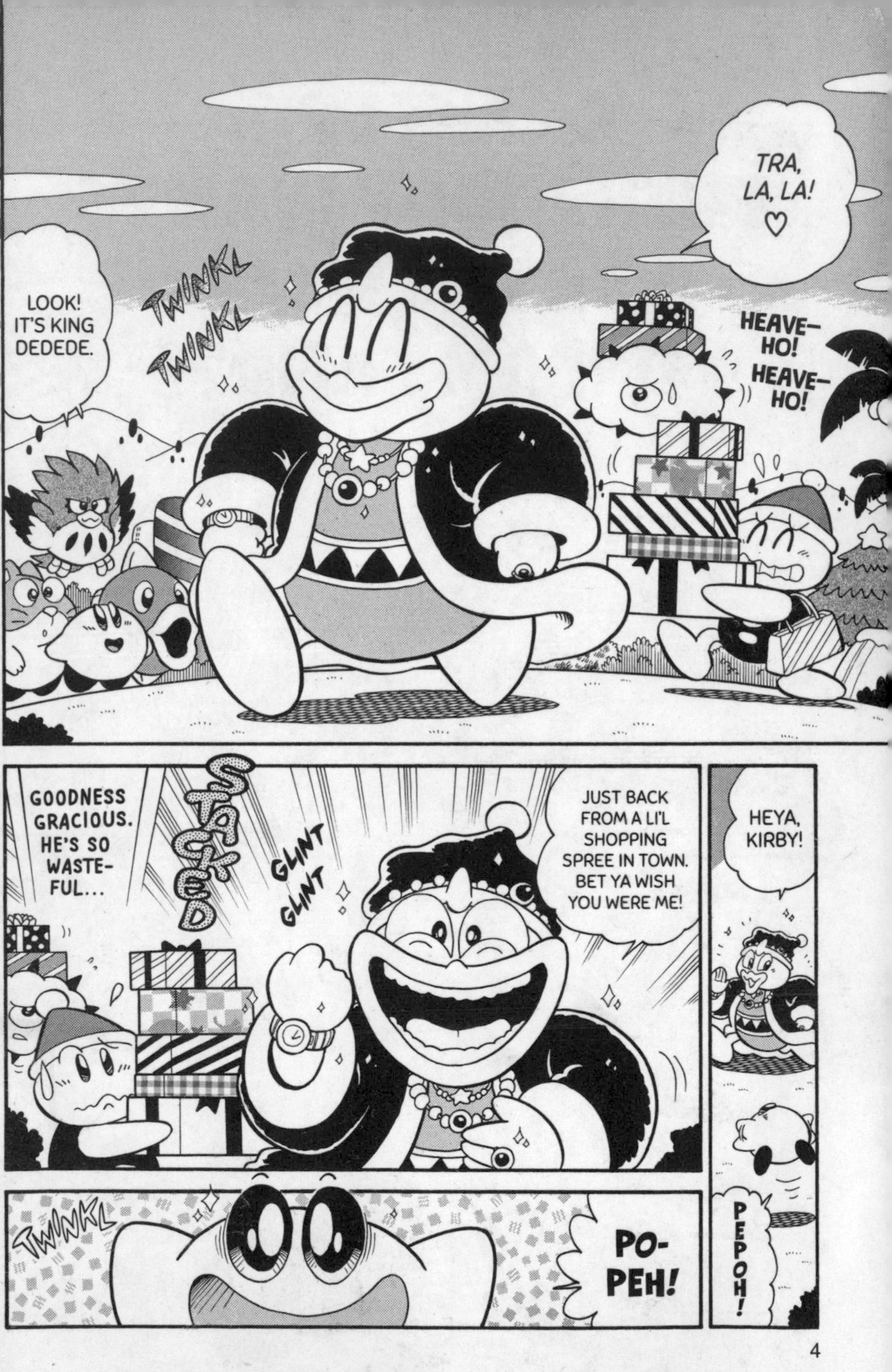
TRA, LA, LA! ♡
HEAVE-HO! HEAVE-HO!
TWINKL TWINKL
LOOK! IT'S KING DEDEDE.
HEYA, KIRBY!
PEPOH!
JUST BACK FROM A LI'L SHOPPING SPREE IN TOWN. BET YA WISH YOU WERE ME!
GLINT GLINT
STACKED
GOODNESS GRACIOUS. HE'S SO WASTE-FUL...
PO-PEH!
TWINKL

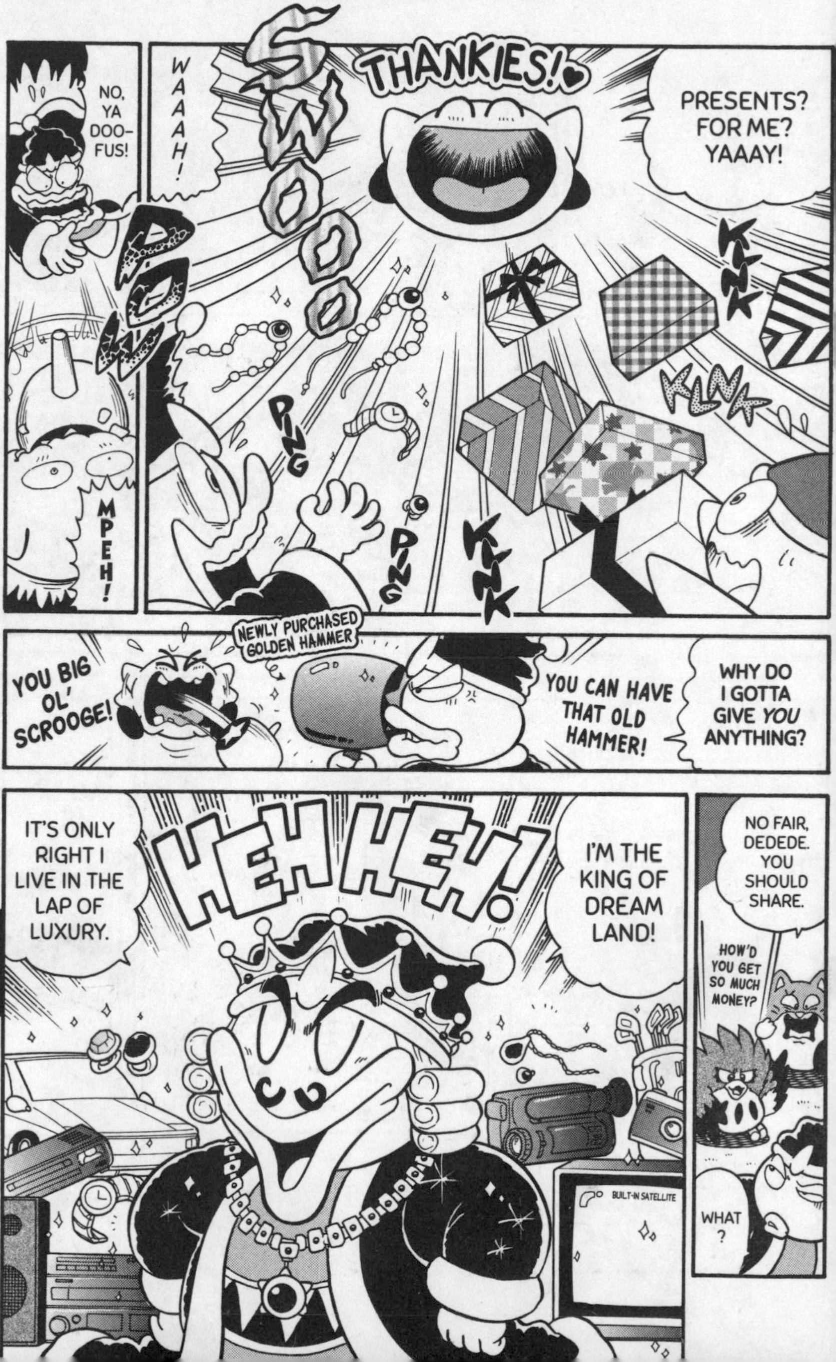
PRESENTS? FOR ME? YAAAY!
THANKIES!♥
KLINK
KLINK
SWOOOO
WAAAAH!
POW
PING
PING
KLINK
NO, YA DOO-FUS!
MPEH!
WHY DO I GOTTA GIVE *YOU* ANYTHING?
YOU CAN HAVE THAT OLD HAMMER!
NEWLY PURCHASED GOLDEN HAMMER
YOU BIG OL' SCROOGE!
NO FAIR, DEDEDE. YOU SHOULD SHARE.
HOW'D YOU GET SO MUCH MONEY?
WHAT?
I'M THE KING OF DREAM LAND!
HEH HEH!
IT'S ONLY RIGHT I LIVE IN THE LAP OF LUXURY.
BUILT-IN SATELLITE

AUTHOR'S COMMENT

I'M SO GLAD KIRBY MADE SOME FRIENDS! THIS IS ONE OF THE STORIES IN WHICH RICK, KINE AND COO PLAY A BIG PART.

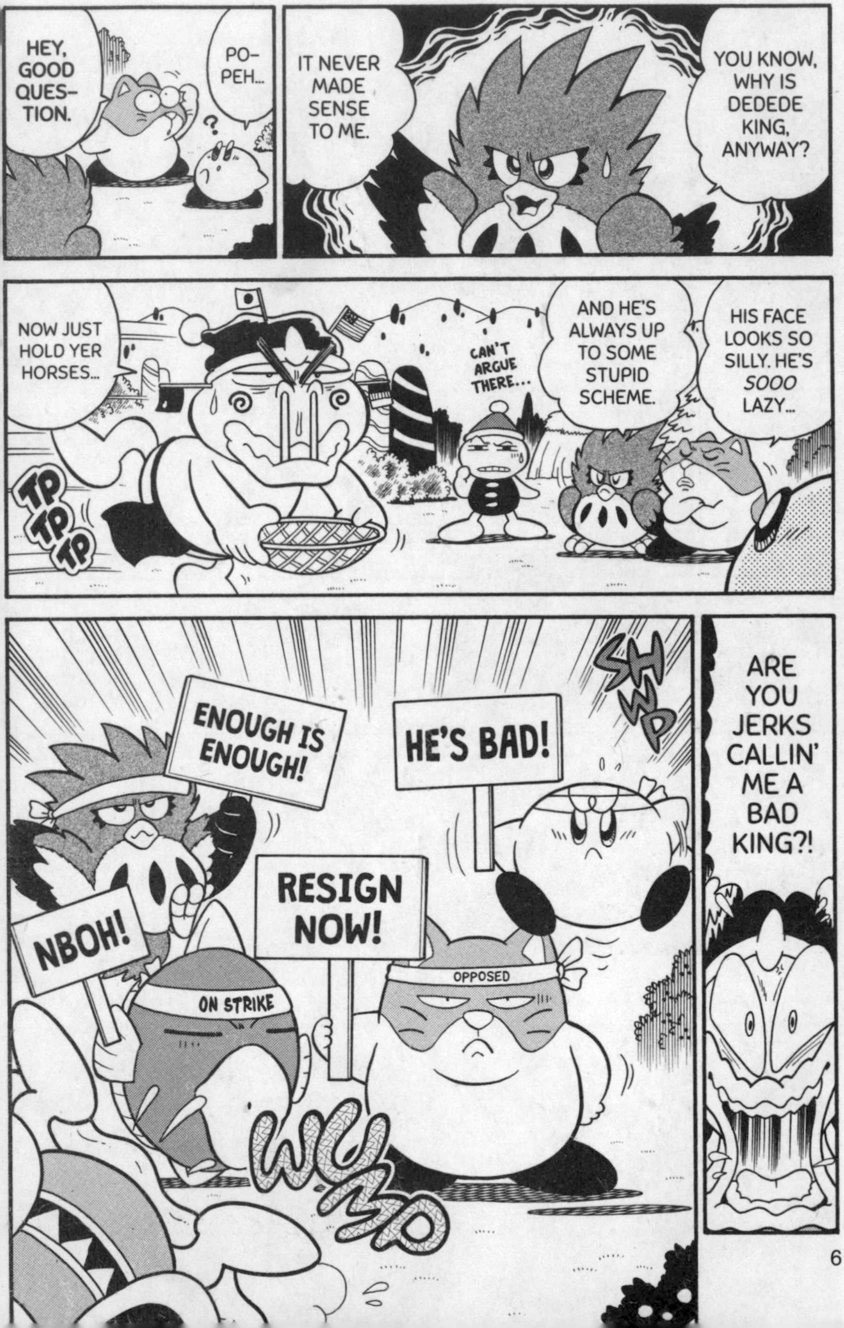

YOU KNOW, WHY IS DEDEDE KING, ANYWAY?
IT NEVER MADE SENSE TO ME.
PO-PEH...
HEY, GOOD QUES-TION.
HIS FACE LOOKS SO SILLY. HE'S *SOOO* LAZY...
AND HE'S ALWAYS UP TO SOME STUPID SCHEME.
CAN'T ARGUE THERE...
NOW JUST HOLD YER HORSES...
TP TP TP
ARE YOU JERKS CALLIN' ME A BAD KING?!
SHWP
HE'S BAD!
ENOUGH IS ENOUGH!
OPPOSED
RESIGN NOW!
NBOH!
ON STRIKE
WUMP

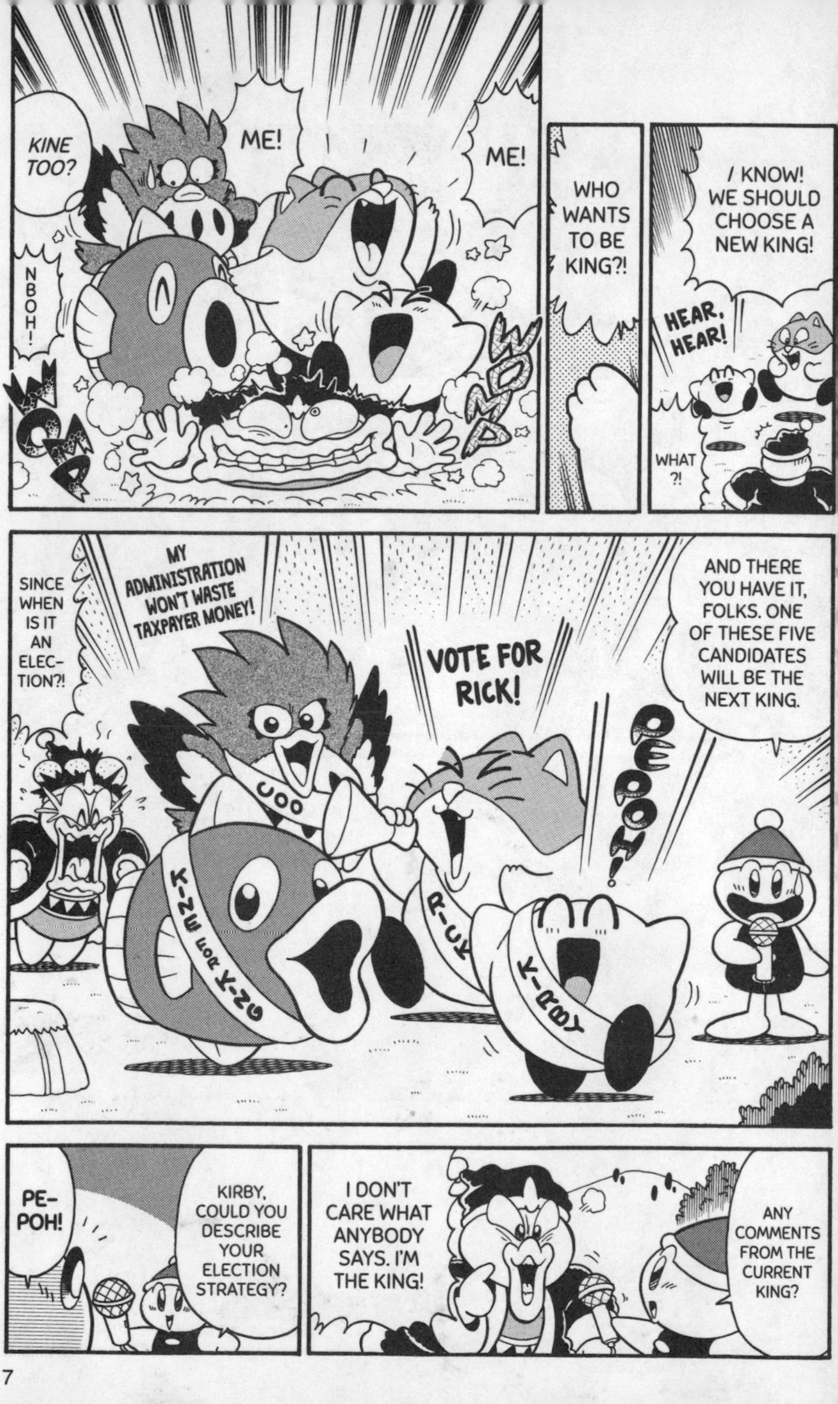
I KNOW! WE SHOULD CHOOSE A NEW KING!
HEAR, HEAR!
WHAT ?!
WHO WANTS TO BE KING?!
ME!
ME!
KINE TOO?
NBOOH!
AND THERE YOU HAVE IT, FOLKS. ONE OF THESE FIVE CANDIDATES WILL BE THE NEXT KING.
PEPOOH!
VOTE FOR RICK!
MY ADMINISTRATION WON'T WASTE TAXPAYER MONEY!
SINCE WHEN IS IT AN ELEC- TION?!
COO
KINE FOR KING
RICK
KIRBY
ANY COMMENTS FROM THE CURRENT KING?
I DON'T CARE WHAT ANYBODY SAYS. I'M THE KING!
KIRBY, COULD YOU DESCRIBE YOUR ELECTION STRATEGY?
PE- POH!

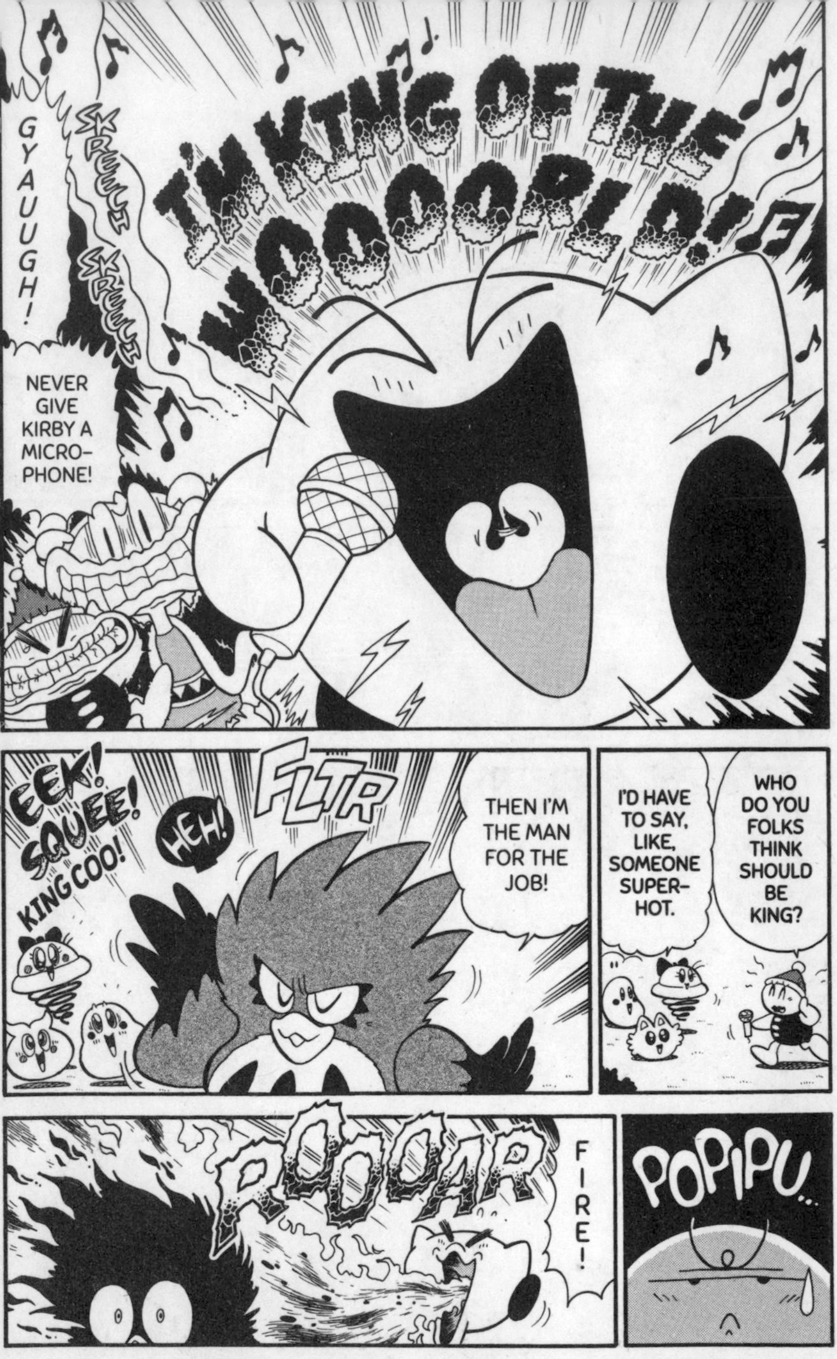
I'M KING OF THE WOOOORLD!
SKREECH SKREECH
GYAUUGH!
NEVER GIVE KIRBY A MICROPHONE!
WHO DO YOU FOLKS THINK SHOULD BE KING?
I'D HAVE TO SAY, LIKE, SOMEONE SUPER-HOT.
THEN I'M THE MAN FOR THE JOB!
FLTR
HEH!
EEK! SQUEEE! KING COO!
POPIPU...
FIRE!
ROOOAR

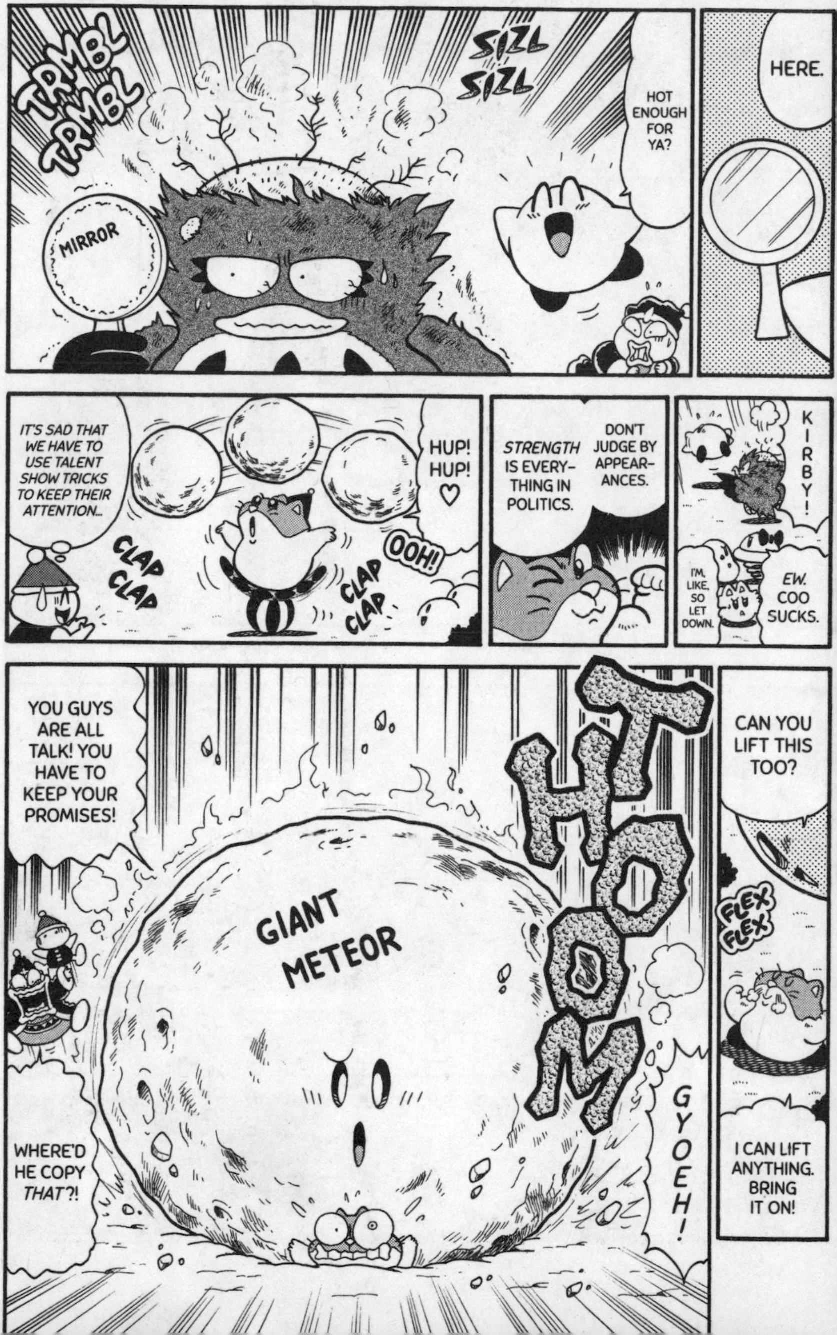
HERE.
HOT ENOUGH FOR YA?
SIZL SIZL
TRMBL TRMBL
MIRROR
KIRBY!
EW. COO SUCKS.
I'M, LIKE, SO LET DOWN.
DON'T JUDGE BY APPEARANCES.
STRENGTH IS EVERYTHING IN POLITICS.
HUP! HUP! ♥
OOH!
CLAP CLAP
CLAP CLAP
IT'S SAD THAT WE HAVE TO USE TALENT SHOW TRICKS TO KEEP THEIR ATTENTION...
CAN YOU LIFT THIS TOO?
FLEX FLEX
I CAN LIFT ANYTHING. BRING IT ON!
THOOM
GYOEH!
GIANT METEOR
YOU GUYS ARE ALL TALK! YOU HAVE TO KEEP YOUR PROMISES!
WHERE'D HE COPY *THAT*?!

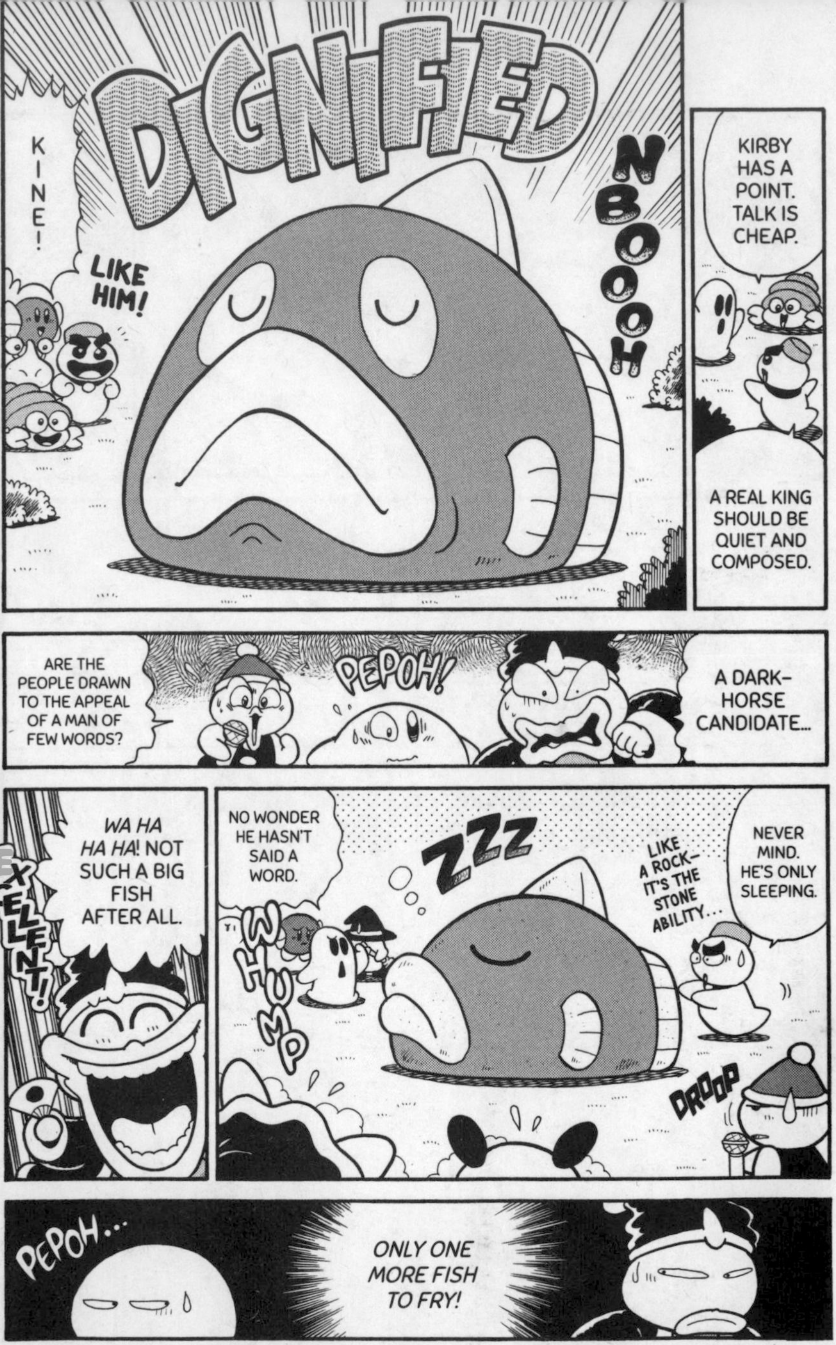
KIRBY HAS A POINT. TALK IS CHEAP.
A REAL KING SHOULD BE QUIET AND COMPOSED.
DIGNIFIED
NBOOOOH
KINE!
LIKE HIM!
A DARK-HORSE CANDIDATE...
PEPOH!
ARE THE PEOPLE DRAWN TO THE APPEAL OF A MAN OF FEW WORDS?
NEVER MIND. HE'S ONLY SLEEPING.
LIKE A ROCK—IT'S THE STONE ABILITY...
ZZZ
NO WONDER HE HASN'T SAID A WORD.
WHUMP
DROOP
WA HA HA HA! NOT SUCH A BIG FISH AFTER ALL.
EXCELLENT!
ONLY ONE MORE FISH TO FRY!
PEPOH...

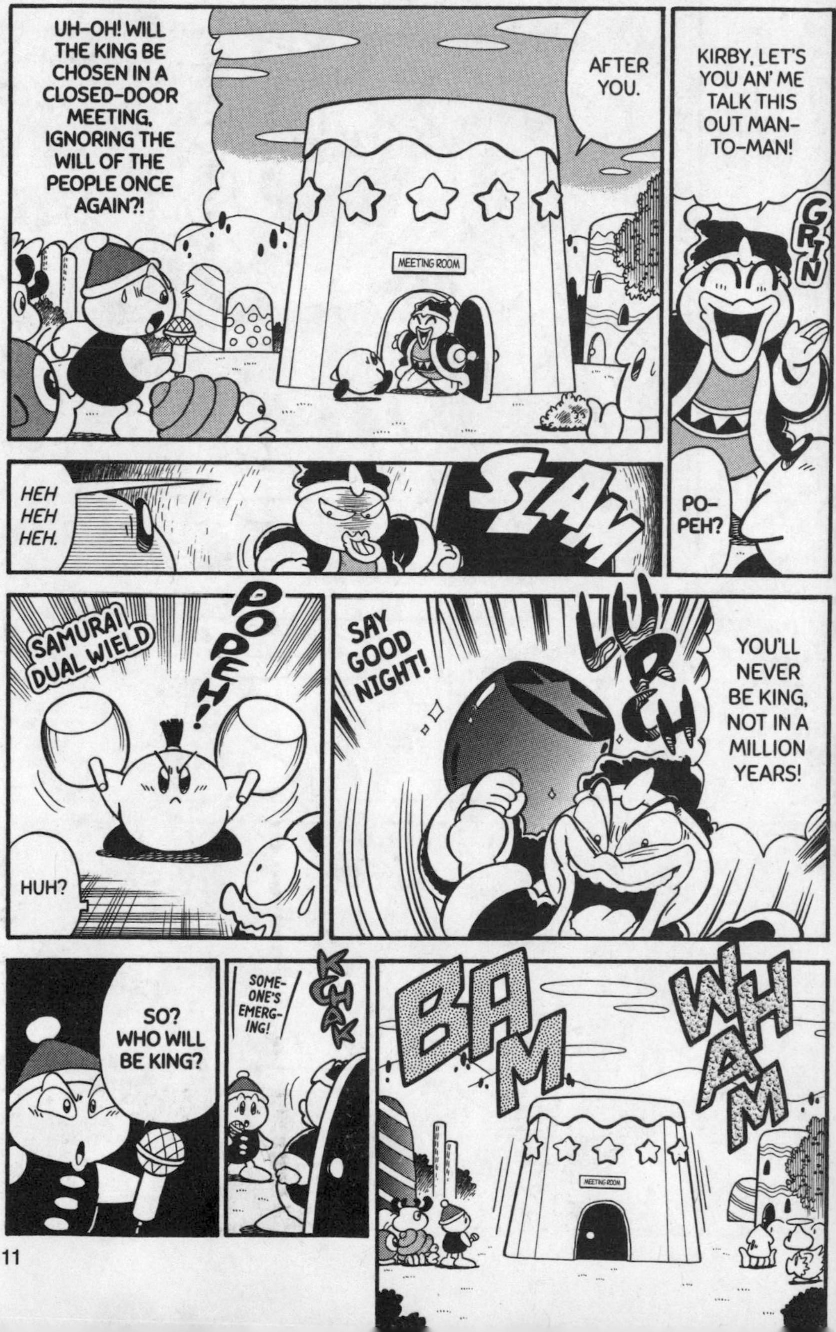
KIRBY, LET'S YOU AN' ME TALK THIS OUT MAN-TO-MAN!
GRIN
PO-PEH?
AFTER YOU.
UH-OH! WILL THE KING BE CHOSEN IN A CLOSED-DOOR MEETING, IGNORING THE WILL OF THE PEOPLE ONCE AGAIN?!
MEETING ROOM
SLAM
HEH HEH HEH.
YOU'LL NEVER BE KING, NOT IN A MILLION YEARS!
LURCH
SAY GOOD NIGHT!
POPEH!
SAMURAI DUAL WIELD
HUH?
WHAM
BAM
MEETING ROOM
KCHAK
SOME-ONE'S EMERG-ING!
SO? WHO WILL BE KING?

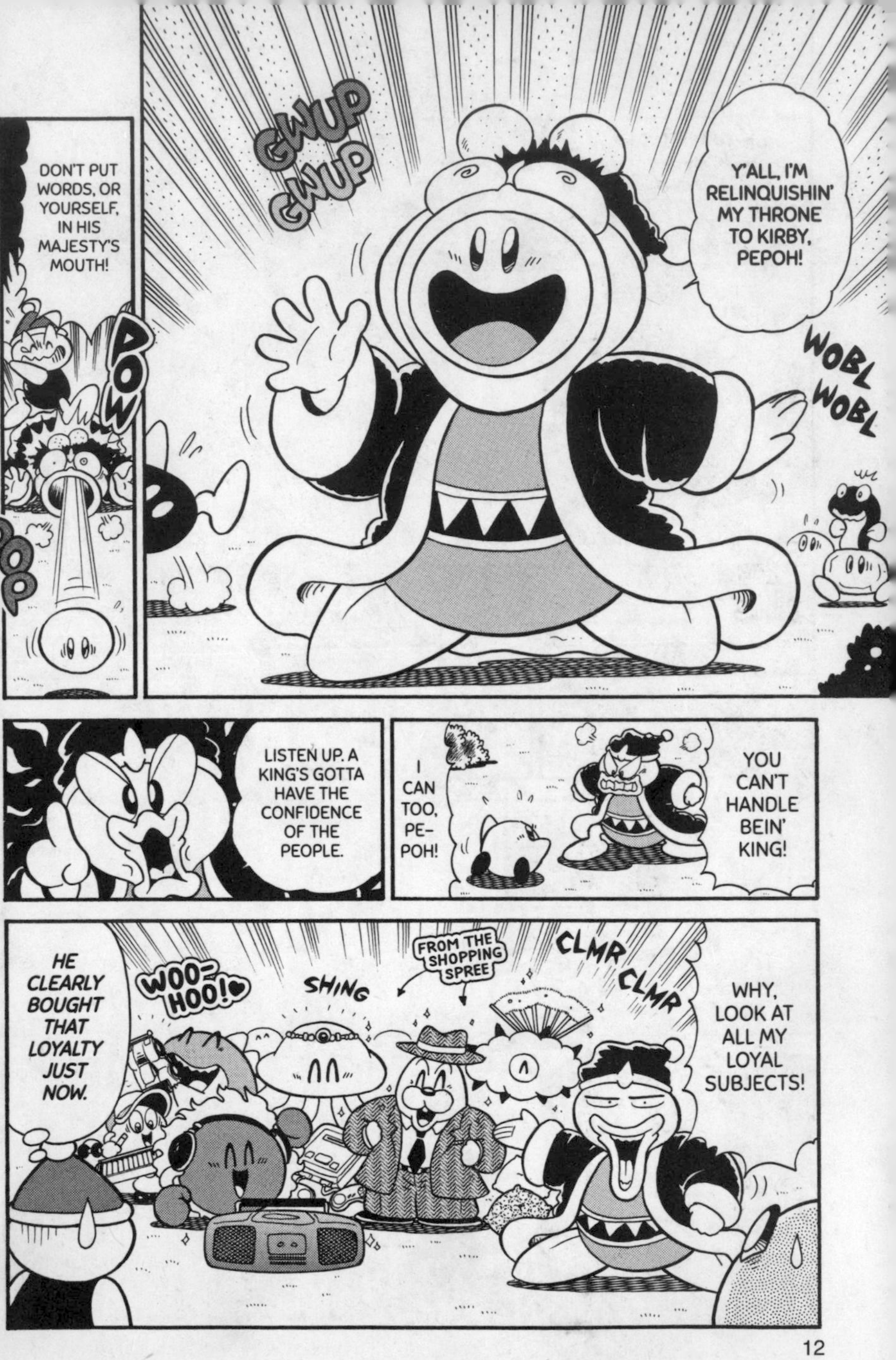
GWUP GWUP
Y'ALL, I'M RELINQUISHIN' MY THRONE TO KIRBY, PEPOH!
WOBL WOBL
DON'T PUT WORDS, OR YOURSELF, IN HIS MAJESTY'S MOUTH!
POW
YOU CAN'T HANDLE BEIN' KING!
I CAN TOO, PE-POH!
LISTEN UP. A KING'S GOTTA HAVE THE CONFIDENCE OF THE PEOPLE.
WHY, LOOK AT ALL MY LOYAL SUBJECTS!
CLMR CLMR
FROM THE SHOPPING SPREE
SHING
WOO-HOO!♥
HE CLEARLY BOUGHT THAT LOYALTY JUST NOW.

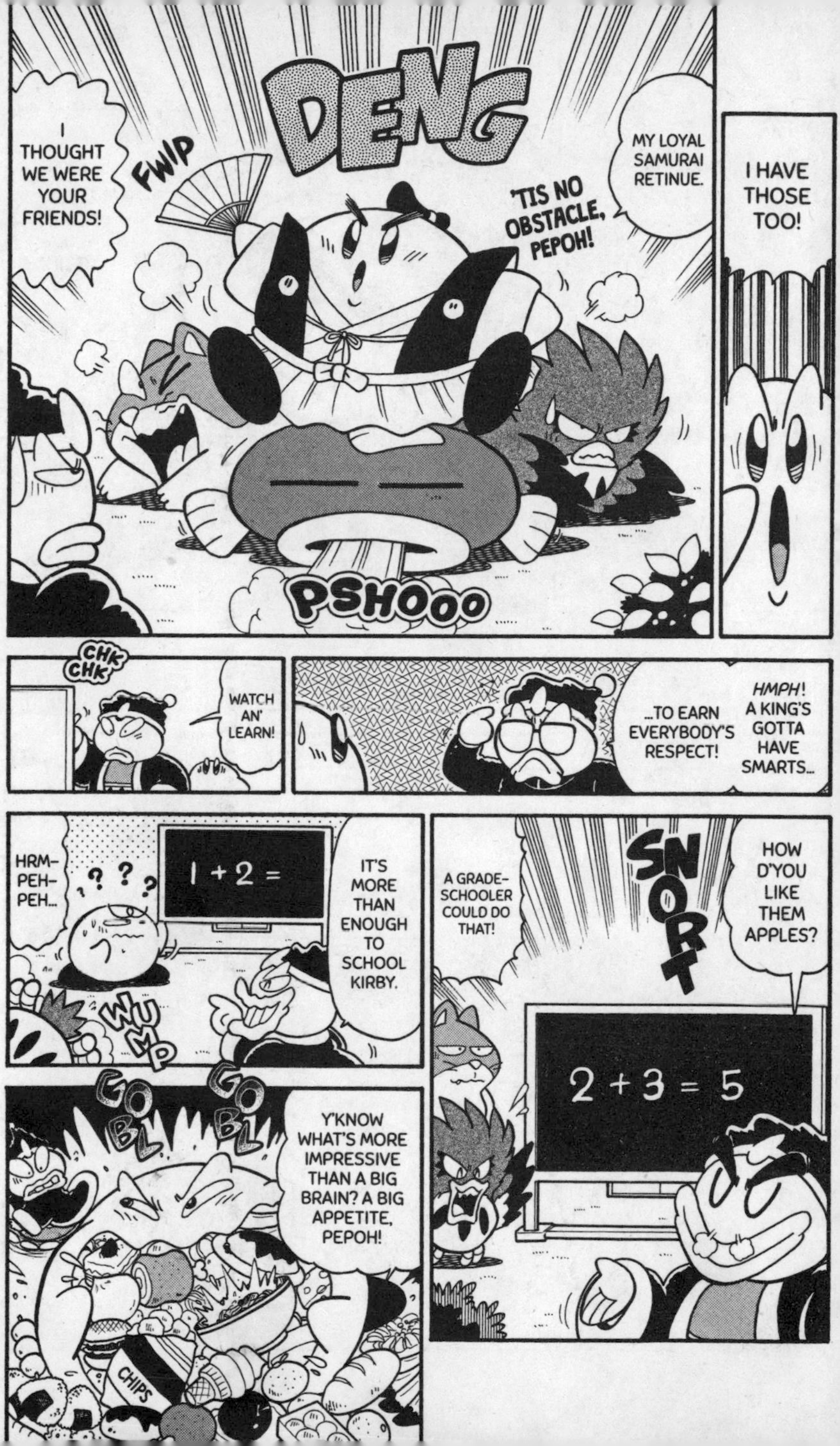
I HAVE THOSE TOO!
MY LOYAL SAMURAI RETINUE.
'TIS NO OBSTACLE, PEPOH!
DENG
FWIP
I THOUGHT WE WERE YOUR FRIENDS!
PSHOOO
HMPH! A KING'S GOTTA HAVE SMARTS...
...TO EARN EVERYBODY'S RESPECT!
WATCH AN' LEARN!
CHK CHK
HOW D'YOU LIKE THEM APPLES?
SNORT
A GRADE-SCHOOLER COULD DO THAT!
2 + 3 = 5
IT'S MORE THAN ENOUGH TO SCHOOL KIRBY.
1 + 2 =
HRM-PEH-PEH...
WUMP
Y'KNOW WHAT'S MORE IMPRESSIVE THAN A BIG BRAIN? A BIG APPETITE, PEPOH!
GOBL GOBL
CHIPS

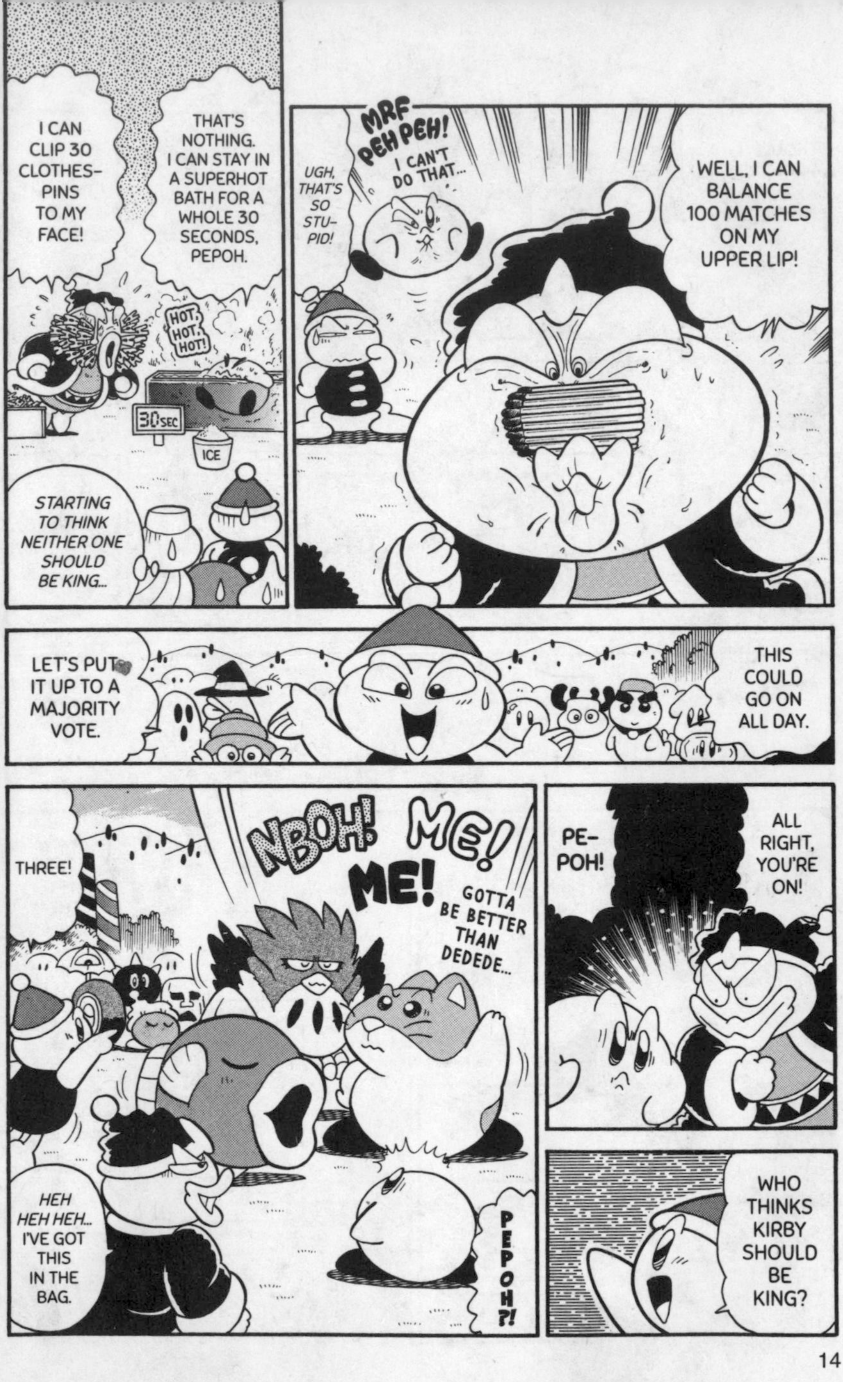
WELL, I CAN BALANCE 100 MATCHES ON MY UPPER LIP!
MRF PEH PEH!
I CAN'T DO THAT...
UGH, THAT'S SO STU-PID!
THAT'S NOTHING. I CAN STAY IN A SUPERHOT BATH FOR A WHOLE 30 SECONDS, PEPOH.
I CAN CLIP 30 CLOTHES-PINS TO MY FACE!
HOT, HOT, HOT!
30SEC
ICE
STARTING TO THINK NEITHER ONE SHOULD BE KING...
THIS COULD GO ON ALL DAY.
LET'S PUT IT UP TO A MAJORITY VOTE.
ALL RIGHT, YOU'RE ON!
PE-POH!
WHO THINKS KIRBY SHOULD BE KING?
ME!
NBOH!
ME!
GOTTA BE BETTER THAN DEDEDE...
THREE!
PEPOH?!
HEH HEH HEH... I'VE GOT THIS IN THE BAG.

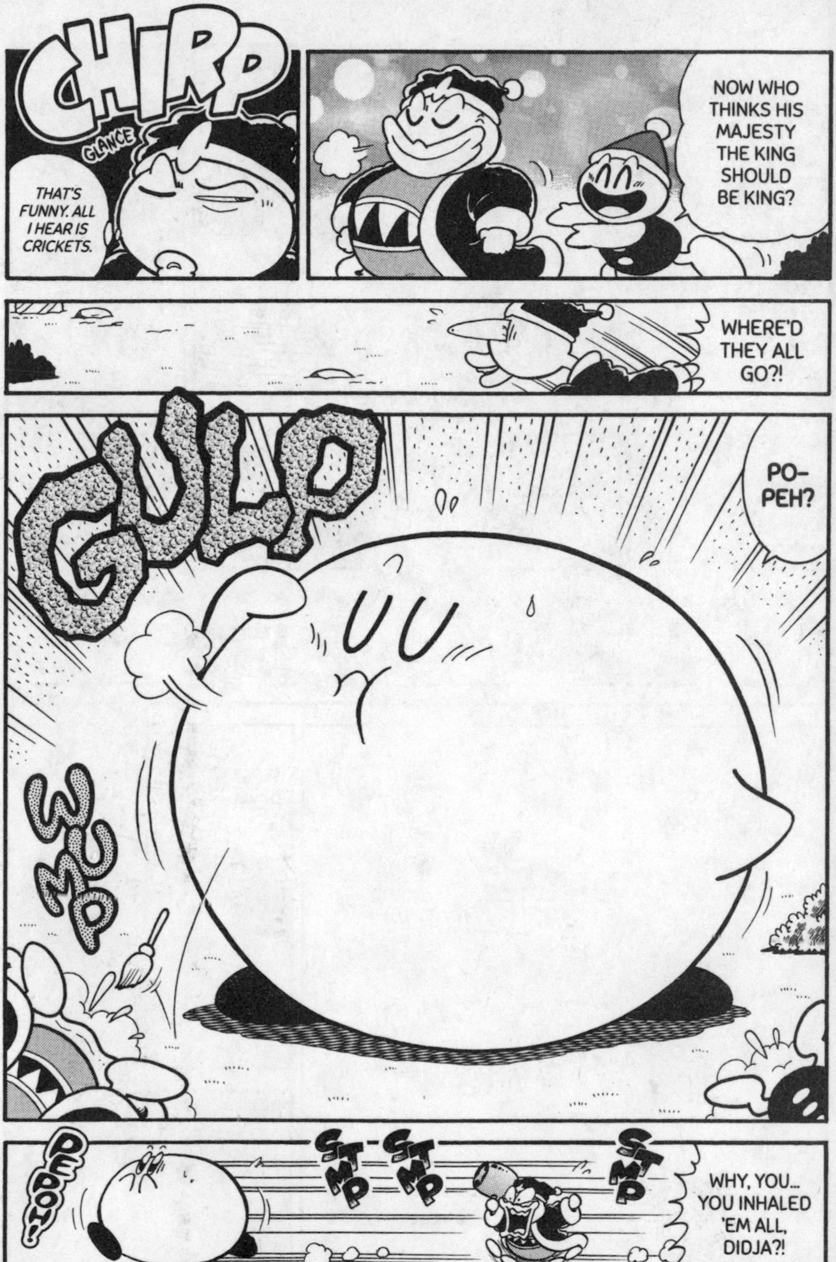
NOW WHO THINKS HIS MAJESTY THE KING SHOULD BE KING?
CHIRP
GLANCE
THAT'S FUNNY. ALL I HEAR IS CRICKETS.
WHERE'D THEY ALL GO?!
PO-PEH?
GULP
WUMP
WHY, YOU... YOU INHALED 'EM ALL, DIDJA?!
STMP
STMP
STMP
DEDOH!

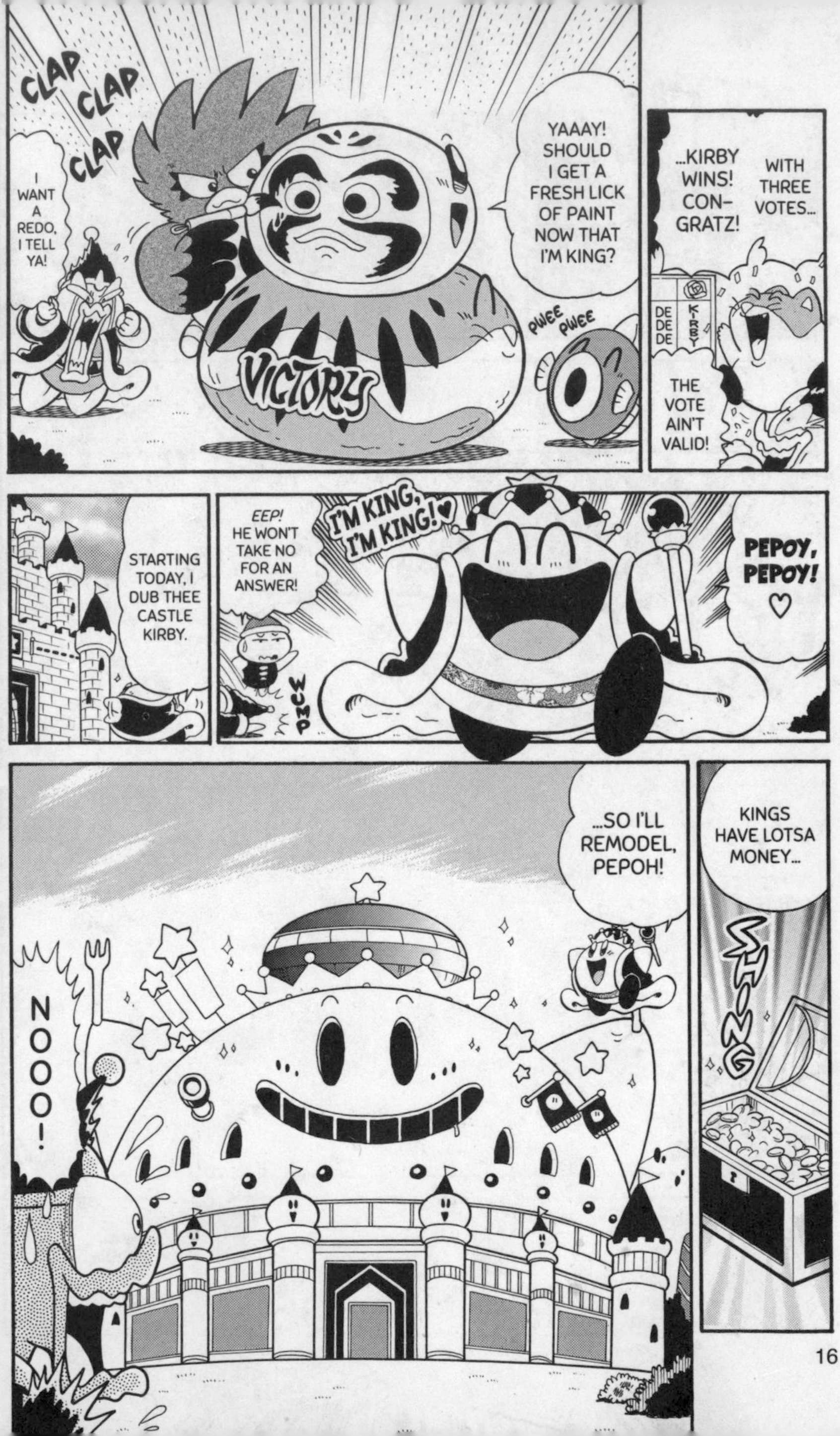
WITH THREE VOTES...
...KIRBY WINS! CONGRATZ!
DE DE DE
KIRBY
THE VOTE AIN'T VALID!
YAAAY! SHOULD I GET A FRESH LICK OF PAINT NOW THAT I'M KING?
PWEE PWEE
VICTORY
CLAP CLAP CLAP
I WANT A REDO, I TELL YA!
PEPOY, PEPOY! ♡
I'M KING, I'M KING!♥
EEP! HE WON'T TAKE NO FOR AN ANSWER!
WUMP
STARTING TODAY, I DUB THEE CASTLE KIRBY.
KINGS HAVE LOTSA MONEY...
SHING
...SO I'LL REMODEL, PEPOH!
NOOOO!

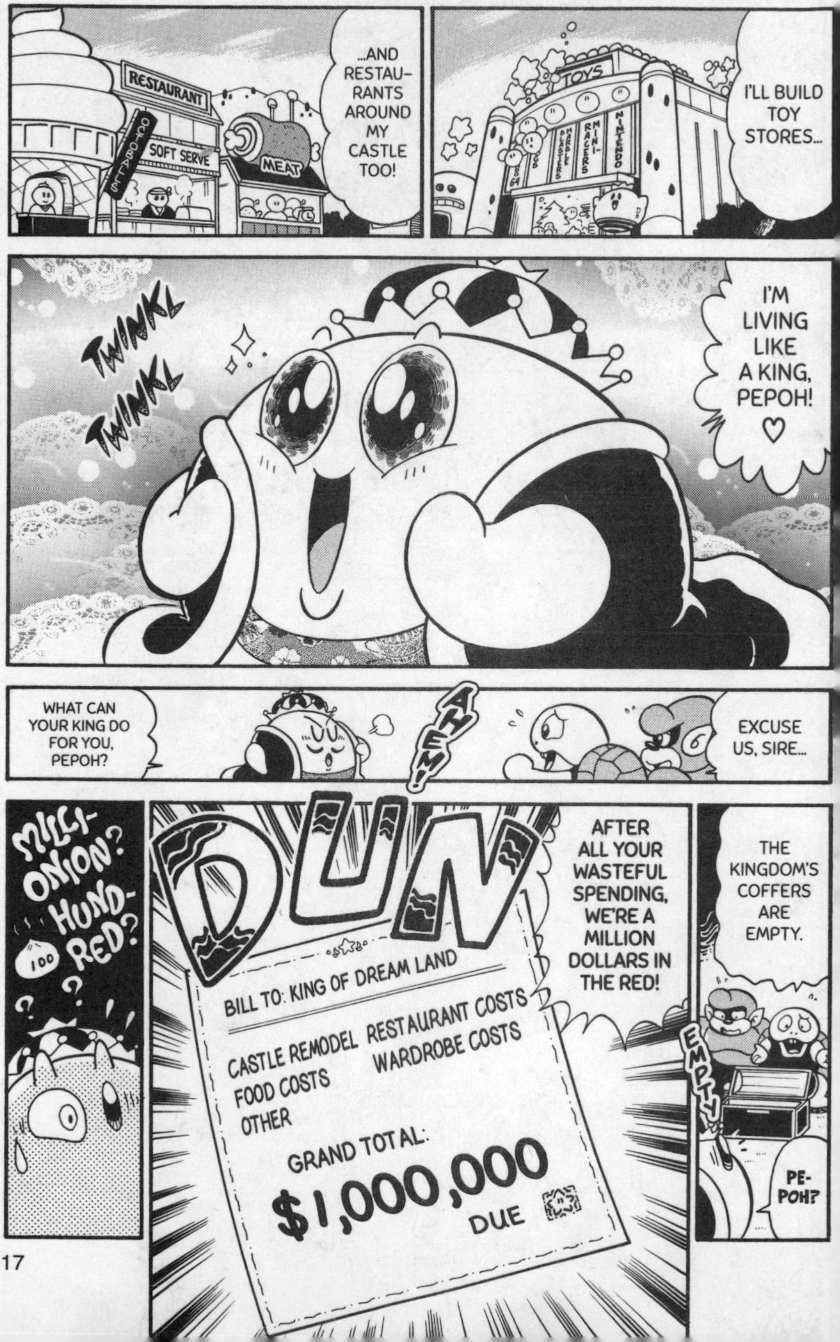

I'LL BUILD TOY STORES...
TOYS
NINTENDO
MINI-RACERS
...AND RESTAURANTS AROUND MY CASTLE TOO!
RESTAURANT
SOFT SERVE
MEAT
I'M LIVING LIKE A KING, PEPOH! ♡
TWINKL
TWINKL
EXCUSE US, SIRE...
AHEM!
WHAT CAN YOUR KING DO FOR YOU, PEPOH?
THE KINGDOM'S COFFERS ARE EMPTY.
EMPTY
PE-POH?
AFTER ALL YOUR WASTEFUL SPENDING, WE'RE A MILLION DOLLARS IN THE RED!
DUN
BILL TO: KING OF DREAM LAND
CASTLE REMODEL
FOOD COSTS
OTHER
RESTAURANT COSTS
WARDROBE COSTS
GRAND TOTAL:
$1,000,000
DUE
MILLI-ONION? HUND-RED?
100

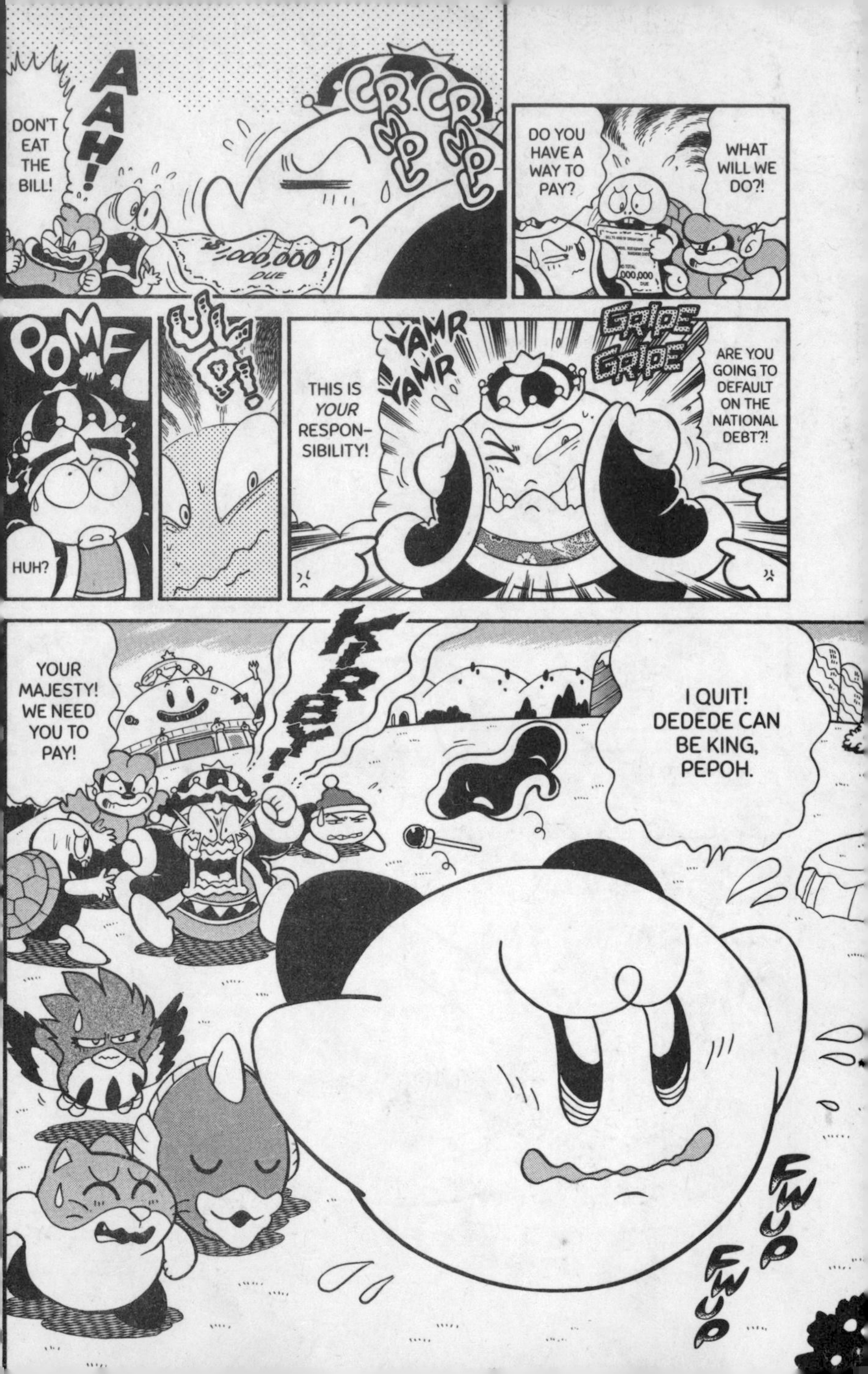
WHAT WILL WE DO?!
DO YOU HAVE A WAY TO PAY?
CRMMPL CRMMPL
AAH!
DON'T EAT THE BILL!
$1,000,000 DUE
GRIPE GRIPE
ARE YOU GOING TO DEFAULT ON THE NATIONAL DEBT?!
YAMR YAMR
THIS IS *YOUR* RESPONSIBILITY!
ULP!
POMF
HUH?
I QUIT! DEDEDE CAN BE KING, PEPOH.
KIRBY!!
YOUR MAJESTY! WE NEED YOU TO PAY!
FWUP FWUP FWUP

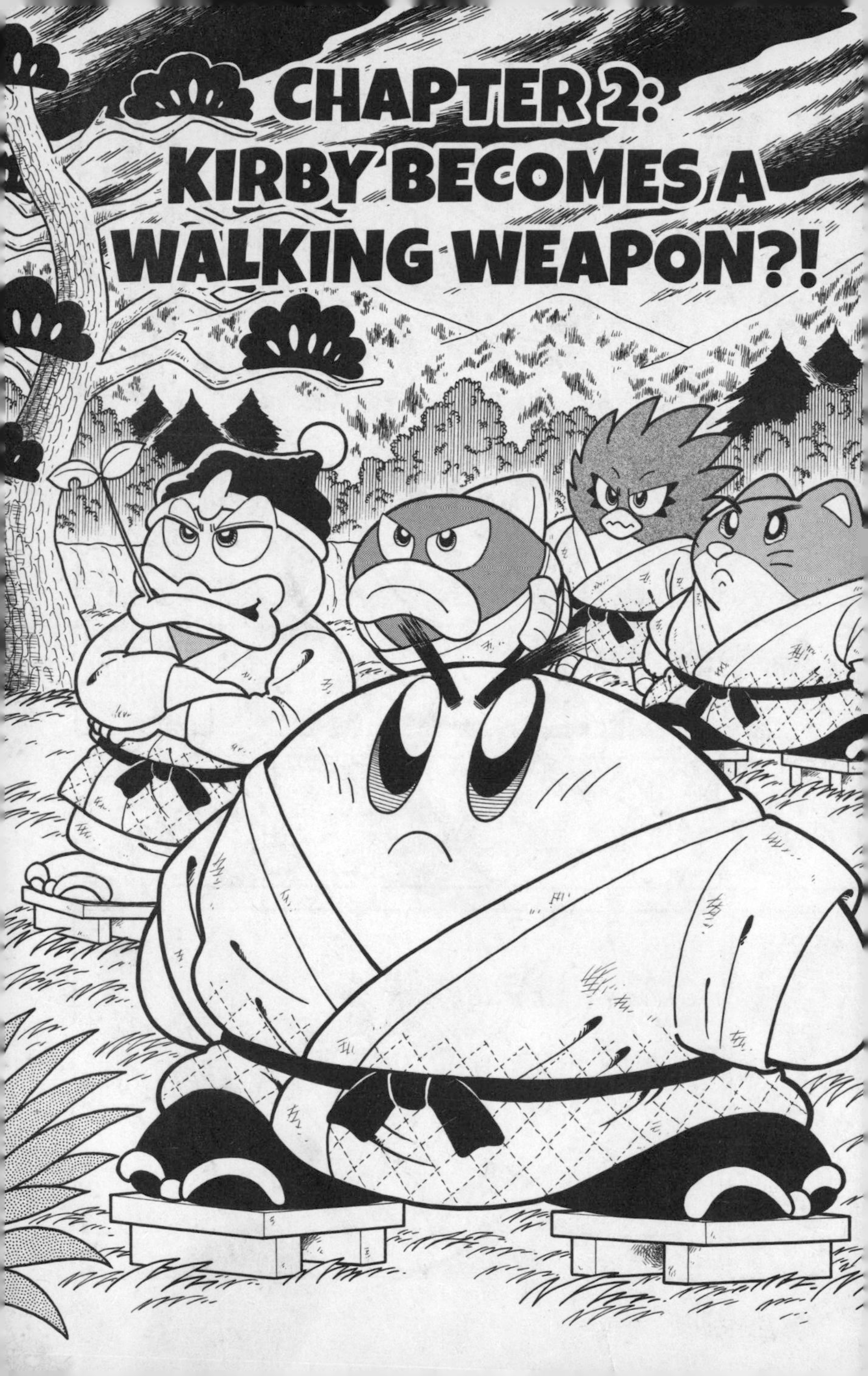
CHAPTER 2:
KIRBY BECOMES A
WALKING WEAPON?!

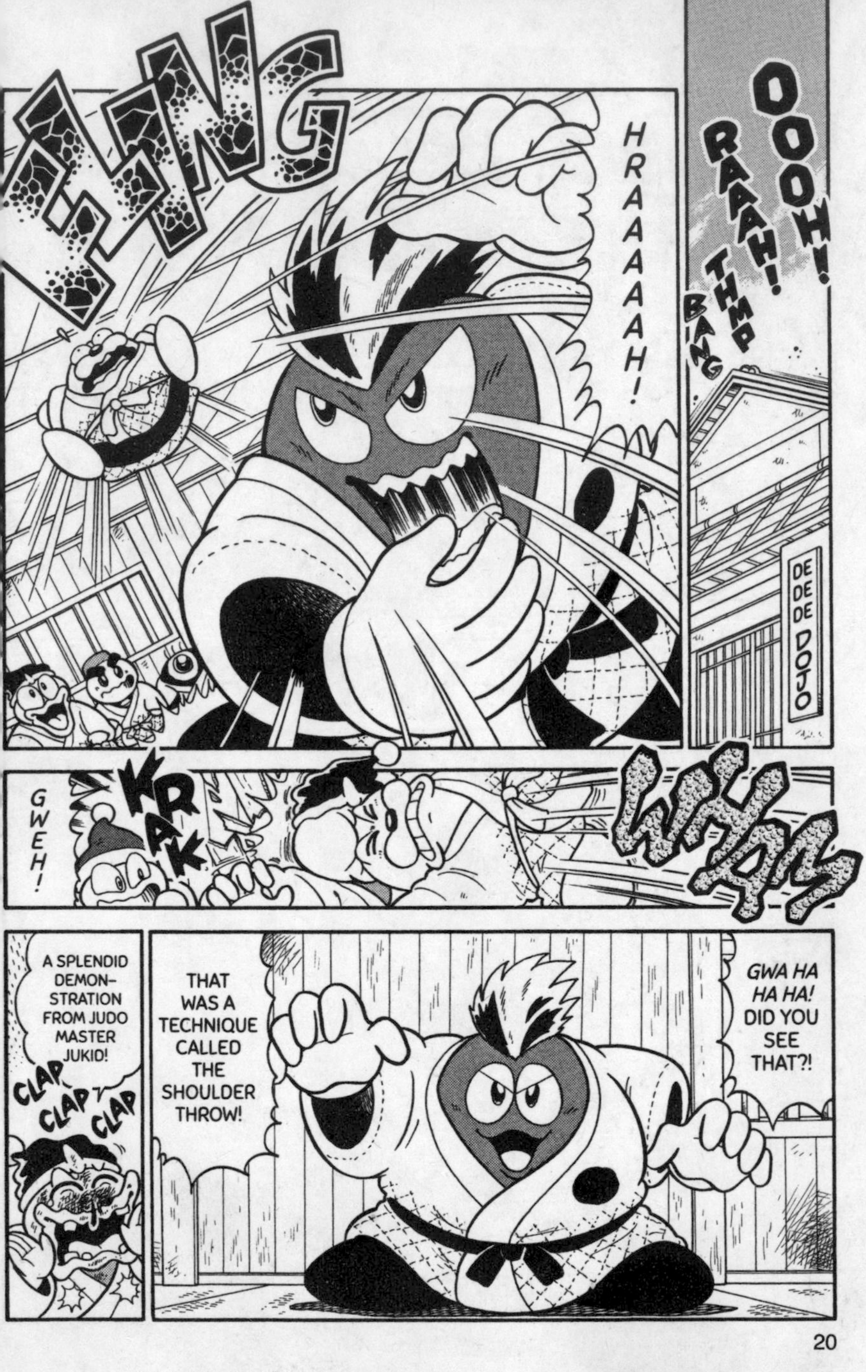
OOOOH!
RAAAAH!
THMP
BANG
DE DE DE DOJO
HRAAAAAAH!
WHAM
KRAK
GWEH!
GWA HA HA HA! DID YOU SEE THAT?!
THAT WAS A TECHNIQUE CALLED THE SHOULDER THROW!
A SPLENDID DEMON-STRATION FROM JUDO MASTER JUKID!
CLAP CLAP CLAP

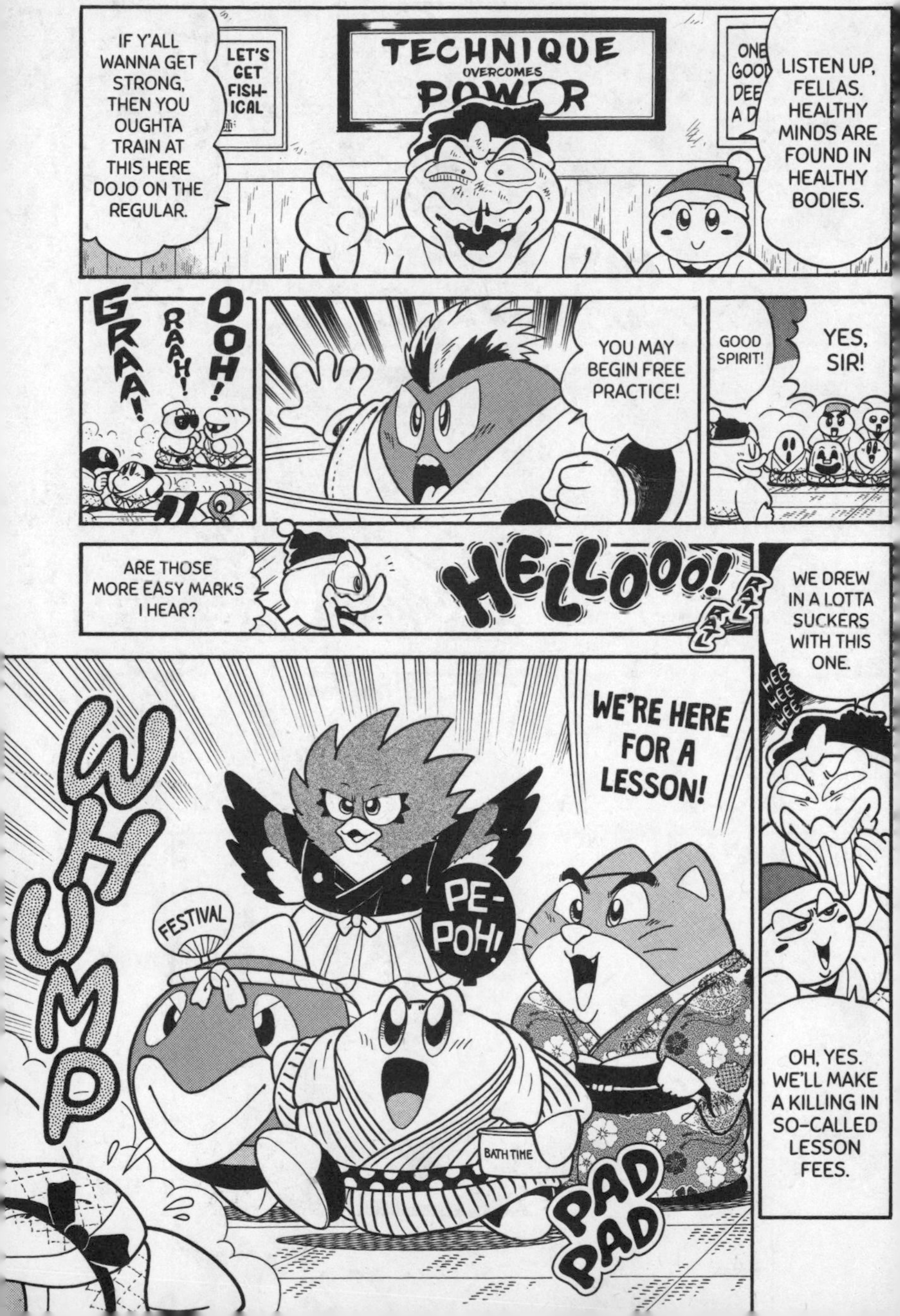
LISTEN UP, FELLAS. HEALTHY MINDS ARE FOUND IN HEALTHY BODIES.
TECHNIQUE OVERCOMES
LET'S GET FISH-ICAL
IF Y'ALL WANNA GET STRONG, THEN YOU OUGHTA TRAIN AT THIS HERE DOJO ON THE REGULAR.
YES, SIR!
GOOD SPIRIT!
YOU MAY BEGIN FREE PRACTICE!
OOH!
RAAH!
GRAA!
WE DREW IN A LOTTA SUCKERS WITH THIS ONE.
HEE HEE HEE
OH, YES. WE'LL MAKE A KILLING IN SO-CALLED LESSON FEES.
HELLOOO!
ARE THOSE MORE EASY MARKS I HEAR?
WE'RE HERE FOR A LESSON!
PE-POH!
FESTIVAL
WHUMP
BATH TIME
PAD PAD

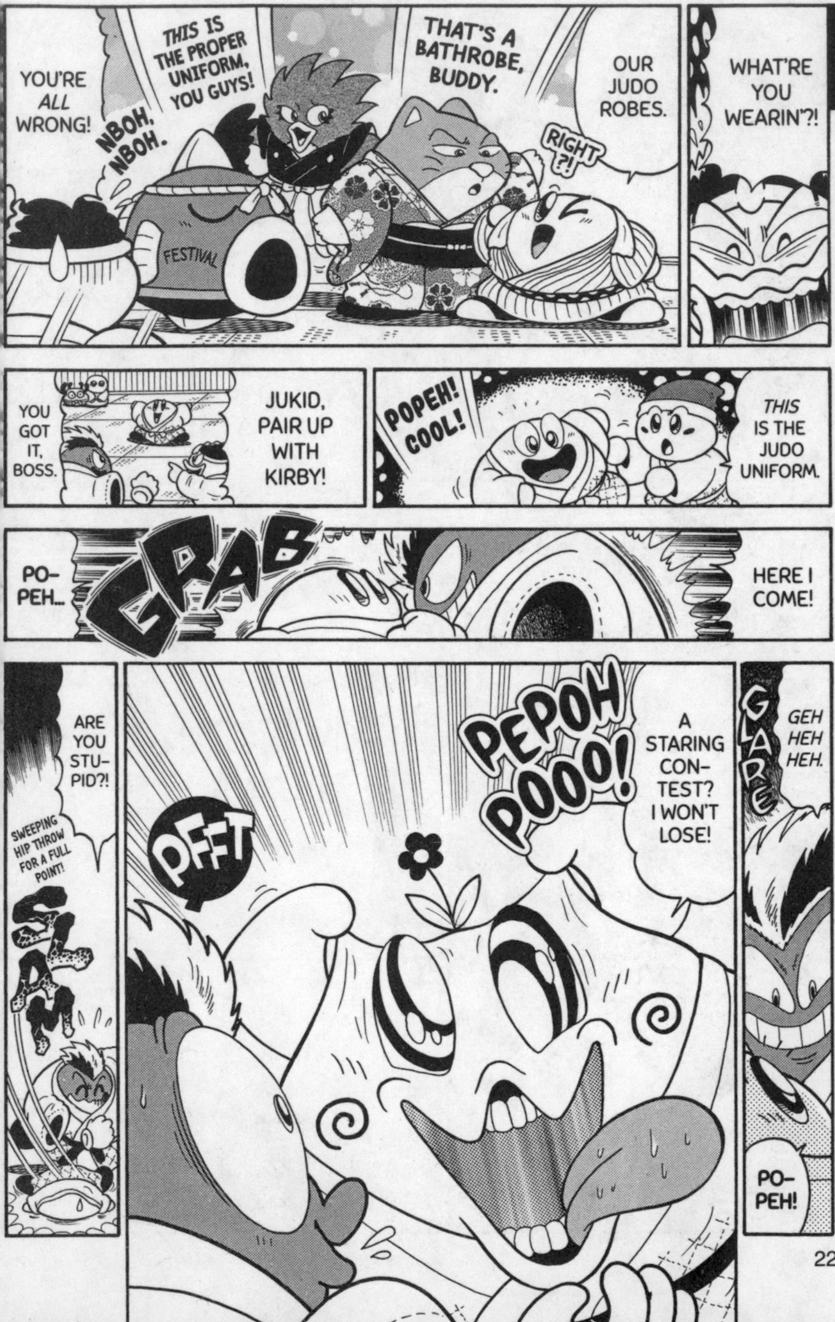
WHAT'RE YOU WEARIN'?!
OUR JUDO ROBES.
RIGHT?!
THAT'S A BATHROBE, BUDDY.
THIS IS THE PROPER UNIFORM, YOU GUYS!
NBOH, NBOH.
FESTIVAL
YOU'RE ALL WRONG!
THIS IS THE JUDO UNIFORM.
POPEH! COOL!
JUKID, PAIR UP WITH KIRBY!
YOU GOT IT, BOSS.
HERE I COME!
GRAB
PO-PEH...
GLARE
GEH HEH HEH.
PO-PEH!
A STARING CONTEST? I WON'T LOSE!
PEPOH POOOO!
PFFT
ARE YOU STUPID?!
SWEEPING HIP THROW FOR A FULL POINT!
SLAM

AUTHOR'S COMMENT

THIS CHAPTER'S COVER ILLUSTRATION IS A PARODY OF THE JUDO ARC OF A MANGA I ADORE CALLED *DOKABEN*. MAN OH MAN, I HAD MY NOSE TO THE GRINDSTONE BACK WHEN I DREW THIS ONE (*LOL*)!

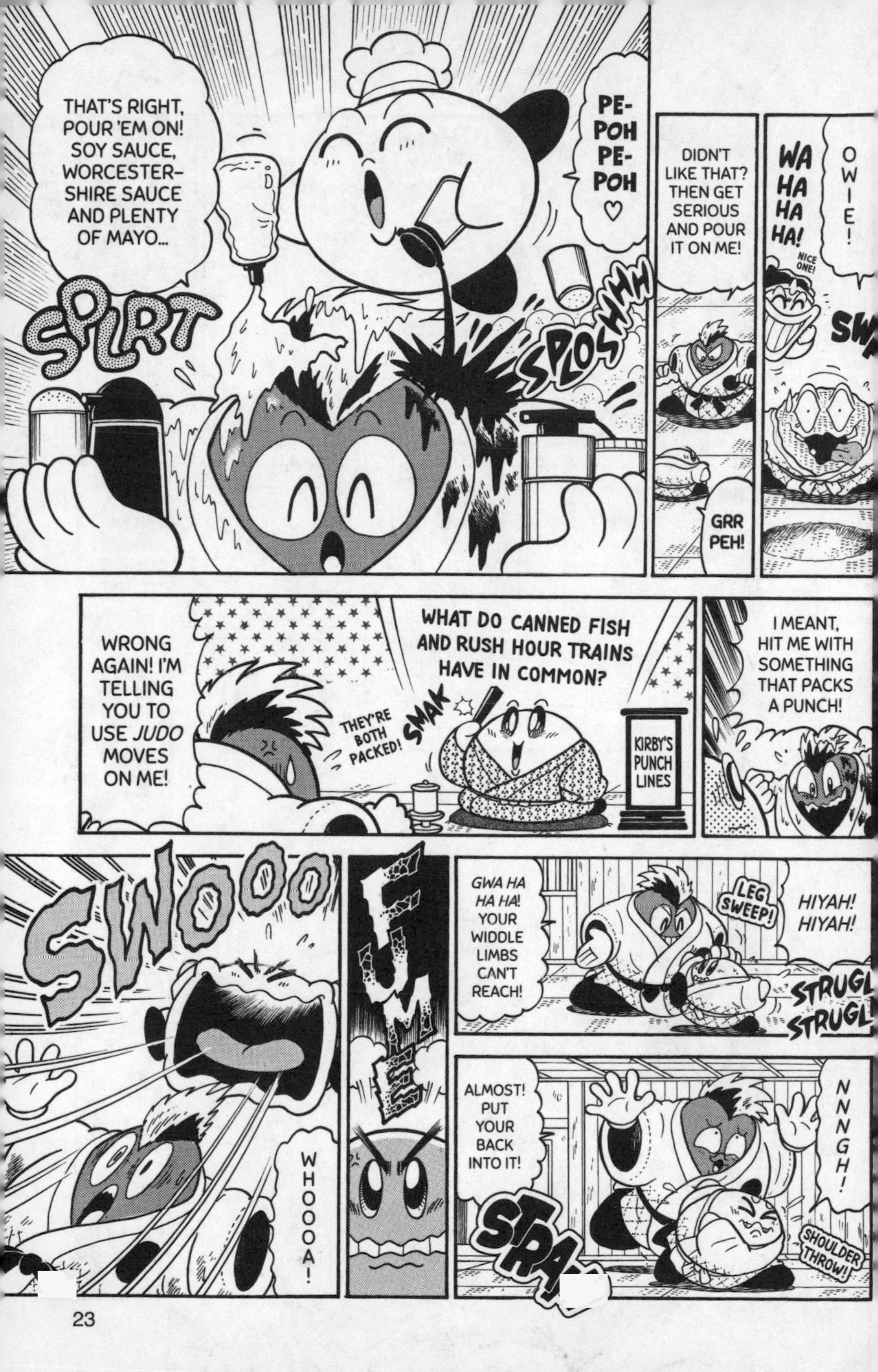
OWIE!
WA HA HA HA!
NICE ONE!
DIDN'T LIKE THAT? THEN GET SERIOUS AND POUR IT ON ME!
GRR PEH!
PE-POH PE-POH ♡
THAT'S RIGHT, POUR 'EM ON! SOY SAUCE, WORCESTERSHIRE SAUCE AND PLENTY OF MAYO...
SPLOSHHH
SPLRT
I MEANT, HIT ME WITH SOMETHING THAT PACKS A PUNCH!
WHAT DO CANNED FISH AND RUSH HOUR TRAINS HAVE IN COMMON?
SMAK
THEY'RE BOTH PACKED!
KIRBY'S PUNCH LINES
WRONG AGAIN! I'M TELLING YOU TO USE *JUDO* MOVES ON ME!
HIYAH! HIYAH!
LEG SWEEP!
GWA HA HA HA! YOUR WIDDLE LIMBS CAN'T REACH!
STRUGL STRUGL
NNNGH!
SHOULDER THROW!
ALMOST! PUT YOUR BACK INTO IT!
FUME
WHOOOA!
SWOOO

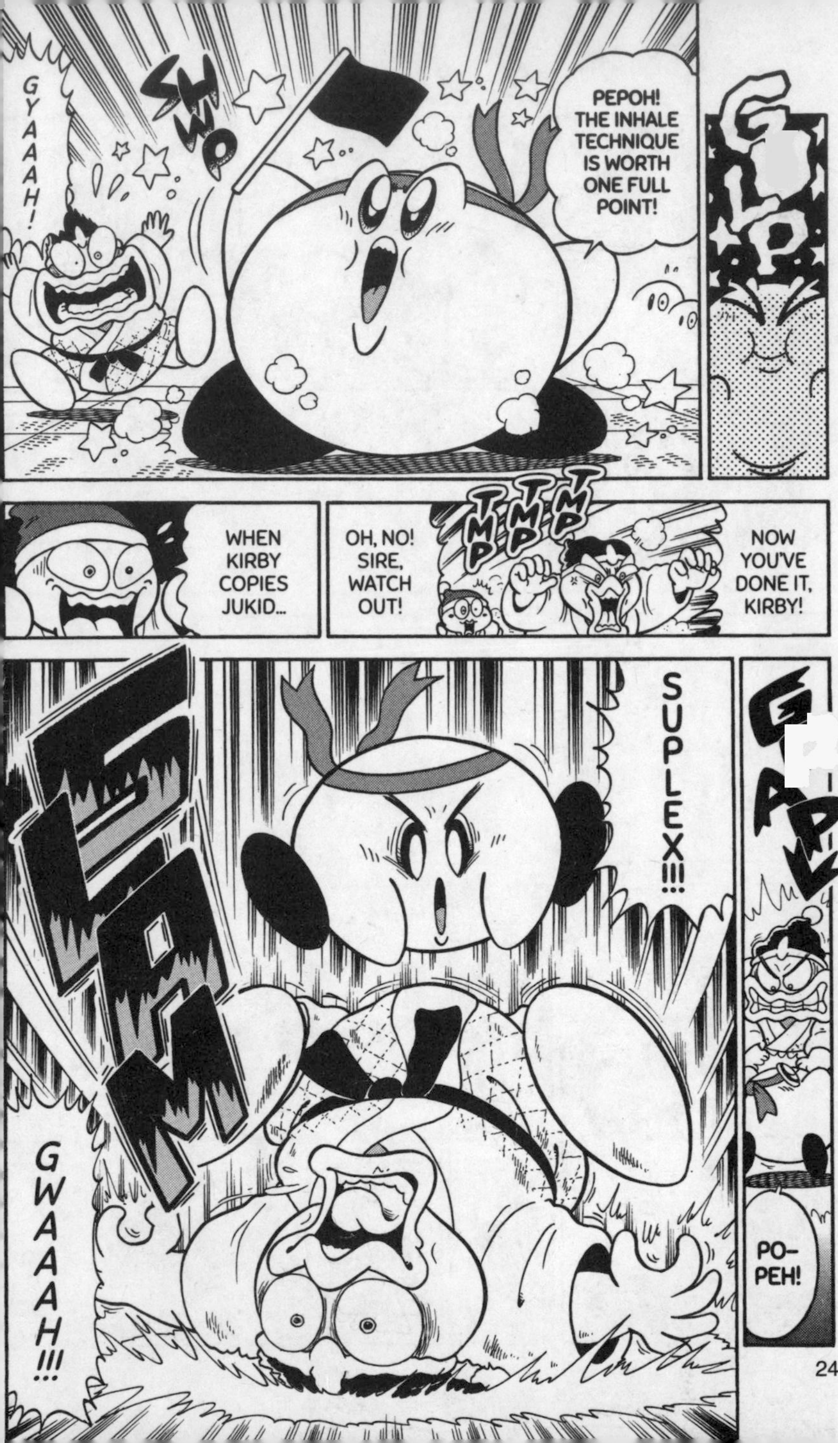
PEPOH! THE INHALE TECHNIQUE IS WORTH ONE FULL POINT!
SHWOP
GYAAAAH!
NOW YOU'VE DONE IT, KIRBY!
TMP TMP TMP
OH, NO! SIRE, WATCH OUT!
WHEN KIRBY COPIES JUKID...
PO-PEH!
SUPLEX!!!
SLAM
GWAAAAH!!!

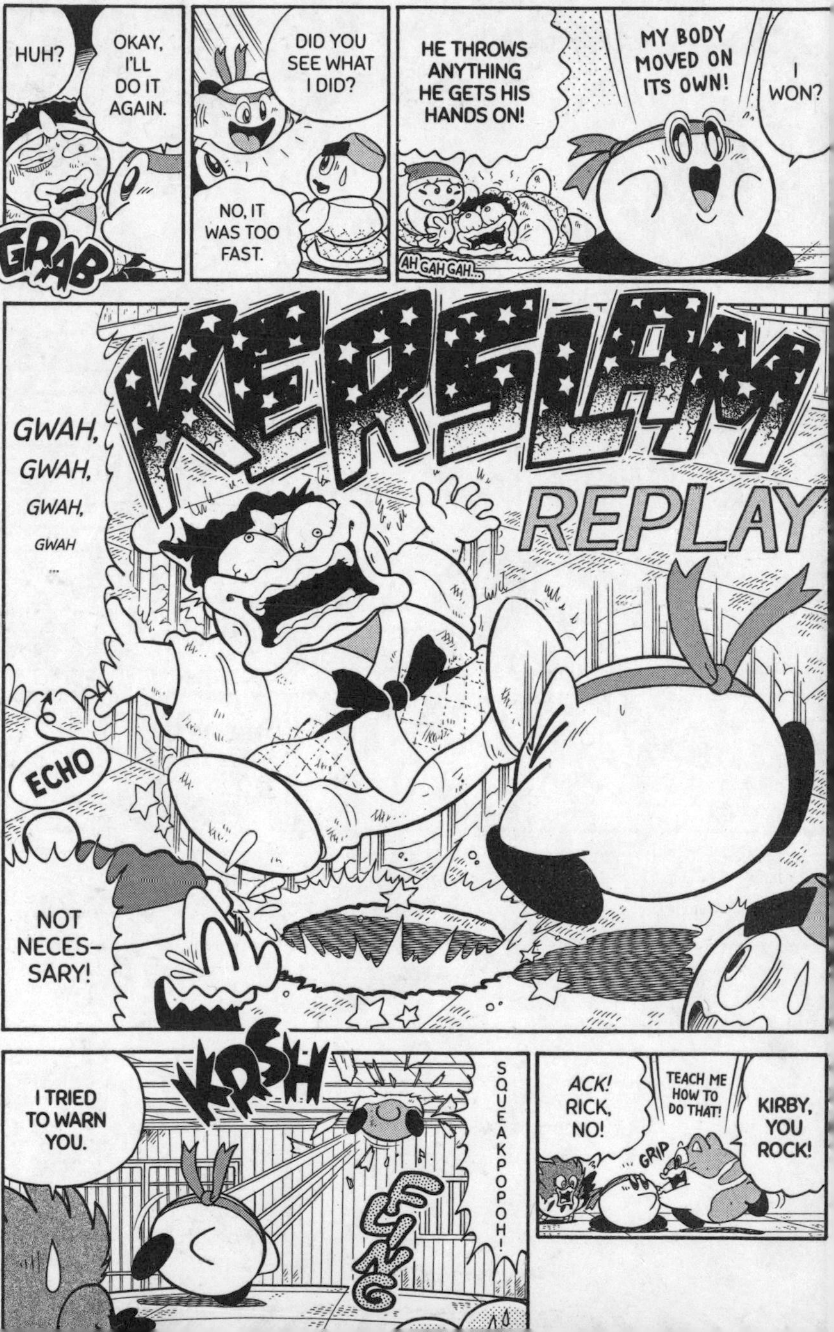
I WON?
MY BODY MOVED ON ITS OWN!
HE THROWS ANYTHING HE GETS HIS HANDS ON!
AH GAH GAH...
DID YOU SEE WHAT I DID?
NO, IT WAS TOO FAST.
OKAY, I'LL DO IT AGAIN.
HUH?
GRAB
KERSLAM
REPLAY
GWAH, GWAH, GWAH, GWAH...
ECHO
NOT NECES-SARY!
KIRBY, YOU ROCK!
TEACH ME HOW TO DO THAT!
ACK! RICK, NO!
GRIP
SQUEAKPOPOH!
KPSH
I TRIED TO WARN YOU.
FLING

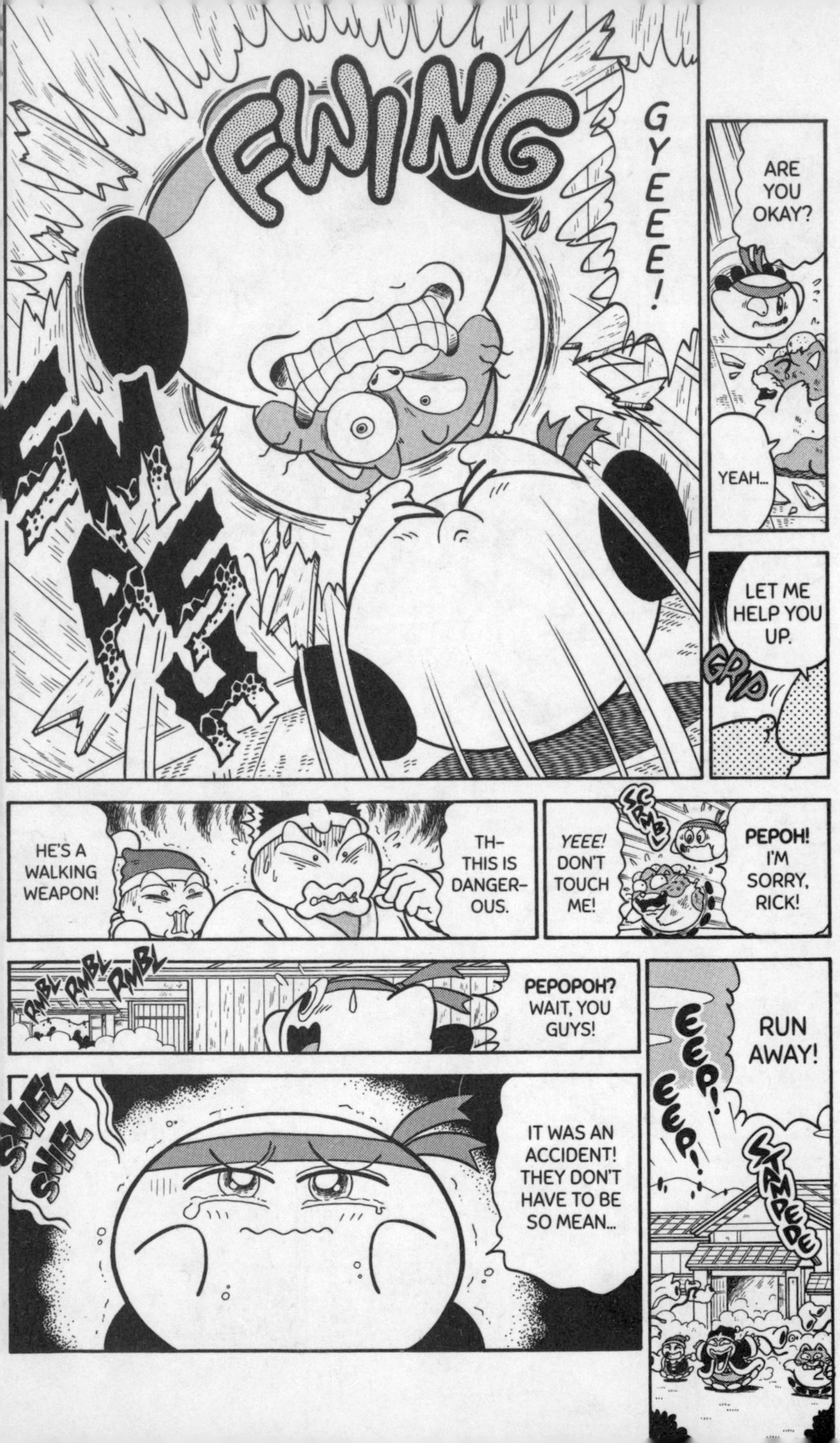
ARE YOU OKAY?
YEAH...
LET ME HELP YOU UP.
GRIP
FWING
GYEEE!
PEPOH! I'M SORRY, RICK!
SCRMBL
YEEE! DON'T TOUCH ME!
TH- THIS IS DANGER-OUS.
HE'S A WALKING WEAPON!
RUN AWAY!
EEP! EEP! EEP!
STAMPEDE
PEPOPOH? WAIT, YOU GUYS!
RMBL RMBL RMBL
IT WAS AN ACCIDENT! THEY DON'T HAVE TO BE SO MEAN...
SNIFL SNIFL

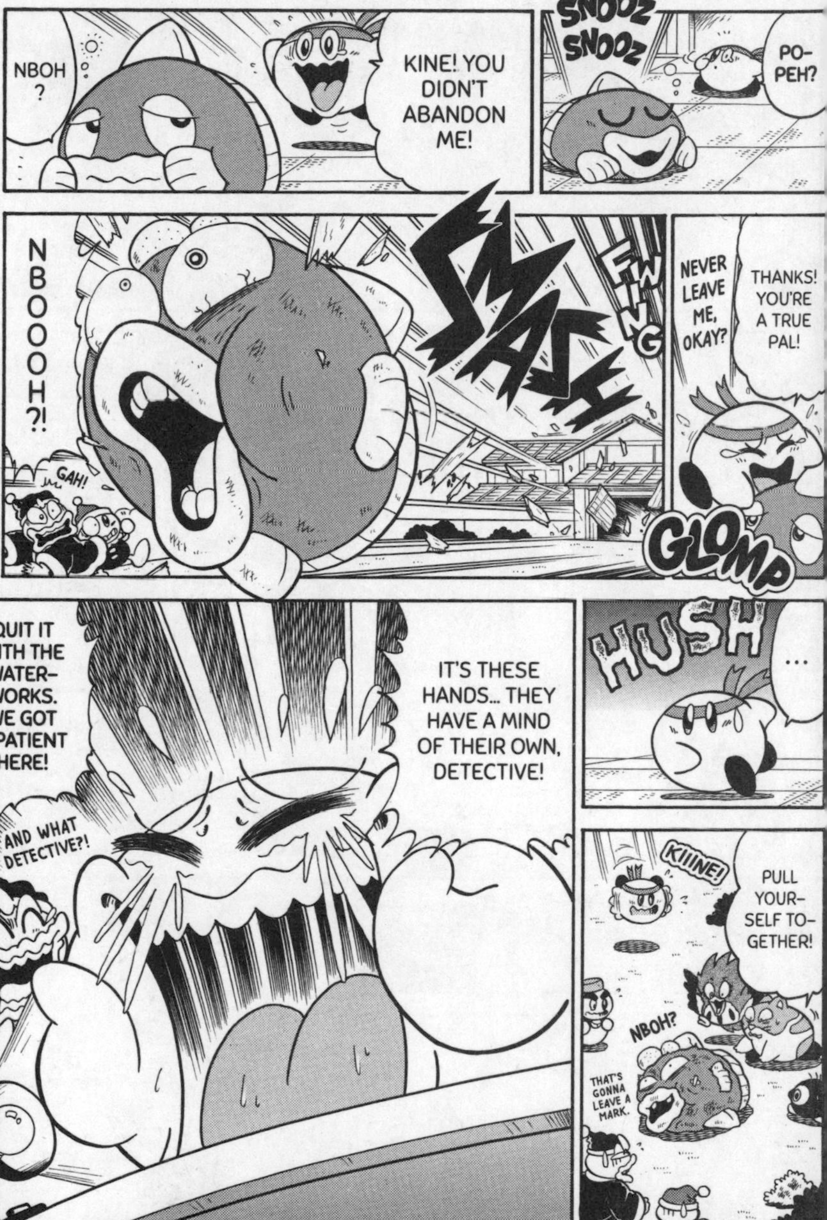
SNOOZ SNOOZ
PO-PEH?
KINE! YOU DIDN'T ABANDON ME!
NBOH ?
THANKS! YOU'RE A TRUE PAL!
NEVER LEAVE ME, OKAY?
GLOMP
FWING
SMASH
NBOOOOH?!
GAH!
...
HUSH
PULL YOURSELF TOGETHER!
KIIINE!
NBOH?
THAT'S GONNA LEAVE A MARK.
IT'S THESE HANDS... THEY HAVE A MIND OF THEIR OWN, DETECTIVE!
QUIT IT WITH THE WATERWORKS. WE GOT A PATIENT HERE!
AND WHAT DETECTIVE?!

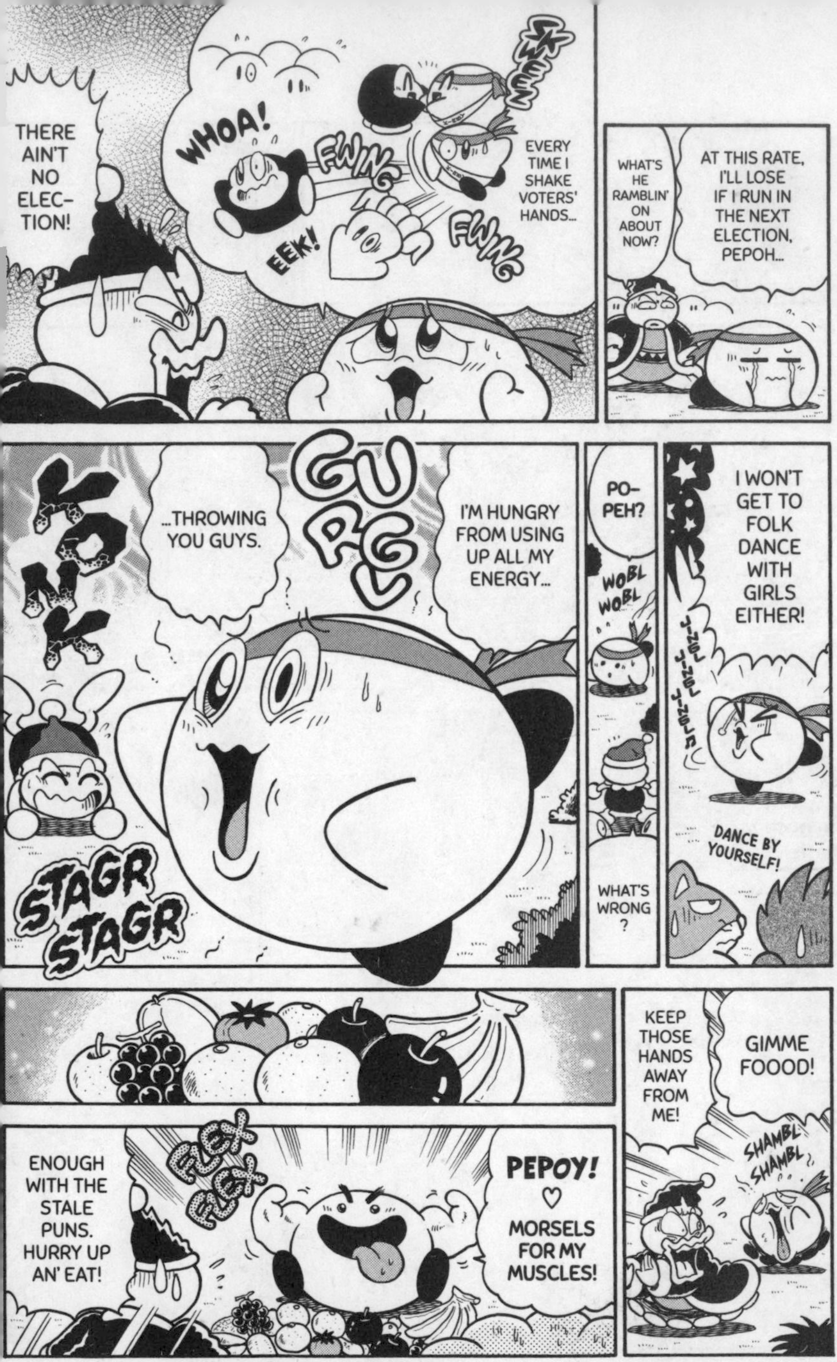
AT THIS RATE, I'LL LOSE IF I RUN IN THE NEXT ELECTION, PEPOH...
WHAT'S HE RAMBLIN' ON ABOUT NOW?
EVERY TIME I SHAKE VOTERS' HANDS...
SKWEEN
WHOA!
FWING
FWING
EEK!
THERE AIN'T NO ELEC-TION!
I WON'T GET TO FOLK DANCE WITH GIRLS EITHER!
JINGL JINGL JINGL
DANCE BY YOURSELF!
PO-PEH?
WOBL WOBL
WHAT'S WRONG?
I'M HUNGRY FROM USING UP ALL MY ENERGY...
GURGL
...THROWING YOU GUYS.
KONK
STAGR STAGR
GIMME FOOOD!
KEEP THOSE HANDS AWAY FROM ME!
SHAMBL SHAMBL
PEPOY! ♡
MORSELS FOR MY MUSCLES!
FLEX FLEX
ENOUGH WITH THE STALE PUNS. HURRY UP AN' EAT!

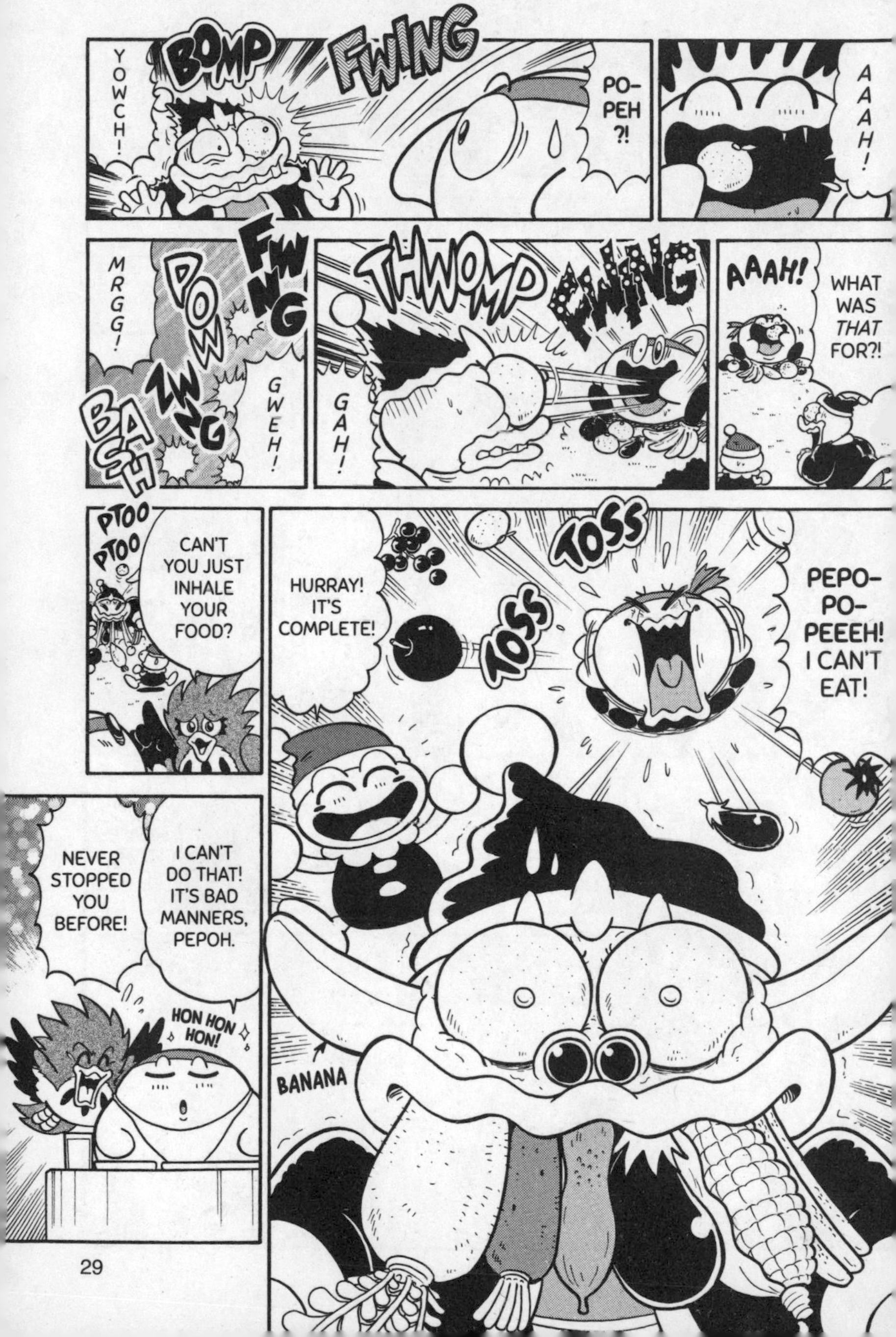
AAAH!
PO-PEH?!
FWING
BOMP
YOWCH!
WHAT WAS *THAT* FOR?!
AAAH!
FWING
THWOMP
GAH!
FWNG
POW
ZWNG
BASH
MRGG!
GWEH!
PEPO-PO-PEEEH! I CAN'T EAT!
TOSS
TOSS
HURRAY! IT'S COMPLETE!
BANANA
CAN'T YOU JUST INHALE YOUR FOOD?
PTOO PTOO
I CAN'T DO THAT! IT'S BAD MANNERS, PEPOH.
NEVER STOPPED YOU BEFORE!
HON HON HON!

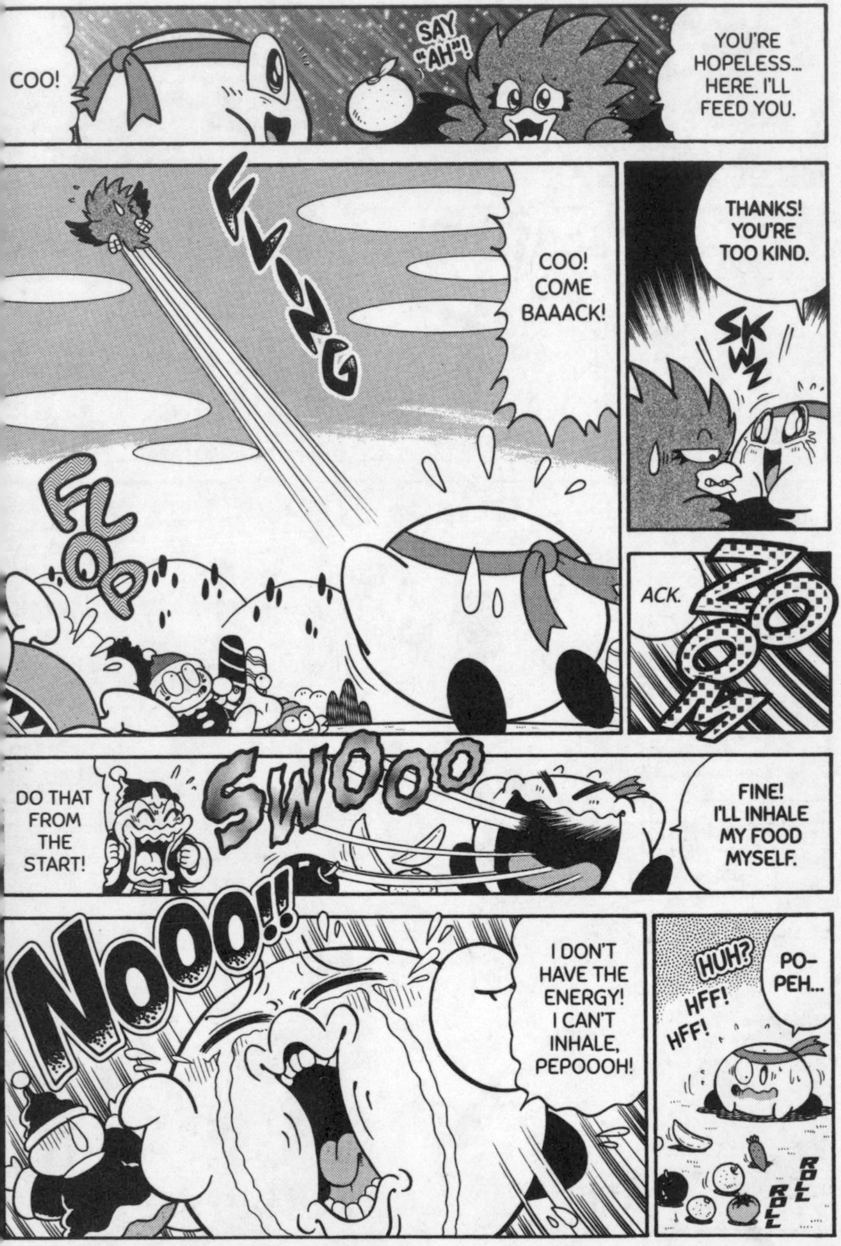
YOU'RE HOPELESS... HERE. I'LL FEED YOU.
SAY "AH"!
COO!
THANKS! YOU'RE TOO KIND.
SKWZ
ZOOM
ACK.
COO! COME BAAACK!
FLING
FLOP
FINE! I'LL INHALE MY FOOD MYSELF.
SWOOO
DO THAT FROM THE START!
PO-PEH...
HUH?
HFF! HFF!
ROLL
ROLL
I DON'T HAVE THE ENERGY! I CAN'T INHALE, PEPOOOH!
NOOO!!

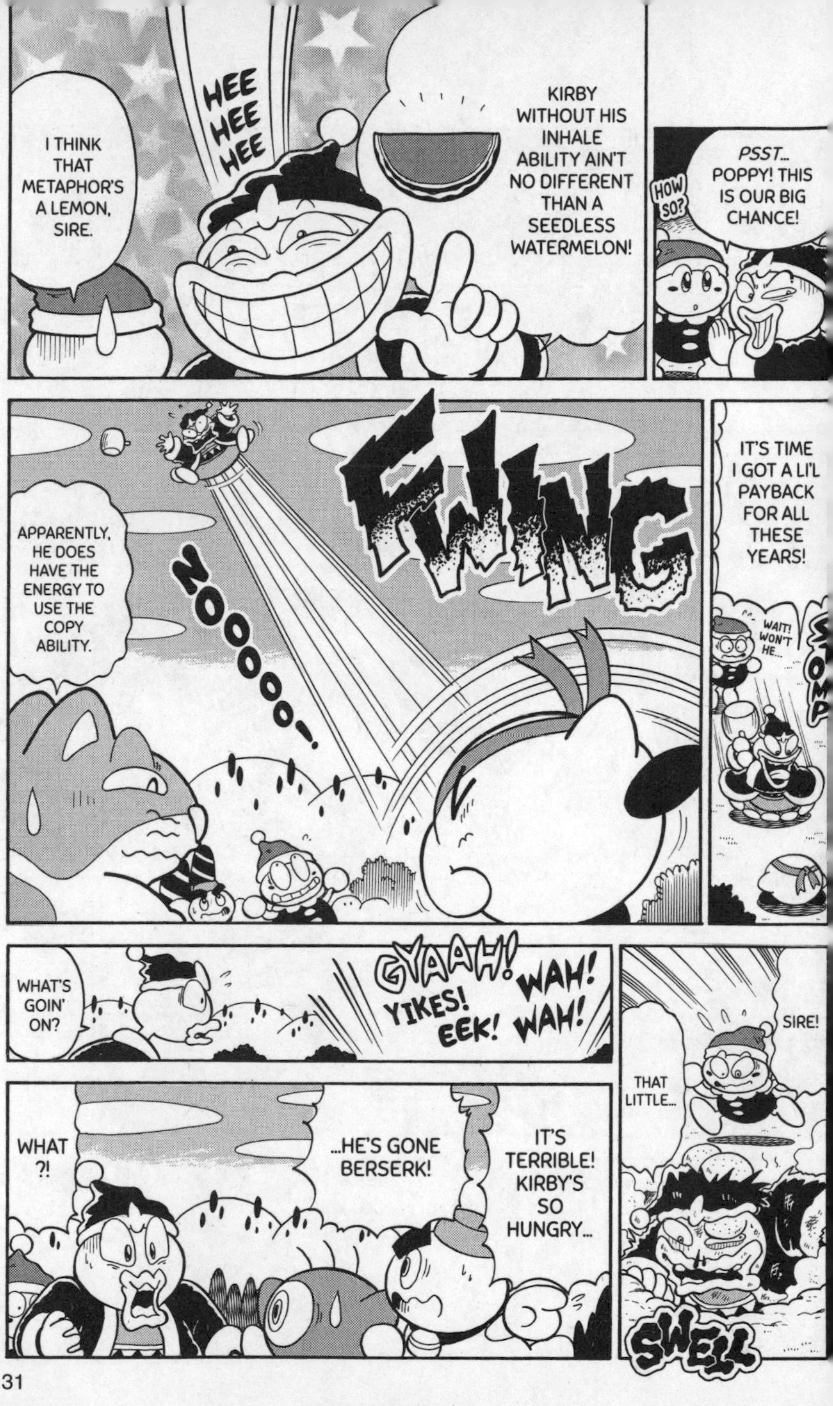
PSST... POPPY! THIS IS OUR BIG CHANCE!
HOW SO?
KIRBY WITHOUT HIS INHALE ABILITY AIN'T NO DIFFERENT THAN A SEEDLESS WATERMELON!
HEE HEE HEE
I THINK THAT METAPHOR'S A LEMON, SIRE.
IT'S TIME I GOT A LI'L PAYBACK FOR ALL THESE YEARS!
WAIT! WON'T HE...
STOMP
FWING
NOOOOOO!
APPARENTLY, HE DOES HAVE THE ENERGY TO USE THE COPY ABILITY.
SIRE!
THAT LITTLE...
SWELL
GYAAH!
WAH! WAH!
YIKES! EEK!
WHAT'S GOIN' ON?
IT'S TERRIBLE! KIRBY'S SO HUNGRY...
...HE'S GONE BERSERK!
WHAT?!

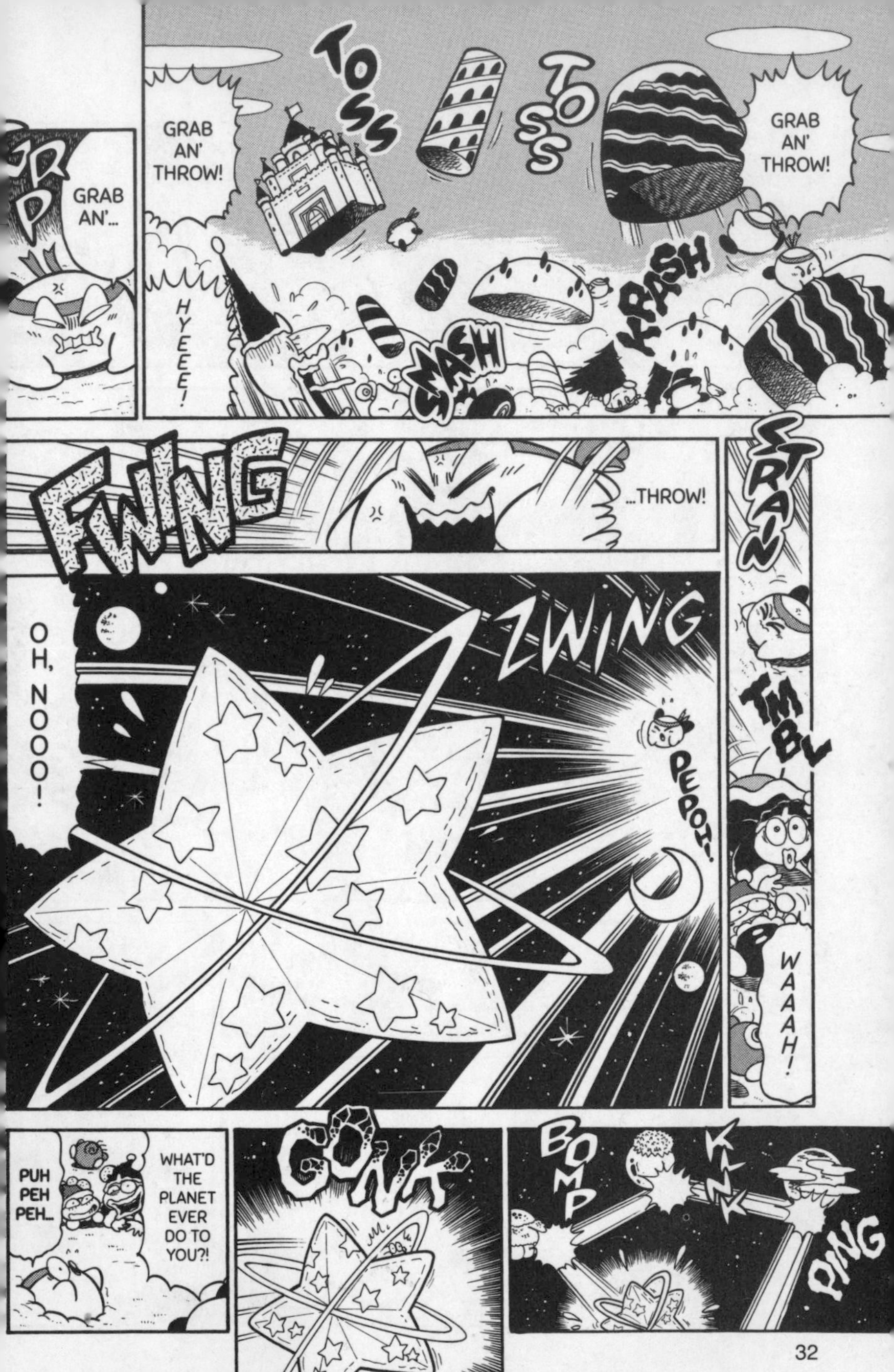
GRAB AN' THROW!
TOSS
GRAB AN' THROW!
TOSS
KRASH
SMASH
HYEEE!
GRAB AN'...
STRAIN
TMBL
WAAAAH!
...THROW!
FWING
ZWING
PEPOH!
OH, NOOOO!
PING
KLINK
BOMP
GONK
WHAT'D THE PLANET EVER DO TO YOU?!
PUH PEH PEH...

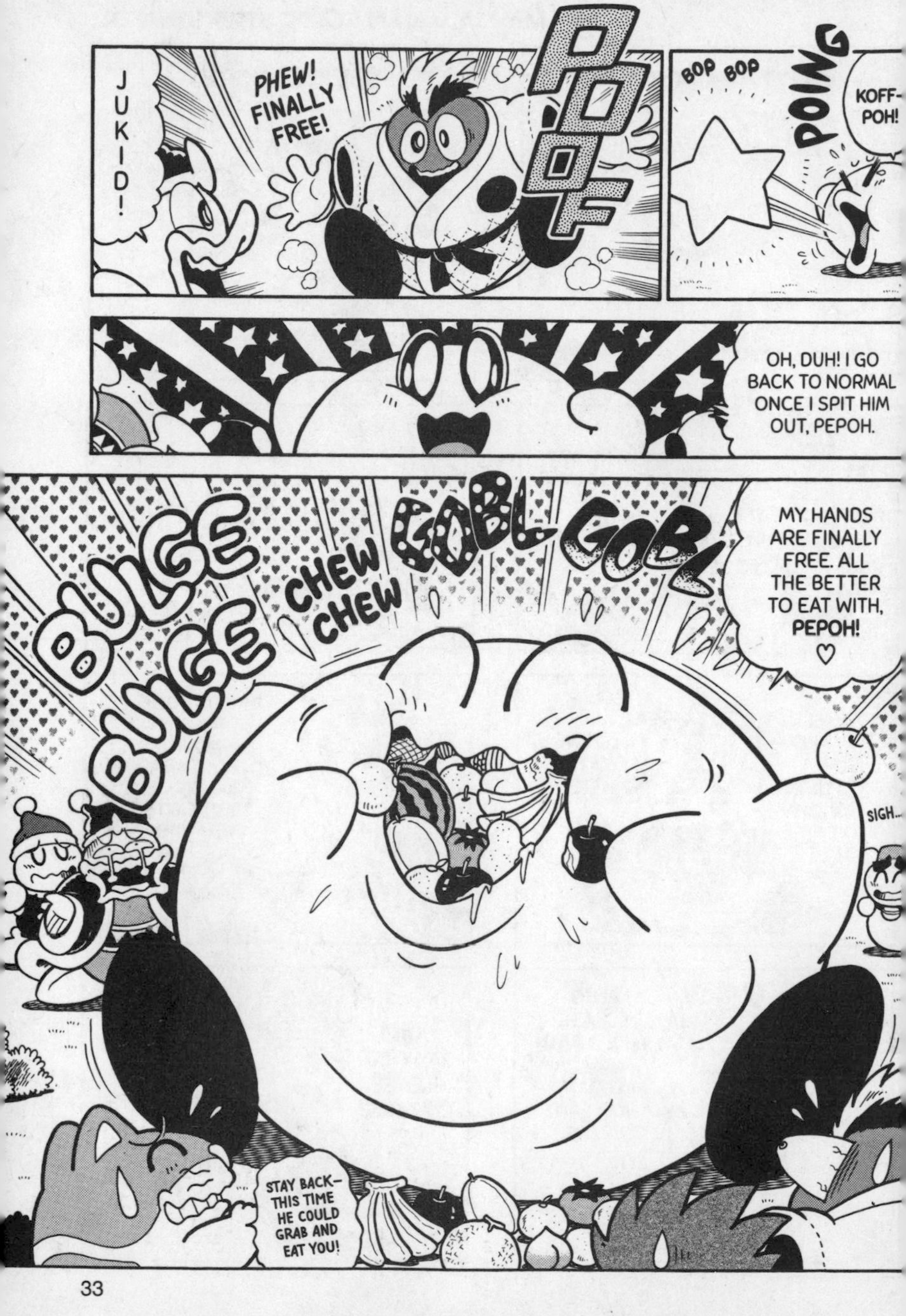
POING
KOFF-POH!
BOP BOP
POOF
PHEW! FINALLY FREE!
JUKID!
OH, DUH! I GO BACK TO NORMAL ONCE I SPIT HIM OUT, PEPOH.
MY HANDS ARE FINALLY FREE. ALL THE BETTER TO EAT WITH, PEPOH! ♡
GOBL GOBL
CHEW CHEW
BULGE BULGE
SIGH...
STAY BACK—THIS TIME HE COULD GRAB AND EAT YOU!

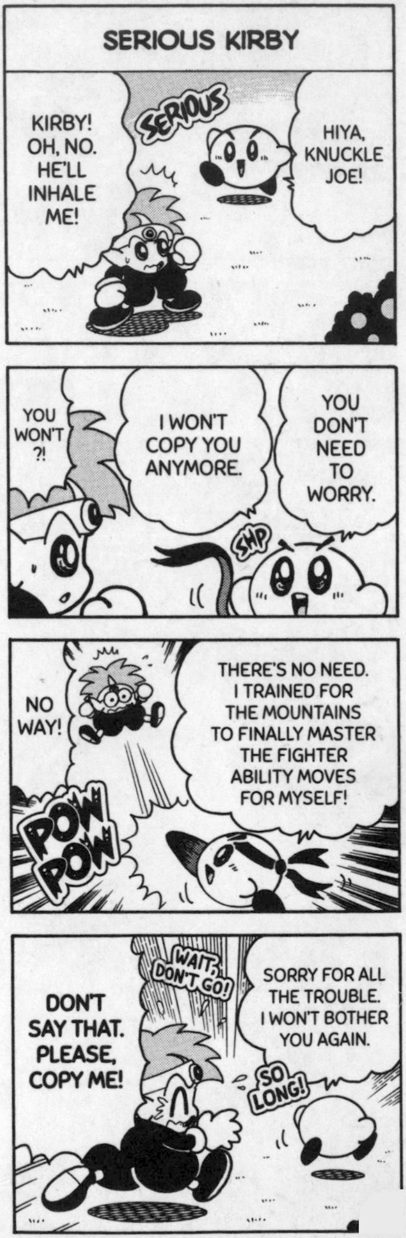
SERIOUS KIRBY
HIYA, KNUCKLE JOE!
SERIOUS
KIRBY! OH, NO. HE'LL INHALE ME!
YOU DON'T NEED TO WORRY.
I WON'T COPY YOU ANYMORE.
SHP
YOU WON'T ?!
THERE'S NO NEED. I TRAINED FOR THE MOUNTAINS TO FINALLY MASTER THE FIGHTER ABILITY MOVES FOR MYSELF!
NO WAY!
POW POW
SORRY FOR ALL THE TROUBLE. I WON'T BOTHER YOU AGAIN.
SO LONG!
WAIT, DON'T GO!
DON'T SAY THAT. PLEASE, COPY ME!

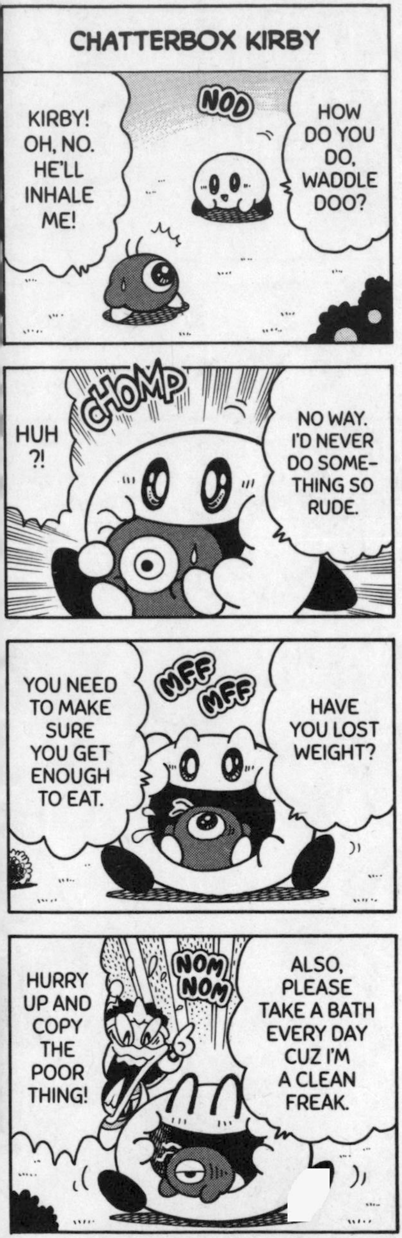
CHATTERBOX KIRBY
HOW DO YOU DO, WADDLE DOO?
NOD
KIRBY! OH, NO. HE'LL INHALE ME!
NO WAY. I'D NEVER DO SOME-THING SO RUDE.
CHOMP
HUH ?!
HAVE YOU LOST WEIGHT?
MFF MFF
YOU NEED TO MAKE SURE YOU GET ENOUGH TO EAT.
ALSO, PLEASE TAKE A BATH EVERY DAY CUZ I'M A CLEAN FREAK.
NOM NOM
HURRY UP AND COPY THE POOR THING!

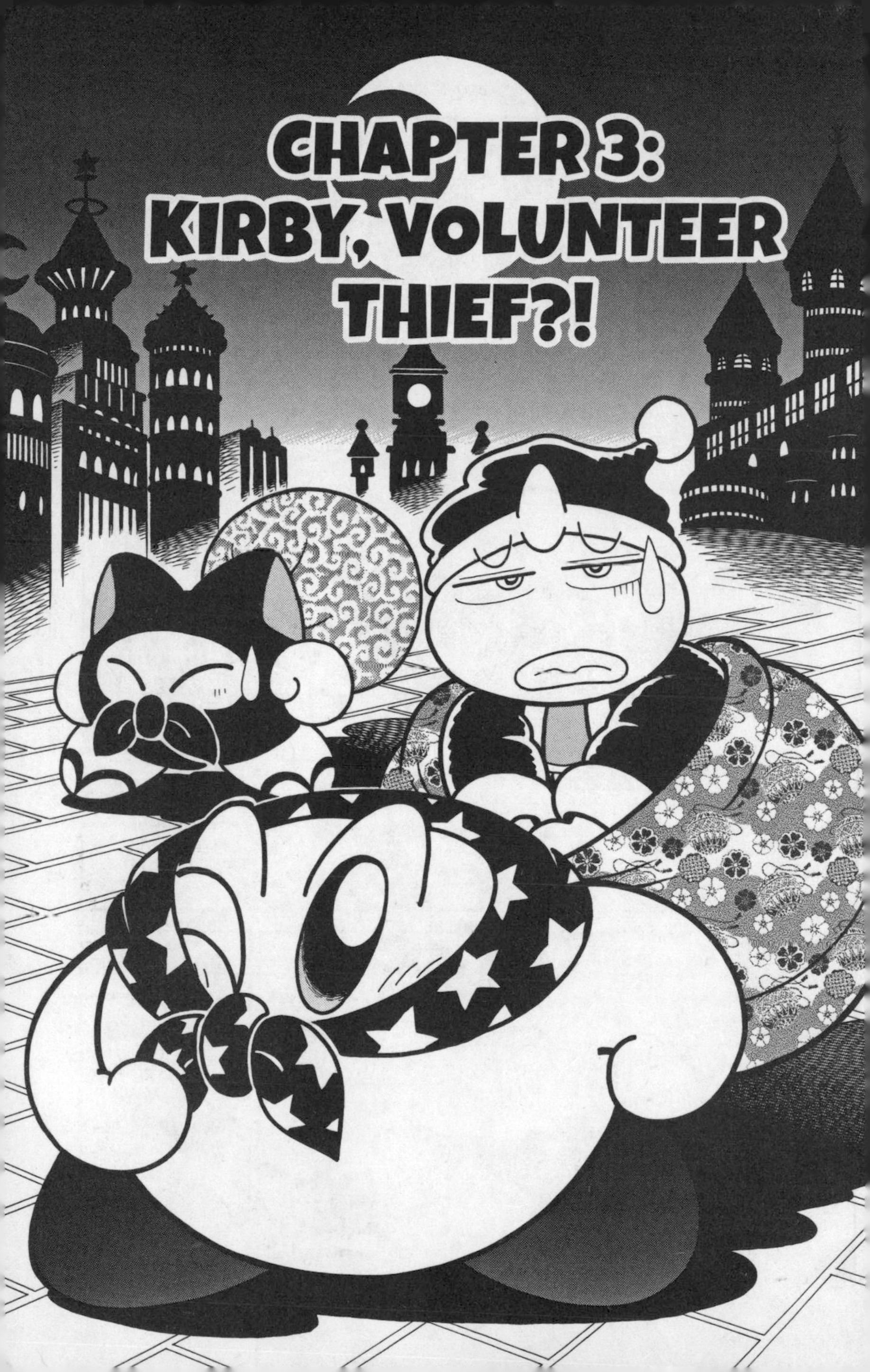
CHAPTER 3:
KIRBY, VOLUNTEER
THIEF?!

AUTHOR'S COMMENT

AFTER OVER A WEEK OF STRUGGLING TO DRAFT A NEW CHAPTER, ONE PHONE CALL WITH MY EDITOR LATER, I MANAGED TO BANG THE STORYBOARDS FOR THIS ONE OUT IN ONLY EIGHT HOURS. THANKS, EDITOR! ♫

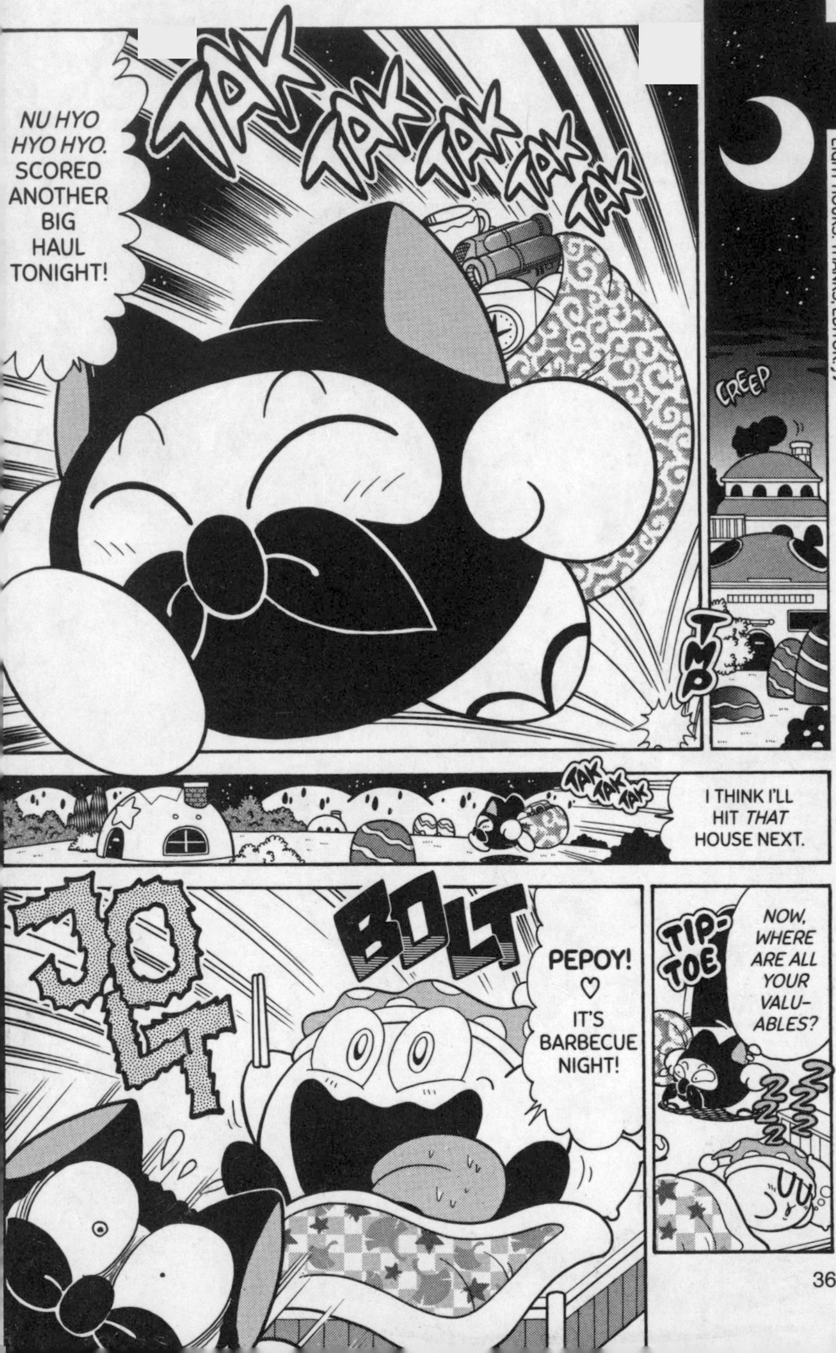
CREEP
TMP
TAK TAK TAK TAK TAK
NU HYO HYO HYO. SCORED ANOTHER BIG HAUL TONIGHT!
TAK TAK TAK
I THINK I'LL HIT *THAT* HOUSE NEXT.
TIP-TOE
NOW, WHERE ARE ALL YOUR VALU-ABLES?
ZZZ
JOLT
BOLT
PEPOY! ♡ IT'S BARBECUE NIGHT!

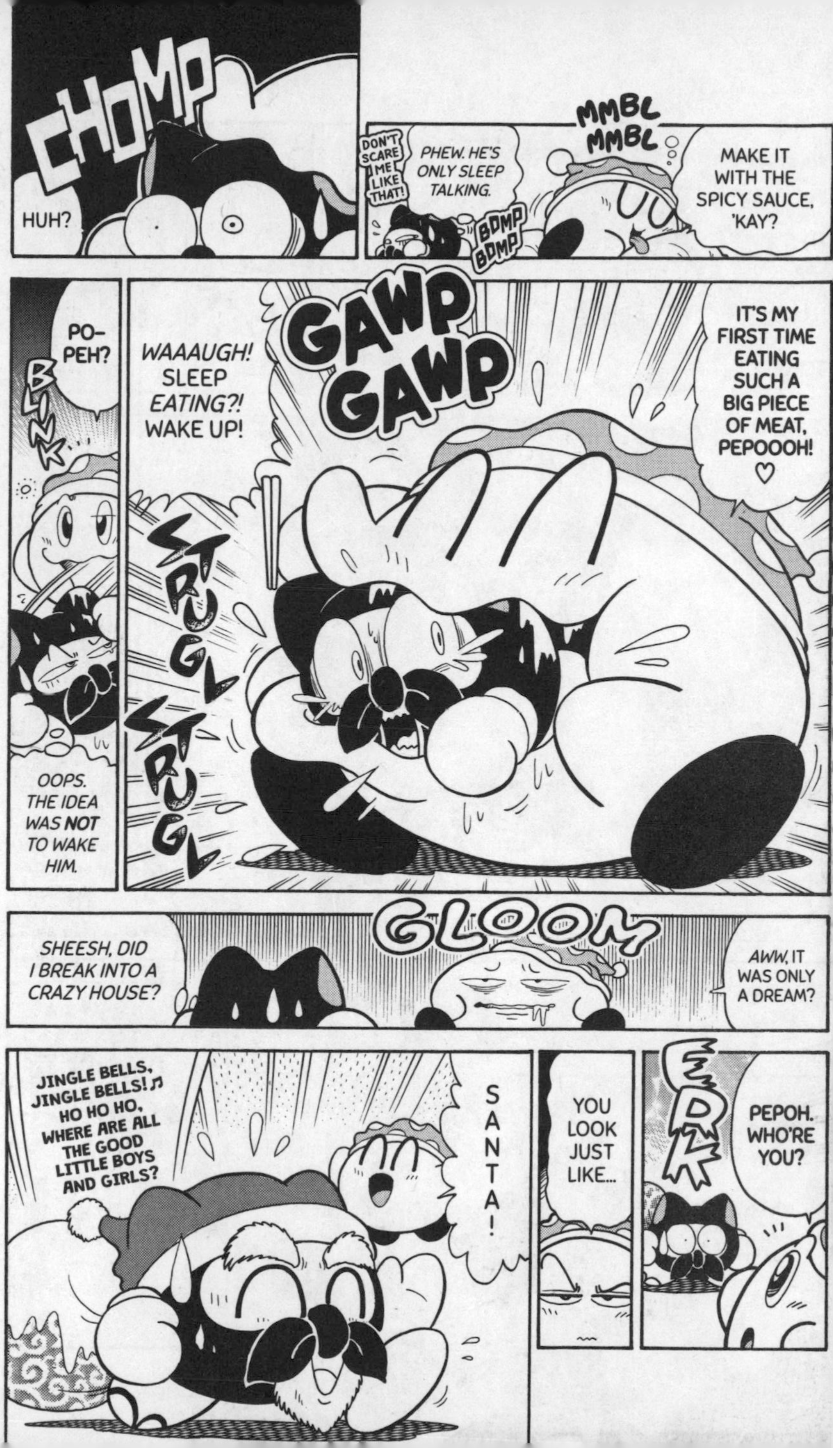
MMBL MMBL
MAKE IT WITH THE SPICY SAUCE, 'KAY?
BDMP BDMP
PHEW. HE'S ONLY SLEEP TALKING.
DON'T SCARE ME LIKE THAT!
CHOMP
HUH?
GAWP GAWP
IT'S MY FIRST TIME EATING SUCH A BIG PIECE OF MEAT, PEPOOOH! ♡
WAAAUGH! SLEEP EATING?! WAKE UP!
STRUGL STRUGL
PO-PEH?
BLINK...
OOPS. THE IDEA WAS NOT TO WAKE HIM.
GLOOM
AWW, IT WAS ONLY A DREAM?
SHEESH, DID I BREAK INTO A CRAZY HOUSE?
ERK
PEPOH. WHO'RE YOU?
YOU LOOK JUST LIKE...
SANTA!
JINGLE BELLS, JINGLE BELLS! ♫ HO HO HO, WHERE ARE ALL THE GOOD LITTLE BOYS AND GIRLS?

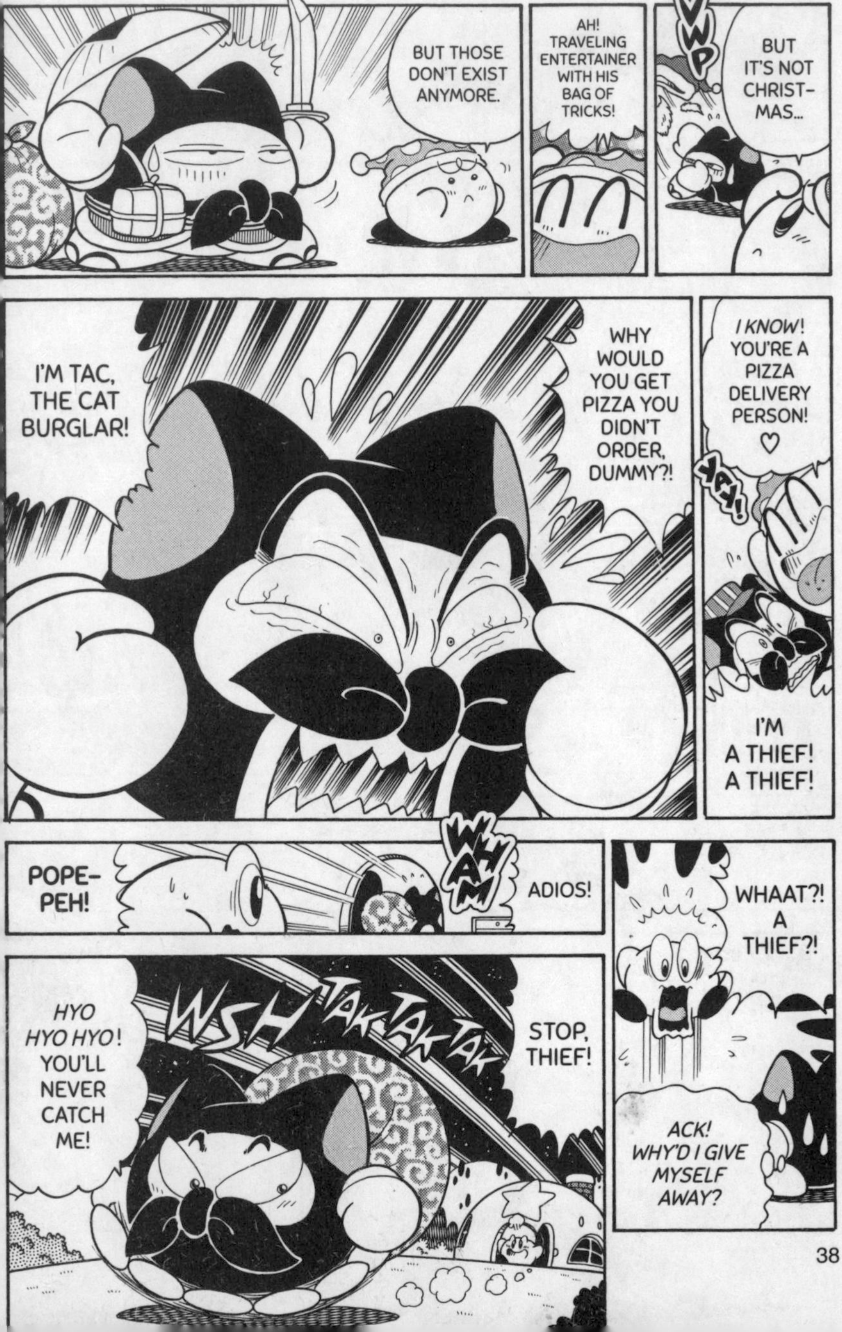
VWP
BUT IT'S NOT CHRIST-MAS...
AH! TRAVELING ENTERTAINER WITH HIS BAG OF TRICKS!
BUT THOSE DON'T EXIST ANYMORE.
I KNOW! YOU'RE A PIZZA DELIVERY PERSON! ♡
I'M A THIEF! A THIEF!
WHY WOULD YOU GET PIZZA YOU DIDN'T ORDER, DUMMY?!
I'M TAC, THE CAT BURGLAR!
WHAAT?! A THIEF?!
ACK! WHY'D I GIVE MYSELF AWAY?
ADIOS!
WHAM
POPE-PEH!
STOP, THIEF!
WSH TAK TAK TAK TAK
HYO HYO HYO! YOU'LL NEVER CATCH ME!

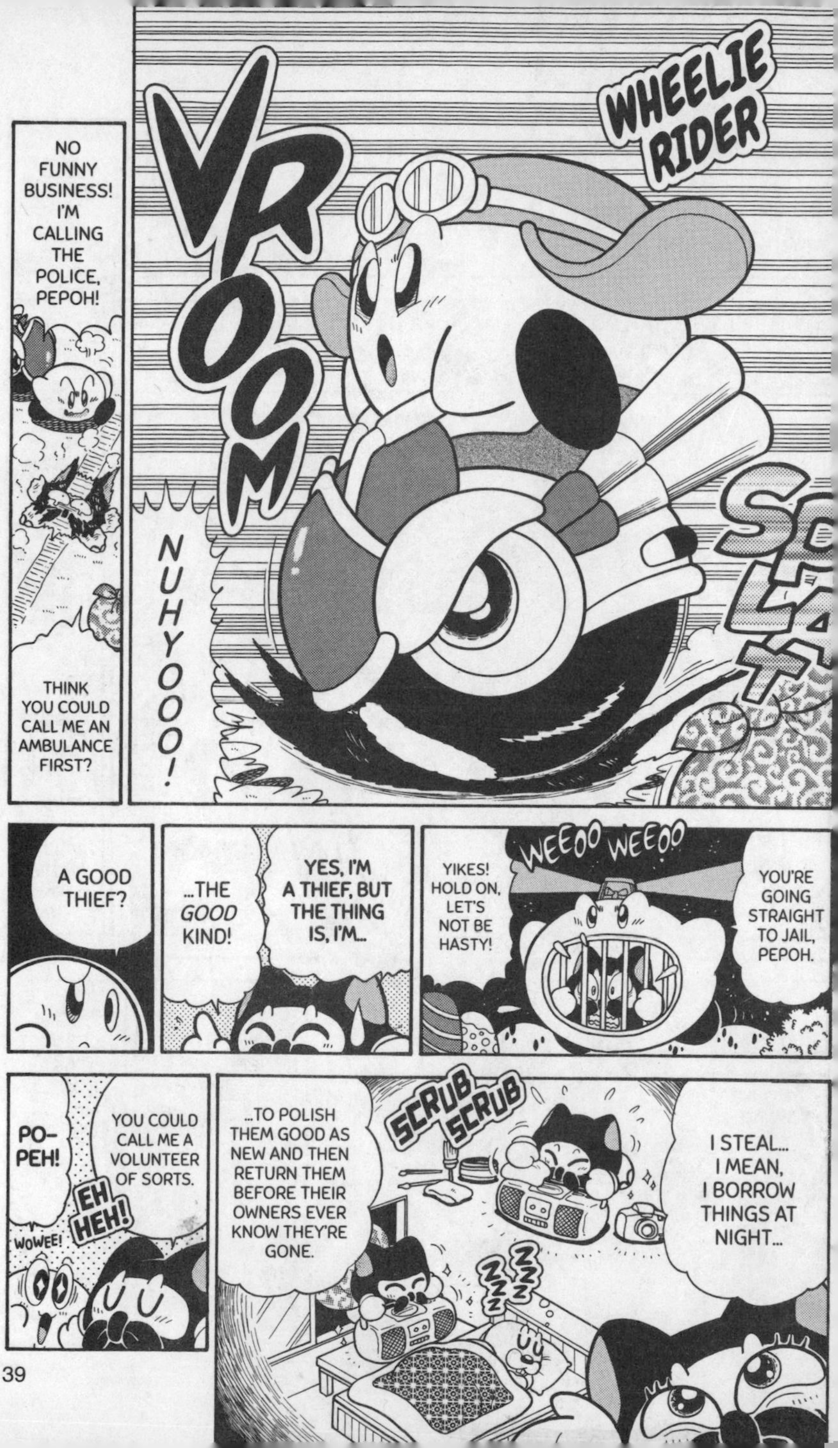
WHEELIE RIDER
VROOM
NUHYOOOO!
NO FUNNY BUSINESS! I'M CALLING THE POLICE, PEPOH!
THINK YOU COULD CALL ME AN AMBULANCE FIRST?
WEEOO WEEOO
YOU'RE GOING STRAIGHT TO JAIL, PEPOH.
YIKES! HOLD ON, LET'S NOT BE HASTY!
YES, I'M A THIEF, BUT THE THING IS, I'M...
...THE *GOOD* KIND!
A GOOD THIEF?
I STEAL... I MEAN, I BORROW THINGS AT NIGHT...
SCRUB SCRUB
...TO POLISH THEM GOOD AS NEW AND THEN RETURN THEM BEFORE THEIR OWNERS EVER KNOW THEY'RE GONE.
ZZZ ZZZ
YOU COULD CALL ME A VOLUNTEER OF SORTS.
EH HEH!
PO-PEH!
WOWEE!

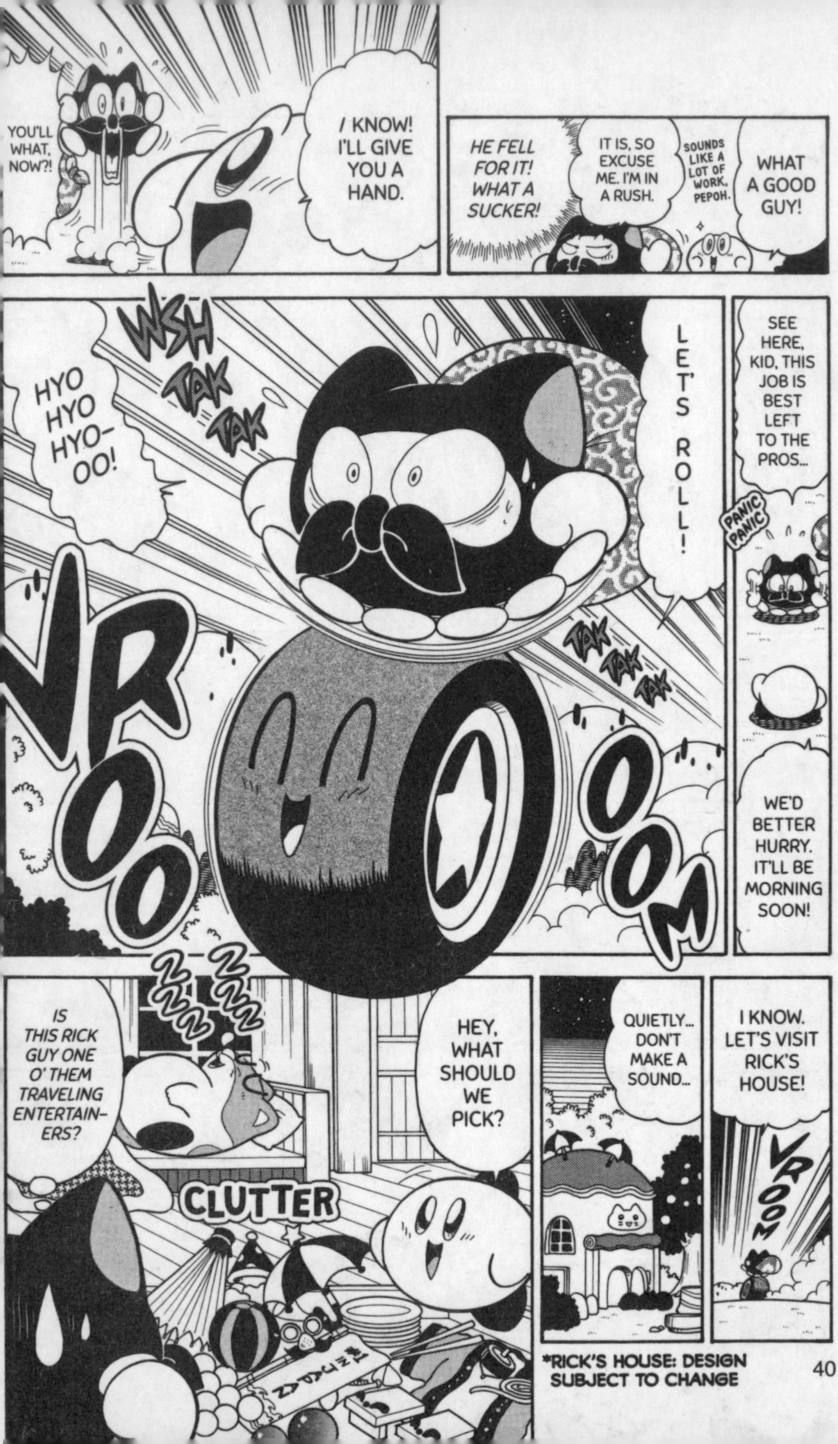
WHAT A GOOD GUY!
SOUNDS LIKE A LOT OF WORK, PEPOH.
IT IS, SO EXCUSE ME. I'M IN A RUSH.
HE FELL FOR IT! WHAT A SUCKER!
I KNOW! I'LL GIVE YOU A HAND.
YOU'LL WHAT, NOW?!
SEE HERE, KID, THIS JOB IS BEST LEFT TO THE PROS...
PANIC PANIC
WE'D BETTER HURRY. IT'LL BE MORNING SOON!
LET'S ROLL!
WSH
TAK TAK
HYO HYO HYO-OO!
VROOOOOM
TAK TAK TAK
I KNOW. LET'S VISIT RICK'S HOUSE!
VROOOM
QUIETLY... DON'T MAKE A SOUND...
HEY, WHAT SHOULD WE PICK?
ZZZ ZZZ
IS THIS RICK GUY ONE O' THEM TRAVELING ENTERTAINERS?
CLUTTER

*RICK'S HOUSE: DESIGN SUBJECT TO CHANGE

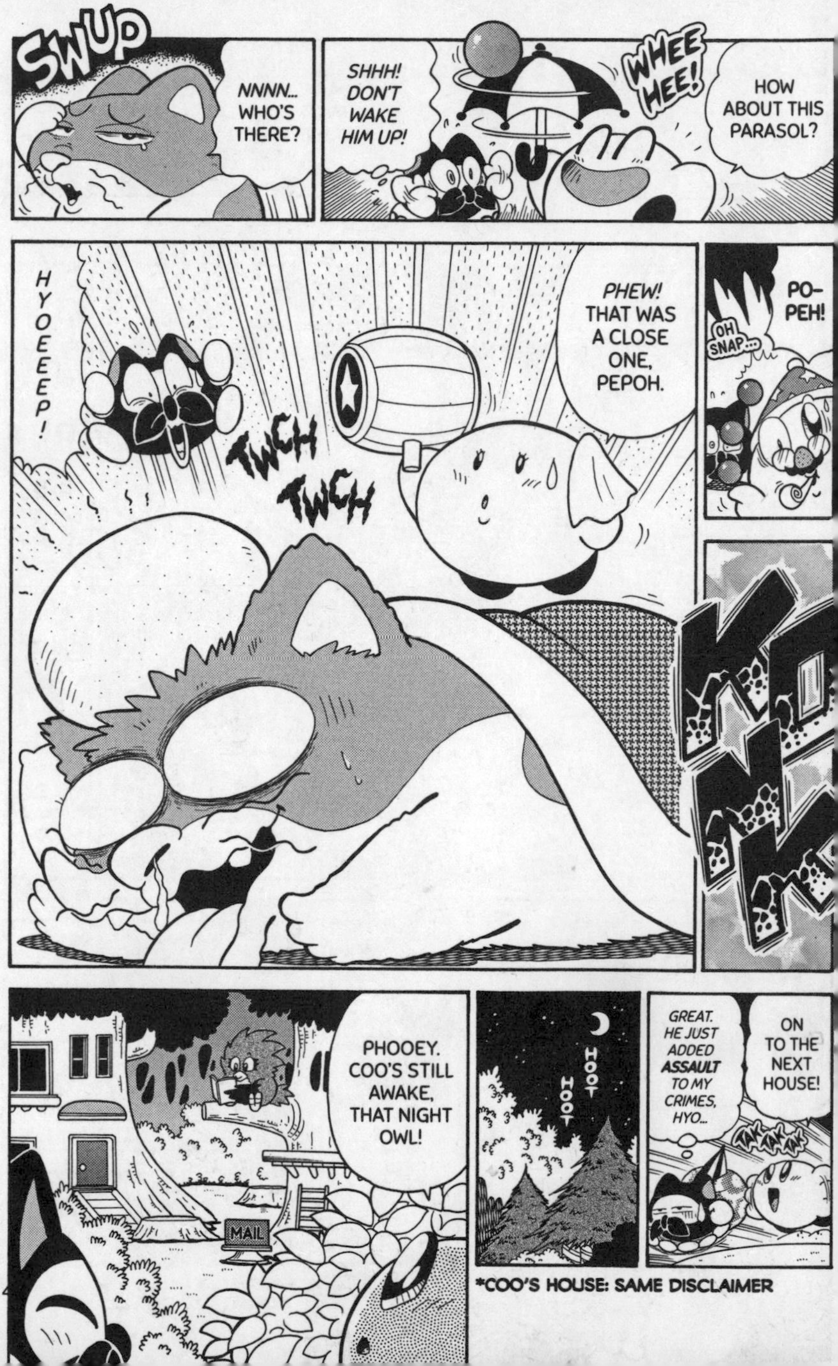
HOW ABOUT THIS PARASOL?
WHEE HEE!
SHHH! DON'T WAKE HIM UP!
SWUP
NNNN... WHO'S THERE?
PO-PEH!
OH SNAP...
PHEW! THAT WAS A CLOSE ONE, PEPOH.
TWCH TWCH
HYOEEEP!
ON TO THE NEXT HOUSE!
GREAT. HE JUST ADDED **ASSAULT** TO MY CRIMES, HYO...
TAK TAK TAK
HOOT HOOT
PHOOEY. COO'S STILL AWAKE, THAT NIGHT OWL!
MAIL
*COO'S HOUSE: SAME DISCLAIMER

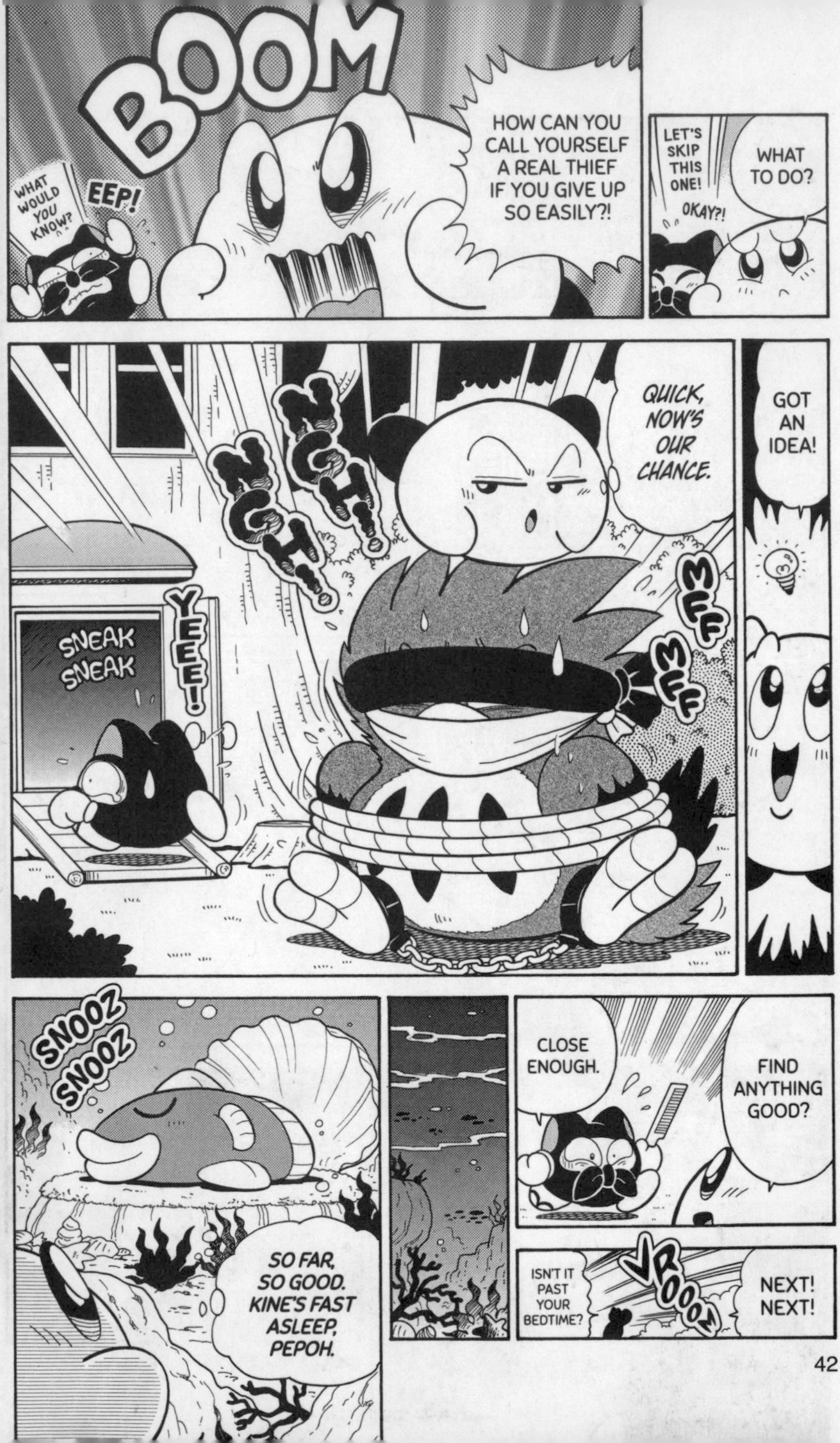
WHAT TO DO?
LET'S SKIP THIS ONE!
OKAY?!
HOW CAN YOU CALL YOURSELF A REAL THIEF IF YOU GIVE UP SO EASILY?!
BOOM
EEP!
WHAT WOULD YOU KNOW?
GOT AN IDEA!
QUICK, NOW'S OUR CHANCE.
MFF
MFF
NGH!
NGH!
YEEE!
SNEAK SNEAK
FIND ANYTHING GOOD?
CLOSE ENOUGH.
NEXT! NEXT!
VROOOM
ISN'T IT PAST YOUR BEDTIME?
SNOOZ SNOOZ
SO FAR, SO GOOD. KINE'S FAST ASLEEP, PEPOH.

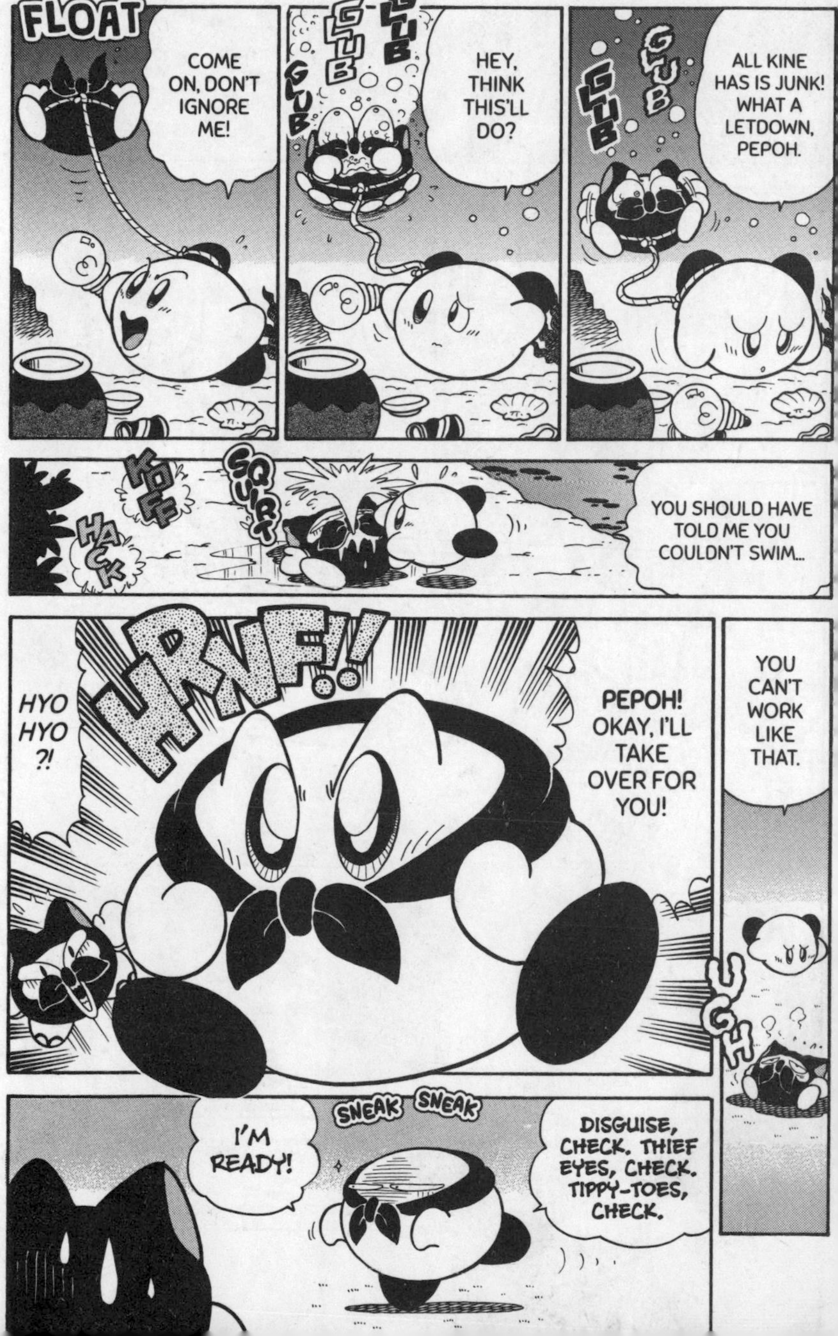
GLUB GLUB
ALL KINE HAS IS JUNK! WHAT A LETDOWN, PEPOH.
GLUB-GLUB
HEY, THINK THIS'LL DO?
FLOAT
COME ON, DON'T IGNORE ME!
YOU SHOULD HAVE TOLD ME YOU COULDN'T SWIM...
SQUIRT
KOFF
HACK
YOU CAN'T WORK LIKE THAT.
UGH
PEPOH! OKAY, I'LL TAKE OVER FOR YOU!
HRNF!!
HYO HYO ?!
DISGUISE, CHECK. THIEF EYES, CHECK. TIPPY-TOES, CHECK.
SNEAK SNEAK
I'M READY!

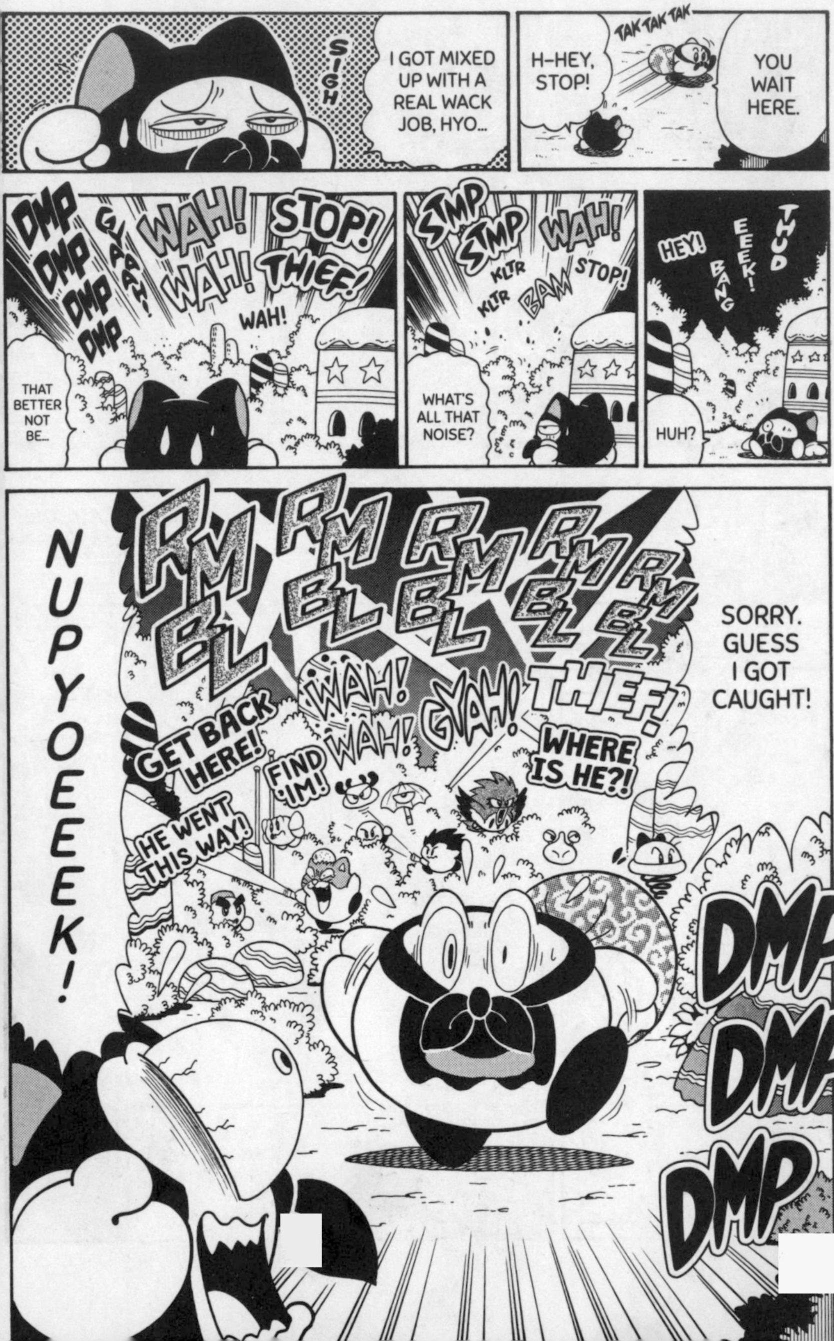
YOU WAIT HERE.
TAK TAK TAK
H-HEY, STOP!
I GOT MIXED UP WITH A REAL WACK JOB, HYO...
SIGH
THUD
EEEK!
BANG
HEY!
HUH?
WAH!
STOP!
STMP STMP
KLTR KLTR
BAM
WHAT'S ALL THAT NOISE?
STOP! THIEF!
WAH! WAH!
GYAAAH!
DMP DMP DMP DMP
WAH!
THAT BETTER NOT BE...
SORRY. GUESS I GOT CAUGHT!
RMBL RMBL RMBL RMBL RMBL
THIEF!
WHERE IS HE?!
GYAH!
WAH! WAH!
FIND 'IM!
GET BACK HERE!
HE WENT THIS WAY!
DMP DMP DMP
NUPYOEEEEK!

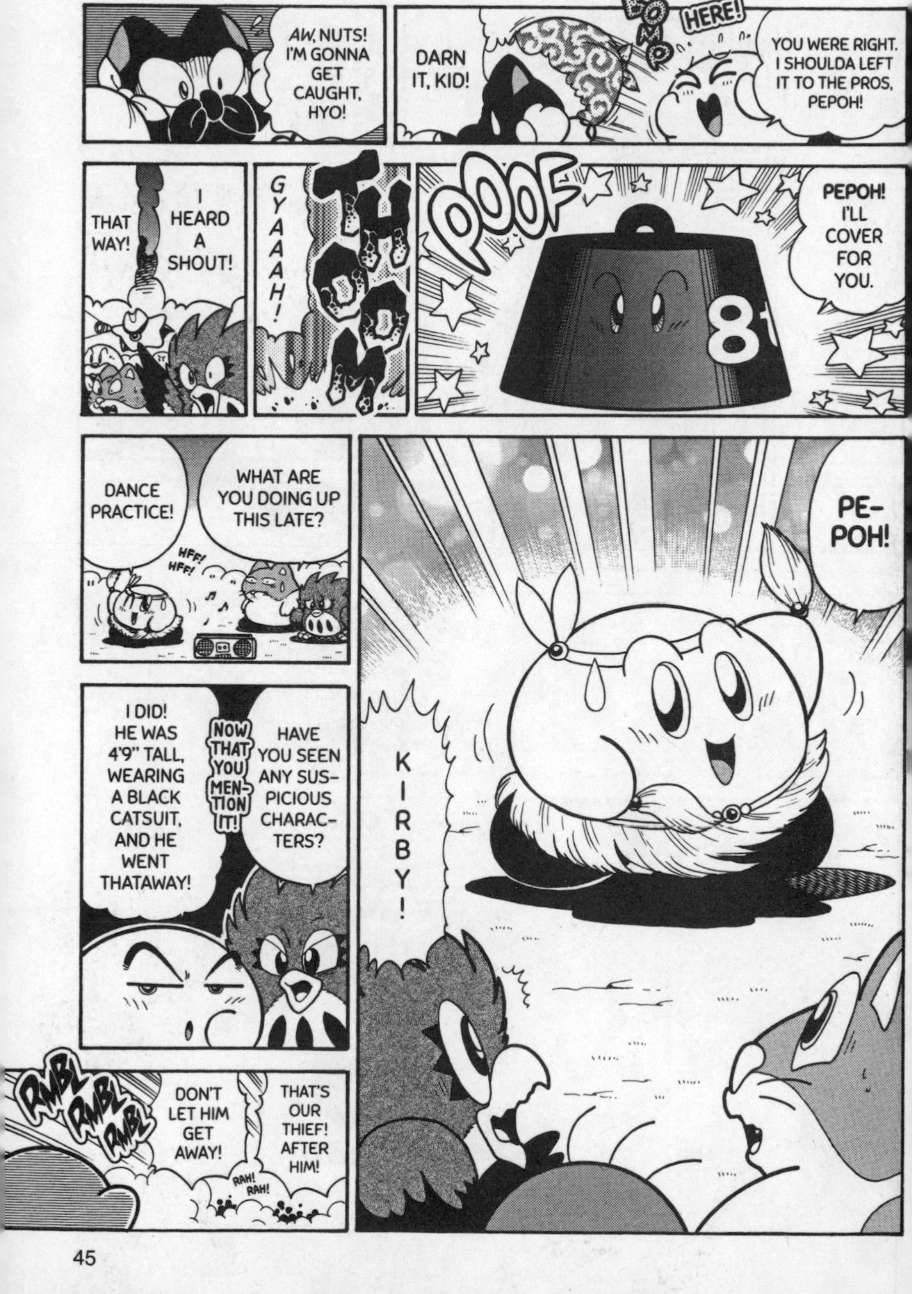

HERE!
YOU WERE RIGHT. I SHOULDA LEFT IT TO THE PROS, PEPOH!
BOMP
DARN IT, KID!
AW, NUTS! I'M GONNA GET CAUGHT, HYO!
PEPOH! I'LL COVER FOR YOU.
POOF
8
THOOOM
GYAAAAH!
I HEARD A SHOUT!
THAT WAY!
PE-POH!
KIRBY!
WHAT ARE YOU DOING UP THIS LATE?
DANCE PRACTICE!
HFF! HFF!
HAVE YOU SEEN ANY SUSPICIOUS CHARACTERS?
NOW THAT YOU MENTION IT!
I DID! HE WAS 4'9" TALL, WEARING A BLACK CATSUIT, AND HE WENT THATAWAY!
THAT'S OUR THIEF! AFTER HIM!
DON'T LET HIM GET AWAY!
RAH! RAH!
RMBL RMBL RMBL

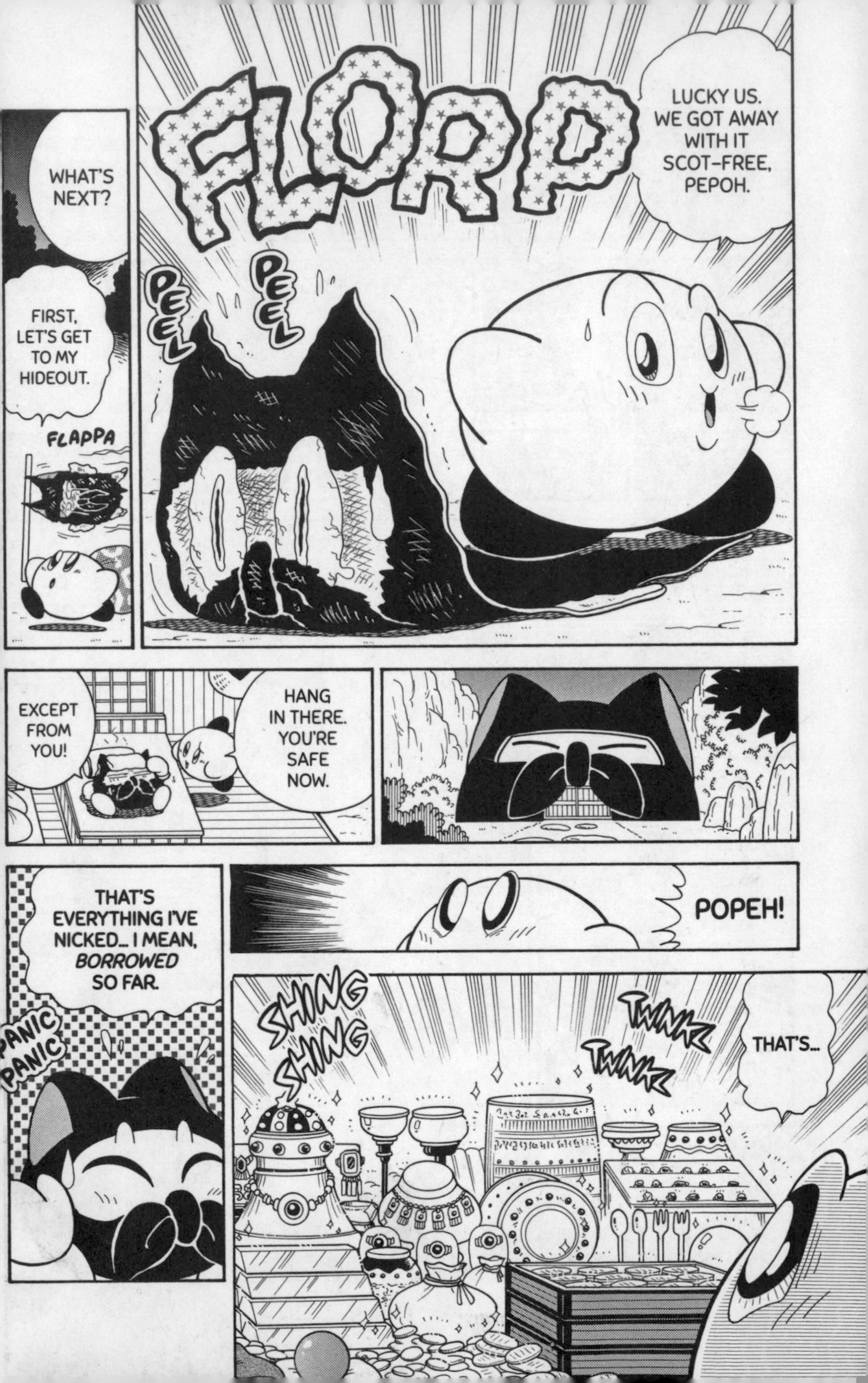
LUCKY US. WE GOT AWAY WITH IT SCOT-FREE, PEPOH.
FLORP
PEEL PEEL
WHAT'S NEXT?
FIRST, LET'S GET TO MY HIDEOUT.
FLAPPA
HANG IN THERE. YOU'RE SAFE NOW.
EXCEPT FROM YOU!
POPEH!
THAT'S...
TWINK TWINK
SHING SHING
THAT'S EVERYTHING I'VE NICKED... I MEAN, *BORROWED* SO FAR.
PANIC PANIC

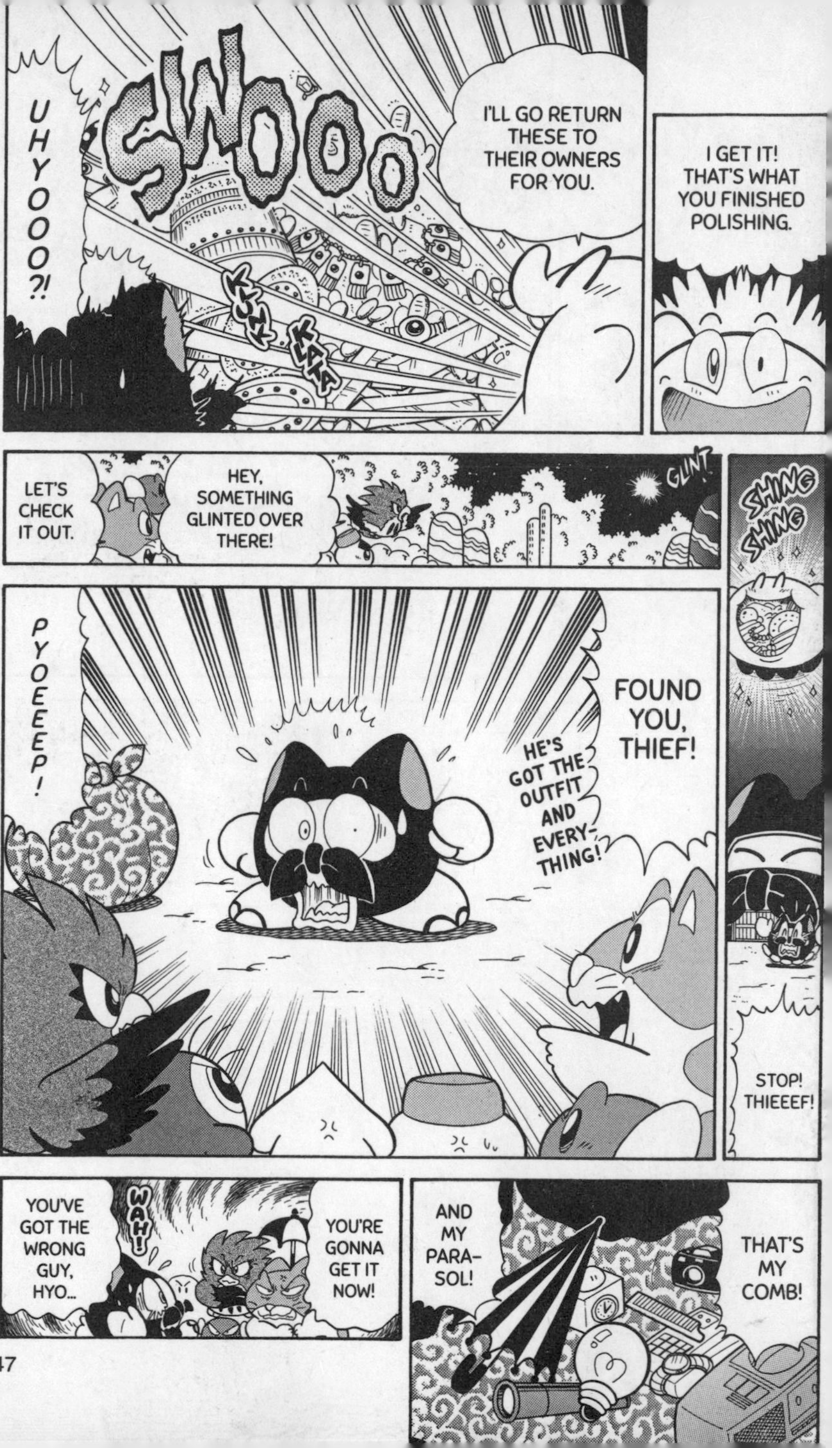
I GET IT! THAT'S WHAT YOU FINISHED POLISHING.
I'LL GO RETURN THESE TO THEIR OWNERS FOR YOU.
SWOOO
KLATA
UHYOOOO?!
SHING SHING
STOP! THIEEEF!
GLINT
HEY, SOMETHING GLINTED OVER THERE!
LET'S CHECK IT OUT.
FOUND YOU, THIEF!
HE'S GOT THE OUTFIT AND EVERY-THING!
PYOEEEP!
THAT'S MY COMB!
AND MY PARA-SOL!
YOU'RE GONNA GET IT NOW!
WAH!
YOU'VE GOT THE WRONG GUY, HYO...

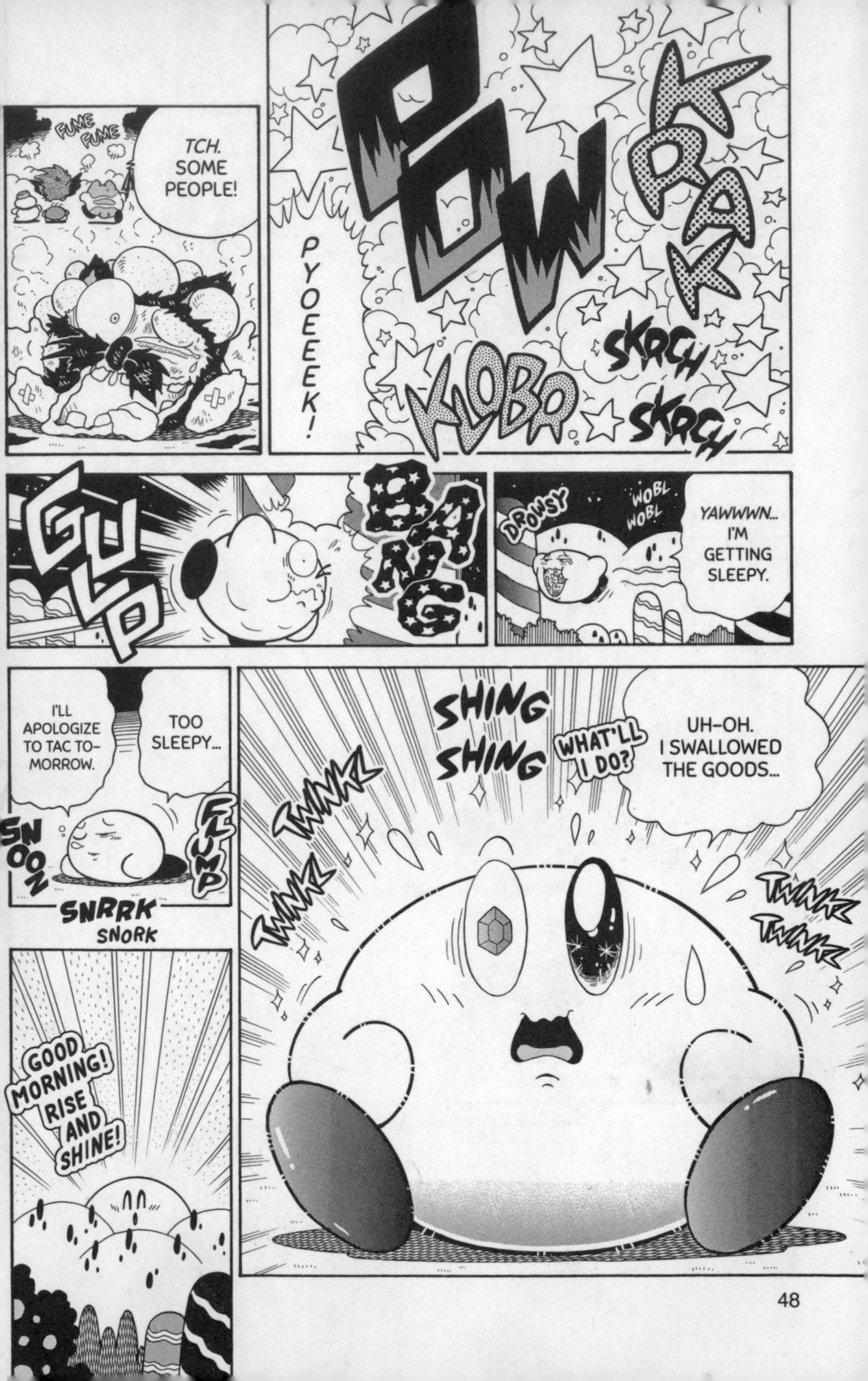
FUME FUME
TCH. SOME PEOPLE!
PYOEEEK!
POW
KRAK
KLOBR
SKRCH
SKRCH
GULP
BANG
DROWSY
WOBL WOBL
YAWWWN... I'M GETTING SLEEPY.
TOO SLEEPY...
I'LL APOLOGIZE TO TAC TO-MORROW.
SNOOZ
FLUMP
SNRRK
SNORK
GOOD MORNING! RISE AND SHINE!
SHING SHING
WHAT'LL I DO?
UH-OH. I SWALLOWED THE GOODS...
TWINKL TWINKL
TWINKL TWINKL

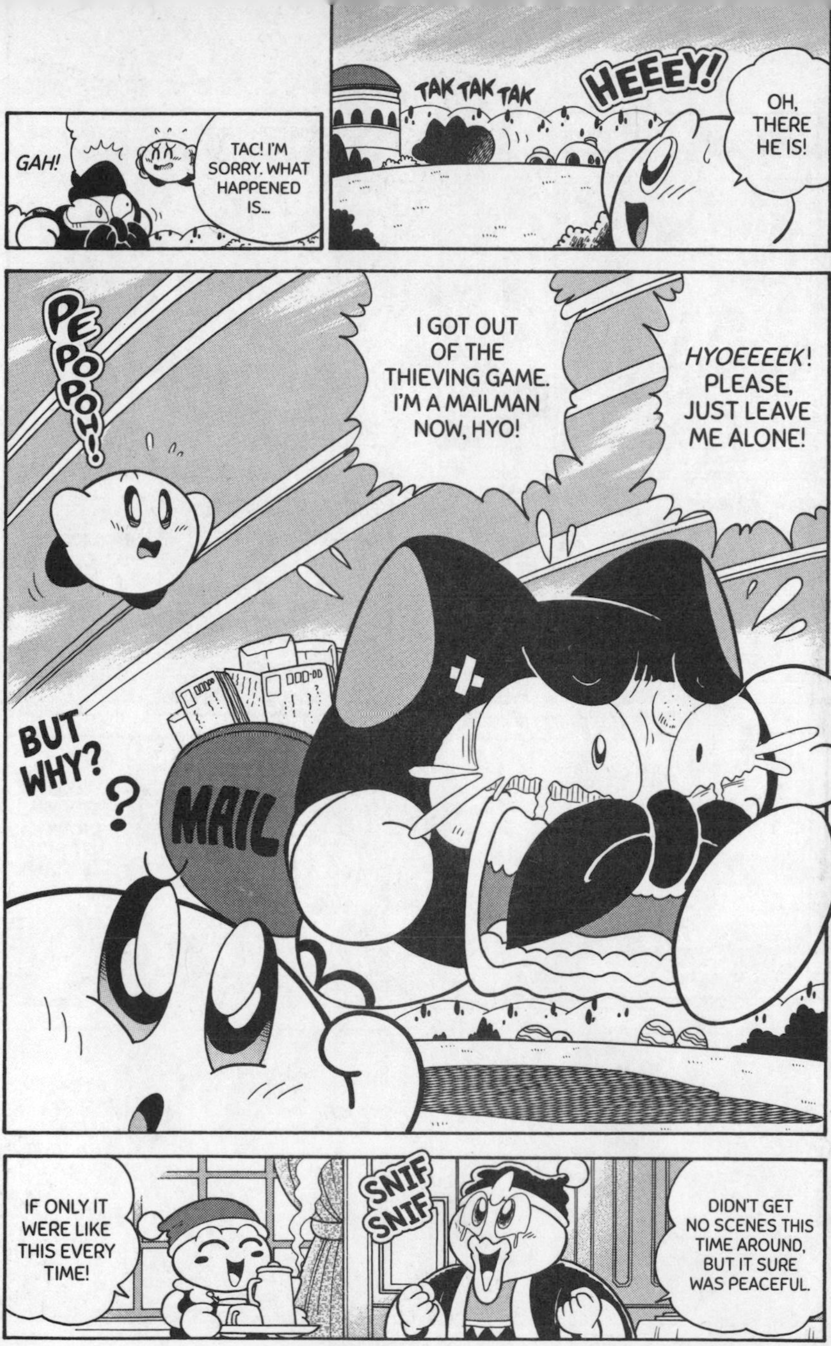
OH, THERE HE IS!
HEEEY!
TAK TAK TAK
TAC! I'M SORRY. WHAT HAPPENED IS...
GAH!
HYOEEEEK! PLEASE, JUST LEAVE ME ALONE!
I GOT OUT OF THE THIEVING GAME. I'M A MAILMAN NOW, HYO!
PEPOPOH!
MAIL
BUT WHY?
DIDN'T GET NO SCENES THIS TIME AROUND, BUT IT SURE WAS PEACEFUL.
SNIF SNIF
IF ONLY IT WERE LIKE THIS EVERY TIME!

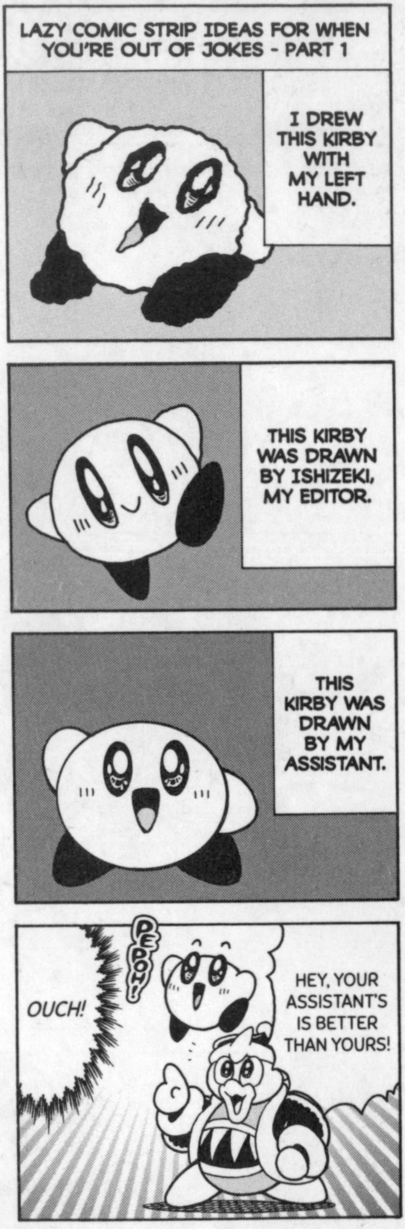
LAZY COMIC STRIP IDEAS FOR WHEN YOU'RE OUT OF JOKES - PART 1
I DREW THIS KIRBY WITH MY LEFT HAND.
THIS KIRBY WAS DRAWN BY ISHIZEKI, MY EDITOR.
THIS KIRBY WAS DRAWN BY MY ASSISTANT.
HEY, YOUR ASSISTANT'S IS BETTER THAN YOURS!
PEPOH!
OUCH!

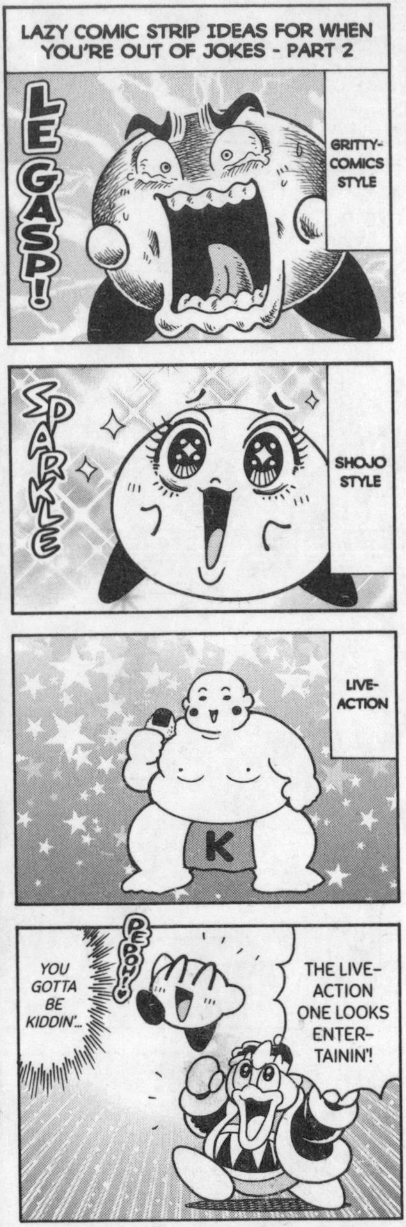
LAZY COMIC STRIP IDEAS FOR WHEN YOU'RE OUT OF JOKES - PART 2
GRITTY-COMICS STYLE
LE GASP!
SHOJO STYLE
SPARKLE
LIVE-ACTION
THE LIVE-ACTION ONE LOOKS ENTER-TAININ'!
PEPOH!
YOU GOTTA BE KIDDIN'...

CHAPTER 4: HERO KIRBY APPEARS!

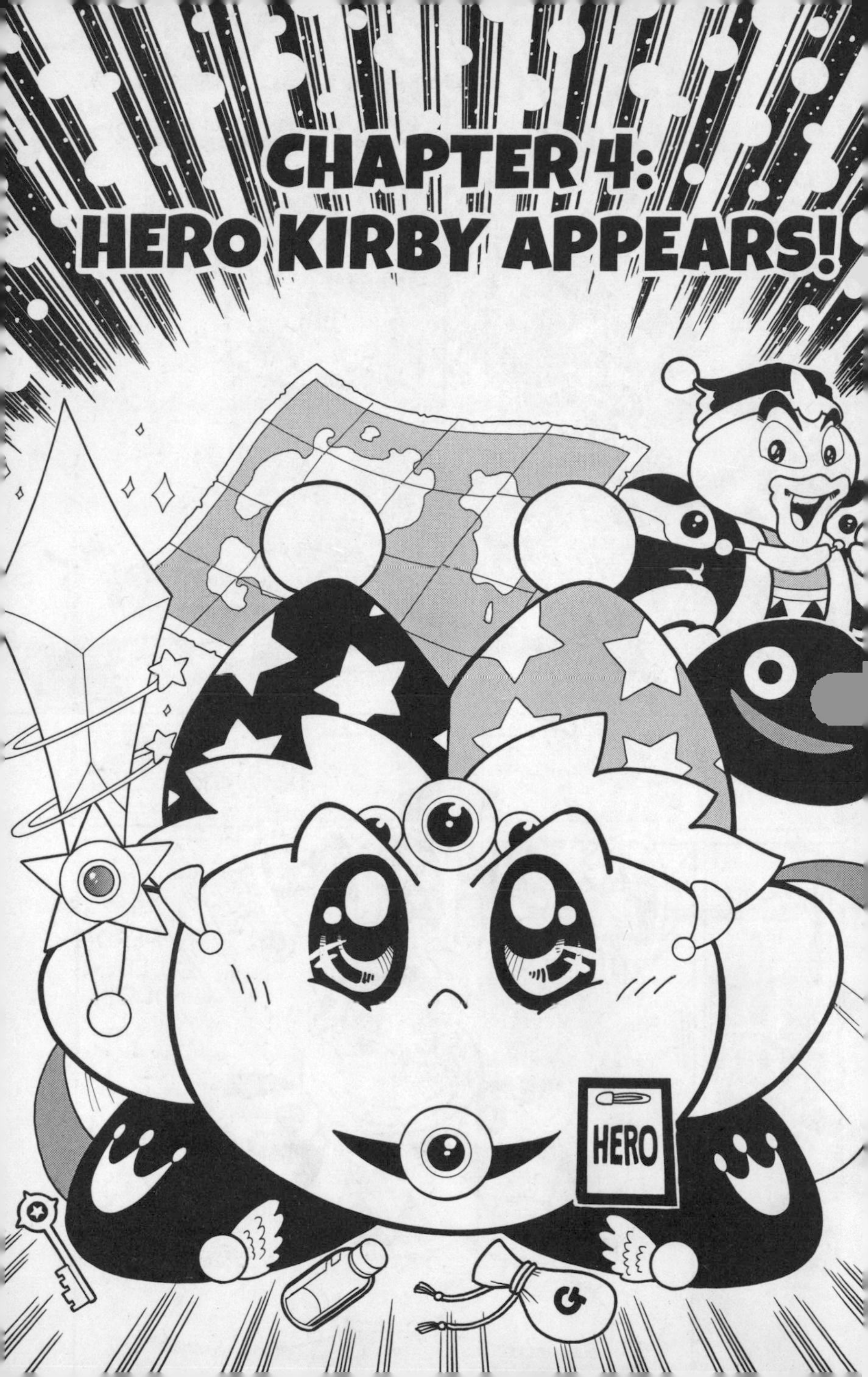
HERO

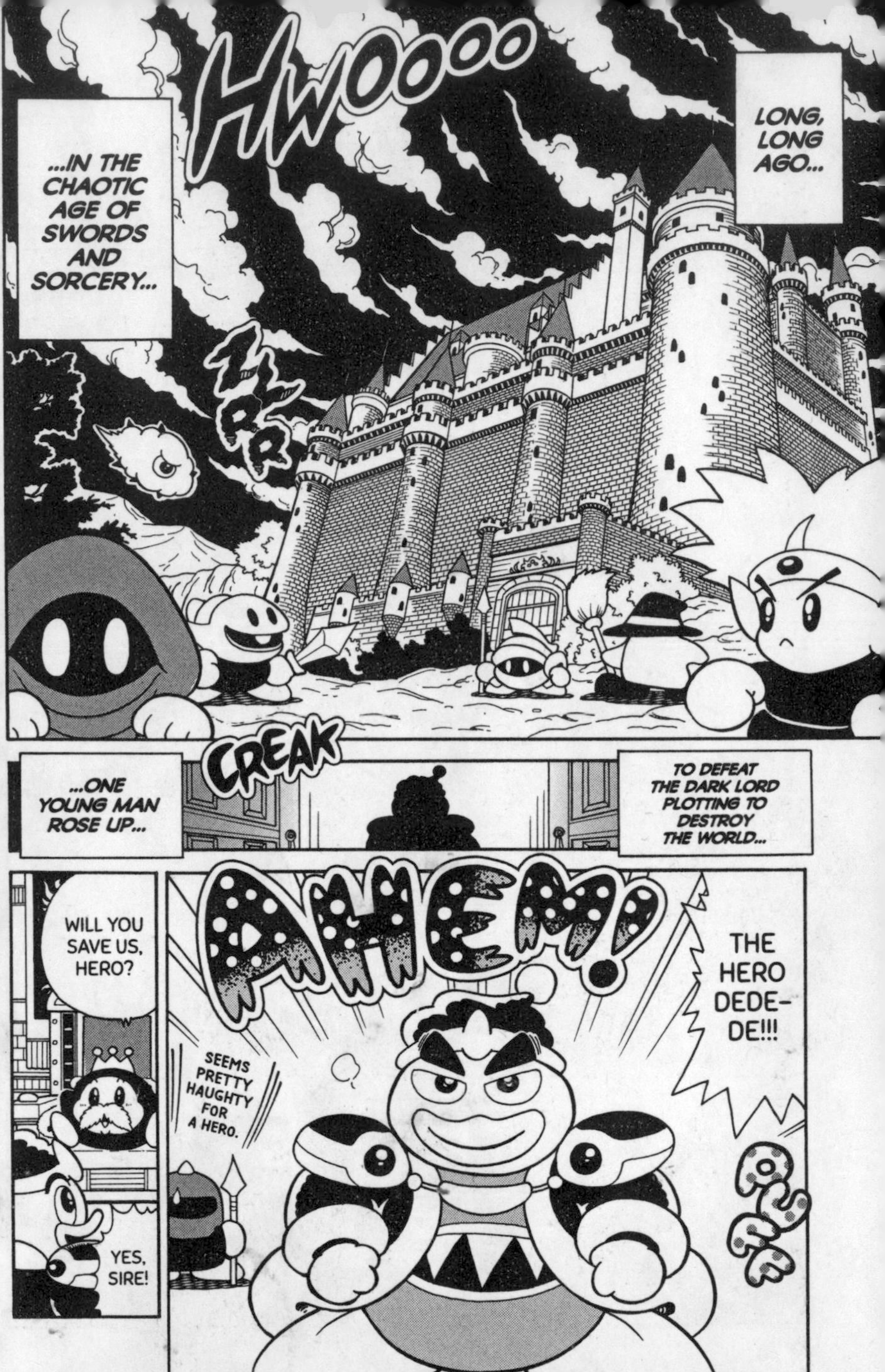
LONG, LONG AGO...
HWOOOO
...IN THE CHAOTIC AGE OF SWORDS AND SORCERY...
TO DEFEAT THE DARK LORD PLOTTING TO DESTROY THE WORLD...
CREAK
...ONE YOUNG MAN ROSE UP...
THE HERO DEDEDE!!!
AHEM!
SEEMS PRETTY HAUGHTY FOR A HERO.
WILL YOU SAVE US, HERO?
YES, SIRE!

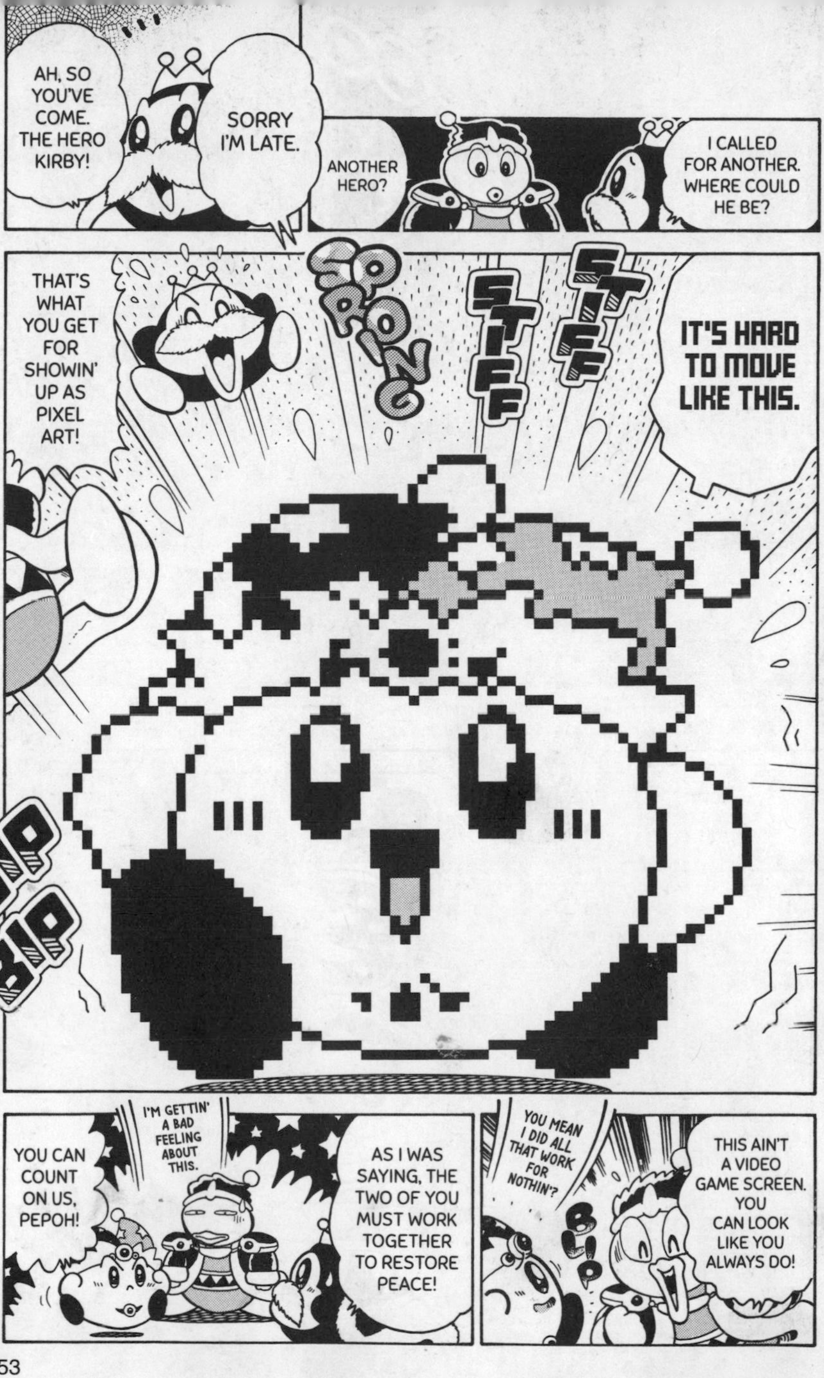

...
I CALLED FOR ANOTHER. WHERE COULD HE BE?
ANOTHER HERO?
AH, SO YOU'VE COME. THE HERO KIRBY!
SORRY I'M LATE.
IT'S HARD TO MOVE LIKE THIS.
STIFF
STIFF
SPRONG
THAT'S WHAT YOU GET FOR SHOWIN' UP AS PIXEL ART!
BIP BIP
THIS AIN'T A VIDEO GAME SCREEN. YOU CAN LOOK LIKE YOU ALWAYS DO!
BIP
YOU MEAN I DID ALL THAT WORK FOR NOTHIN'?
AS I WAS SAYING, THE TWO OF YOU MUST WORK TOGETHER TO RESTORE PEACE!
I'M GETTIN' A BAD FEELING ABOUT THIS.
YOU CAN COUNT ON US, PEPOH!

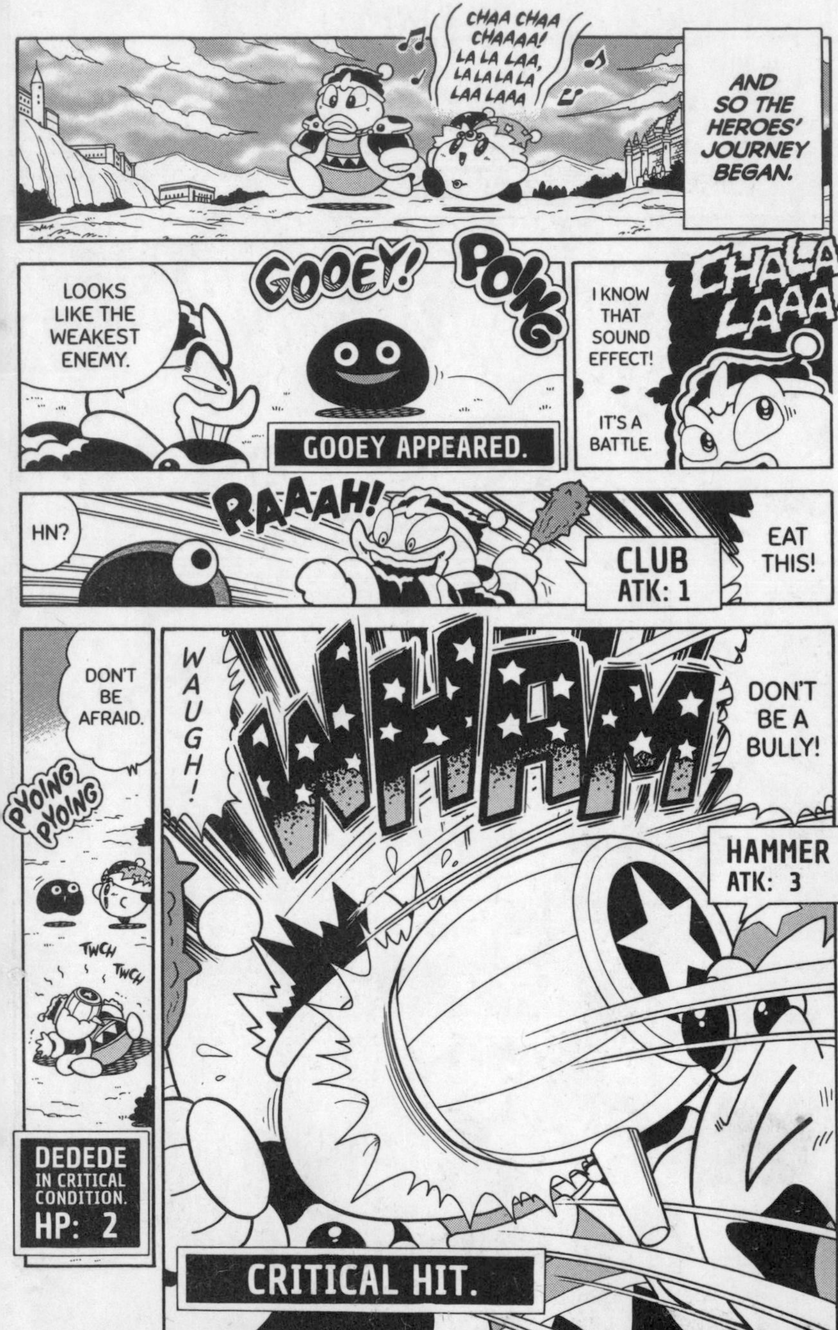
AND SO THE HEROES' JOURNEY BEGAN.
CHAA CHAA CHAAAA! LA LA LAA, LA LA LA LA LAA LAAA
CHALA LAAA
I KNOW THAT SOUND EFFECT!
IT'S A BATTLE.
GOOEY!
POING
LOOKS LIKE THE WEAKEST ENEMY.
GOOEY APPEARED.
EAT THIS!
CLUB ATK: 1
RAAAH!
HN?
DON'T BE A BULLY!
HAMMER ATK: 3
WHAM
WAUGH!
CRITICAL HIT.
DON'T BE AFRAID.
PYOING PYOING
TWCH TWCH
DEDEDE IN CRITICAL CONDITION. HP: 2

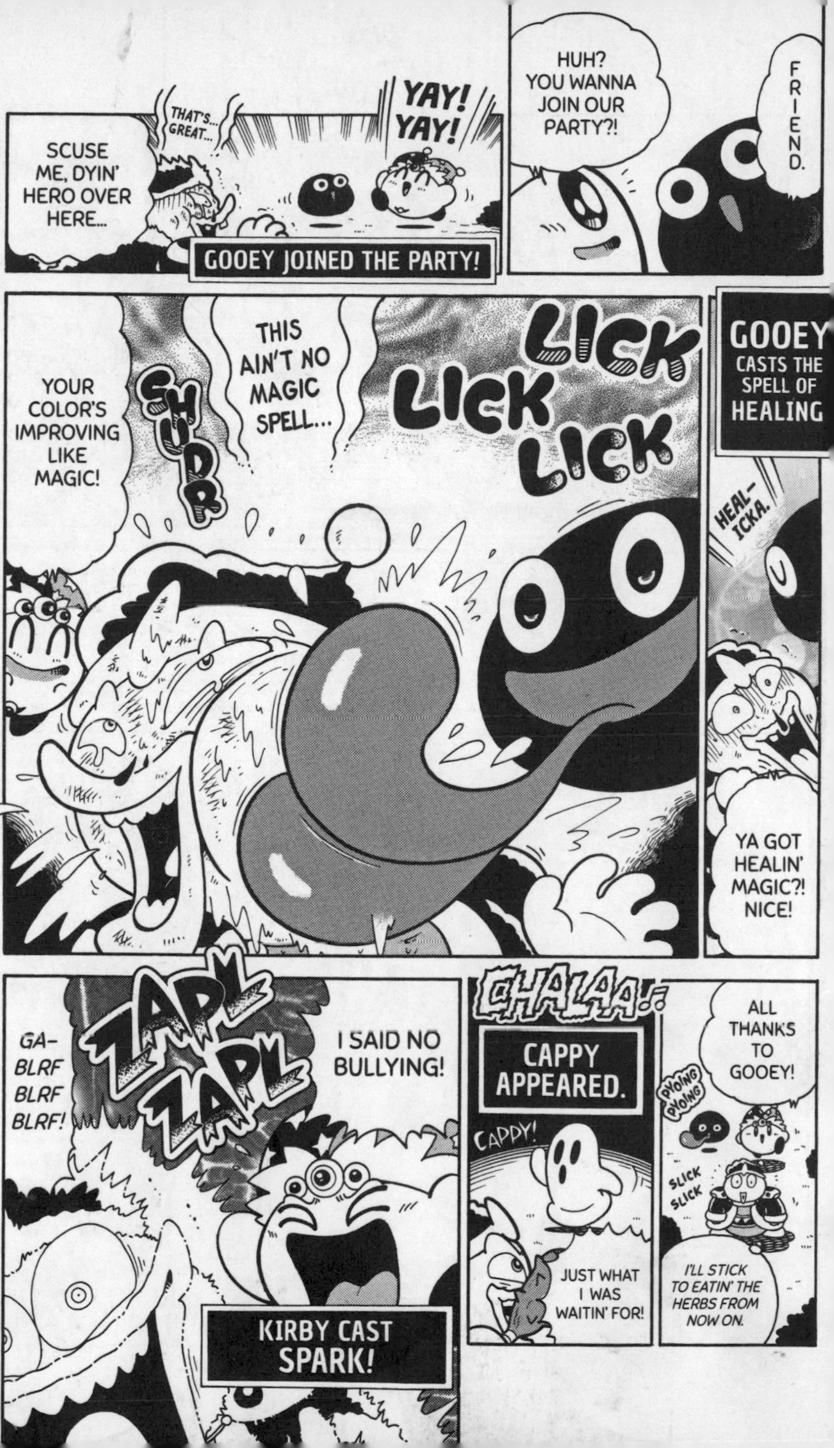
FRIEND.
HUH? YOU WANNA JOIN OUR PARTY?!
YAY! YAY!
THAT'S... GREAT...
SCUSE ME, DYIN' HERO OVER HERE...
GOOEY JOINED THE PARTY!
GOOEY CASTS THE SPELL OF HEALING
HEAL-ICKA.
YA GOT HEALIN' MAGIC?! NICE!
LICK LICK LICK
THIS AIN'T NO MAGIC SPELL...
SHUDDR
YOUR COLOR'S IMPROVING LIKE MAGIC!
ALL THANKS TO GOOEY!
PYOING PYOING
SLICK SLICK
I'LL STICK TO EATIN' THE HERBS FROM NOW ON.
CHALAA!
CAPPY APPEARED.
CAPPY!
JUST WHAT I WAS WAITIN' FOR!
I SAID NO BULLYING!
ZAP! ZAP! ZAP!
GA-BLRF BLRF BLRF!
KIRBY CAST SPARK!

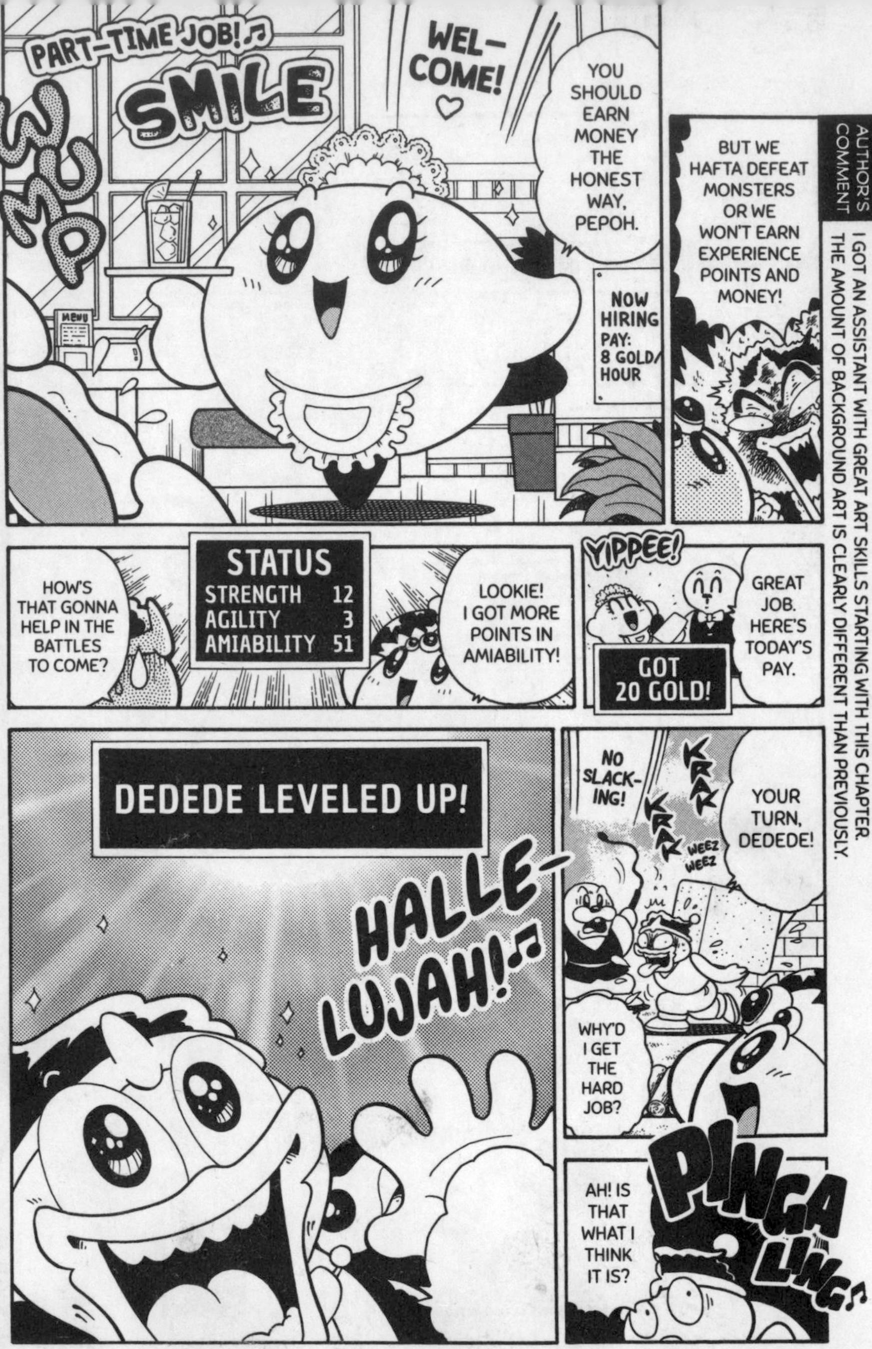
BUT WE HAFTA DEFEAT MONSTERS OR WE WON'T EARN EXPERIENCE POINTS AND MONEY!
WEL-COME!
YOU SHOULD EARN MONEY THE HONEST WAY, PEPOH.
NOW HIRING PAY: 8 GOLD/ HOUR
PART-TIME JOB!♫
SMILE
WMUP
MENU
YIPPEE!
GREAT JOB. HERE'S TODAY'S PAY.
GOT 20 GOLD!
LOOKIE! I GOT MORE POINTS IN AMIABILITY!
STATUS
STRENGTH 12
AGILITY 3
AMIABILITY 51
HOW'S THAT GONNA HELP IN THE BATTLES TO COME?
YOUR TURN, DEDEDE!
KRAK
KRAK
NO SLACK-ING!
WEEZ WEEZ
WHY'D I GET THE HARD JOB?
PINGA LING♫
AH! IS THAT WHAT I THINK IT IS?
DEDEDE LEVELED UP!
HALLE-LUJAH!♫

AUTHOR'S COMMENT

I GOT AN ASSISTANT WITH GREAT ART SKILLS STARTING WITH THIS CHAPTER. THE AMOUNT OF BACKGROUND ART IS CLEARLY DIFFERENT THAN PREVIOUSLY.

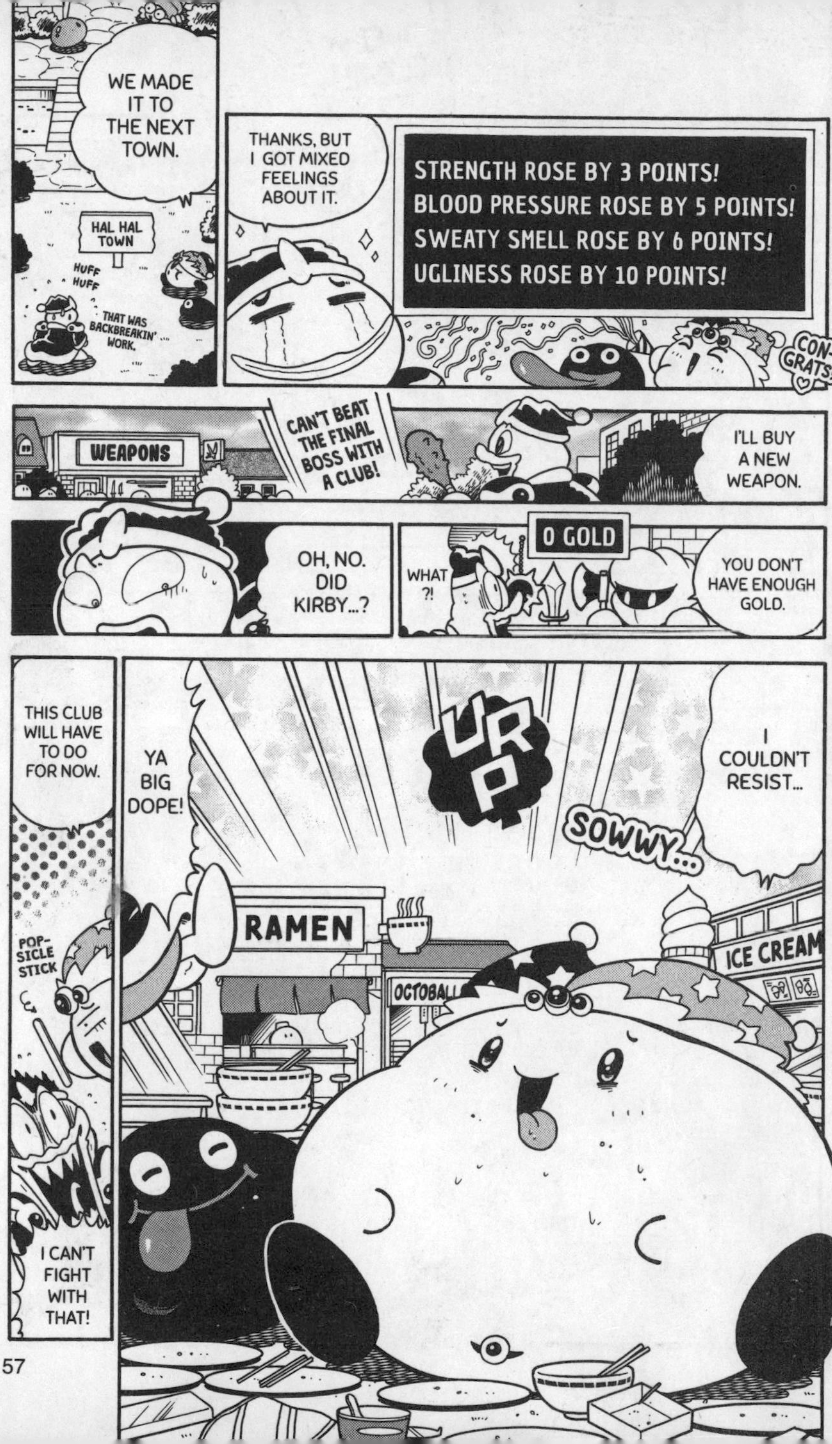
STRENGTH ROSE BY 3 POINTS!
BLOOD PRESSURE ROSE BY 5 POINTS!
SWEATY SMELL ROSE BY 6 POINTS!
UGLINESS ROSE BY 10 POINTS!
THANKS, BUT I GOT MIXED FEELINGS ABOUT IT.
CON-GRATS!
WE MADE IT TO THE NEXT TOWN.
HAL HAL TOWN
HUFF HUFF
THAT WAS BACKBREAKIN' WORK.
I'LL BUY A NEW WEAPON.
CAN'T BEAT THE FINAL BOSS WITH A CLUB!
WEAPONS
YOU DON'T HAVE ENOUGH GOLD.
0 GOLD
WHAT ?!
OH, NO. DID KIRBY...?
I COULDN'T RESIST...
SOWWY...
URP
YA BIG DOPE!
ICE CREAM
RAMEN
THIS CLUB WILL HAVE TO DO FOR NOW.
POP-SICLE STICK
I CAN'T FIGHT WITH THAT!

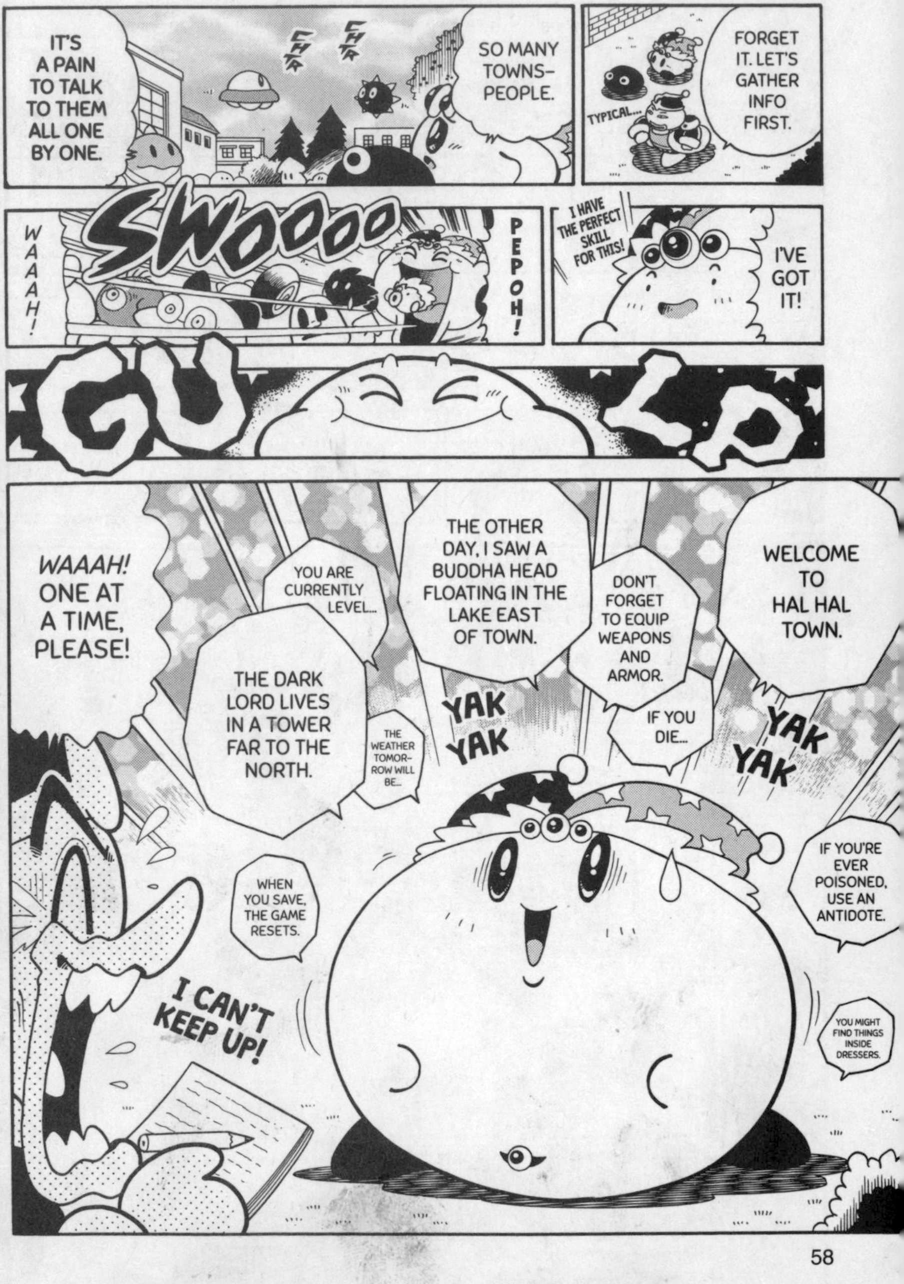
FORGET IT. LET'S GATHER INFO FIRST.
TYPICAL...
SO MANY TOWNS-PEOPLE.
CHTR
CHTR
IT'S A PAIN TO TALK TO THEM ALL ONE BY ONE.
I'VE GOT IT!
I HAVE THE PERFECT SKILL FOR THIS!
PEPOH!
SWOOOO
WAAAAH!
GULP
WELCOME TO HAL HAL TOWN.
YAK YAK
IF YOU DIE...
DON'T FORGET TO EQUIP WEAPONS AND ARMOR.
THE OTHER DAY, I SAW A BUDDHA HEAD FLOATING IN THE LAKE EAST OF TOWN.
YOU ARE CURRENTLY LEVEL...
WAAAH! ONE AT A TIME, PLEASE!
YAK YAK
THE WEATHER TOMOR-ROW WILL BE...
THE DARK LORD LIVES IN A TOWER FAR TO THE NORTH.
IF YOU'RE EVER POISONED, USE AN ANTIDOTE.
YOU MIGHT FIND THINGS INSIDE DRESSERS.
WHEN YOU SAVE, THE GAME RESETS.
I CAN'T KEEP UP!

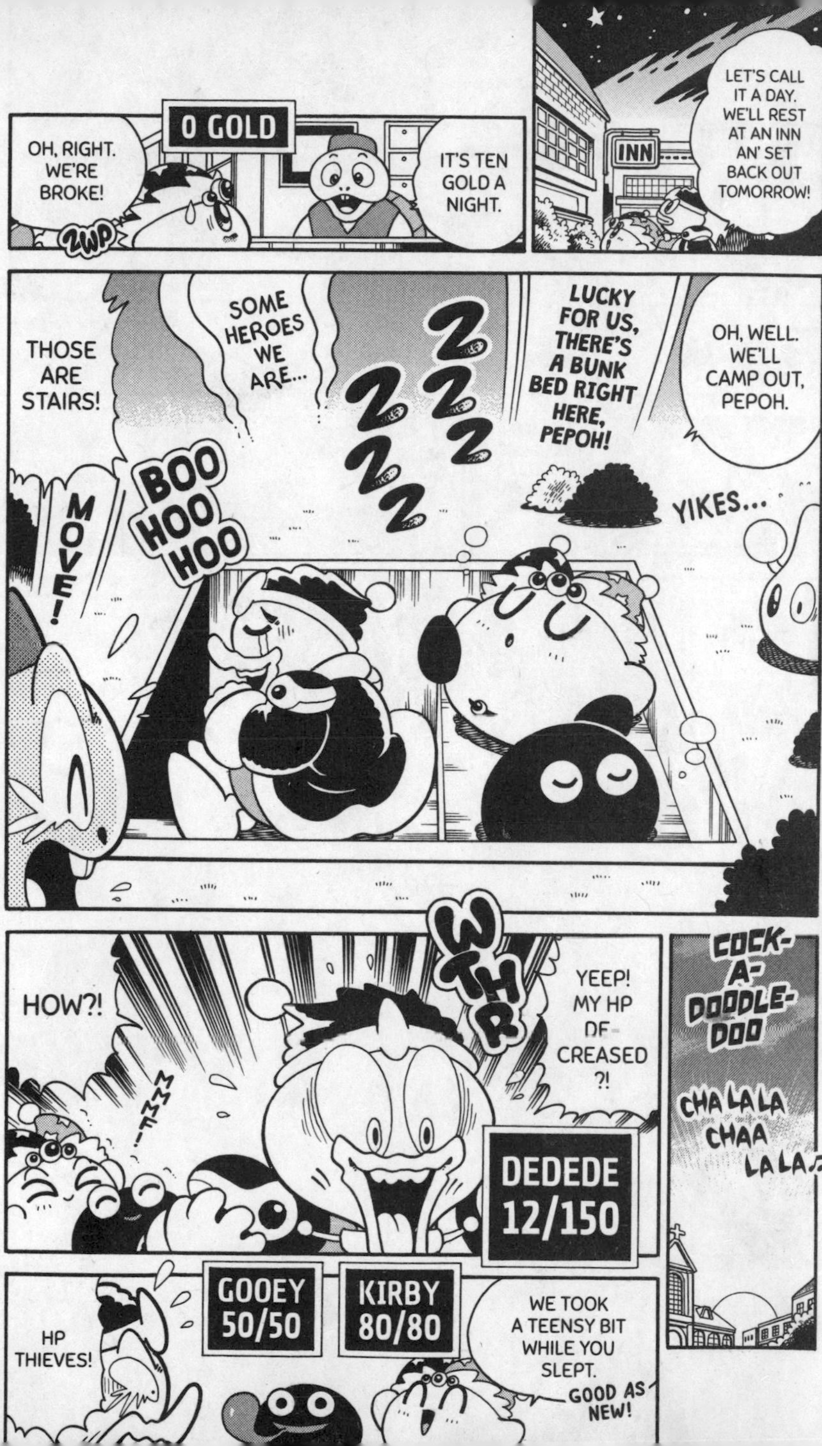
LET'S CALL IT A DAY. WE'LL REST AT AN INN AN' SET BACK OUT TOMORROW!
INN
0 GOLD
IT'S TEN GOLD A NIGHT.
OH, RIGHT. WE'RE BROKE!
ZWP
OH, WELL. WE'LL CAMP OUT, PEPOH.
LUCKY FOR US, THERE'S A BUNK BED RIGHT HERE, PEPOH!
ZZZZZ
SOME HEROES WE ARE...
THOSE ARE STAIRS!
YIKES...
BOO HOO HOO
MOVE!
COCK-A-DOODLE-DOO
CHA LA LA CHAA LA LA♫
WTHR
YEEP! MY HP DE-CREASED?!
HOW?!
MMMF!
DEDEDE 12/150
WE TOOK A TEENSY BIT WHILE YOU SLEPT.
KIRBY 80/80
GOOEY 50/50
GOOD AS NEW!
HP THIEVES!

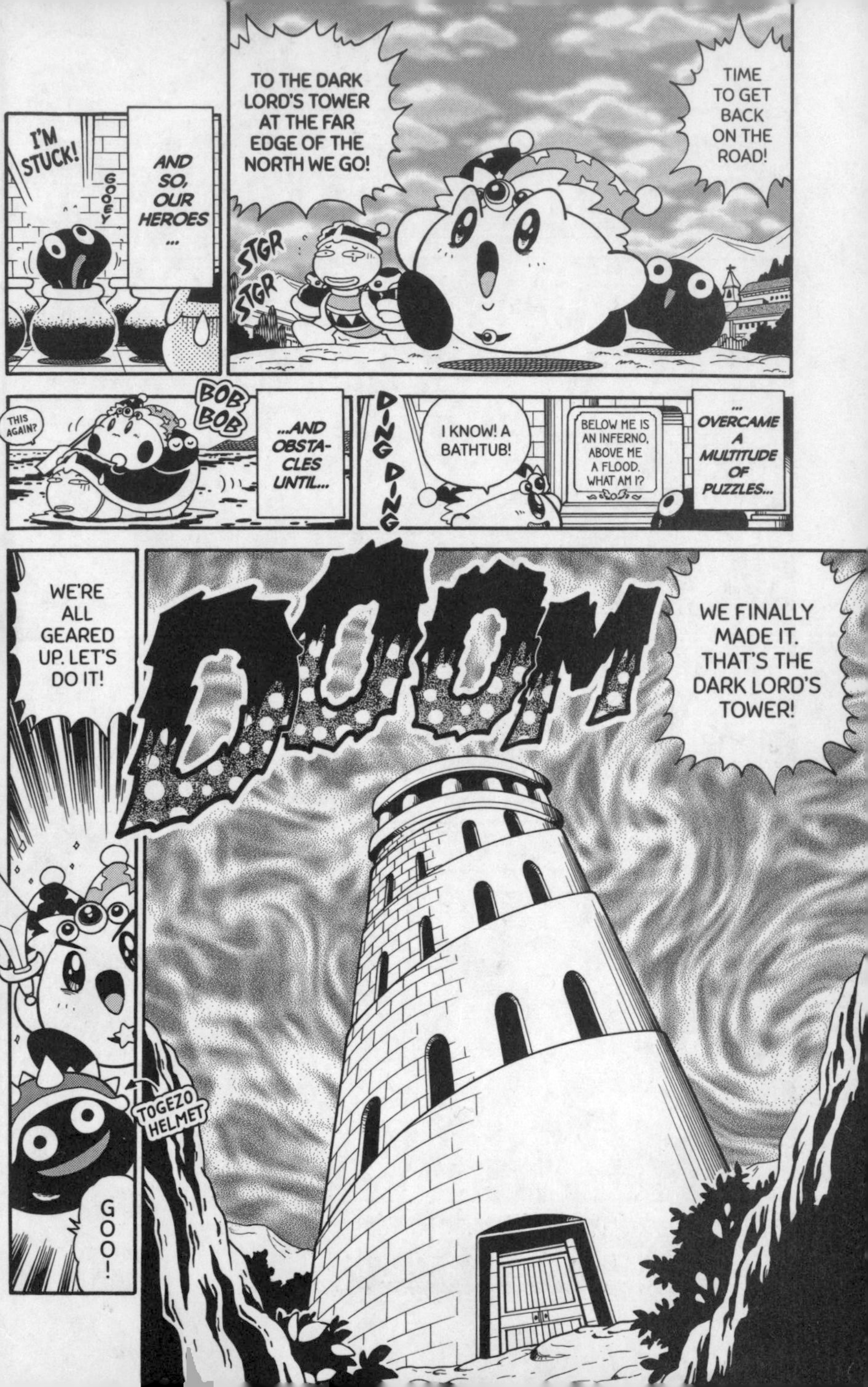
TIME TO GET BACK ON THE ROAD!
TO THE DARK LORD'S TOWER AT THE FAR EDGE OF THE NORTH WE GO!
STGR STGR
AND SO, OUR HEROES ...
I'M STUCK!
GOOEY
... OVERCAME A MULTITUDE OF PUZZLES...
BELOW ME IS AN INFERNO, ABOVE ME A FLOOD. WHAT AM I?
I KNOW! A BATHTUB!
DING DING
...AND OBSTACLES UNTIL...
BOB BOB
THIS AGAIN?
WE FINALLY MADE IT. THAT'S THE DARK LORD'S TOWER!
DOOM
WE'RE ALL GEARED UP. LET'S DO IT!
TOGEZO HELMET
GOO GOO!

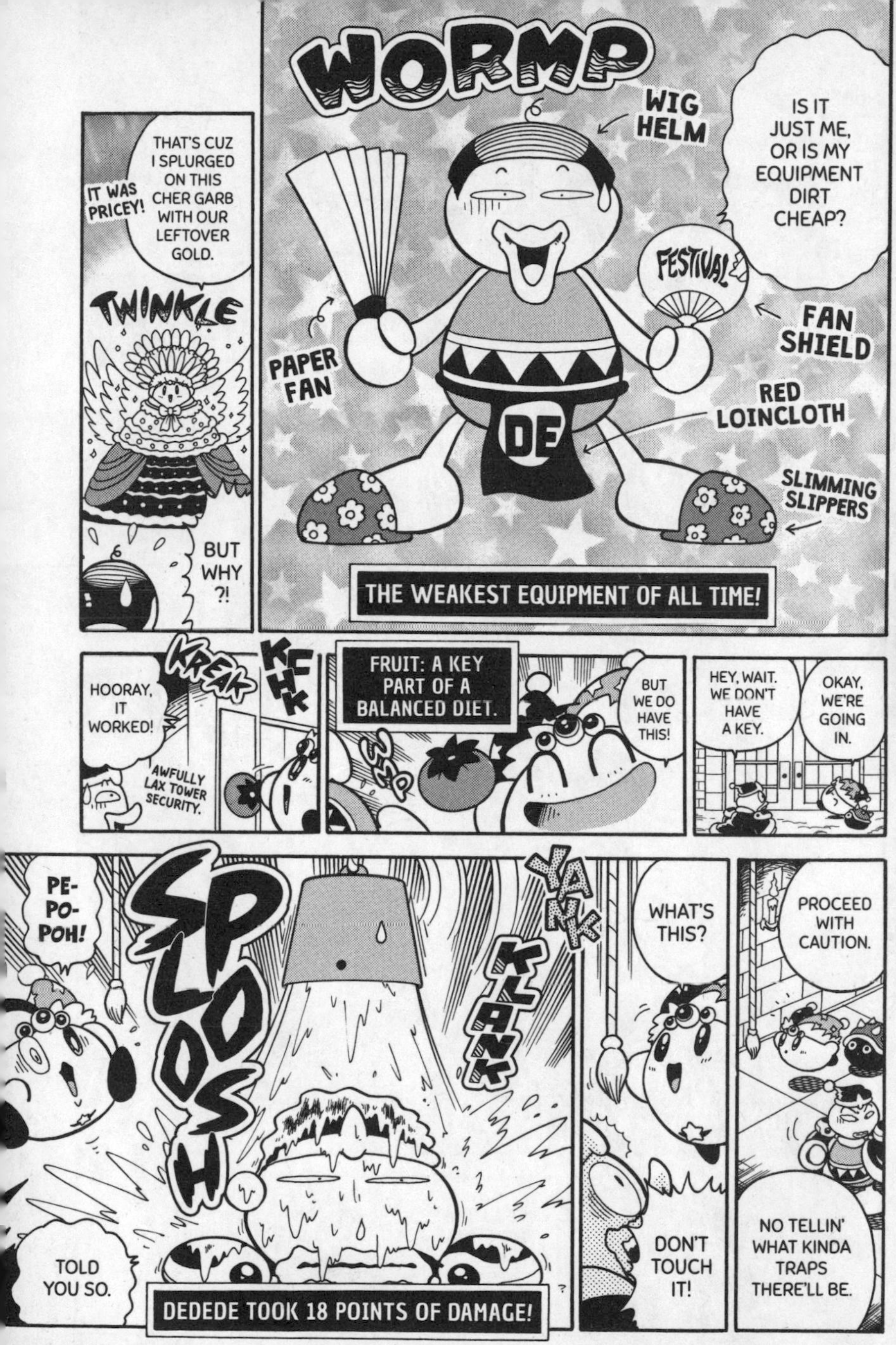
IS IT JUST ME, OR IS MY EQUIPMENT DIRT CHEAP?
WIG HELM
WORMP
FESTIVAL
FAN SHIELD
PAPER FAN
RED LOINCLOTH
SLIMMING SLIPPERS
THE WEAKEST EQUIPMENT OF ALL TIME!
THAT'S CUZ I SPLURGED ON THIS CHER GARB WITH OUR LEFTOVER GOLD.
IT WAS PRICEY!
TWINKLE
BUT WHY ?!
OKAY, WE'RE GOING IN.
HEY, WAIT. WE DON'T HAVE A KEY.
BUT WE DO HAVE THIS!
FRUIT: A KEY PART OF A BALANCED DIET.
KCHK
KREAK
HOORAY, IT WORKED!
AWFULLY LAX TOWER SECURITY.
PROCEED WITH CAUTION.
NO TELLIN' WHAT KINDA TRAPS THERE'LL BE.
WHAT'S THIS?
DON'T TOUCH IT!
YANK
KLANK
SPLOOSH
PE-PO-POH!
TOLD YOU SO.
DEDEDE TOOK 18 POINTS OF DAMAGE!

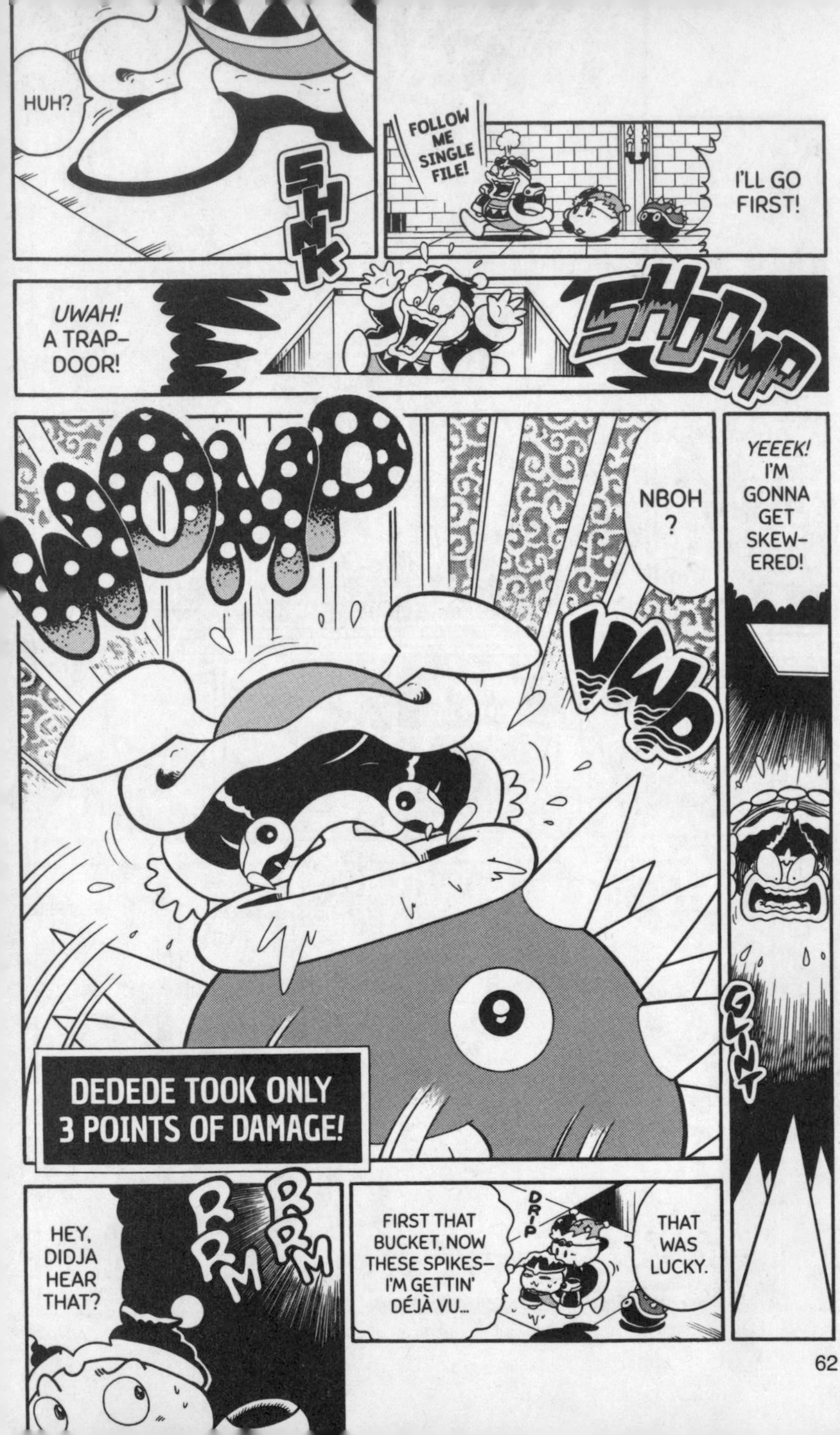
I'LL GO FIRST!
FOLLOW ME SINGLE FILE!
HUH?
SHNK
SHOOMP
UWAH! A TRAP-DOOR!
YEEEK! I'M GONNA GET SKEW-ERED!
GLINT
NBOH?
VWD
WOMP
DEDEDE TOOK ONLY 3 POINTS OF DAMAGE!
THAT WAS LUCKY.
DRIP
FIRST THAT BUCKET, NOW THESE SPIKES— I'M GETTIN' DÉJÀ VU...
RRM
RRM
HEY, DIDJA HEAR THAT?

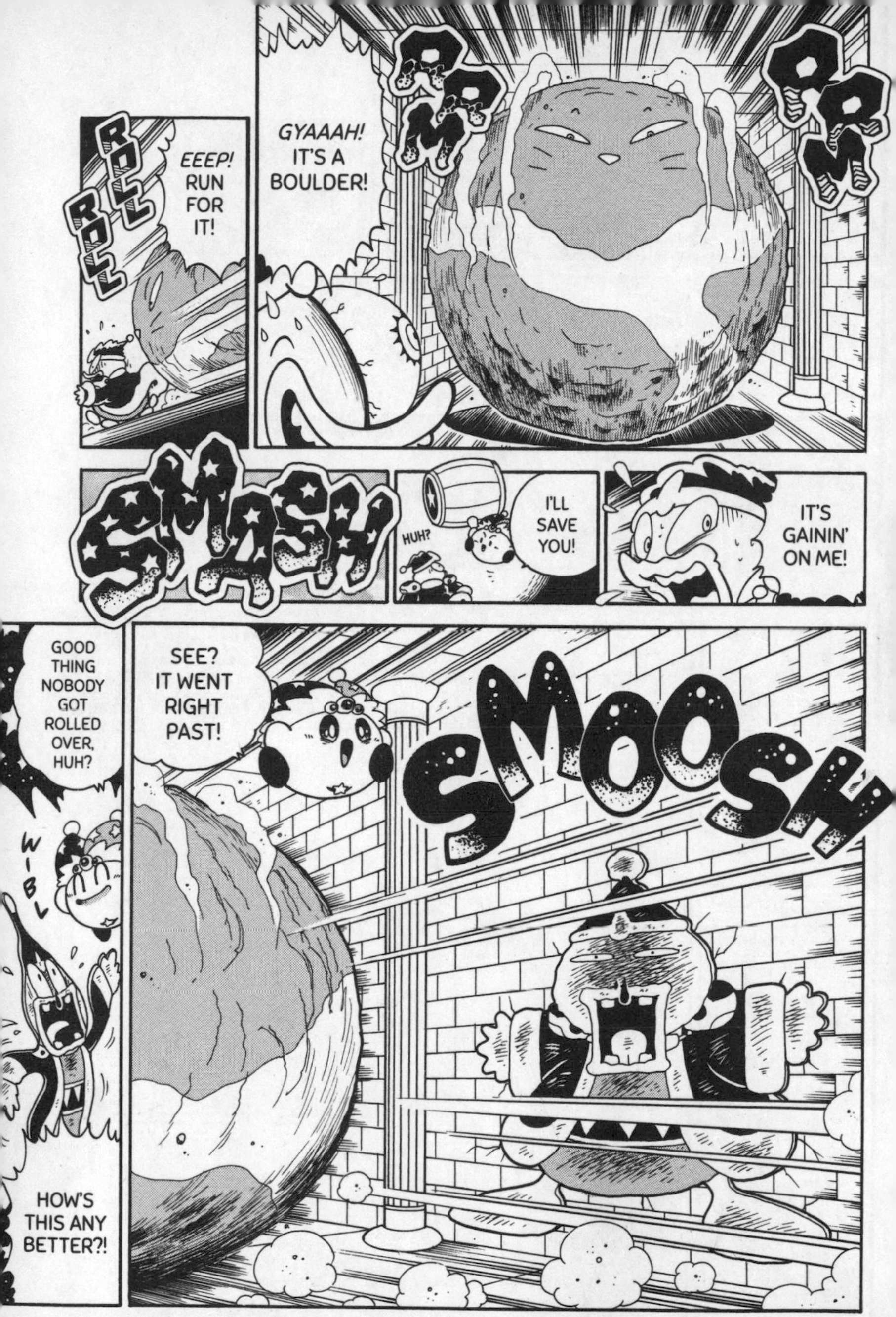
GYAAAH! IT'S A BOULDER!
ROLL ROLL
EEEP! RUN FOR IT!
IT'S GAININ' ON ME!
I'LL SAVE YOU!
HUH?
SMASH
SEE? IT WENT RIGHT PAST!
SMOOSH
GOOD THING NOBODY GOT ROLLED OVER, HUH?
WIBL
HOW'S THIS ANY BETTER?!

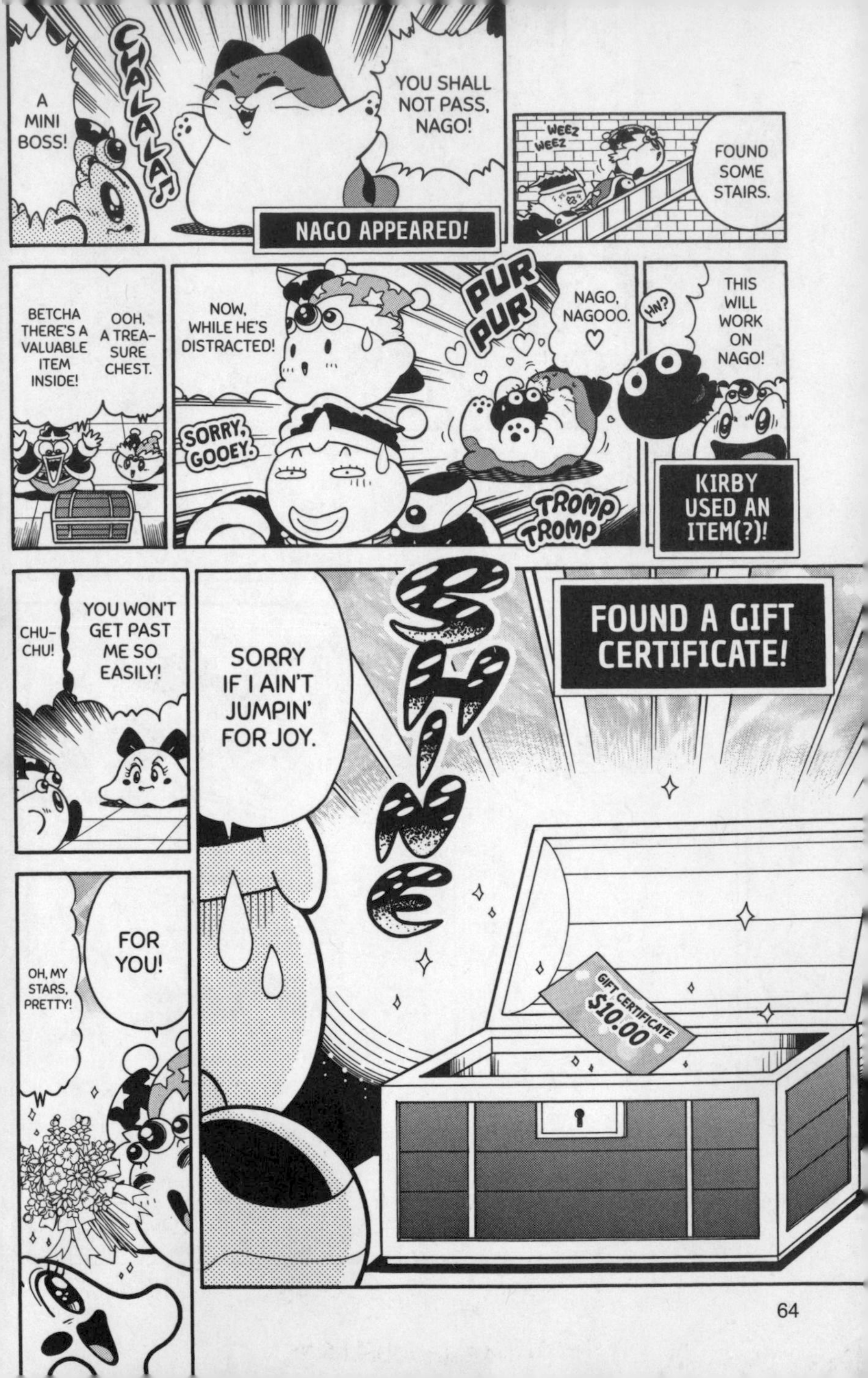

WEEZ WEEZ
FOUND SOME STAIRS.
YOU SHALL NOT PASS, NAGO!
CHALALA♪
A MINI BOSS!
NAGO APPEARED!
THIS WILL WORK ON NAGO!
HN?
KIRBY USED AN ITEM(?)!
NAGO, NAGOOO. ♡
PUR PUR
NOW, WHILE HE'S DISTRACTED!
SORRY, GOOEY.
TROMP TROMP
OOH, A TREASURE CHEST.
BETCHA THERE'S A VALUABLE ITEM INSIDE!
FOUND A GIFT CERTIFICATE!
GIFT CERTIFICATE $10.00
SORRY IF I AIN'T JUMPIN' FOR JOY.
YOU WON'T GET PAST ME SO EASILY!
CHU-CHU!
FOR YOU!
OH, MY STARS, PRETTY!

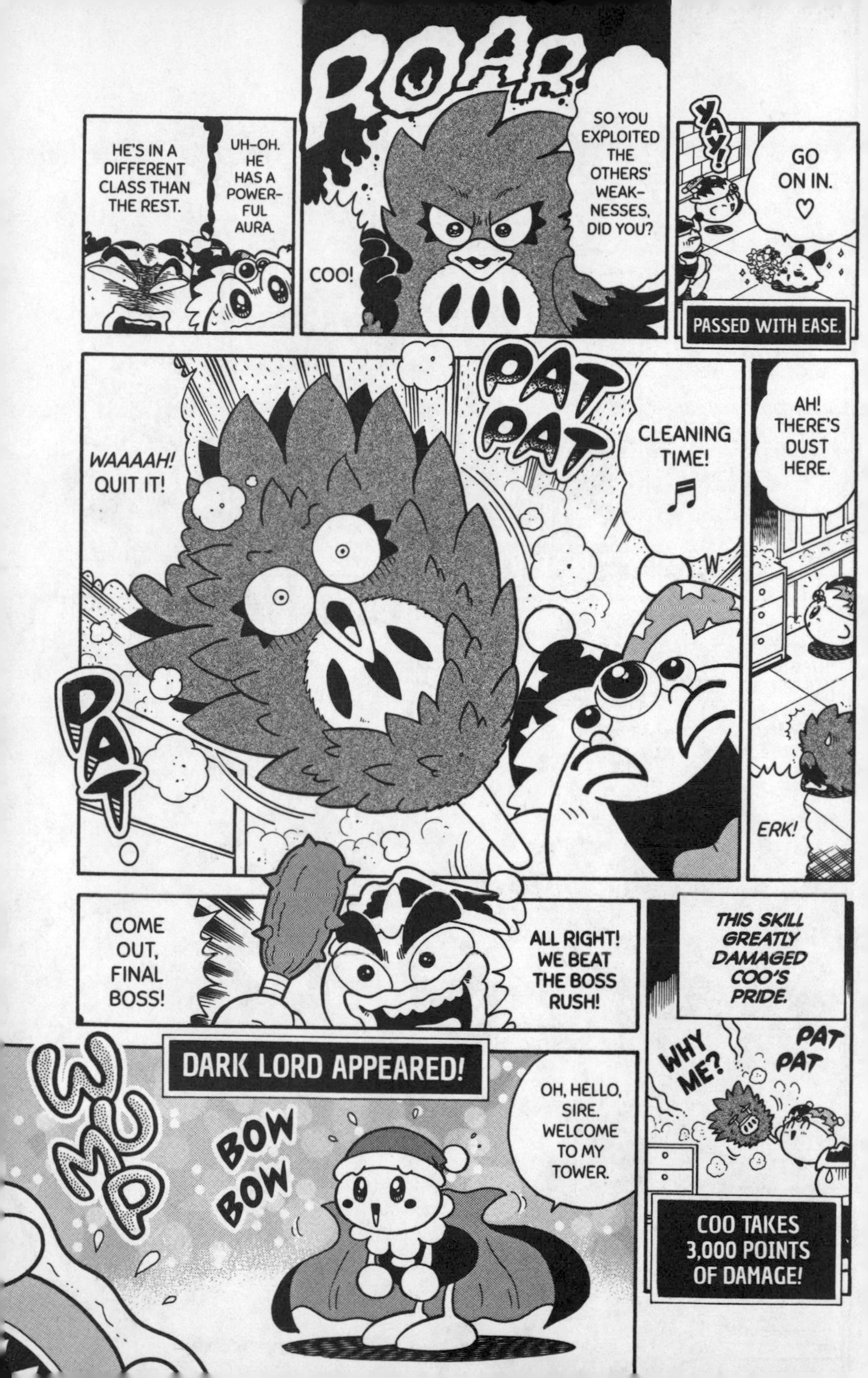
YAY!
GO ON IN. ♡
PASSED WITH EASE.
ROAR
SO YOU EXPLOITED THE OTHERS' WEAKNESSES, DID YOU?
COO!
UH-OH. HE HAS A POWERFUL AURA.
HE'S IN A DIFFERENT CLASS THAN THE REST.
AH! THERE'S DUST HERE.
ERK!
PAT PAT
CLEANING TIME! ♫
WAAAAH! QUIT IT!
PAT
THIS SKILL GREATLY DAMAGED COO'S PRIDE.
PAT PAT
WHY ME?
COO TAKES 3,000 POINTS OF DAMAGE!
ALL RIGHT! WE BEAT THE BOSS RUSH!
COME OUT, FINAL BOSS!
DARK LORD APPEARED!
OH, HELLO, SIRE. WELCOME TO MY TOWER.
BOW BOW

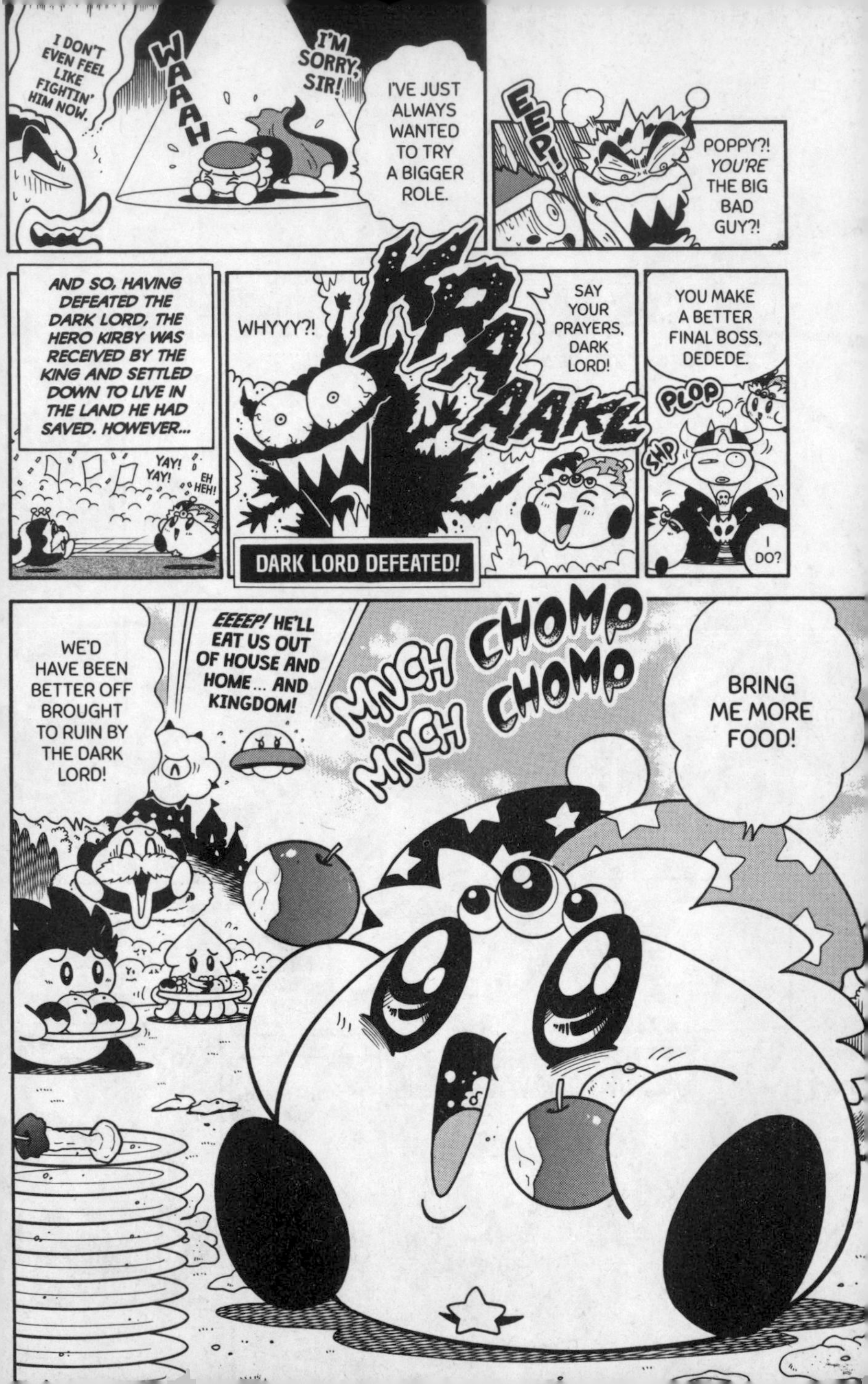
EEEP!
POPPY?! YOU'RE THE BIG BAD GUY?!
I'VE JUST ALWAYS WANTED TO TRY A BIGGER ROLE.
I'M SORRY, SIR!
WAAAAH
I DON'T EVEN FEEL LIKE FIGHTIN' HIM NOW.
YOU MAKE A BETTER FINAL BOSS, DEDEDE.
PLOP
SHP
I DO?
SAY YOUR PRAYERS, DARK LORD!
KRAAAKL
WHYYY?!
DARK LORD DEFEATED!
AND SO, HAVING DEFEATED THE DARK LORD, THE HERO KIRBY WAS RECEIVED BY THE KING AND SETTLED DOWN TO LIVE IN THE LAND HE HAD SAVED. HOWEVER...
YAY! YAY!
EH HEH!
BRING ME MORE FOOD!
MNCH CHOMP MNCH CHOMP
EEEEP! HE'LL EAT US OUT OF HOUSE AND HOME... AND KINGDOM!
WE'D HAVE BEEN BETTER OFF BROUGHT TO RUIN BY THE DARK LORD!

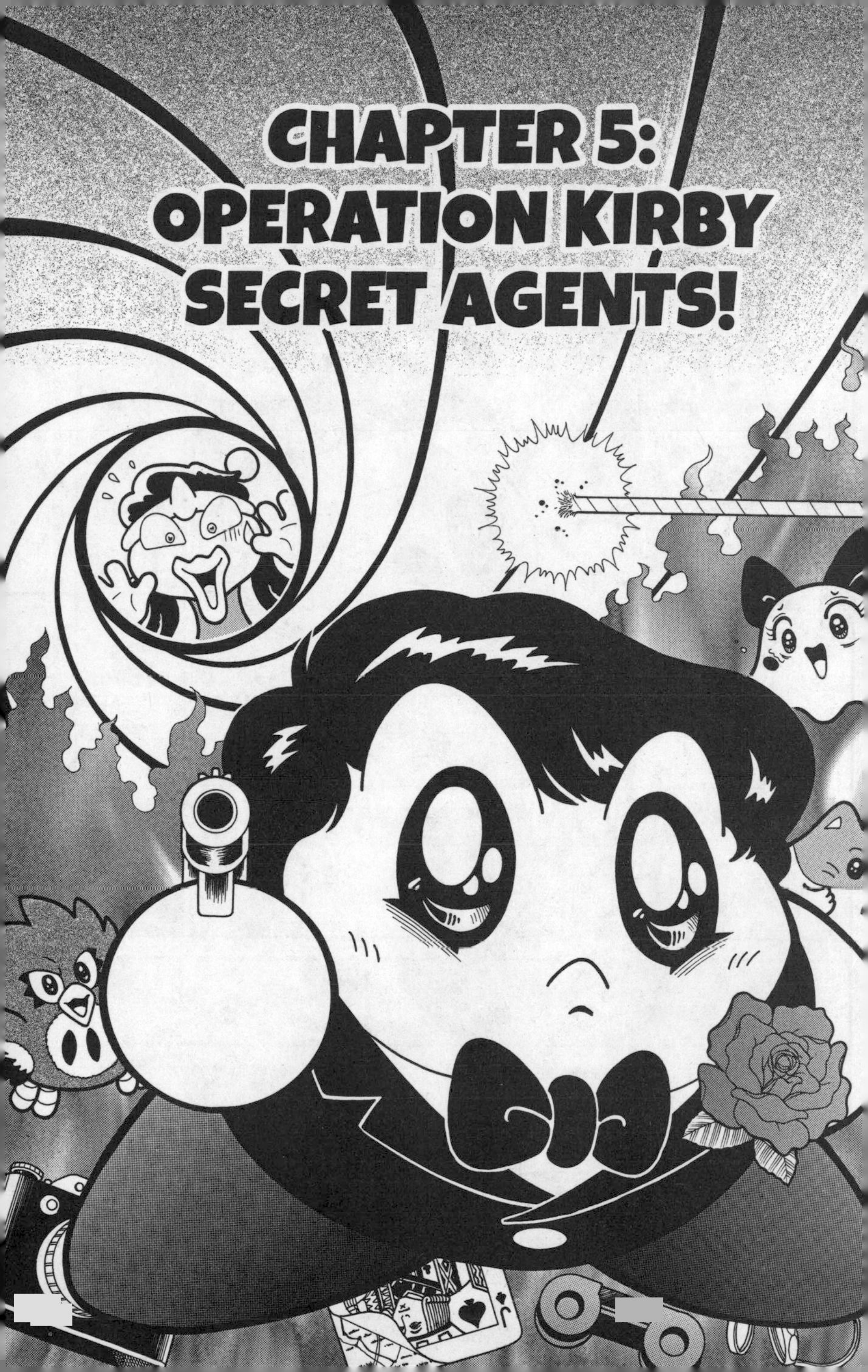
CHAPTER 5:
OPERATION KIRBY
SECRET AGENTS!

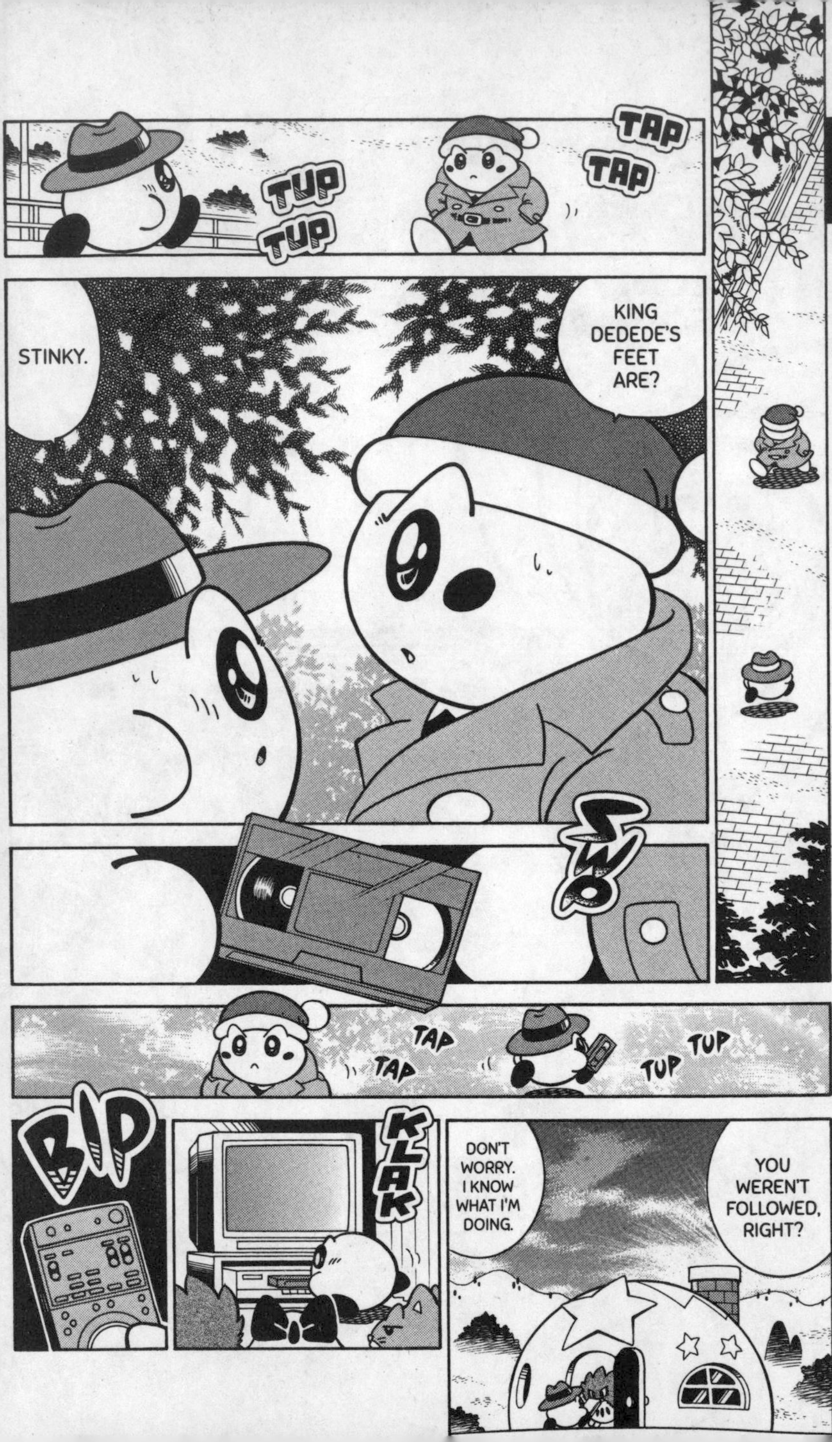
TAP
TAP
TUP
TUP
KING DEDEDE'S FEET ARE?
STINKY.
SWOP
TUP
TUP
TAP
TAP
YOU WEREN'T FOLLOWED, RIGHT?
DON'T WORRY. I KNOW WHAT I'M DOING.
KLAK
BIP

AUTHOR'S COMMENT

THE OBLIGATORY SECRET AGENTS CHAPTER. IT WAS TOUGH TO WRAP UP IN ONLY 15 PAGES, AND FOR THE LARGE NUMBER OF PANELS PER PAGE, IT'S SURPRISINGLY FAST-PACED AND EASY TO READ.

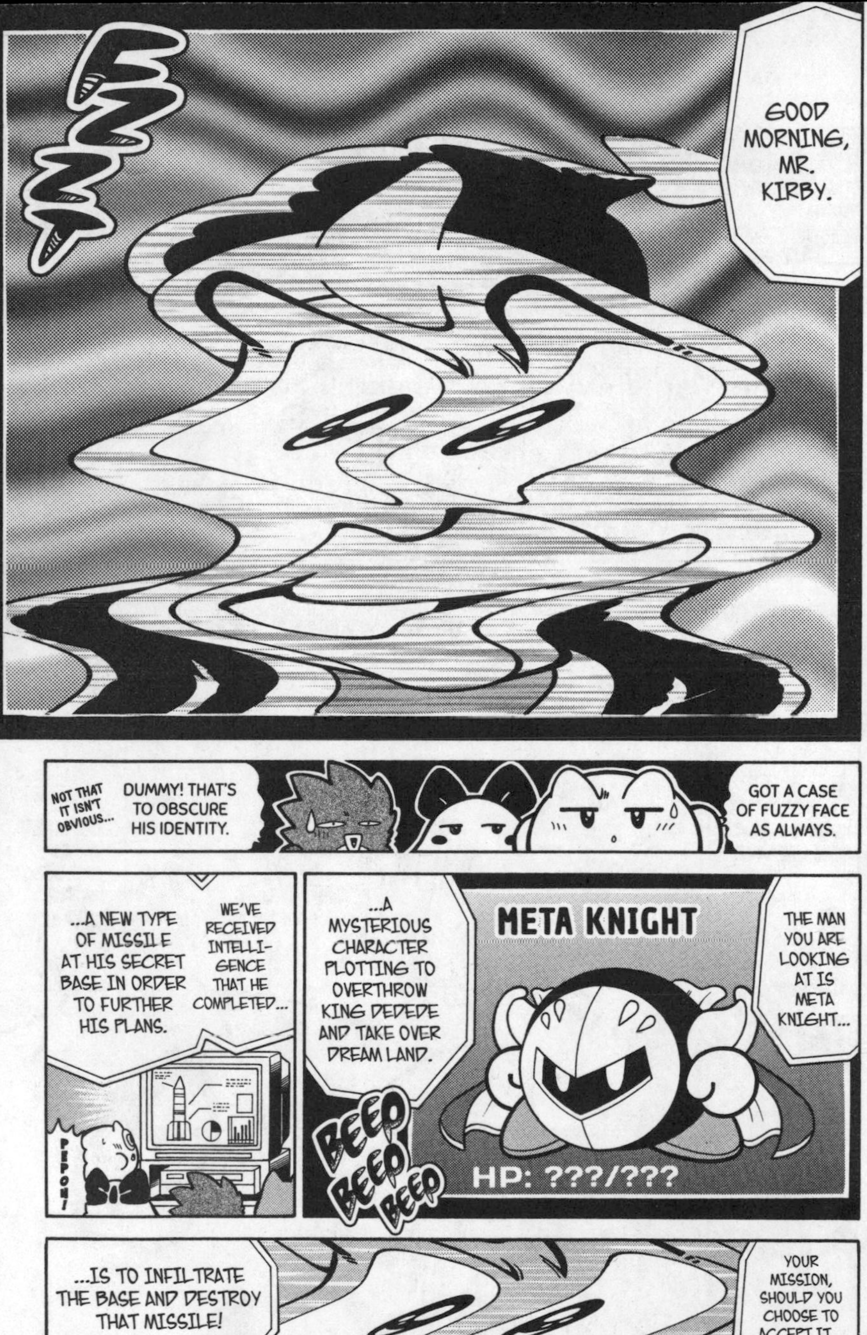
GOOD MORNING, MR. KIRBY.
FZZZT
GOT A CASE OF FUZZY FACE AS ALWAYS.
DUMMY! THAT'S TO OBSCURE HIS IDENTITY.
NOT THAT IT ISN'T OBVIOUS...
THE MAN YOU ARE LOOKING AT IS META KNIGHT...
META KNIGHT
...A MYSTERIOUS CHARACTER PLOTTING TO OVERTHROW KING DEDEDE AND TAKE OVER DREAM LAND.
HP: ???/???
BEEP BEEP BEEP
WE'VE RECEIVED INTELLI-GENCE THAT HE COMPLETED...
...A NEW TYPE OF MISSILE AT HIS SECRET BASE IN ORDER TO FURTHER HIS PLANS.
PEPON!
YOUR MISSION, SHOULD YOU CHOOSE TO ACCEPT IT...
...IS TO INFILTRATE THE BASE AND DESTROY THAT MISSILE!

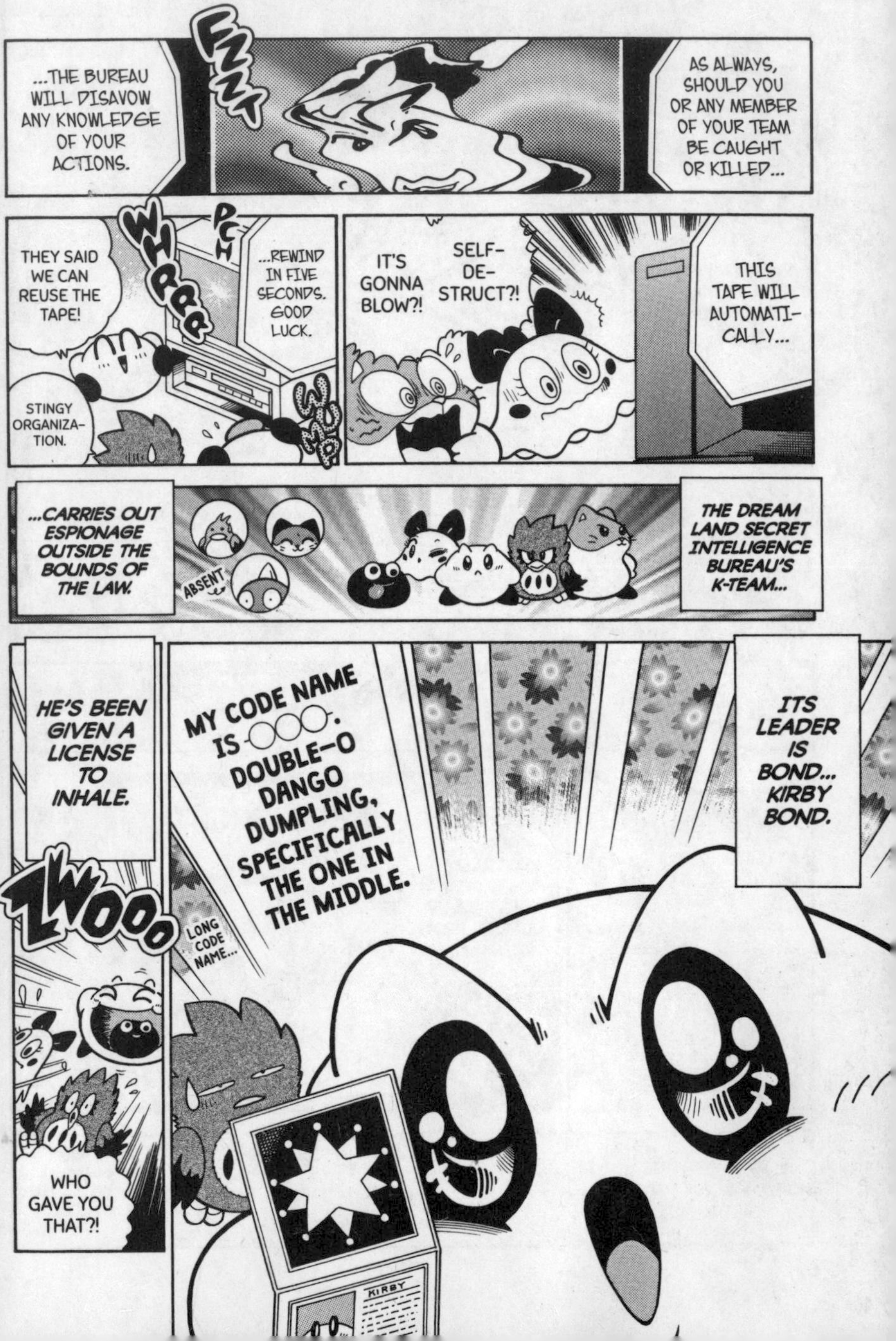
AS ALWAYS, SHOULD YOU OR ANY MEMBER OF YOUR TEAM BE CAUGHT OR KILLED...
...THE BUREAU WILL DISAVOW ANY KNOWLEDGE OF YOUR ACTIONS.
THIS TAPE WILL AUTOMATI-CALLY...
SELF-DE-STRUCT?!
IT'S GONNA BLOW?!
...REWIND IN FIVE SECONDS. GOOD LUCK.
PCH
WHRRR
WUMP
THEY SAID WE CAN REUSE THE TAPE!
STINGY ORGANIZA-TION.
THE DREAM LAND SECRET INTELLIGENCE BUREAU'S K-TEAM...
ABSENT
...CARRIES OUT ESPIONAGE OUTSIDE THE BOUNDS OF THE LAW.
ITS LEADER IS BOND... KIRBY BOND.
MY CODE NAME IS ○○○. DOUBLE-O DANGO DUMPLING, SPECIFICALLY THE ONE IN THE MIDDLE.
KIRBY
HE'S BEEN GIVEN A LICENSE TO INHALE.
ZWOOO
LONG CODE NAME...
WHO GAVE YOU THAT?!

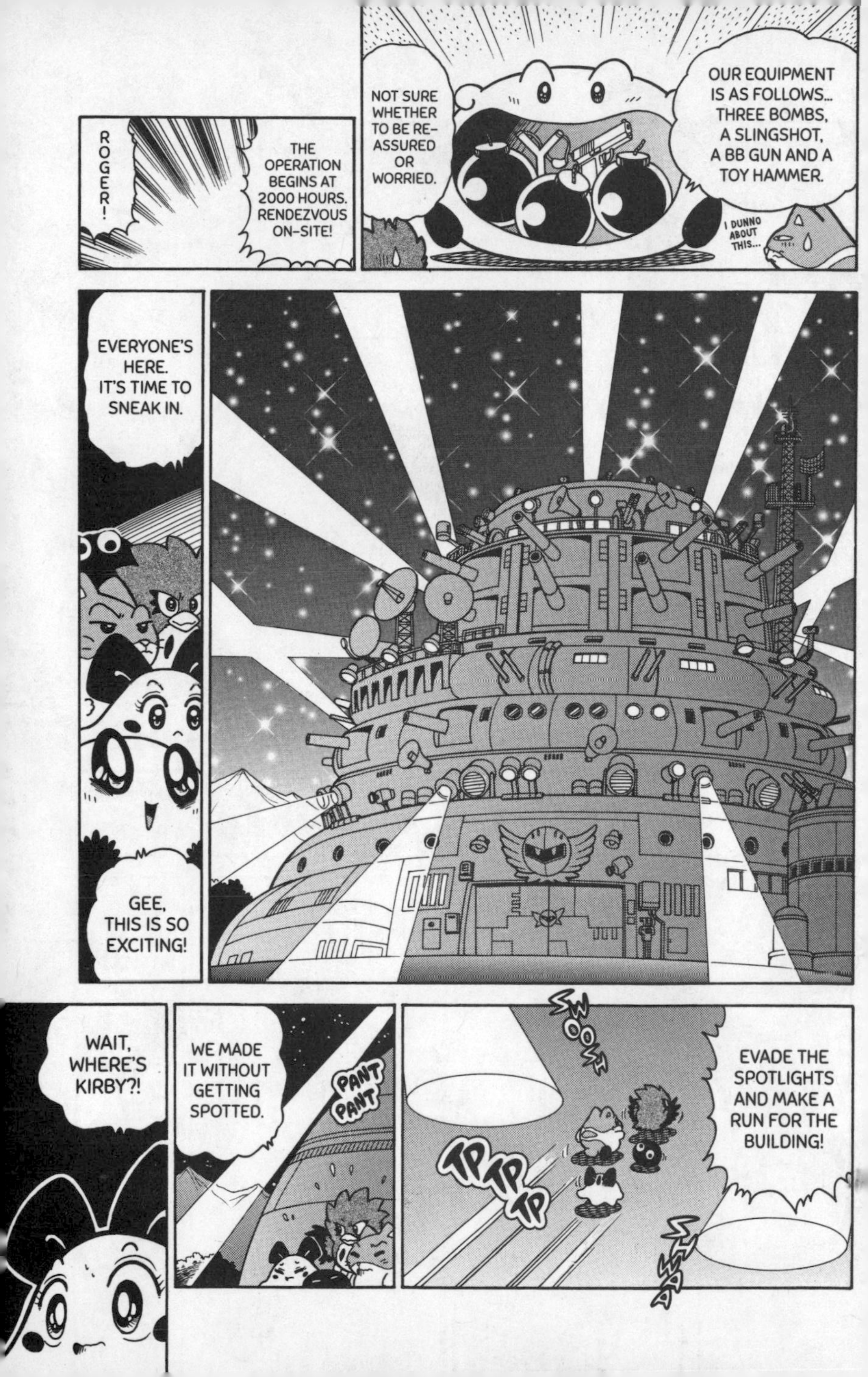
OUR EQUIPMENT IS AS FOLLOWS... THREE BOMBS, A SLINGSHOT, A BB GUN AND A TOY HAMMER.
I DUNNO ABOUT THIS...
NOT SURE WHETHER TO BE RE-ASSURED OR WORRIED.
THE OPERATION BEGINS AT 2000 HOURS. RENDEZVOUS ON-SITE!
ROGER!
EVERYONE'S HERE. IT'S TIME TO SNEAK IN.
GEE, THIS IS SO EXCITING!
EVADE THE SPOTLIGHTS AND MAKE A RUN FOR THE BUILDING!
TP TP TP
WE MADE IT WITHOUT GETTING SPOTTED.
PANT PANT
WAIT, WHERE'S KIRBY?!

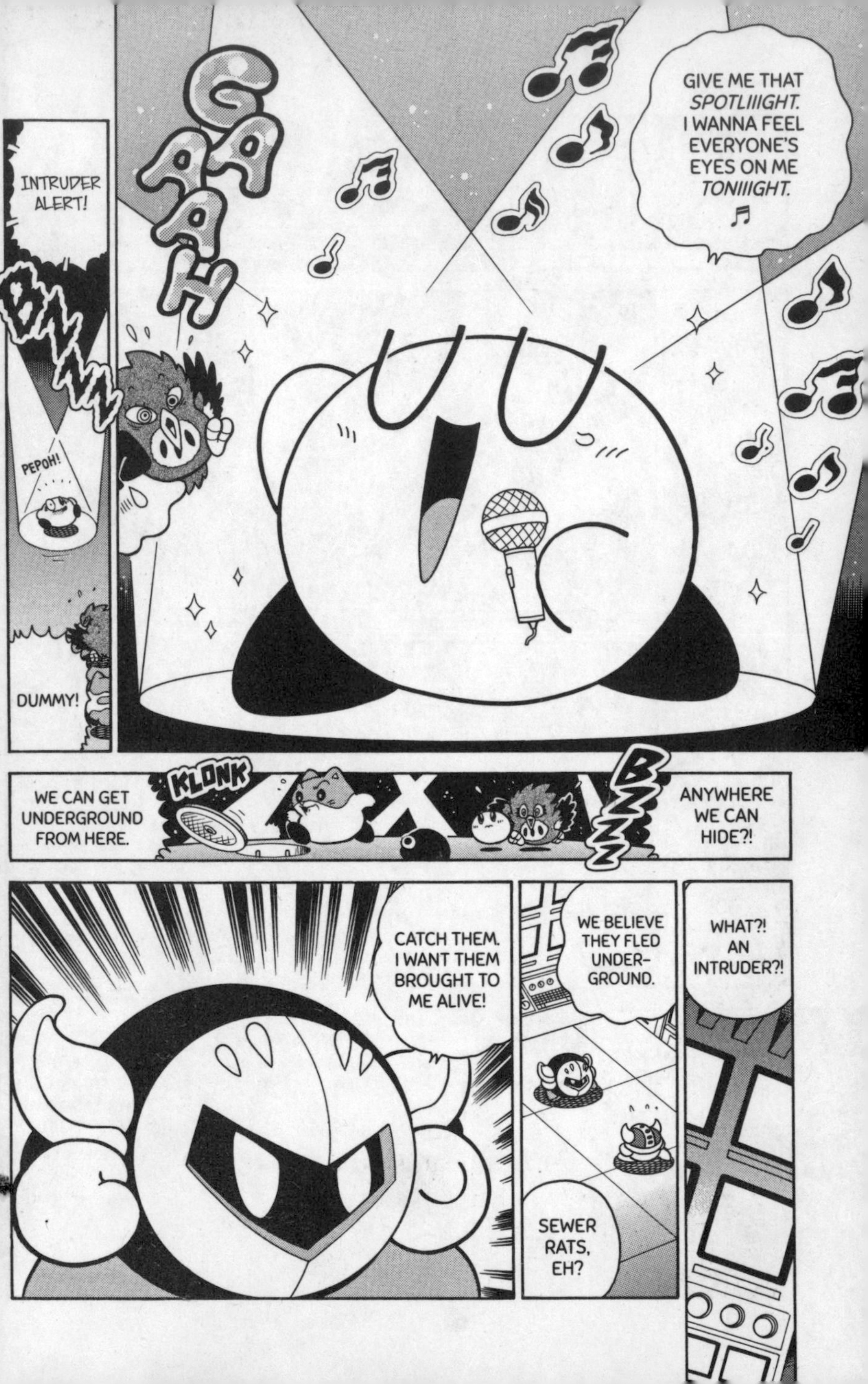
GIVE ME THAT SPOTLIIIGHT. I WANNA FEEL EVERYONE'S EYES ON ME TONIIIGHT. ♬
GAAAH
INTRUDER ALERT!
PEPOH!
DUMMY!
ANYWHERE WE CAN HIDE?!
KLONK
WE CAN GET UNDERGROUND FROM HERE.
WHAT?! AN INTRUDER?!
WE BELIEVE THEY FLED UNDER-GROUND.
SEWER RATS, EH?
CATCH THEM. I WANT THEM BROUGHT TO ME ALIVE!

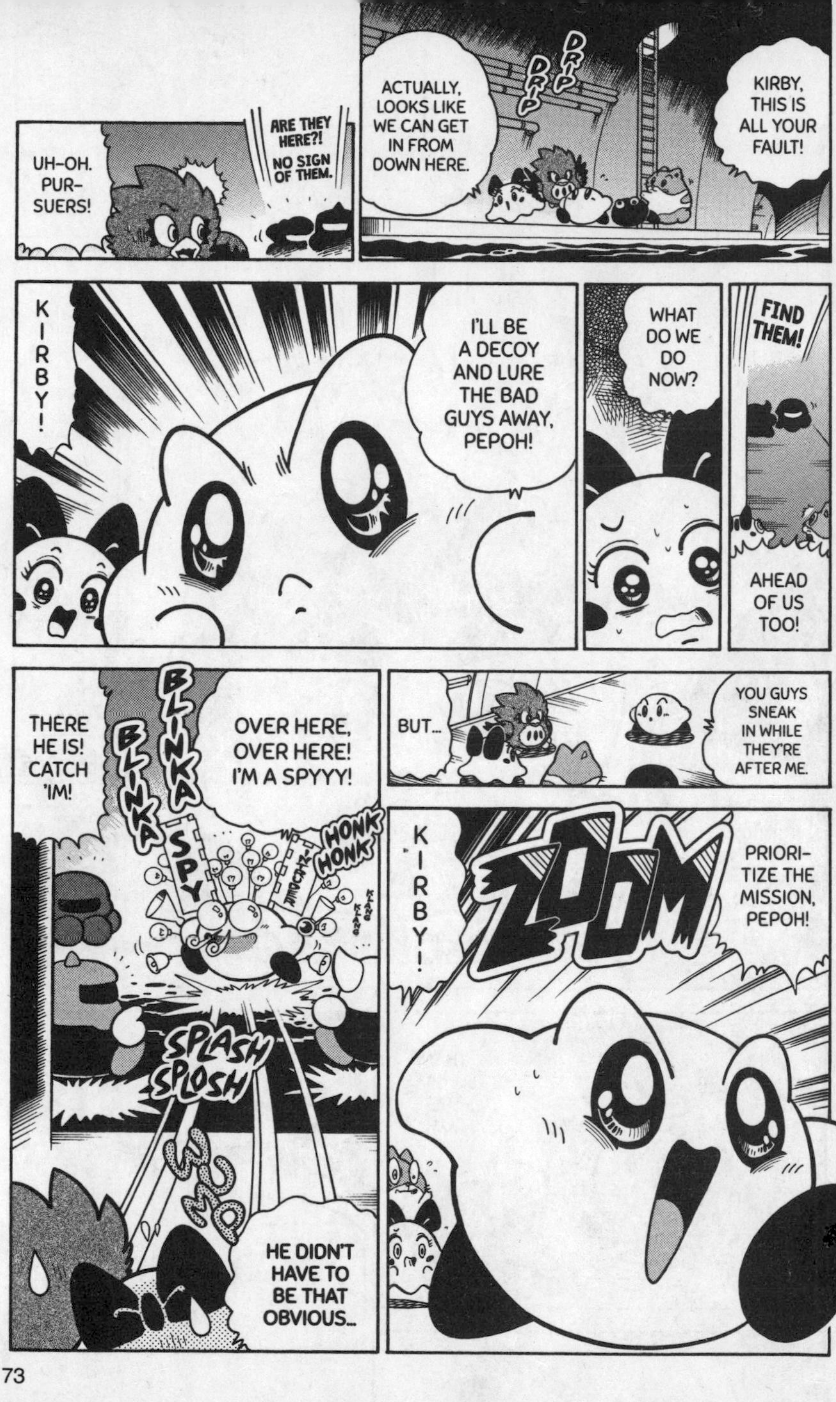
KIRBY, THIS IS ALL YOUR FAULT!
DRIP DRIP
ACTUALLY, LOOKS LIKE WE CAN GET IN FROM DOWN HERE.
ARE THEY HERE?! NO SIGN OF THEM.
UH-OH. PURSUERS!
FIND THEM!
AHEAD OF US TOO!
WHAT DO WE DO NOW?
I'LL BE A DECOY AND LURE THE BAD GUYS AWAY, PEPOH!
KIRBY!
YOU GUYS SNEAK IN WHILE THEY'RE AFTER ME.
BUT...
PRIORITIZE THE MISSION, PEPOH!
ZOOM
KIRBY!
OVER HERE, OVER HERE! I'M A SPYYY!
BLINKA BLINKA
THERE HE IS! CATCH 'IM!
SPY
HONK HONK
SPLASH SPLOSH
HE DIDN'T HAVE TO BE THAT OBVIOUS...

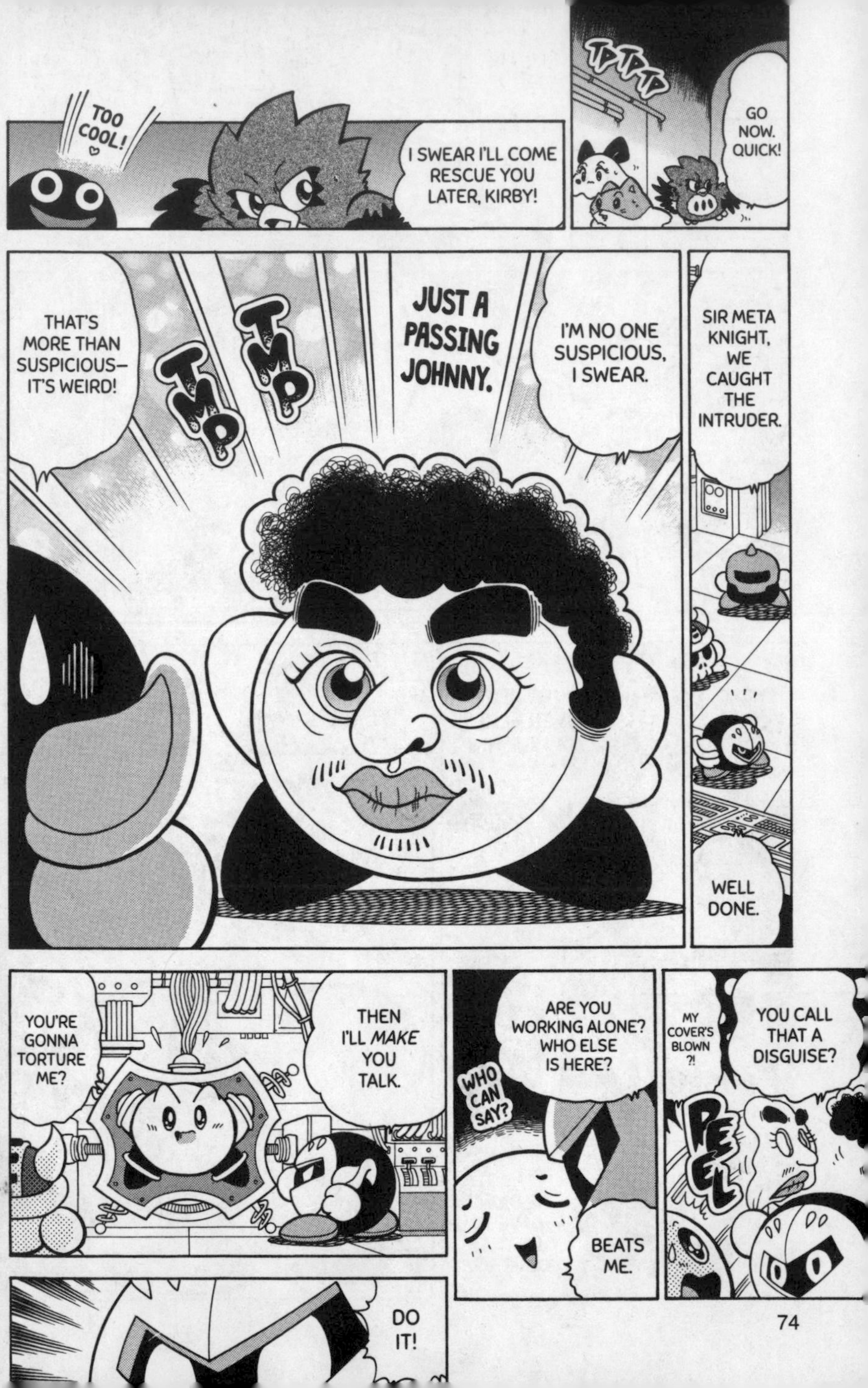
TP TP TP
GO NOW. QUICK!
I SWEAR I'LL COME RESCUE YOU LATER, KIRBY!
TOO COOL! ♡
SIR META KNIGHT, WE CAUGHT THE INTRUDER.
WELL DONE.
I'M NO ONE SUSPICIOUS, I SWEAR.
JUST A PASSING JOHNNY.
TMP TMP
THAT'S MORE THAN SUSPICIOUS— IT'S WEIRD!
YOU CALL THAT A DISGUISE?
MY COVER'S BLOWN ?!
PEEL
ARE YOU WORKING ALONE? WHO ELSE IS HERE?
WHO CAN SAY?
BEATS ME.
THEN I'LL *MAKE* YOU TALK.
YOU'RE GONNA TORTURE ME?
DO IT!

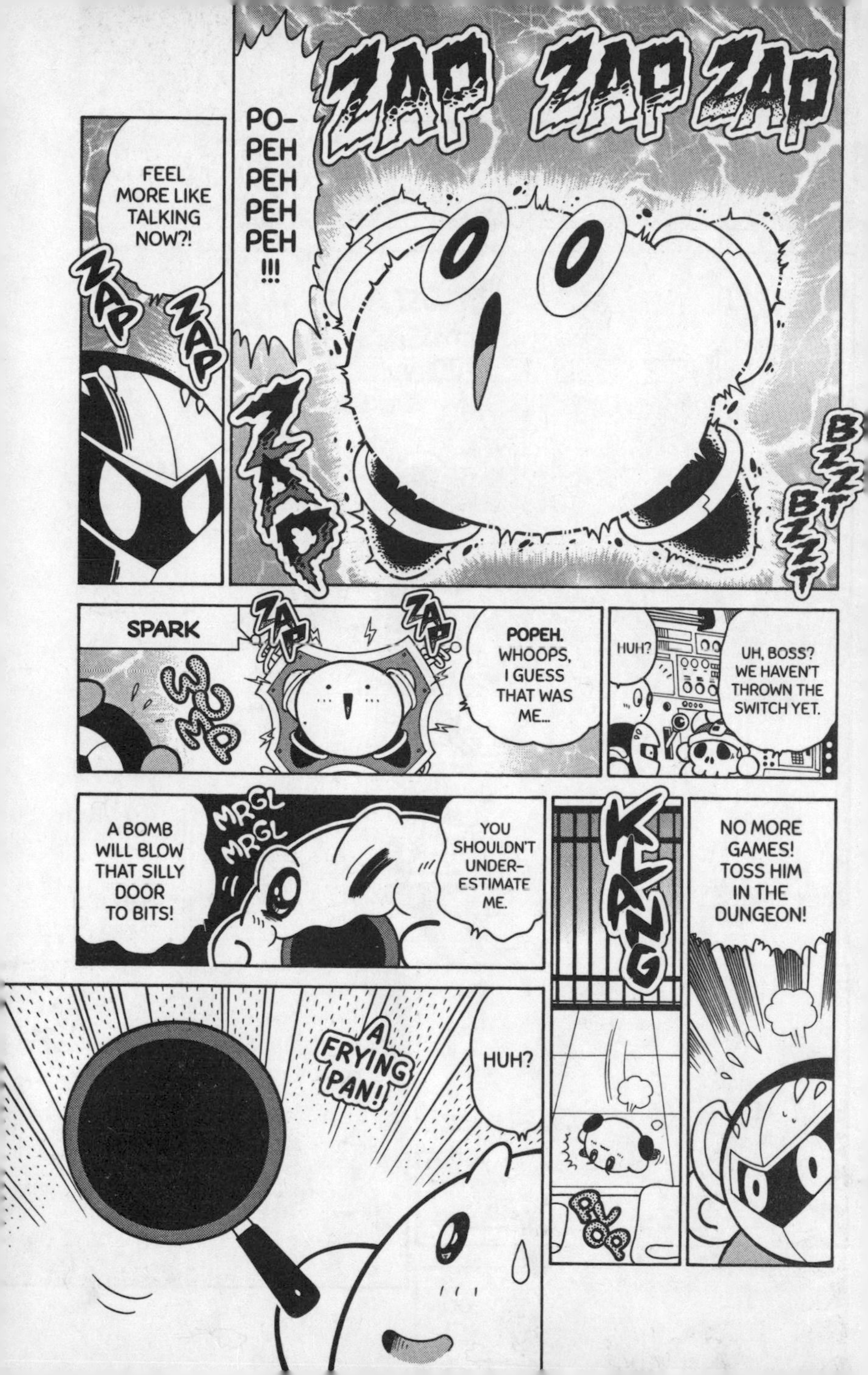
ZAP ZAP ZAP
PO-PEH PEH PEH PEH PEH!!!
ZAP
BZZT BZZT
FEEL MORE LIKE TALKING NOW?!
ZAP ZAP
HUH?
UH, BOSS? WE HAVEN'T THROWN THE SWITCH YET.
POPEH. WHOOPS, I GUESS THAT WAS ME...
ZAP ZAP
SPARK
NO MORE GAMES! TOSS HIM IN THE DUNGEON!
KLANG
PLOP
YOU SHOULDN'T UNDER-ESTIMATE ME.
MRGL MRGL
A BOMB WILL BLOW THAT SILLY DOOR TO BITS!
HUH?
A FRYING PAN!

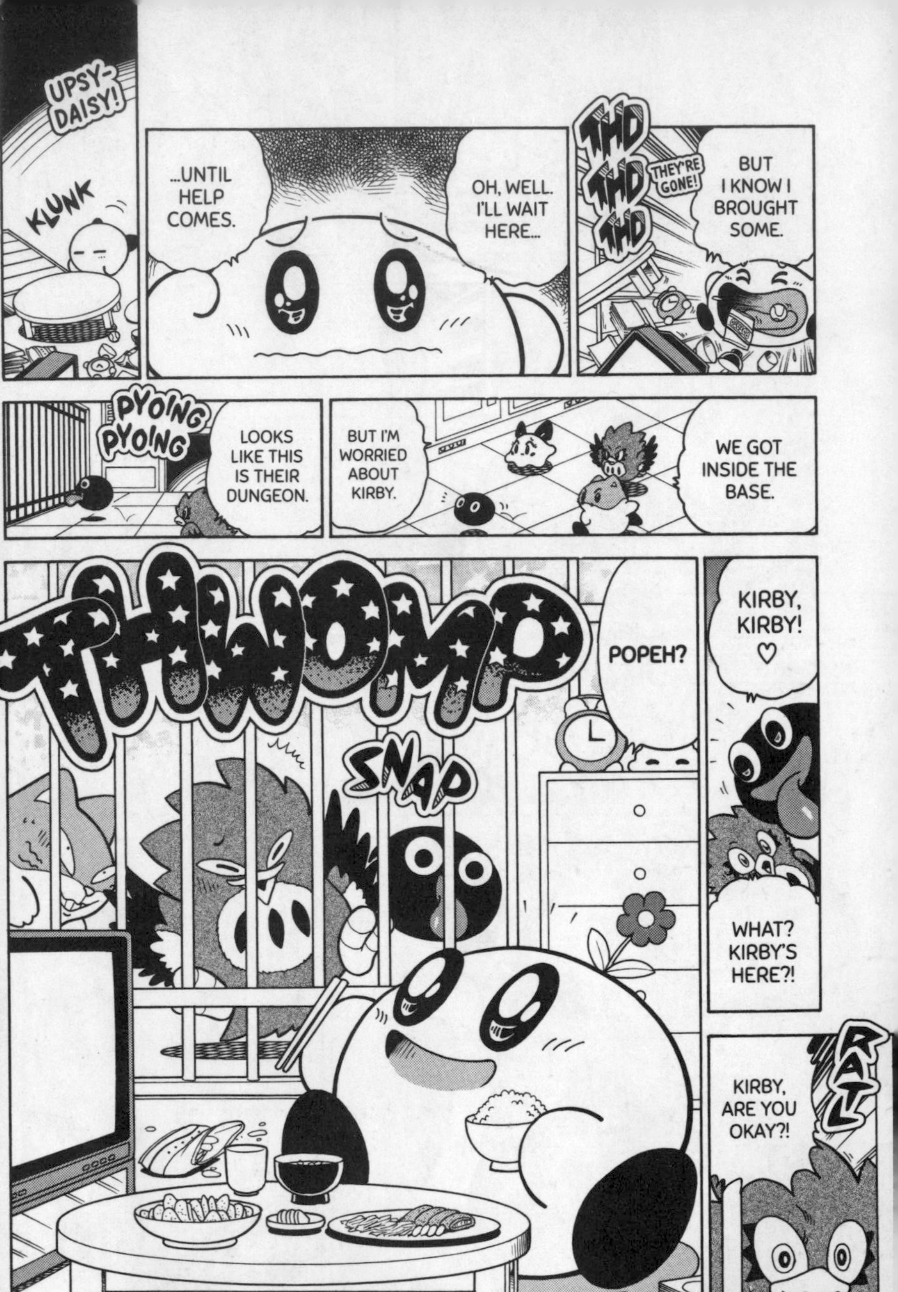
THD
THD
THD
THEY'RE GONE!
BUT I KNOW I BROUGHT SOME.
OH, WELL. I'LL WAIT HERE...
...UNTIL HELP COMES.
UPSY-DAISY!
KLUNK
WE GOT INSIDE THE BASE.
BUT I'M WORRIED ABOUT KIRBY.
PYOING PYOING
LOOKS LIKE THIS IS THEIR DUNGEON.
KIRBY, KIRBY! ♡
WHAT? KIRBY'S HERE?!
RATL
KIRBY, ARE YOU OKAY?!
POPEH?
THWOMP
SNAP

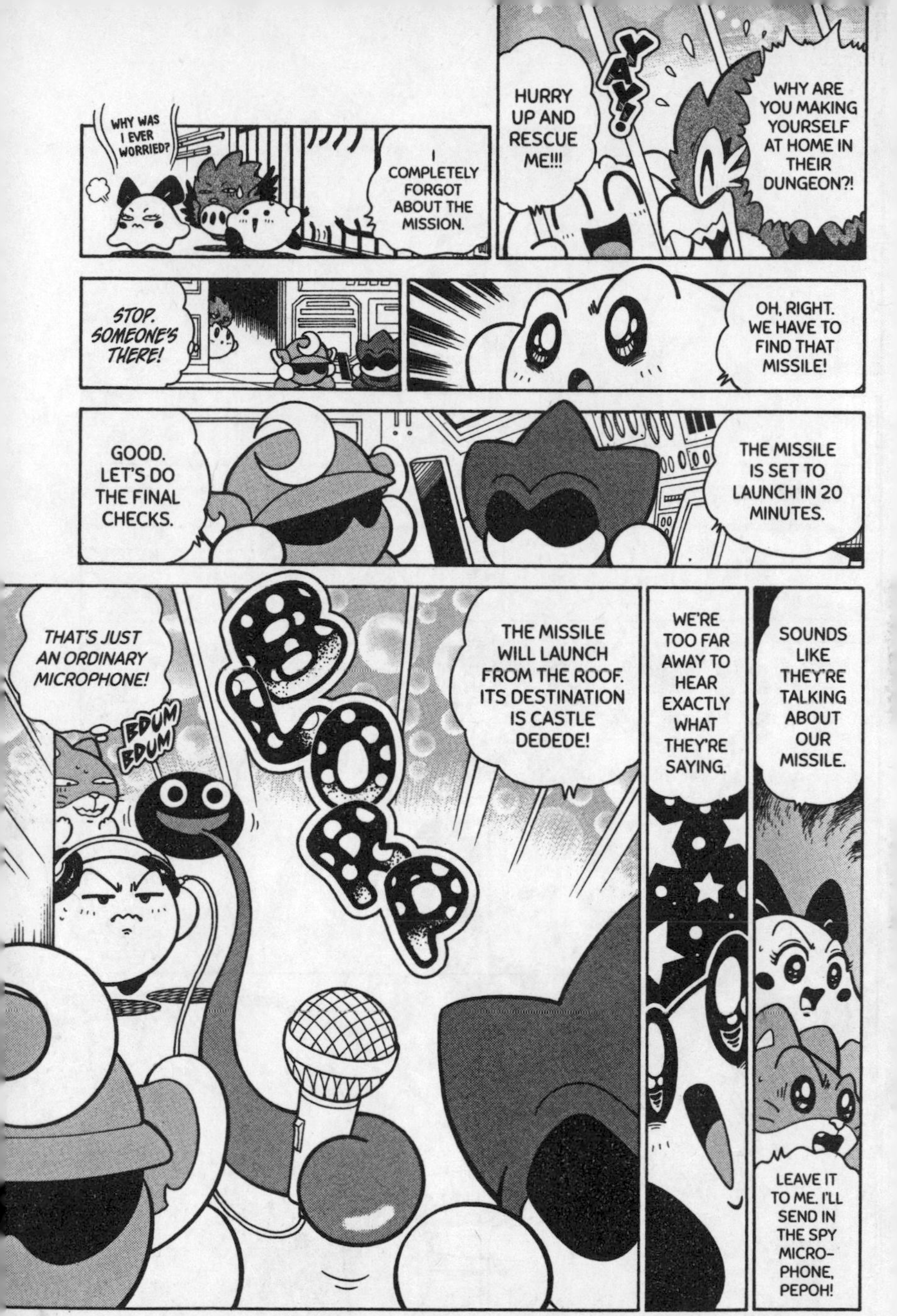
WHY ARE YOU MAKING YOURSELF AT HOME IN THEIR DUNGEON?!
HURRY UP AND RESCUE ME!!!
I COMPLETELY FORGOT ABOUT THE MISSION.
WHY WAS I EVER WORRIED?
OH, RIGHT. WE HAVE TO FIND THAT MISSILE!
STOP. SOMEONE'S THERE!
THE MISSILE IS SET TO LAUNCH IN 20 MINUTES.
GOOD. LET'S DO THE FINAL CHECKS.
SOUNDS LIKE THEY'RE TALKING ABOUT OUR MISSILE.
LEAVE IT TO ME. I'LL SEND IN THE SPY MICRO-PHONE, PEPOH!
WE'RE TOO FAR AWAY TO HEAR EXACTLY WHAT THEY'RE SAYING.
THE MISSILE WILL LAUNCH FROM THE ROOF. ITS DESTINATION IS CASTLE DEDEDE!
BLOOP
THAT'S JUST AN ORDINARY MICROPHONE!
BDUM BDUM

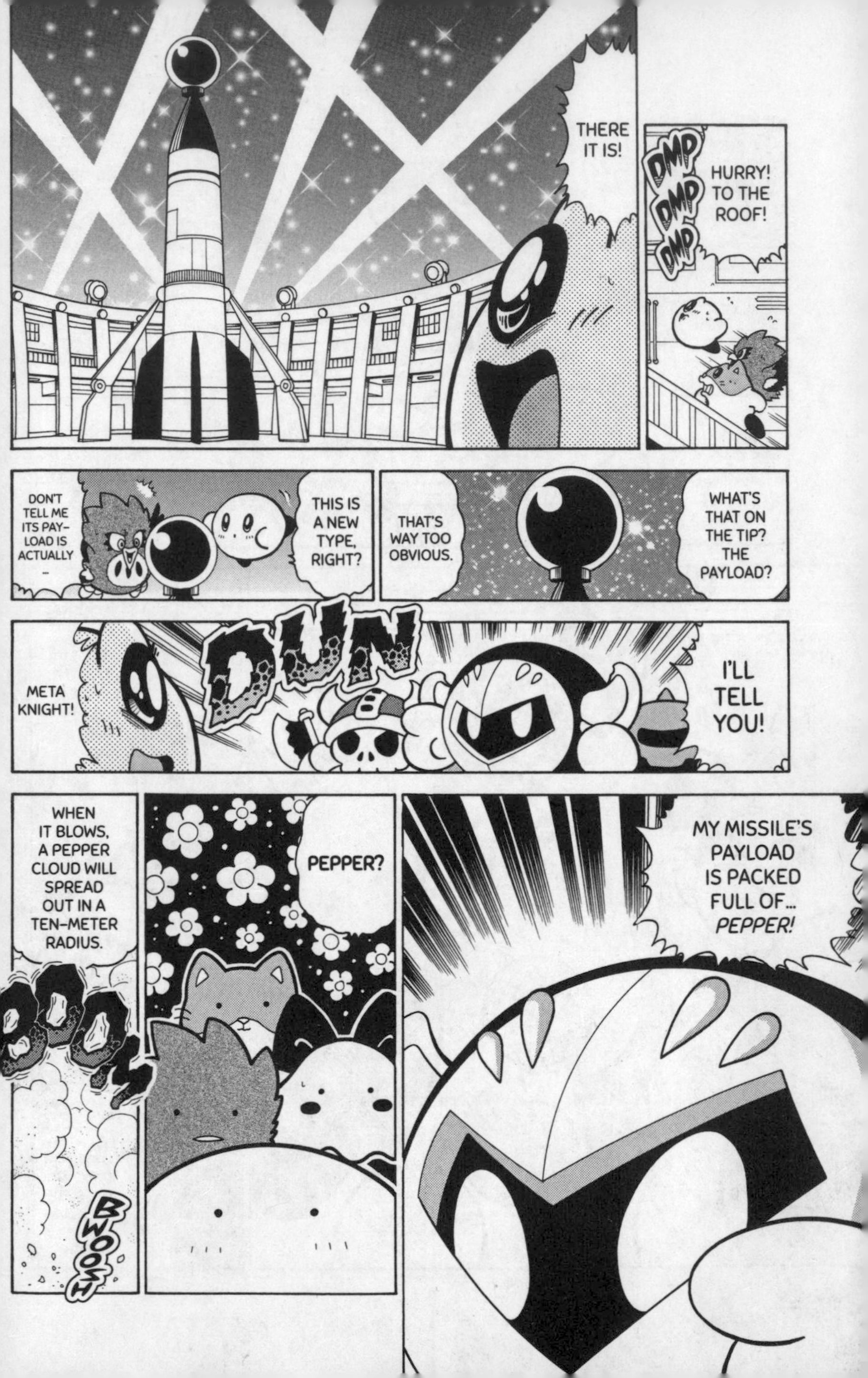
DMP DMP DMP
HURRY! TO THE ROOF!
THERE IT IS!
WHAT'S THAT ON THE TIP? THE PAYLOAD?
THAT'S WAY TOO OBVIOUS.
THIS IS A NEW TYPE, RIGHT?
DON'T TELL ME ITS PAY-LOAD IS ACTUALLY –
I'LL TELL YOU!
DUN
META KNIGHT!
MY MISSILE'S PAYLOAD IS PACKED FULL OF... *PEPPER!*
PEPPER?
WHEN IT BLOWS, A PEPPER CLOUD WILL SPREAD OUT IN A TEN-METER RADIUS.
BWOOSH

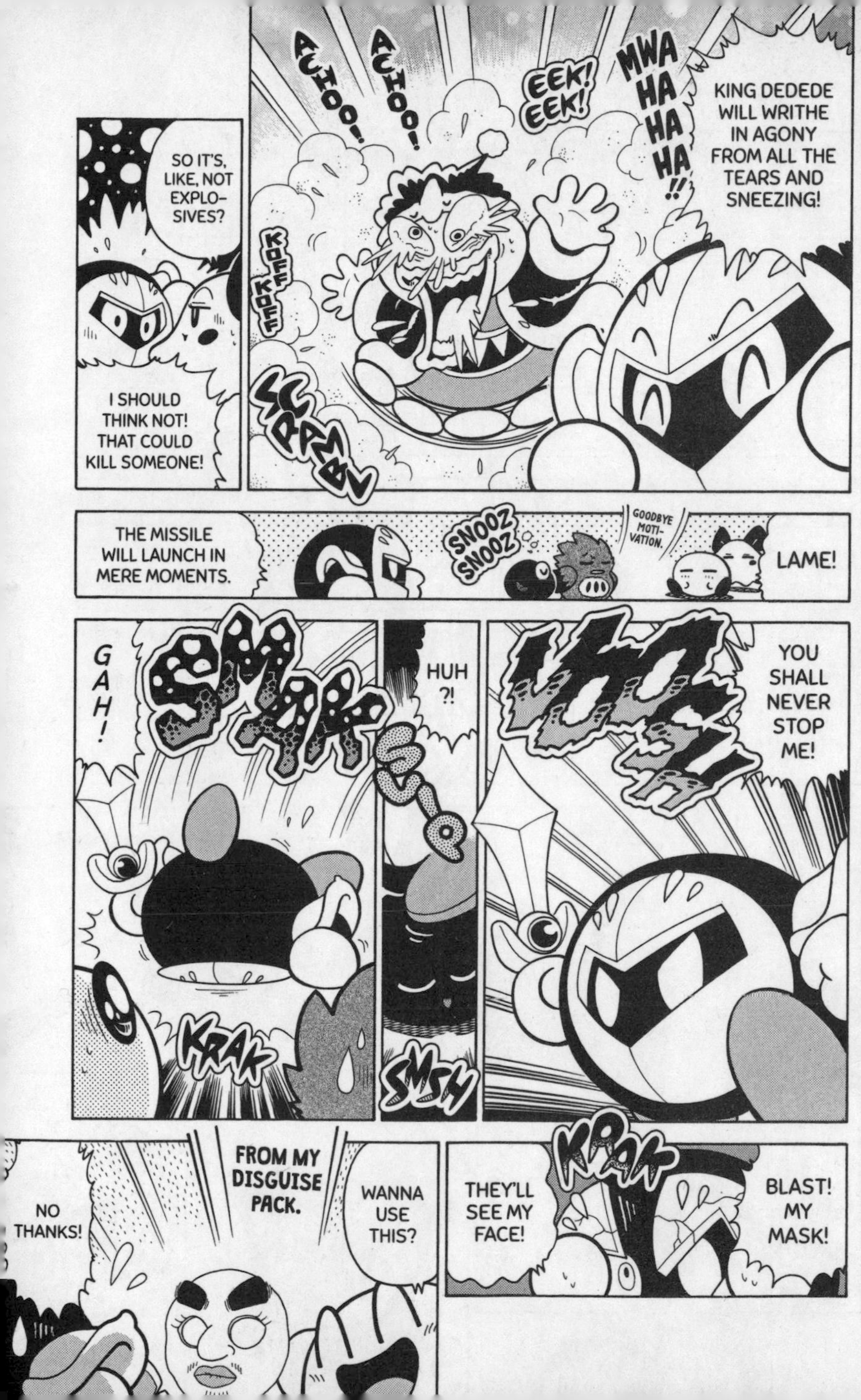
KING DEDEDE WILL WRITHE IN AGONY FROM ALL THE TEARS AND SNEEZING!
MWA HA HA HA!!
EEK! EEK!
ACHOO! ACHOO!
KOFF KOFF
SO IT'S, LIKE, NOT EXPLOSIVES?
I SHOULD THINK NOT! THAT COULD KILL SOMEONE!
LAME!
GOODBYE MOTIVATION.
SNOOZ SNOOZ
THE MISSILE WILL LAUNCH IN MERE MOMENTS.
YOU SHALL NEVER STOP ME!
HUH?!
SMSH
SMAK
GAH!
KRAK
BLAST! MY MASK!
KRAK
THEY'LL SEE MY FACE!
WANNA USE THIS?
FROM MY DISGUISE PACK.
NO THANKS!

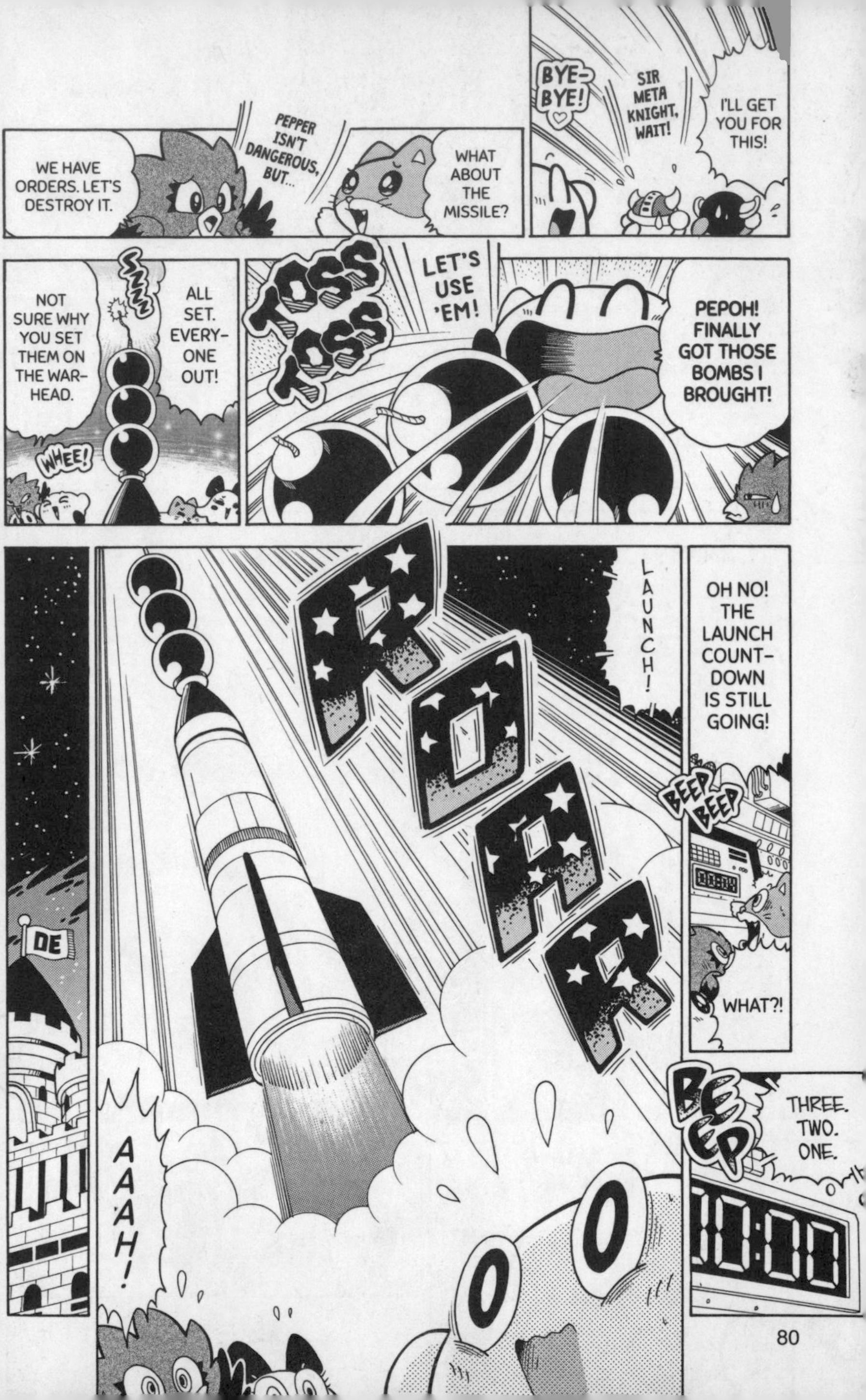
I'LL GET YOU FOR THIS!
SIR META KNIGHT, WAIT!
BYE-BYE!
WHAT ABOUT THE MISSILE?
PEPPER ISN'T DANGEROUS, BUT...
WE HAVE ORDERS. LET'S DESTROY IT.
PEPOH! FINALLY GOT THOSE BOMBS I BROUGHT!
LET'S USE 'EM!
TOSS TOSS
ALL SET. EVERY-ONE OUT!
SZZZ
NOT SURE WHY YOU SET THEM ON THE WAR-HEAD.
WHEE!
OH NO! THE LAUNCH COUNT-DOWN IS STILL GOING!
BEEP BEEP
WHAT?!
THREE. TWO. ONE.
BEEP
LAUNCH!
ROAR
AAAAH!

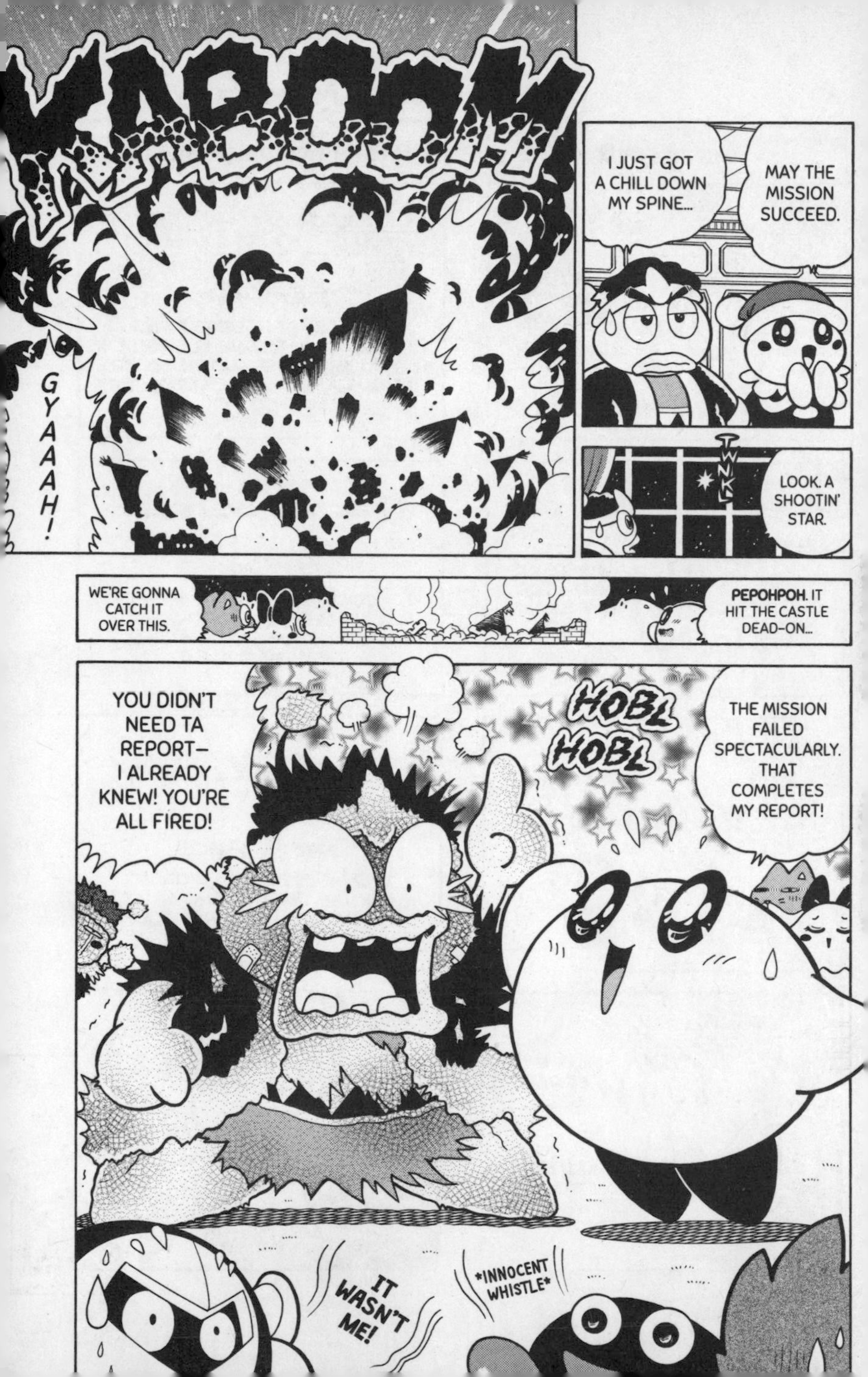
MAY THE MISSION SUCCEED.
I JUST GOT A CHILL DOWN MY SPINE...
LOOK. A SHOOTIN' STAR.
TWNKL
KABOOM
GYAAAAH!
PEPOHPOH. IT HIT THE CASTLE DEAD-ON...
WE'RE GONNA CATCH IT OVER THIS.
THE MISSION FAILED SPECTACULARLY. THAT COMPLETES MY REPORT!
HOBL HOBL
YOU DIDN'T NEED TA REPORT— I ALREADY KNEW! YOU'RE ALL FIRED!
INNOCENT WHISTLE
IT WASN'T ME!

KIRBY MANGA MANIA: COMIC STRIP THEATER!

KIRBY'S WORDS OF WISDOM

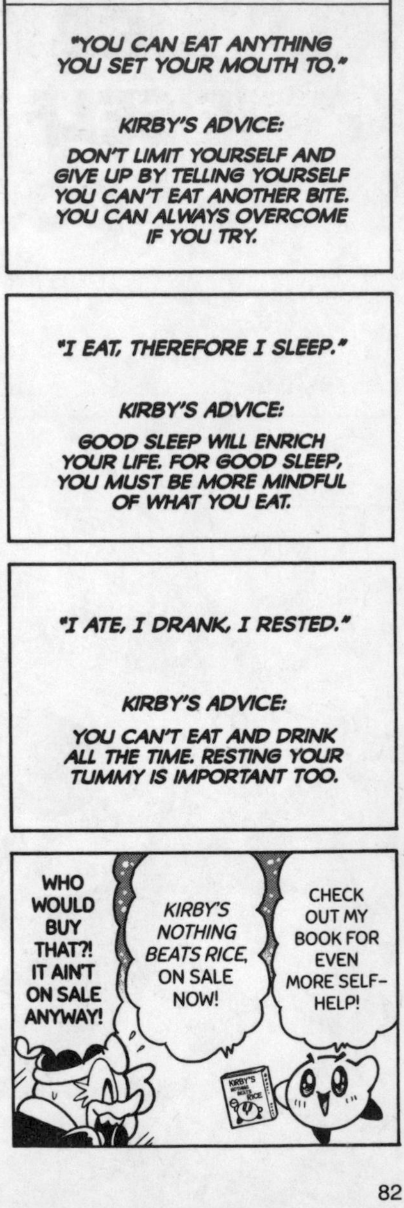
"YOU CAN EAT ANYTHING YOU SET YOUR MOUTH TO."
KIRBY'S ADVICE:
DON'T LIMIT YOURSELF AND GIVE UP BY TELLING YOURSELF YOU CAN'T EAT ANOTHER BITE. YOU CAN ALWAYS OVERCOME IF YOU TRY.
"I EAT, THEREFORE I SLEEP."
KIRBY'S ADVICE:
GOOD SLEEP WILL ENRICH YOUR LIFE. FOR GOOD SLEEP, YOU MUST BE MORE MINDFUL OF WHAT YOU EAT.
"I ATE, I DRANK, I RESTED."
KIRBY'S ADVICE:
YOU CAN'T EAT AND DRINK ALL THE TIME. RESTING YOUR TUMMY IS IMPORTANT TOO.
CHECK OUT MY BOOK FOR EVEN MORE SELF-HELP!
KIRBY'S NOTHING BEATS RICE, ON SALE NOW!
WHO WOULD BUY THAT?! IT AIN'T ON SALE ANYWAY!

KIRBY'S POEM

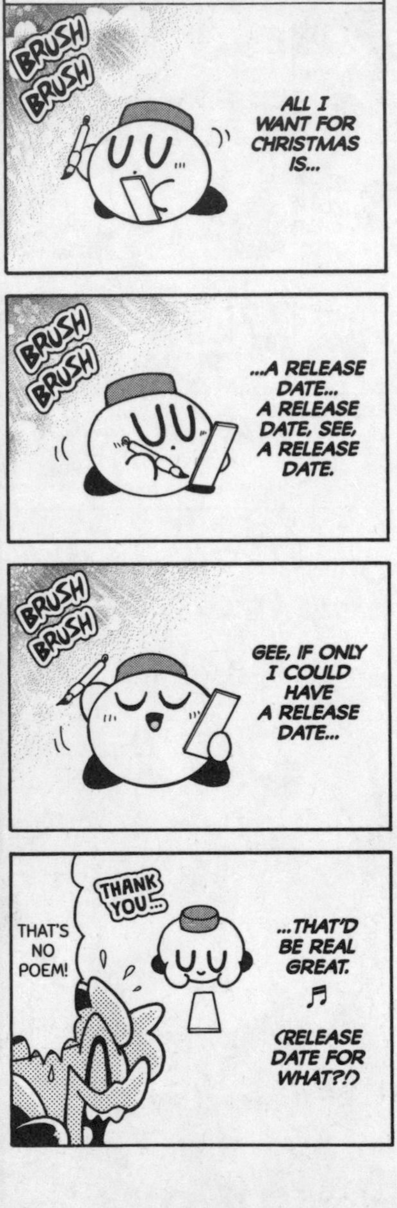
ALL I WANT FOR CHRISTMAS IS...
BRUSH BRUSH
...A RELEASE DATE... A RELEASE DATE, SEE, A RELEASE DATE.
BRUSH BRUSH
GEE, IF ONLY I COULD HAVE A RELEASE DATE...
BRUSH BRUSH
...THAT'D BE REAL GREAT. ♬
THANK YOU...
THAT'S NO POEM!
(RELEASE DATE FOR WHAT?!)

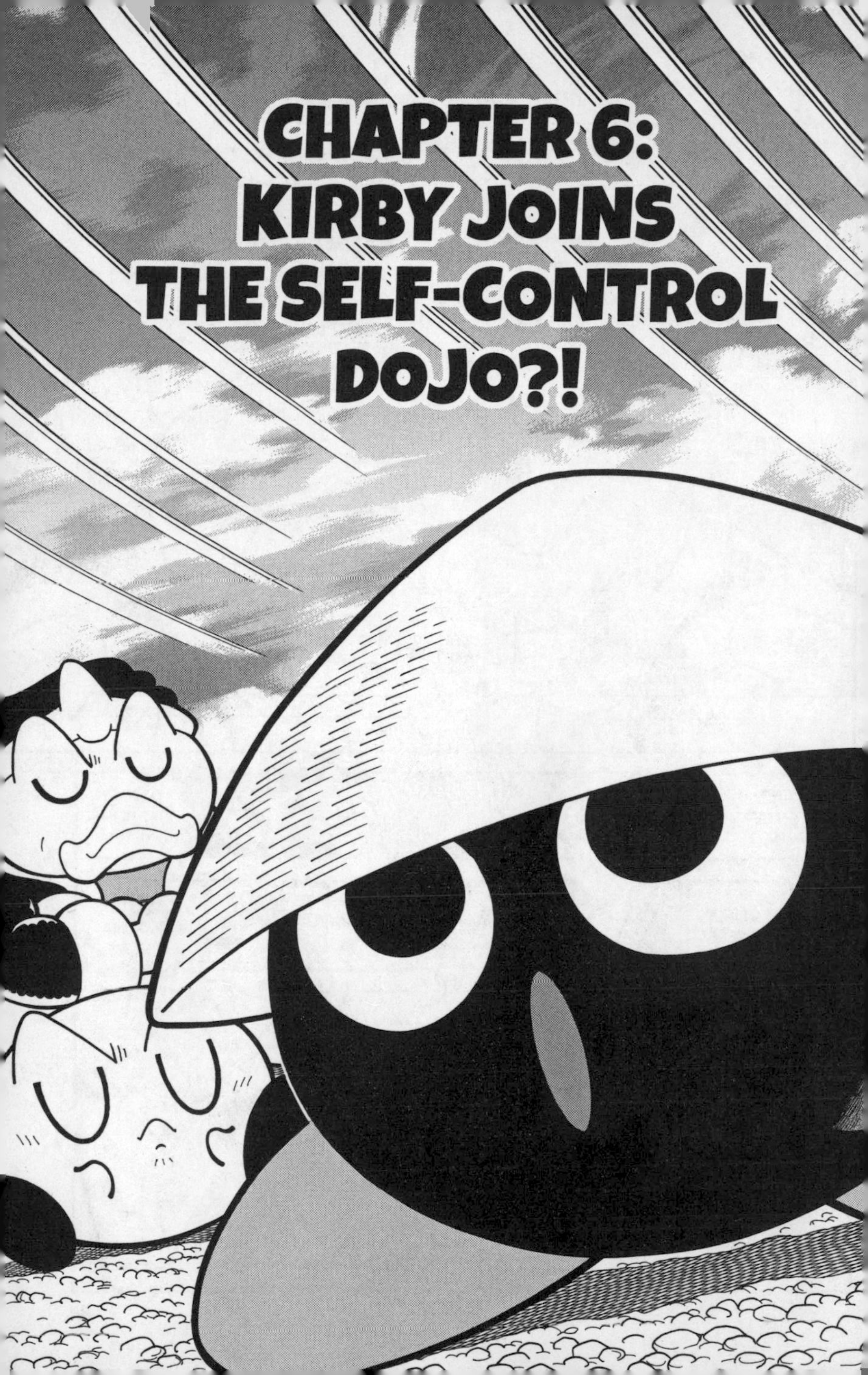
CHAPTER 6:
KIRBY JOINS
THE SELF-CONTROL
DOJO?!

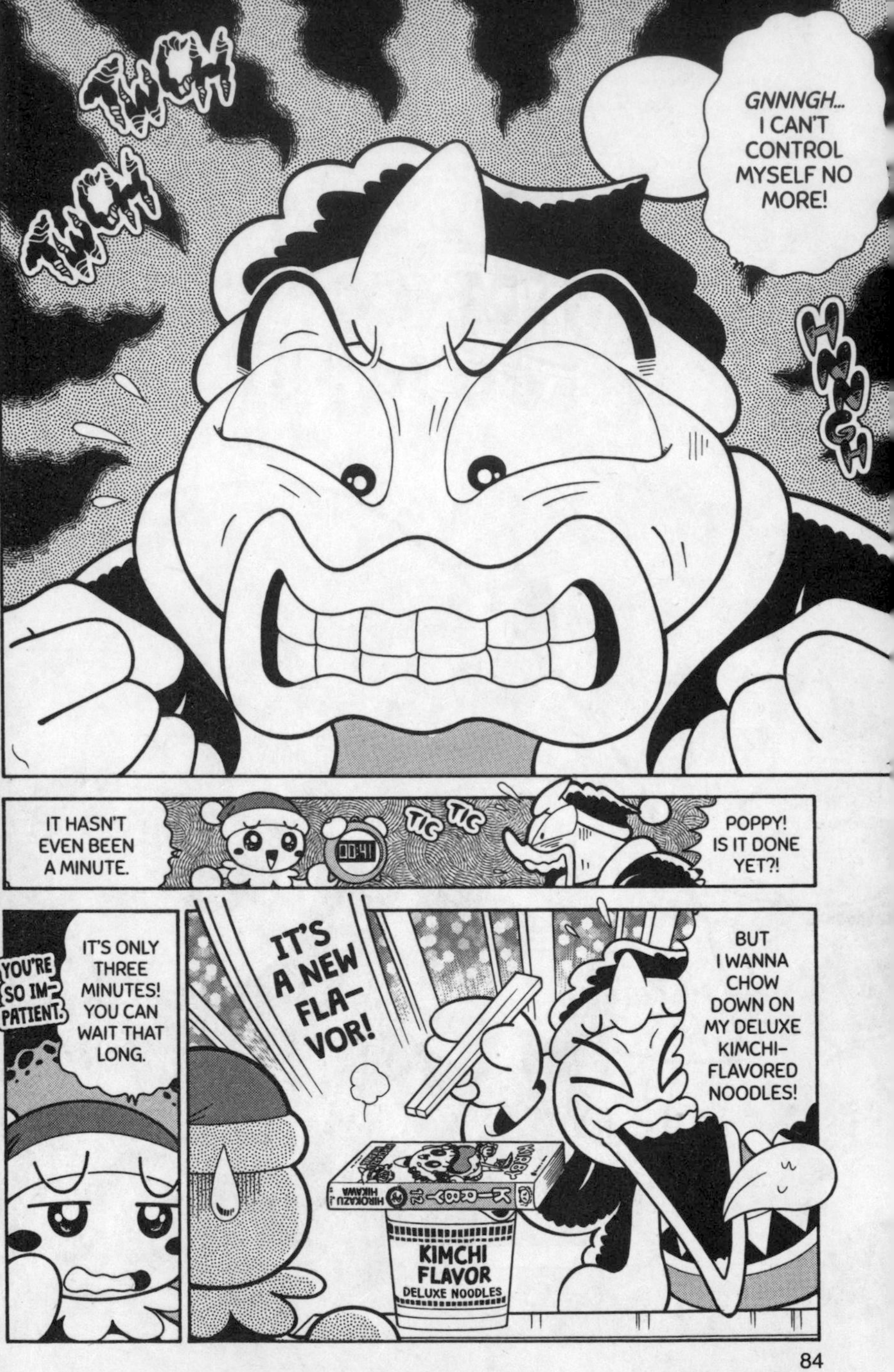
GNNNGH... I CAN'T CONTROL MYSELF NO MORE!
HNNGH
WOH WOH
POPPY! IS IT DONE YET?!
TIC TIC
00:41
IT HASN'T EVEN BEEN A MINUTE.
BUT I WANNA CHOW DOWN ON MY DELUXE KIMCHI-FLAVORED NOODLES!
IT'S A NEW FLA-VOR!
KIMCHI FLAVOR
DELUXE NOODLES
IT'S ONLY THREE MINUTES! YOU CAN WAIT THAT LONG.
YOU'RE SO IM-PATIENT.

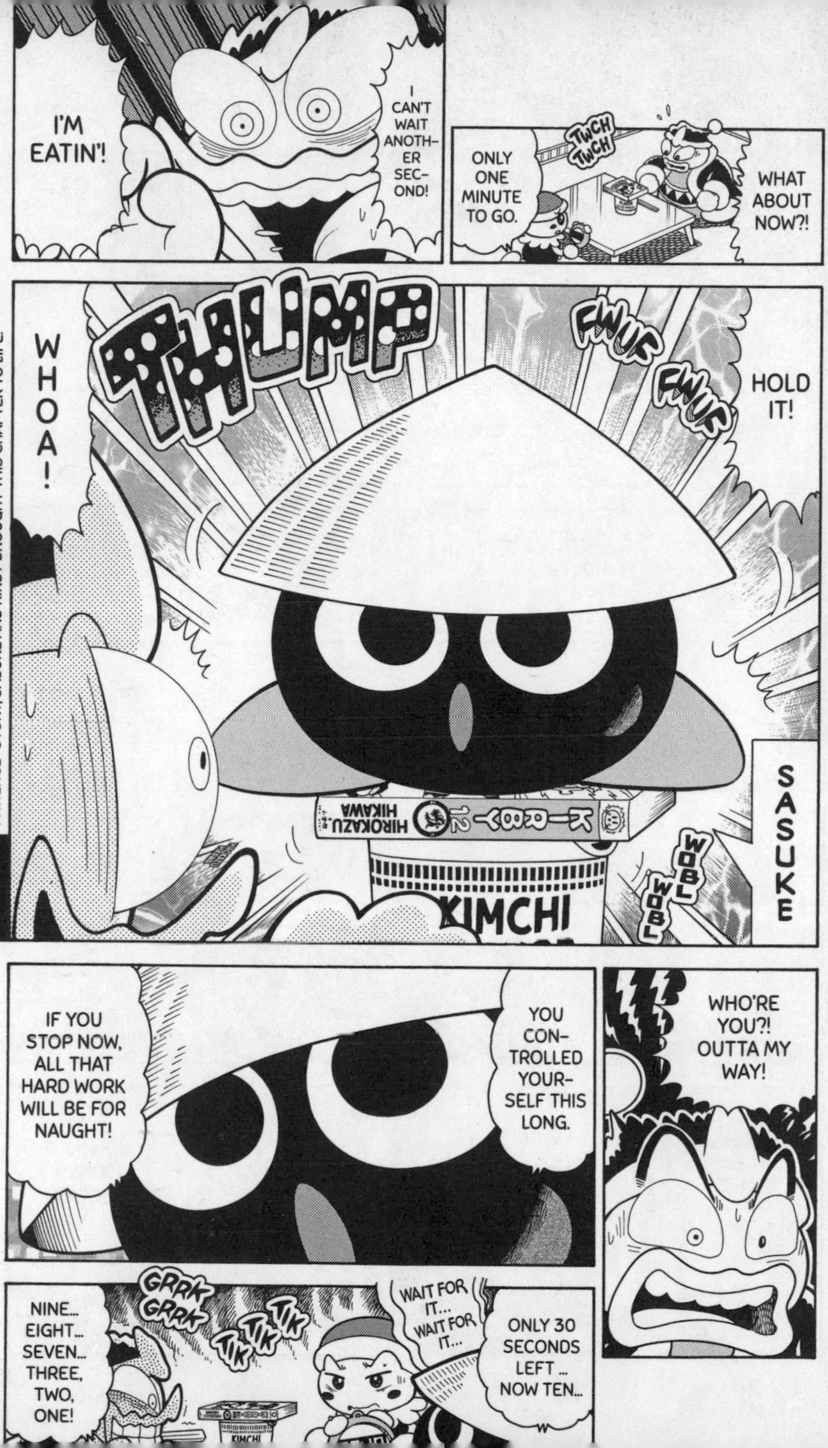
TWCH TWCH
WHAT ABOUT NOW?!
ONLY ONE MINUTE TO GO.
I CAN'T WAIT ANOTHER SECOND!
I'M EATIN'!
FWUF FWUF
HOLD IT!
THUMP
WHOA!
SASUKE
WOBL WOBL
KIMCHI
WHO'RE YOU?! OUTTA MY WAY!
YOU CONTROLLED YOURSELF THIS LONG.
IF YOU STOP NOW, ALL THAT HARD WORK WILL BE FOR NAUGHT!
ONLY 30 SECONDS LEFT ... NOW TEN...
WAIT FOR IT... WAIT FOR IT...
TIK TIK TIK
GRRK GRRK
NINE... EIGHT... SEVEN... THREE, TWO, ONE!

AUTHOR'S COMMENT

ANOTHER STORY THAT GOT THE GO-AHEAD FROM MY EDITOR ON THE FIRST DRAFT! JUST WHEN IT SEEMED LIKE IT WOULD TURN OUT TO BE JUST ANOTHER "LESSON IN PATIENCE" STORY, SASUKE AND KIRBY BROUGHT THIS CHAPTER TO LIFE.

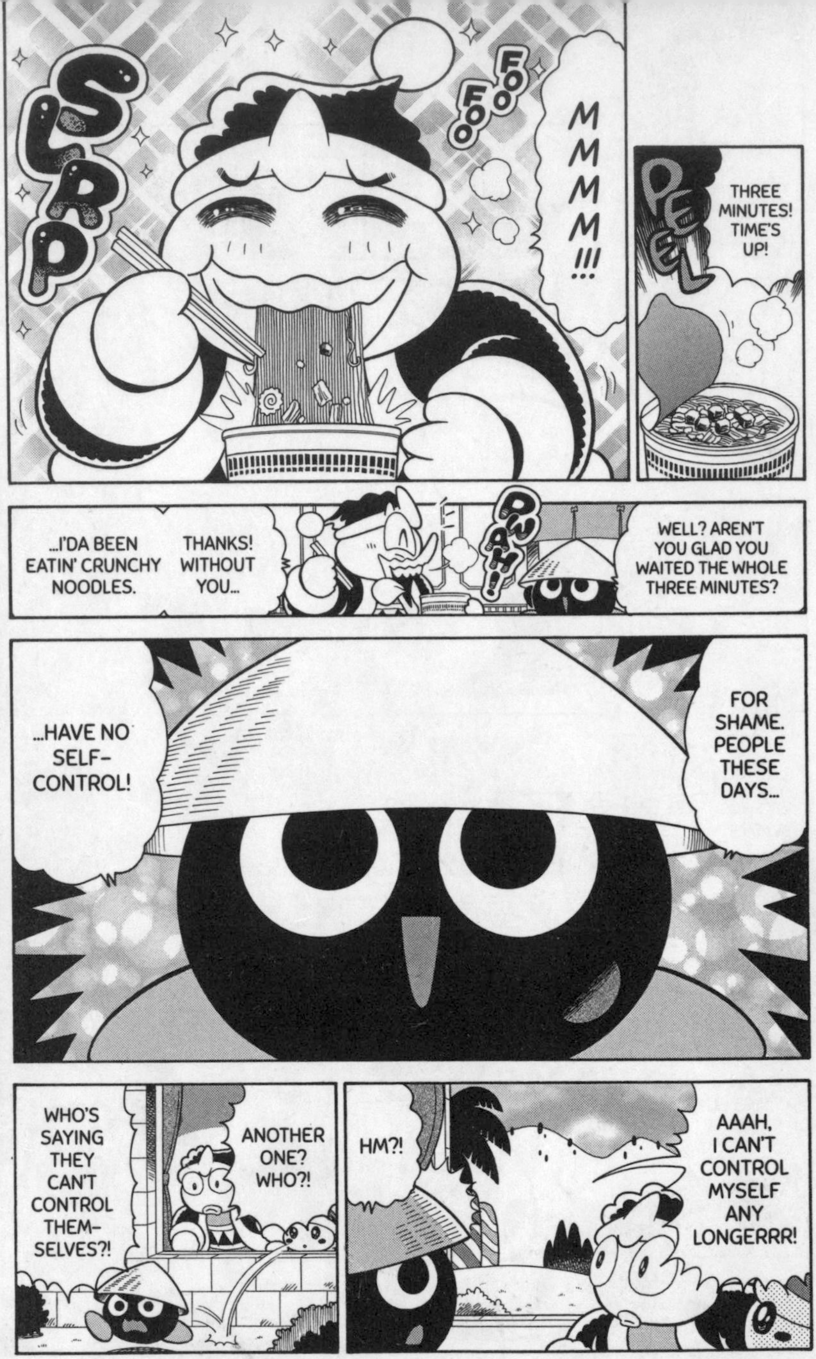
PEEL
THREE MINUTES! TIME'S UP!
SLRP
FOO FOO
MMMMM!!!
WELL? AREN'T YOU GLAD YOU WAITED THE WHOLE THREE MINUTES?
PWAH!
THANKS! WITHOUT YOU...
...I'DA BEEN EATIN' CRUNCHY NOODLES.
FOR SHAME. PEOPLE THESE DAYS...
...HAVE NO SELF-CONTROL!
AAAH, I CAN'T CONTROL MYSELF ANY LONGERRR!
HM?!
ANOTHER ONE? WHO?!
WHO'S SAYING THEY CAN'T CONTROL THEMSELVES?!

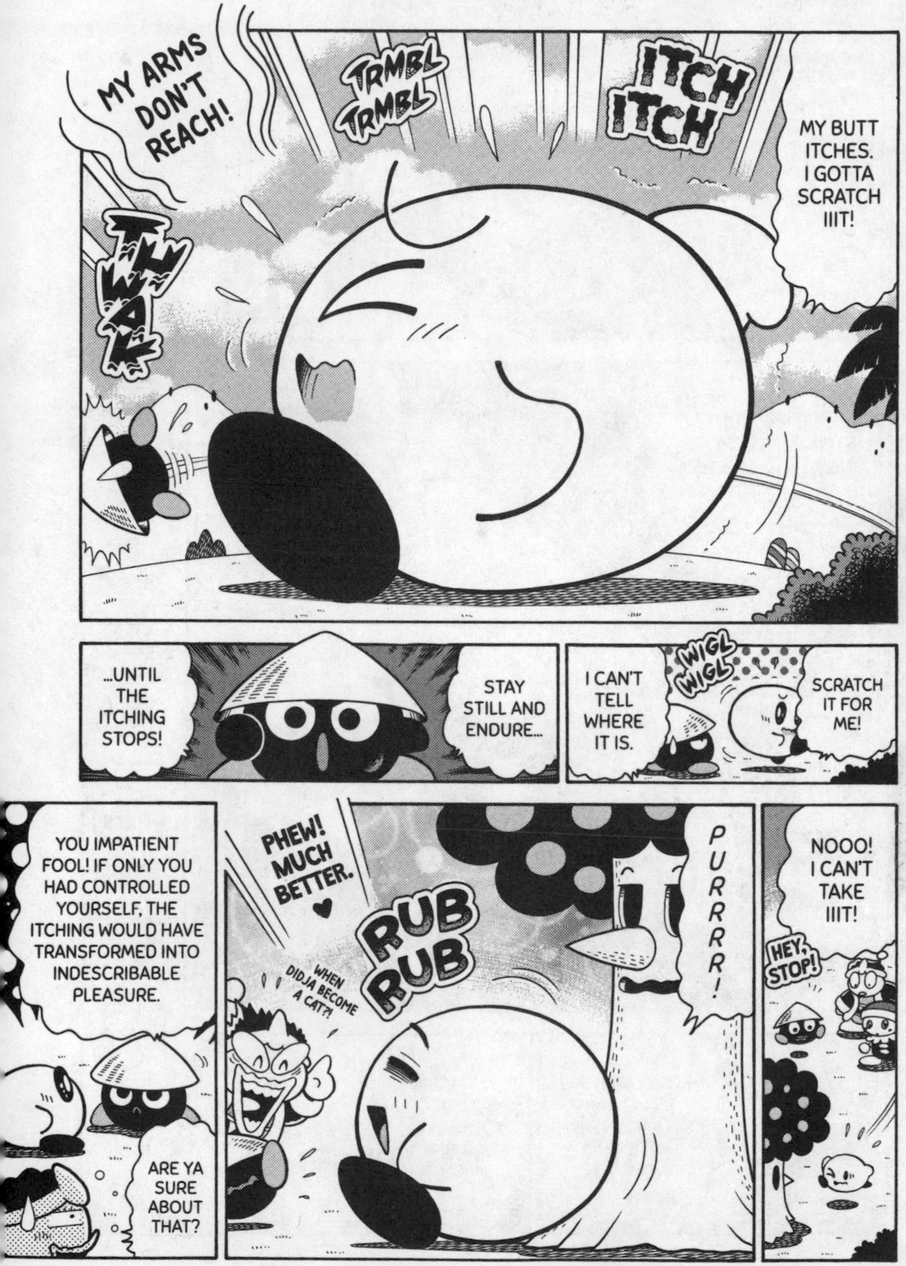

MY BUTT ITCHES. I GOTTA SCRATCH IIIT!
ITCH ITCH
TRMBL TRMBL
MY ARMS DON'T REACH!
THWAK
SCRATCH IT FOR ME!
WIGL WIGL
I CAN'T TELL WHERE IT IS.
STAY STILL AND ENDURE...
...UNTIL THE ITCHING STOPS!
NOOO! I CAN'T TAKE IIIT!
HEY, STOP!
PURRRR!
PHEW! MUCH BETTER.
RUB RUB
WHEN DIDJA BECOME A CAT?!
YOU IMPATIENT FOOL! IF ONLY YOU HAD CONTROLLED YOURSELF, THE ITCHING WOULD HAVE TRANSFORMED INTO INDESCRIBABLE PLEASURE.
ARE YA SURE ABOUT THAT?

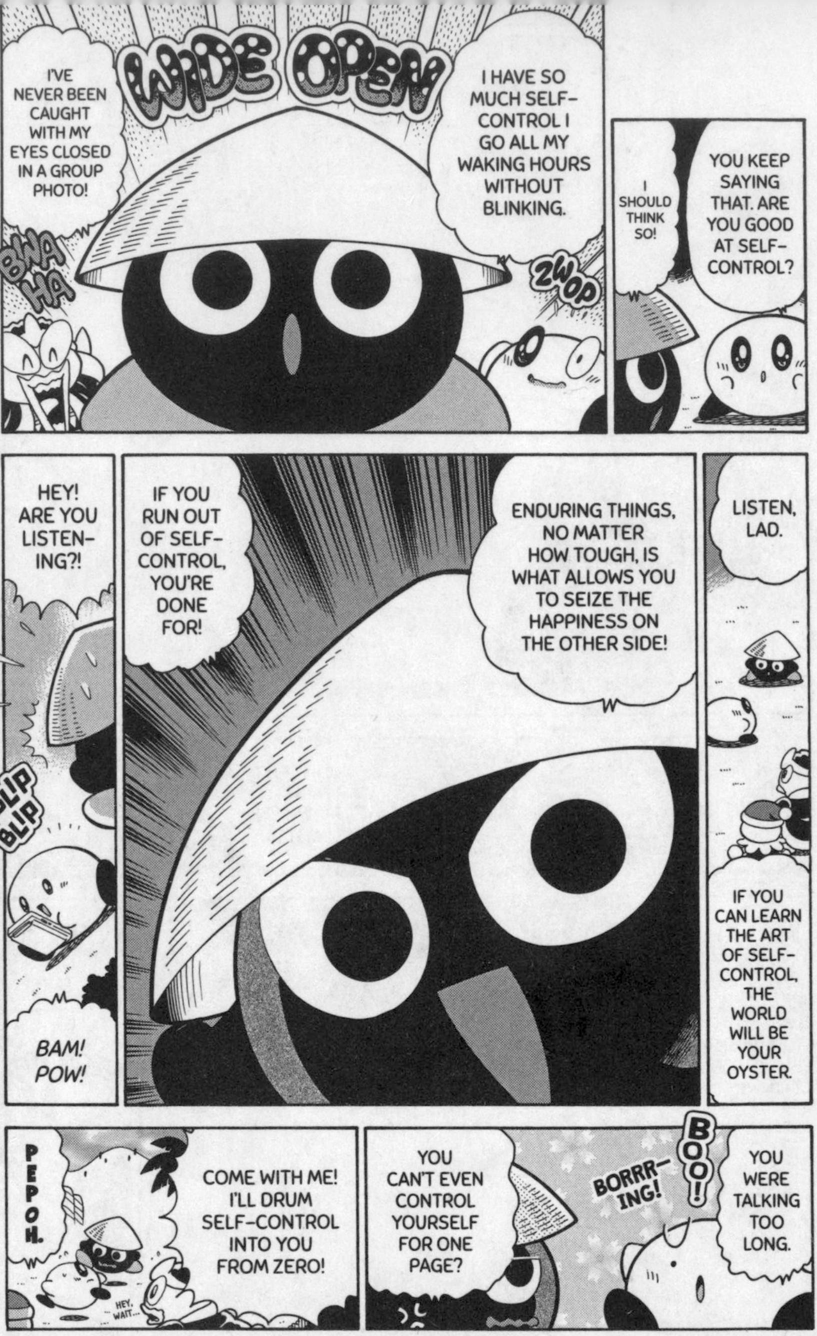
YOU KEEP SAYING THAT. ARE YOU GOOD AT SELF-CONTROL?
I SHOULD THINK SO!
I HAVE SO MUCH SELF-CONTROL I GO ALL MY WAKING HOURS WITHOUT BLINKING.
WIDE OPEN
I'VE NEVER BEEN CAUGHT WITH MY EYES CLOSED IN A GROUP PHOTO!
ZWOP
BWAHA HA
LISTEN, LAD.
IF YOU CAN LEARN THE ART OF SELF-CONTROL, THE WORLD WILL BE YOUR OYSTER.
ENDURING THINGS, NO MATTER HOW TOUGH, IS WHAT ALLOWS YOU TO SEIZE THE HAPPINESS ON THE OTHER SIDE!
IF YOU RUN OUT OF SELF-CONTROL, YOU'RE DONE FOR!
HEY! ARE YOU LISTENING?!
BLIP BLIP
BAM! POW!
BOO!
YOU WERE TALKING TOO LONG.
BORRR-ING!
YOU CAN'T EVEN CONTROL YOURSELF FOR ONE PAGE?
COME WITH ME! I'LL DRUM SELF-CONTROL INTO YOU FROM ZERO!
PEPOH.
HEY, WAIT...

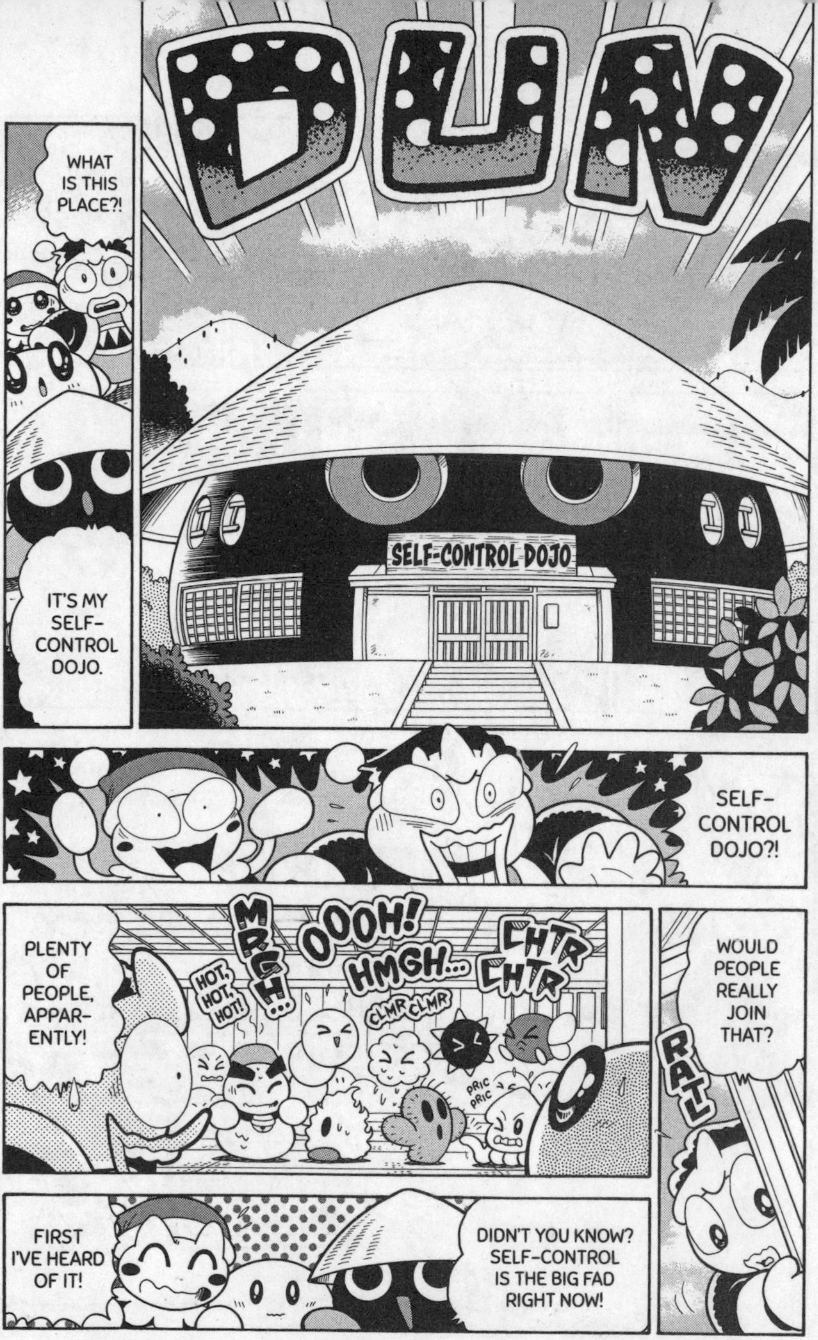
DUN
SELF-CONTROL DOJO
WHAT IS THIS PLACE?!
IT'S MY SELF-CONTROL DOJO.
SELF-CONTROL DOJO?!
WOULD PEOPLE REALLY JOIN THAT?
RATL
CHTR CHTR
OOOH!
HMGH...
MRGH!!
CLMR CLMR
HOT, HOT, HOT!
PRIC PRIC
PLENTY OF PEOPLE, APPAR-ENTLY!
DIDN'T YOU KNOW? SELF-CONTROL IS THE BIG FAD RIGHT NOW!
FIRST I'VE HEARD OF IT!

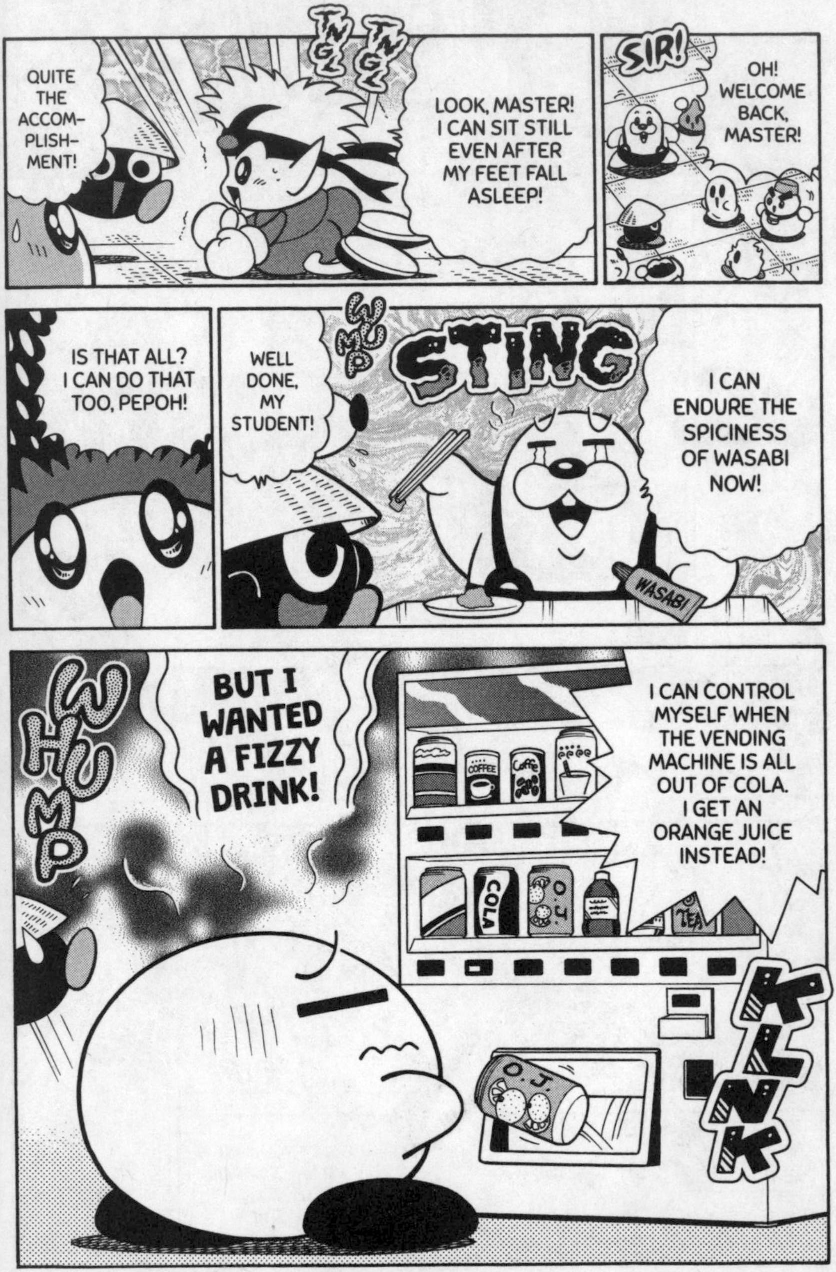
OH! WELCOME BACK, MASTER!
SIR!
TNG TNG
LOOK, MASTER! I CAN SIT STILL EVEN AFTER MY FEET FALL ASLEEP!
QUITE THE ACCOM-PLISH-MENT!
I CAN ENDURE THE SPICINESS OF WASABI NOW!
STING
WMP
WELL DONE, MY STUDENT!
WASABI
IS THAT ALL? I CAN DO THAT TOO, PEPOH!
I CAN CONTROL MYSELF WHEN THE VENDING MACHINE IS ALL OUT OF COLA. I GET AN ORANGE JUICE INSTEAD!
KLINK
COFFEE
COLA
O.J.
TEA
BUT I WANTED A FIZZY DRINK!
WHUMP

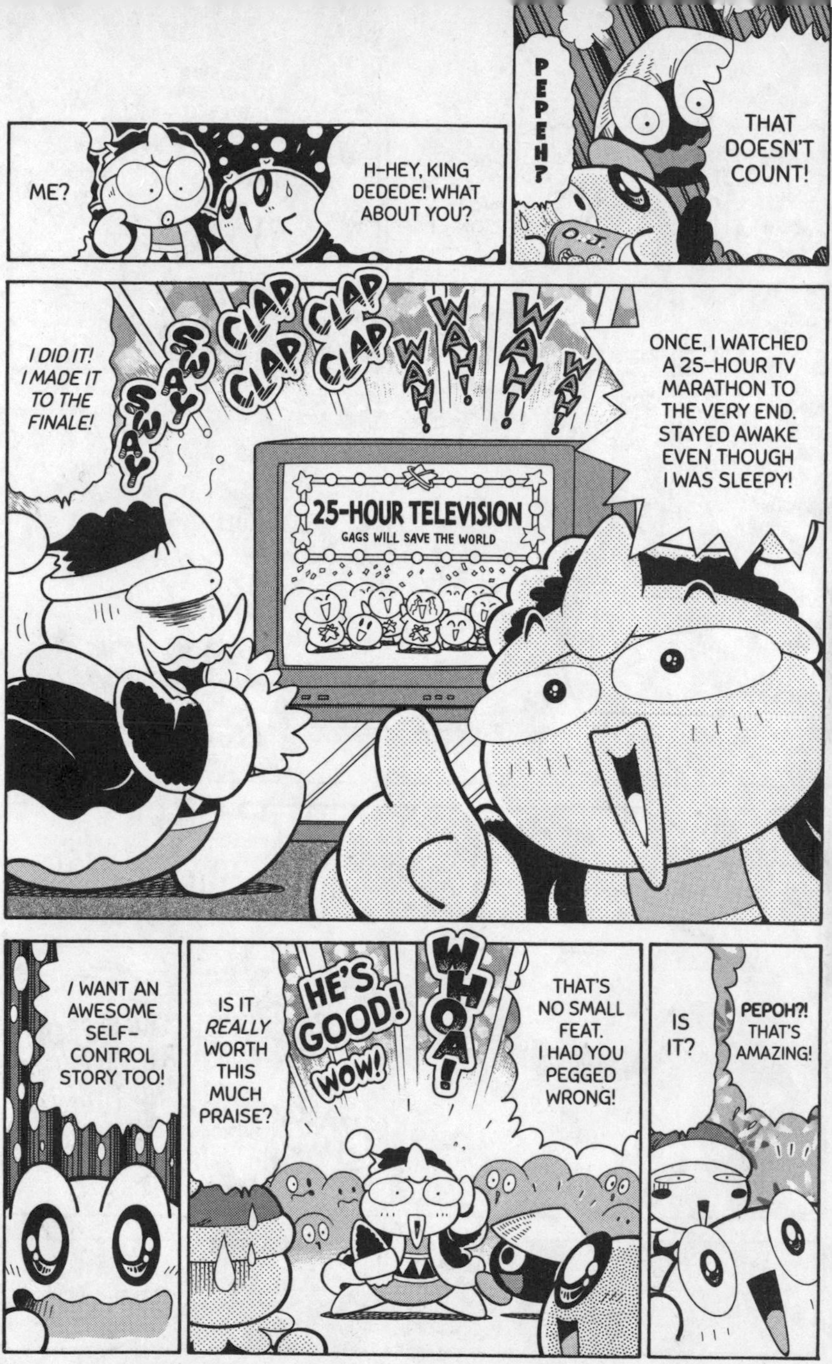
PEPEH?
THAT DOESN'T COUNT!
H-HEY, KING DEDEDE! WHAT ABOUT YOU?
ME?
ONCE, I WATCHED A 25-HOUR TV MARATHON TO THE VERY END. STAYED AWAKE EVEN THOUGH I WAS SLEEPY!
WAH! WAH!
WAH! WAH!
CLAP CLAP CLAP CLAP
SWAY SWAY
I DID IT! I MADE IT TO THE FINALE!
25-HOUR TELEVISION
GAGS WILL SAVE THE WORLD
PEPOH?! THAT'S AMAZING!
IS IT?
THAT'S NO SMALL FEAT. I HAD YOU PEGGED WRONG!
WHOA!
HE'S GOOD!
WOW!
IS IT *REALLY* WORTH THIS MUCH PRAISE?
I WANT AN AWESOME SELF-CONTROL STORY TOO!

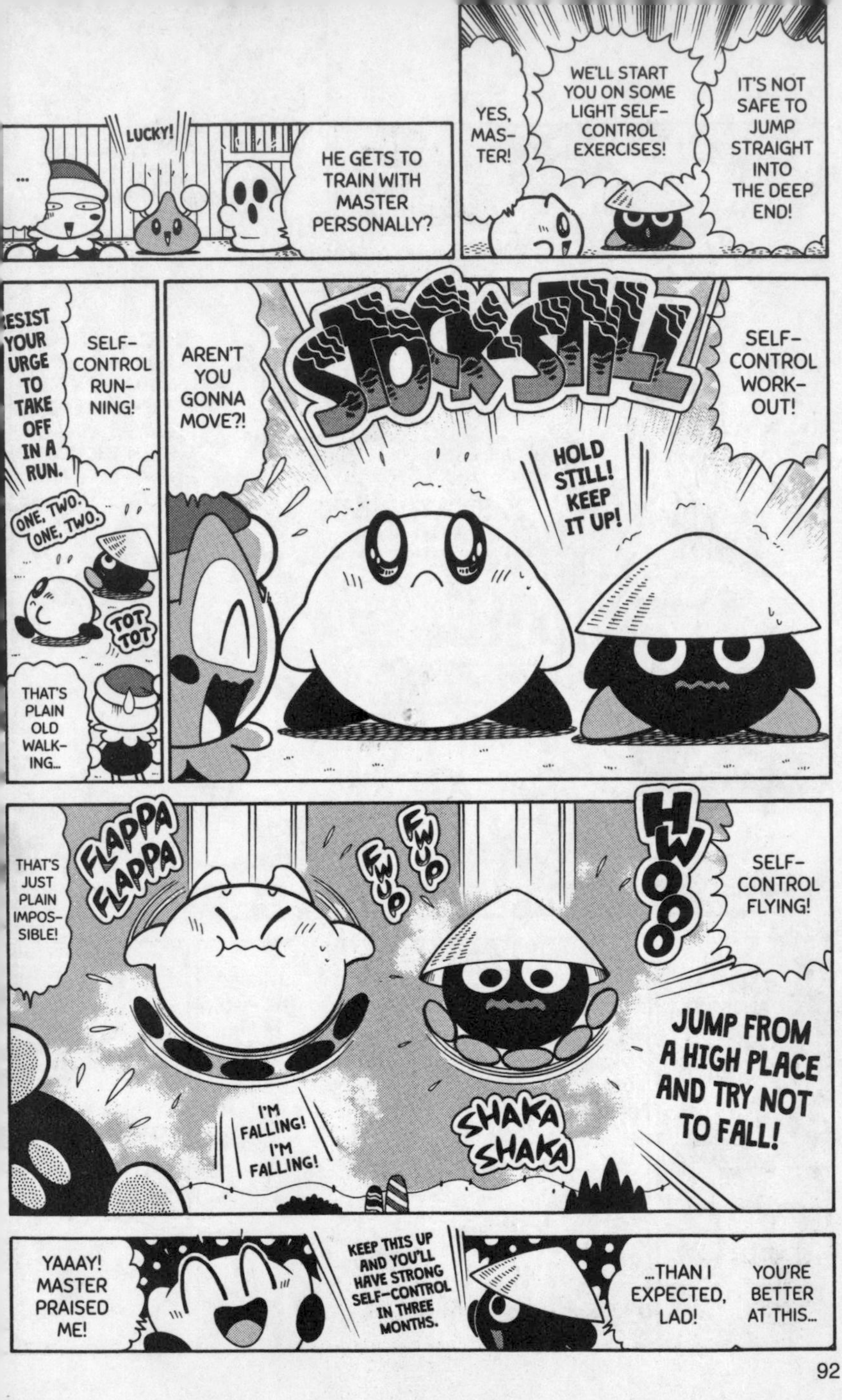
IT'S NOT SAFE TO JUMP STRAIGHT INTO THE DEEP END!
WE'LL START YOU ON SOME LIGHT SELF-CONTROL EXERCISES!
YES, MASTER!
HE GETS TO TRAIN WITH MASTER PERSONALLY?
LUCKY!
...
SELF-CONTROL WORKOUT!
HOLD STILL! KEEP IT UP!
AREN'T YOU GONNA MOVE?!
SELF-CONTROL RUNNING!
ESIST YOUR URGE TO TAKE OFF IN A RUN.
ONE, TWO. ONE, TWO.
TOT TOT
THAT'S PLAIN OLD WALKING...
SELF-CONTROL FLYING!
HWOOO
JUMP FROM A HIGH PLACE AND TRY NOT TO FALL!
FWUP FWUP
FLAPPA FLAPPA
SHAKA SHAKA
I'M FALLING! I'M FALLING!
THAT'S JUST PLAIN IMPOSSIBLE!
YOU'RE BETTER AT THIS...
...THAN I EXPECTED, LAD!
KEEP THIS UP AND YOU'LL HAVE STRONG SELF-CONTROL IN THREE MONTHS.
YAAAY! MASTER PRAISED ME!

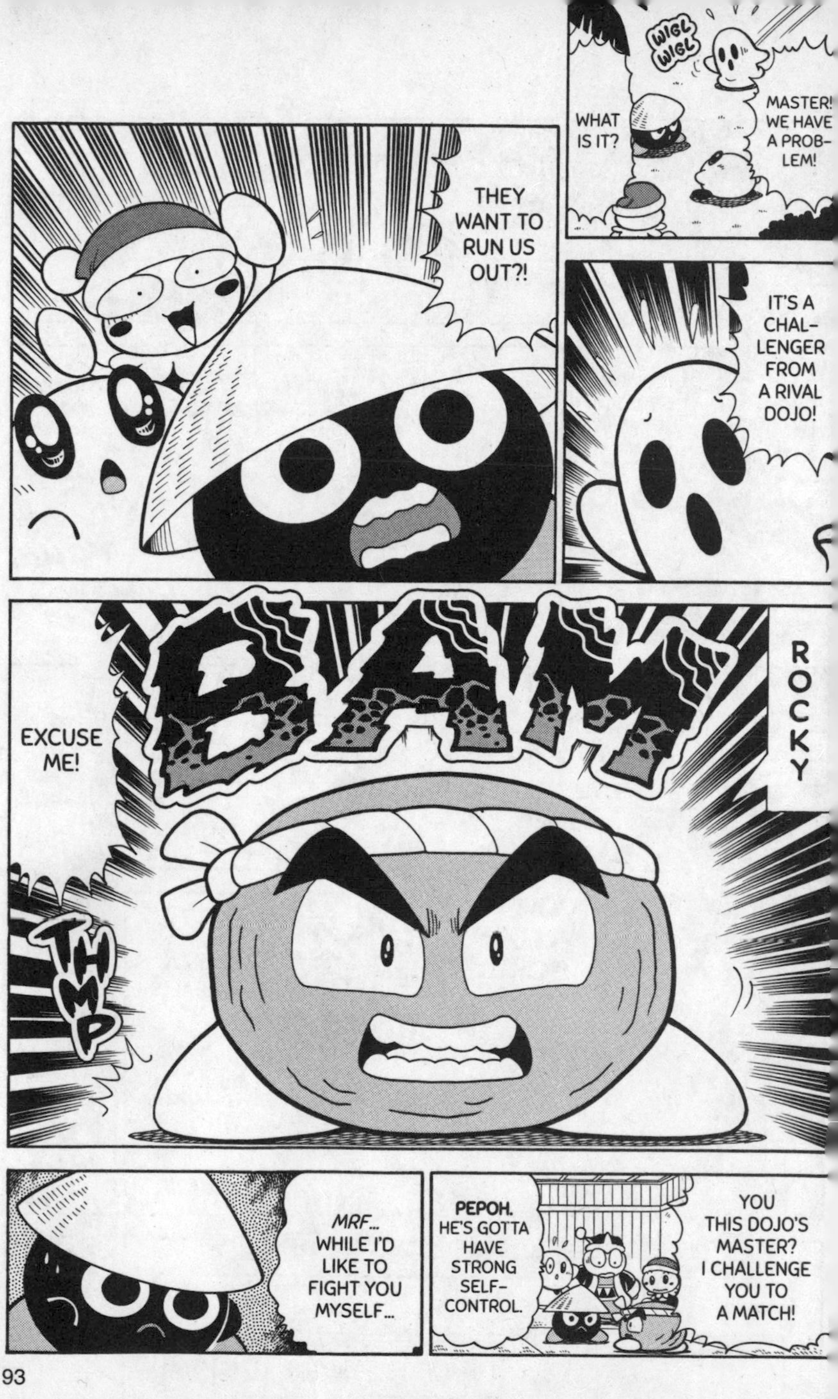

WIGL WIGL
MASTER! WE HAVE A PROB-LEM!
WHAT IS IT?
IT'S A CHAL-LENGER FROM A RIVAL DOJO!
THEY WANT TO RUN US OUT?!
ROCKY
BAM
EXCUSE ME!
THUMP
YOU THIS DOJO'S MASTER? I CHALLENGE YOU TO A MATCH!
PEPOH. HE'S GOTTA HAVE STRONG SELF-CONTROL.
MRF... WHILE I'D LIKE TO FIGHT YOU MYSELF...

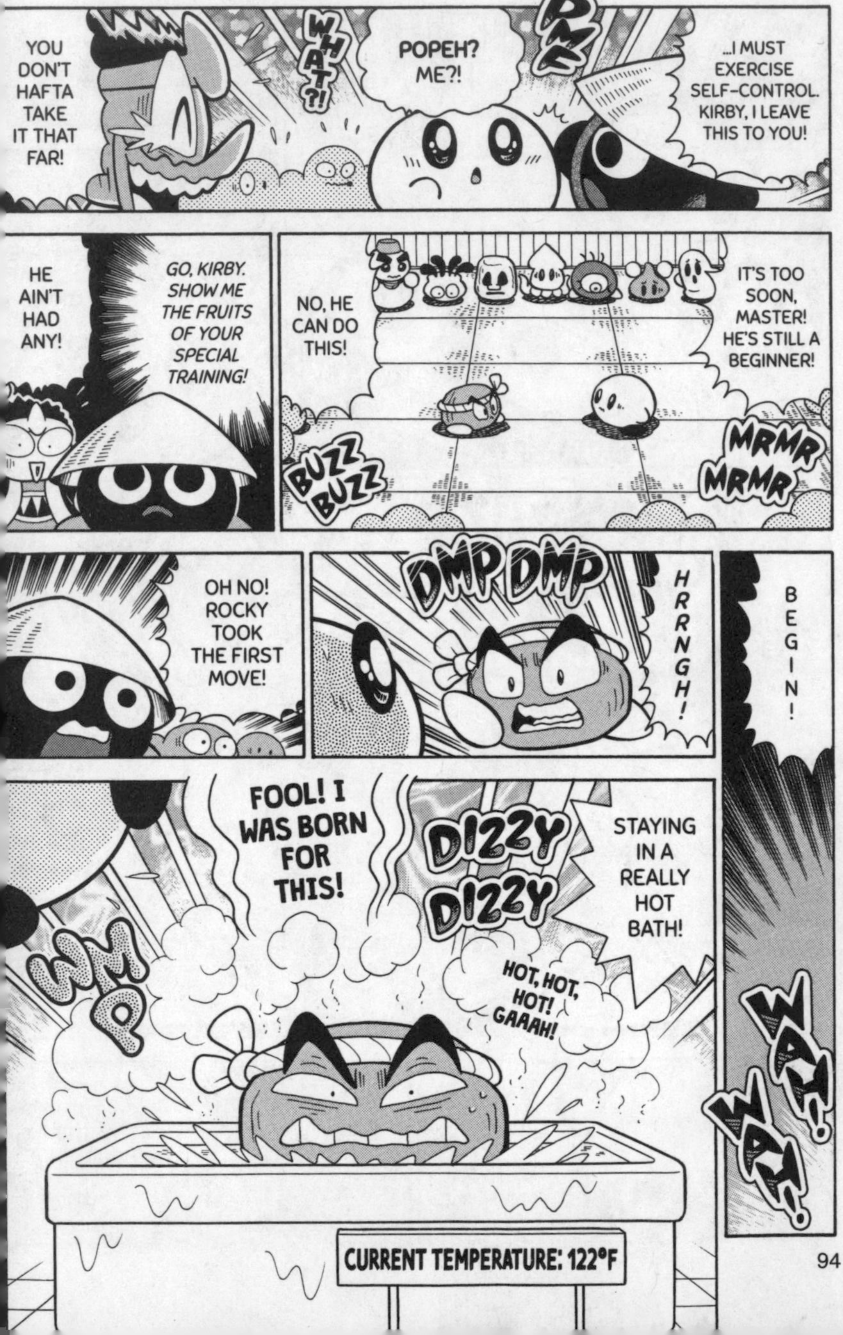
...I MUST EXERCISE SELF-CONTROL. KIRBY, I LEAVE THIS TO YOU!
POPEH? ME?!
WHAT?!
YOU DON'T HAFTA TAKE IT THAT FAR!
IT'S TOO SOON, MASTER! HE'S STILL A BEGINNER!
MRMR MRMR
NO, HE CAN DO THIS!
BUZZ BUZZ
GO, KIRBY. SHOW ME THE FRUITS OF YOUR SPECIAL TRAINING!
HE AIN'T HAD ANY!
BEGIN!
WAH! WAH!
HRRNGH!
DMP DMP
OH NO! ROCKY TOOK THE FIRST MOVE!
STAYING IN A REALLY HOT BATH!
DIZZY DIZZY
HOT, HOT, HOT! GAAAH!
FOOL! I WAS BORN FOR THIS!
WMP
CURRENT TEMPERATURE: 122°F

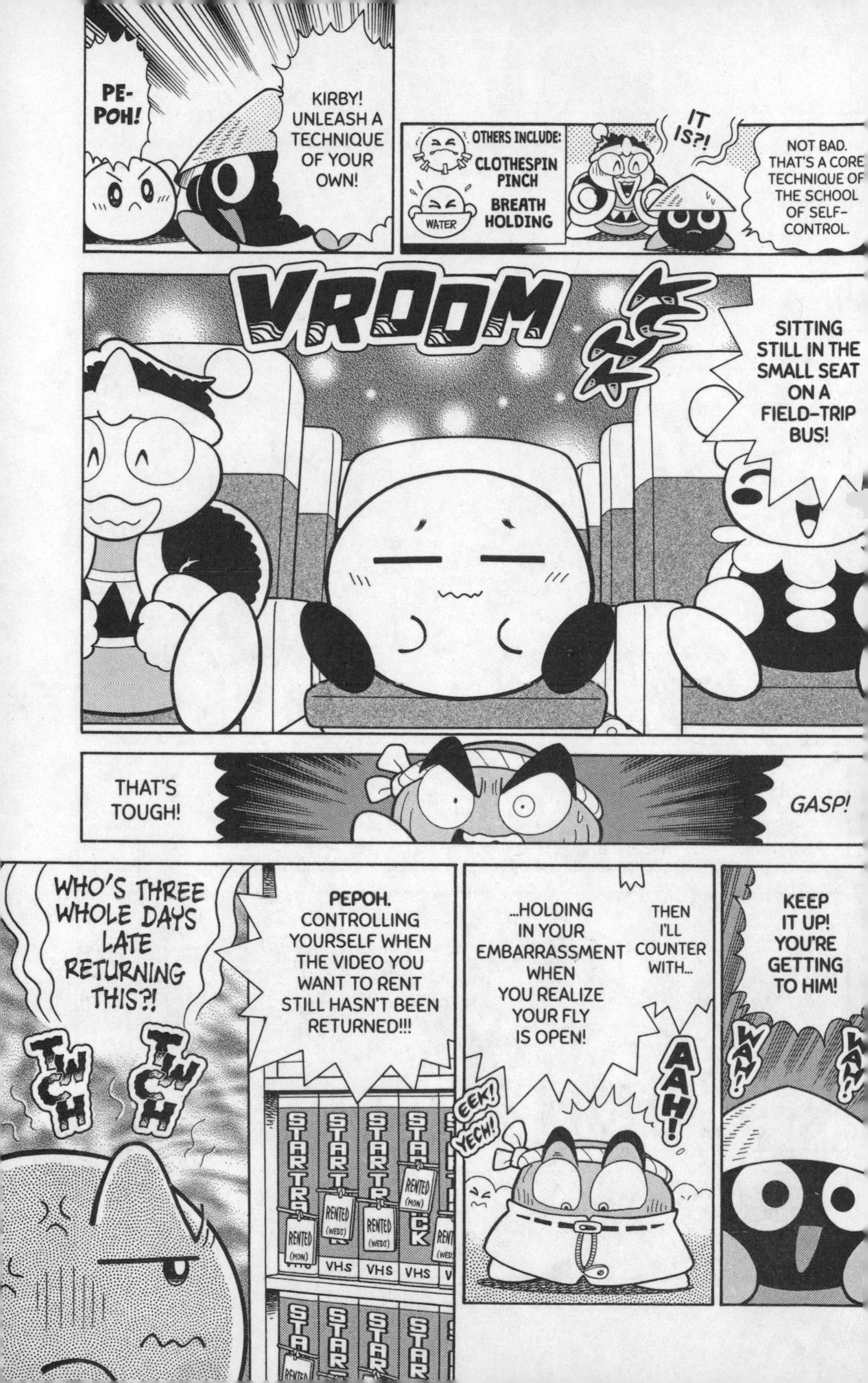
NOT BAD. THAT'S A CORE TECHNIQUE OF THE SCHOOL OF SELF-CONTROL.
IT IS?!
OTHERS INCLUDE:
CLOTHESPIN PINCH
BREATH HOLDING
WATER
KIRBY! UNLEASH A TECHNIQUE OF YOUR OWN!
PE-POH!
VROOM
SITTING STILL IN THE SMALL SEAT ON A FIELD-TRIP BUS!
GASP!
THAT'S TOUGH!
KEEP IT UP! YOU'RE GETTING TO HIM!
WAH!
WAH!
THEN I'LL COUNTER WITH...
...HOLDING IN YOUR EMBARRASSMENT WHEN YOU REALIZE YOUR FLY IS OPEN!
AAH!
EEK!
YECH!
PEPOH. CONTROLLING YOURSELF WHEN THE VIDEO YOU WANT TO RENT STILL HASN'T BEEN RETURNED!!!
RENTED (MON)
RENTED (WEDS)
VHS
WHO'S THREE WHOLE DAYS LATE RETURNING THIS?!
TWITCH
TWITCH

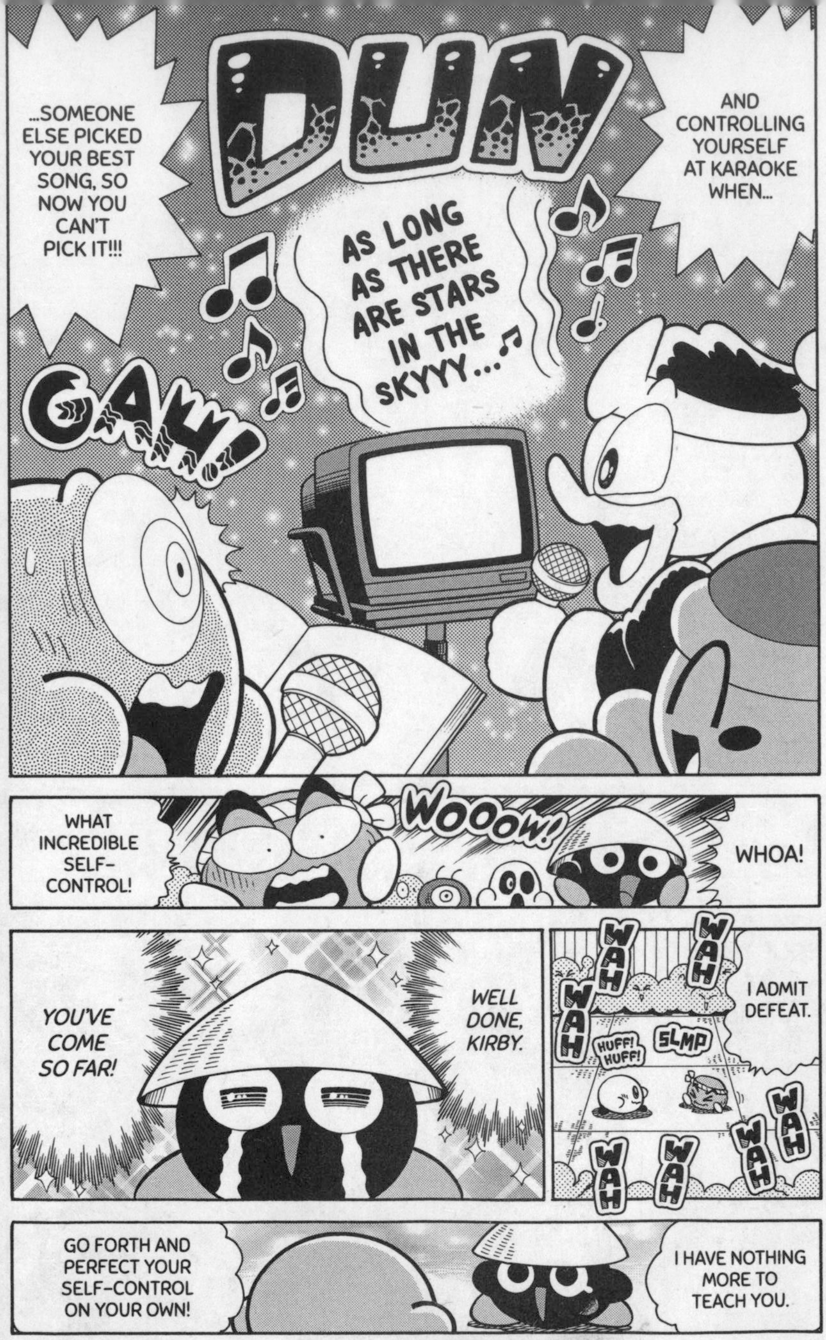

AND CONTROLLING YOURSELF AT KARAOKE WHEN...
DUN
AS LONG AS THERE ARE STARS IN THE SKYYY...♪
...SOMEONE ELSE PICKED YOUR BEST SONG, SO NOW YOU CAN'T PICK IT!!!
WHOA!
WOOOOW!
WHAT INCREDIBLE SELF-CONTROL!
I ADMIT DEFEAT.
WAH WAH WAH WAH WAH WAH WAH
SLMP
HUFF! HUFF!
WELL DONE, KIRBY.
YOU'VE COME SO FAR!
I HAVE NOTHING MORE TO TEACH YOU.
GO FORTH AND PERFECT YOUR SELF-CONTROL ON YOUR OWN!

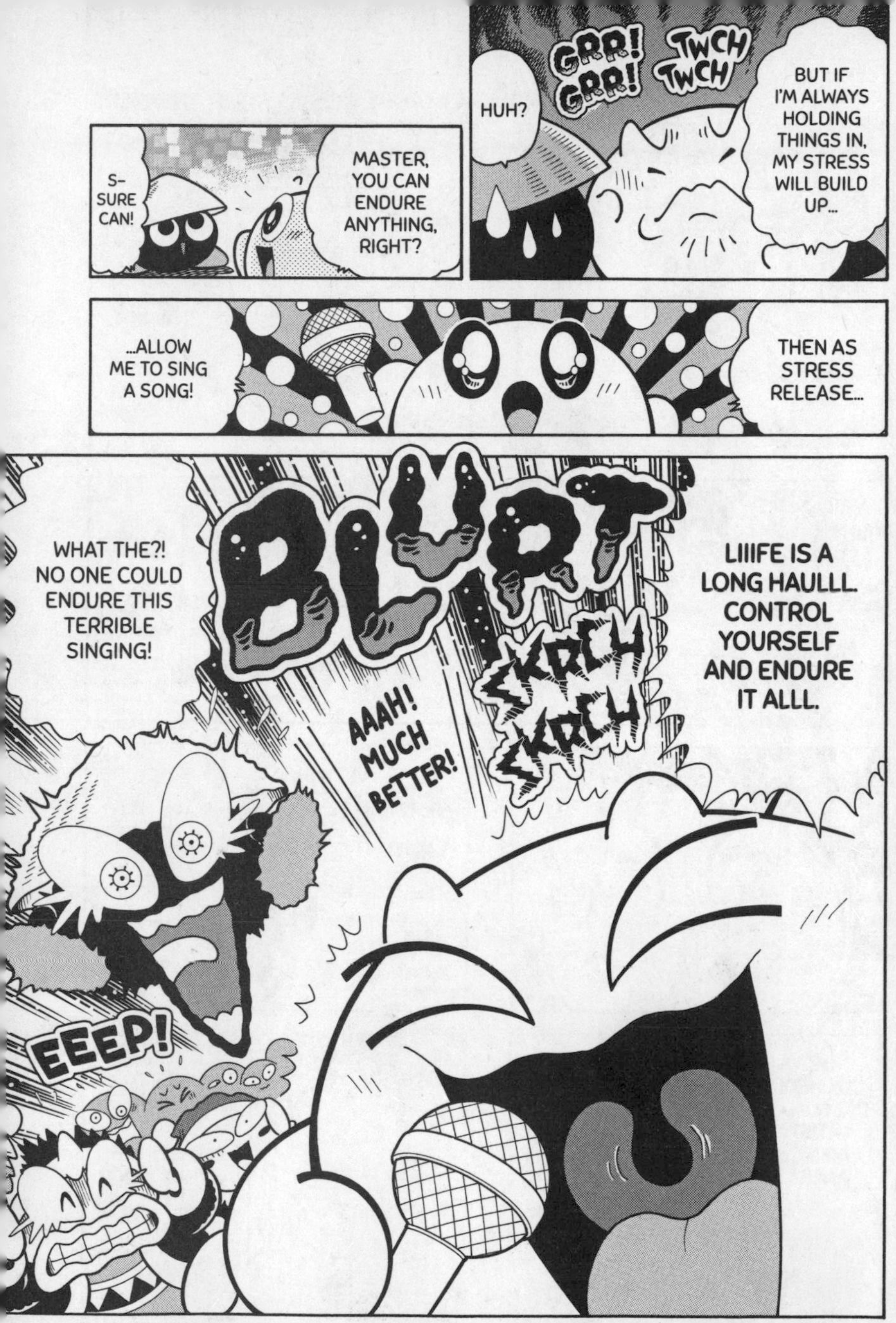

BUT IF I'M ALWAYS HOLDING THINGS IN, MY STRESS WILL BUILD UP...
TWCH TWCH
GRR! GRR!
HUH?
MASTER, YOU CAN ENDURE ANYTHING, RIGHT?
S-SURE CAN!
THEN AS STRESS RELEASE...
...ALLOW ME TO SING A SONG!
BLURT
LIIIFE IS A LONG HAULLL. CONTROL YOURSELF AND ENDURE IT ALLL.
SKRCH SKRCH
AAAH! MUCH BETTER!
WHAT THE?! NO ONE COULD ENDURE THIS TERRIBLE SINGING!
EEEP!

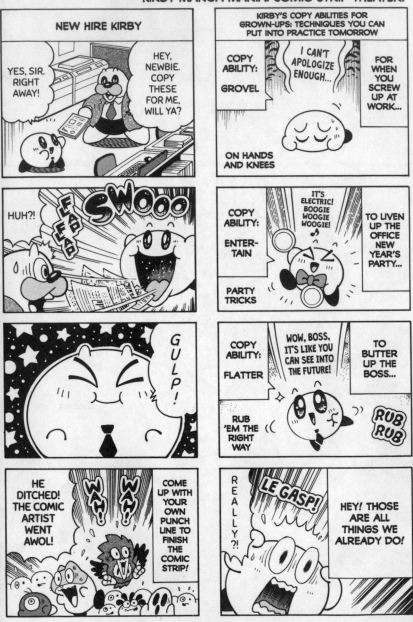

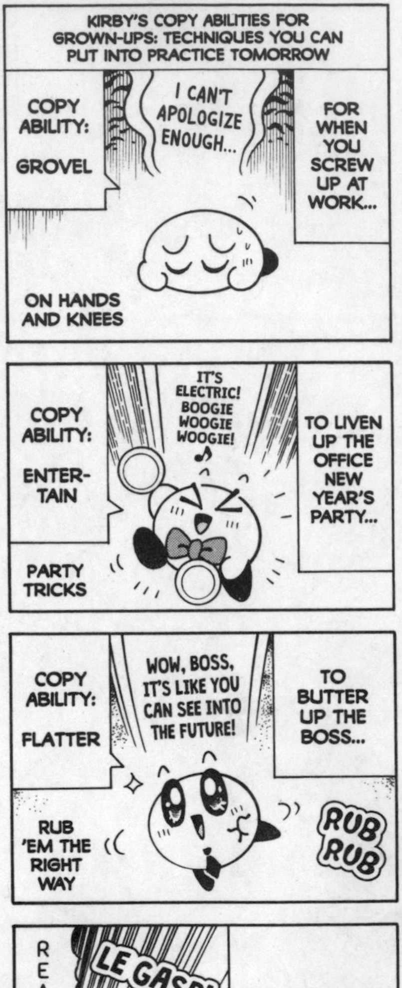
KIRBY'S COPY ABILITIES FOR GROWN-UPS: TECHNIQUES YOU CAN PUT INTO PRACTICE TOMORROW
FOR WHEN YOU SCREW UP AT WORK...
I CAN'T APOLOGIZE ENOUGH...
COPY ABILITY: GROVEL
ON HANDS AND KNEES
TO LIVEN UP THE OFFICE NEW YEAR'S PARTY...
IT'S ELECTRIC! BOOGIE WOOGIE WOOGIE!
COPY ABILITY: ENTER-TAIN
PARTY TRICKS
TO BUTTER UP THE BOSS...
WOW, BOSS, IT'S LIKE YOU CAN SEE INTO THE FUTURE!
COPY ABILITY: FLATTER
RUB RUB
RUB 'EM THE RIGHT WAY
HEY! THOSE ARE ALL THINGS WE ALREADY DO!
LE GASP!
REALLY?!

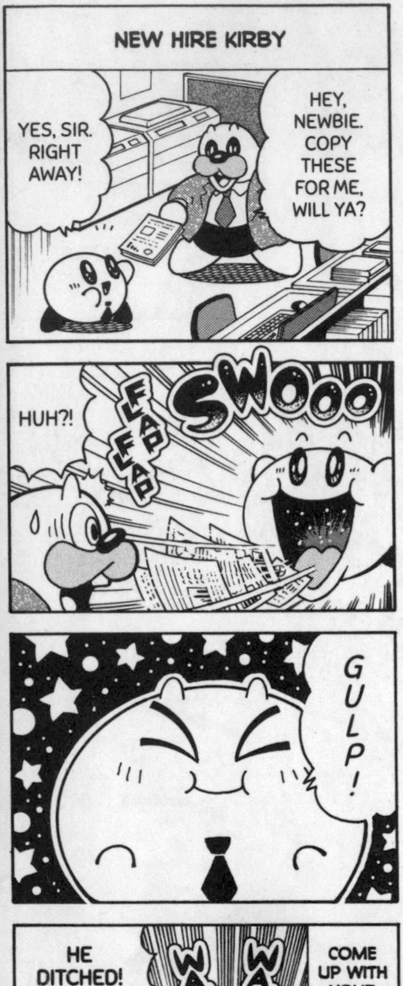
NEW HIRE KIRBY
HEY, NEWBIE. COPY THESE FOR ME, WILL YA?
YES, SIR. RIGHT AWAY!
SWOOO
FLAP FLAP
HUH?!
GULP!
COME UP WITH YOUR OWN PUNCH LINE TO FINISH THE COMIC STRIP!
WAH!
WAH!
HE DITCHED! THE COMIC ARTIST WENT AWOL!

CHAPTER 7: GO FOR THE GOLD! THE DREAM LAND OLYMPICS

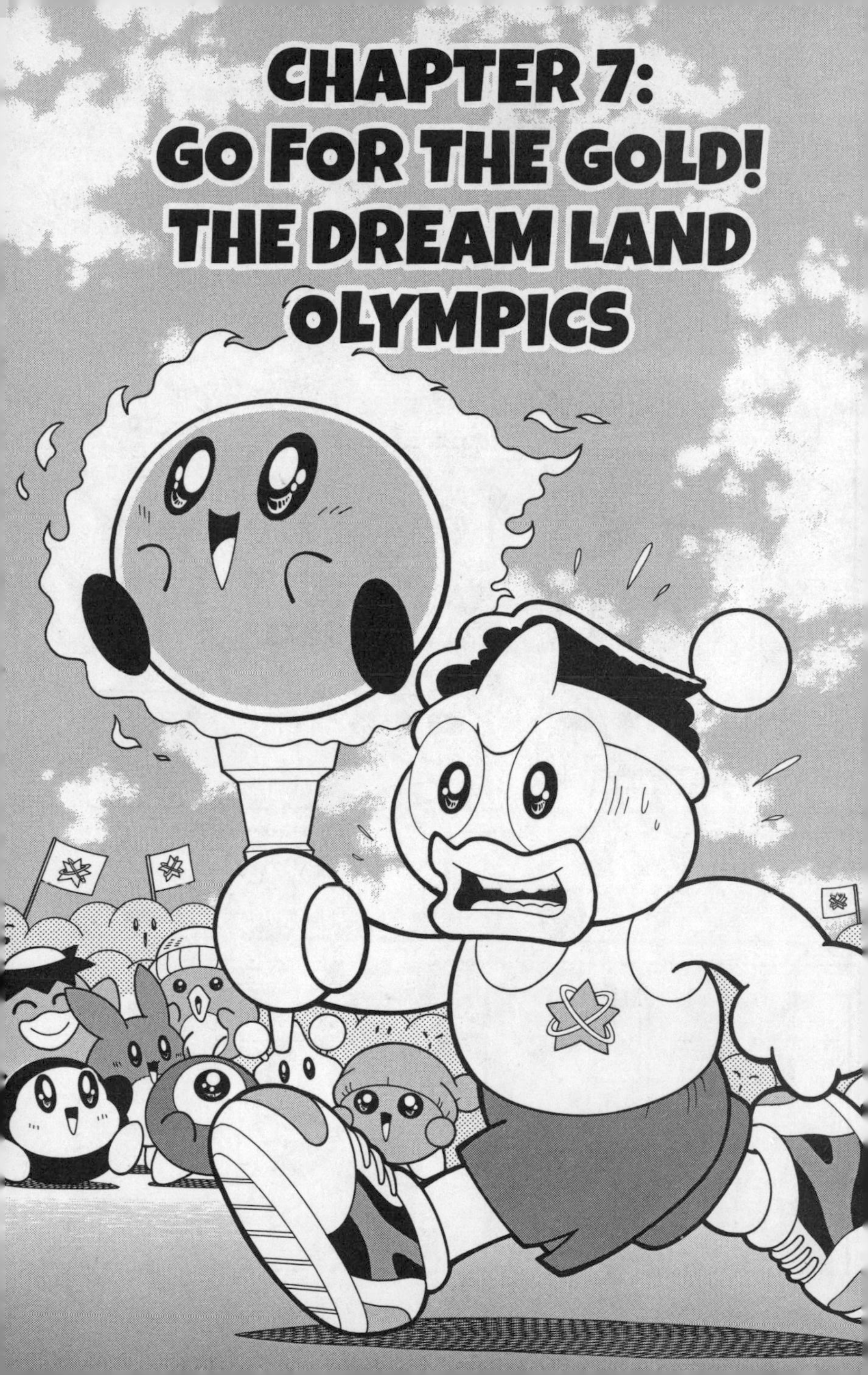

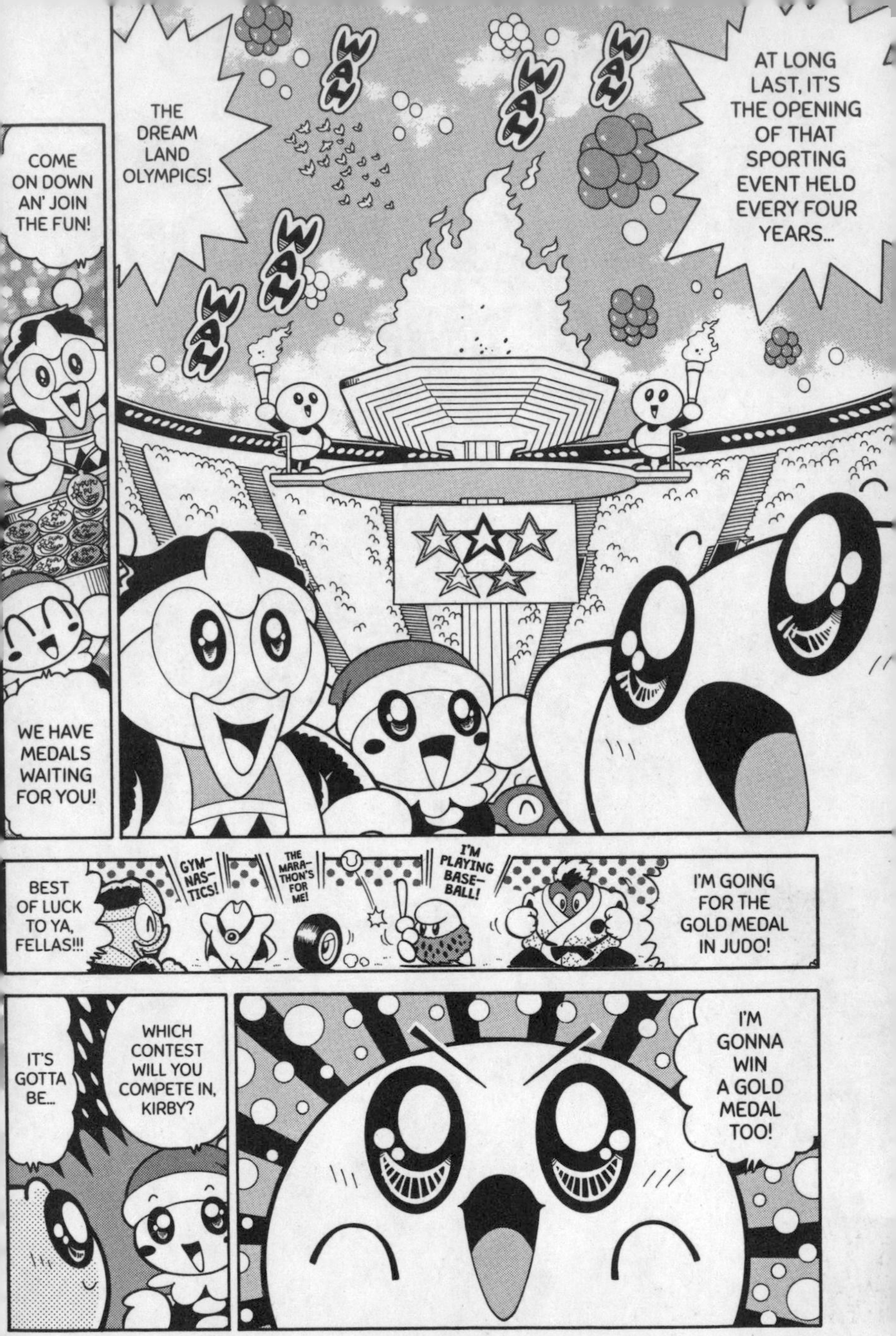
AT LONG LAST, IT'S THE OPENING OF THAT SPORTING EVENT HELD EVERY FOUR YEARS...
WAH WAH WAH
THE DREAM LAND OLYMPICS!
WAH WAH WAH
COME ON DOWN AN' JOIN THE FUN!
WE HAVE MEDALS WAITING FOR YOU!
I'M GOING FOR THE GOLD MEDAL IN JUDO!
I'M PLAYING BASE-BALL!
THE MARA-THON'S FOR ME!
GYM-NAS-TICS!
BEST OF LUCK TO YA, FELLAS!!!
I'M GONNA WIN A GOLD MEDAL TOO!
WHICH CONTEST WILL YOU COMPETE IN, KIRBY?
IT'S GOTTA BE...

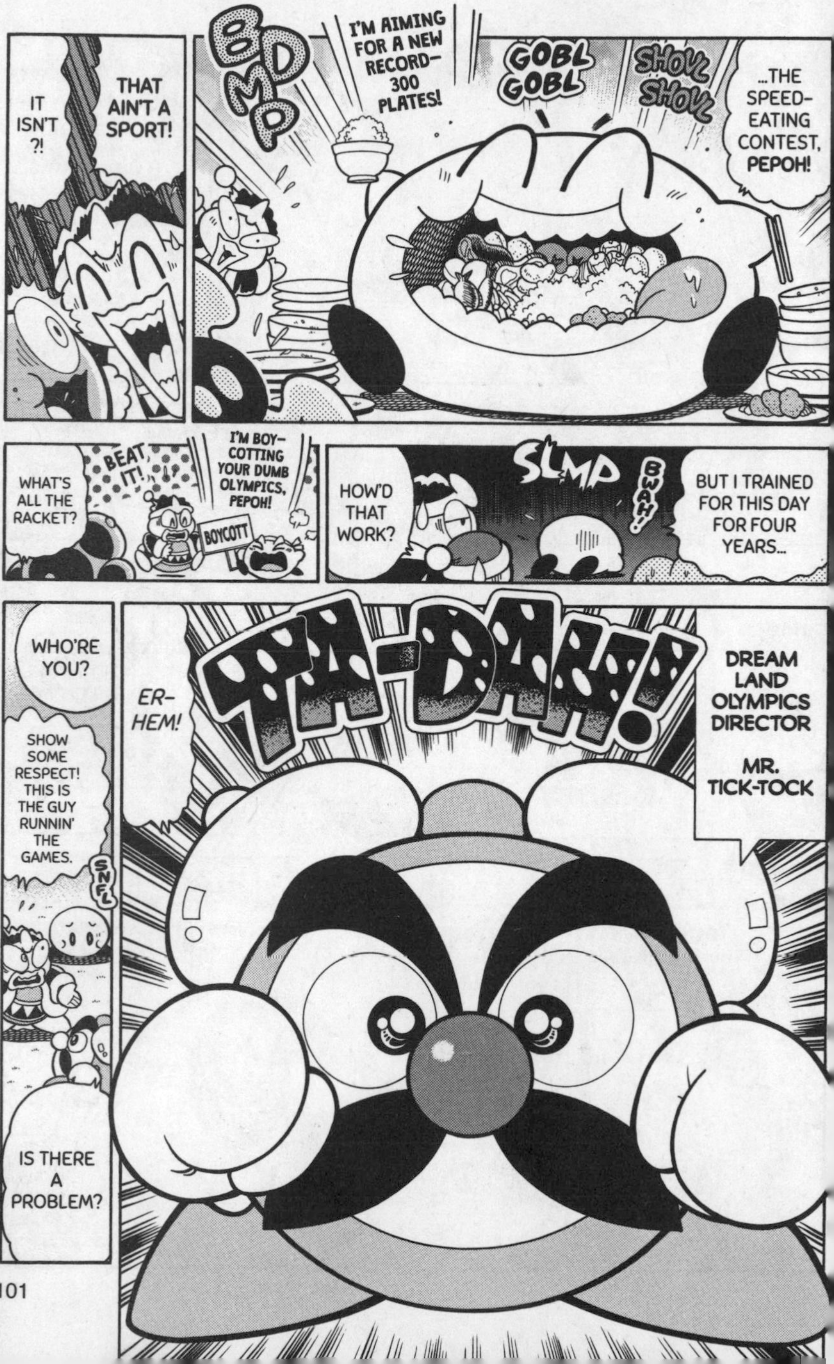
...THE SPEED-EATING CONTEST, PEPOH!
SHOVL SHOVL
GOBL GOBL
I'M AIMING FOR A NEW RECORD—300 PLATES!
BDMP
THAT AIN'T A SPORT!
IT ISN'T ?!
BUT I TRAINED FOR THIS DAY FOR FOUR YEARS...
BWAH!
SLMP
HOW'D THAT WORK?
I'M BOYCOTTING YOUR DUMB OLYMPICS, PEPOH!
BEAT IT!
BOYCOTT
WHAT'S ALL THE RACKET?
DREAM LAND OLYMPICS DIRECTOR
MR. TICK-TOCK
TA-DAH!!
ER-HEM!
WHO'RE YOU?
SHOW SOME RESPECT! THIS IS THE GUY RUNNIN' THE GAMES.
SNFL
IS THERE A PROBLEM?

AUTHOR'S COMMENT

THIS IS ANOTHER CHOICE FROM VOLUME 14. THINKING BACK ON IT NOW, THAT VOLUME WAS MY PEAK—THE STORIES, THE PANELING, THE DIALOGUE—IT WAS PERFECT. IT'S GOOD COMICS! (TOOTING MY OWN HORN)

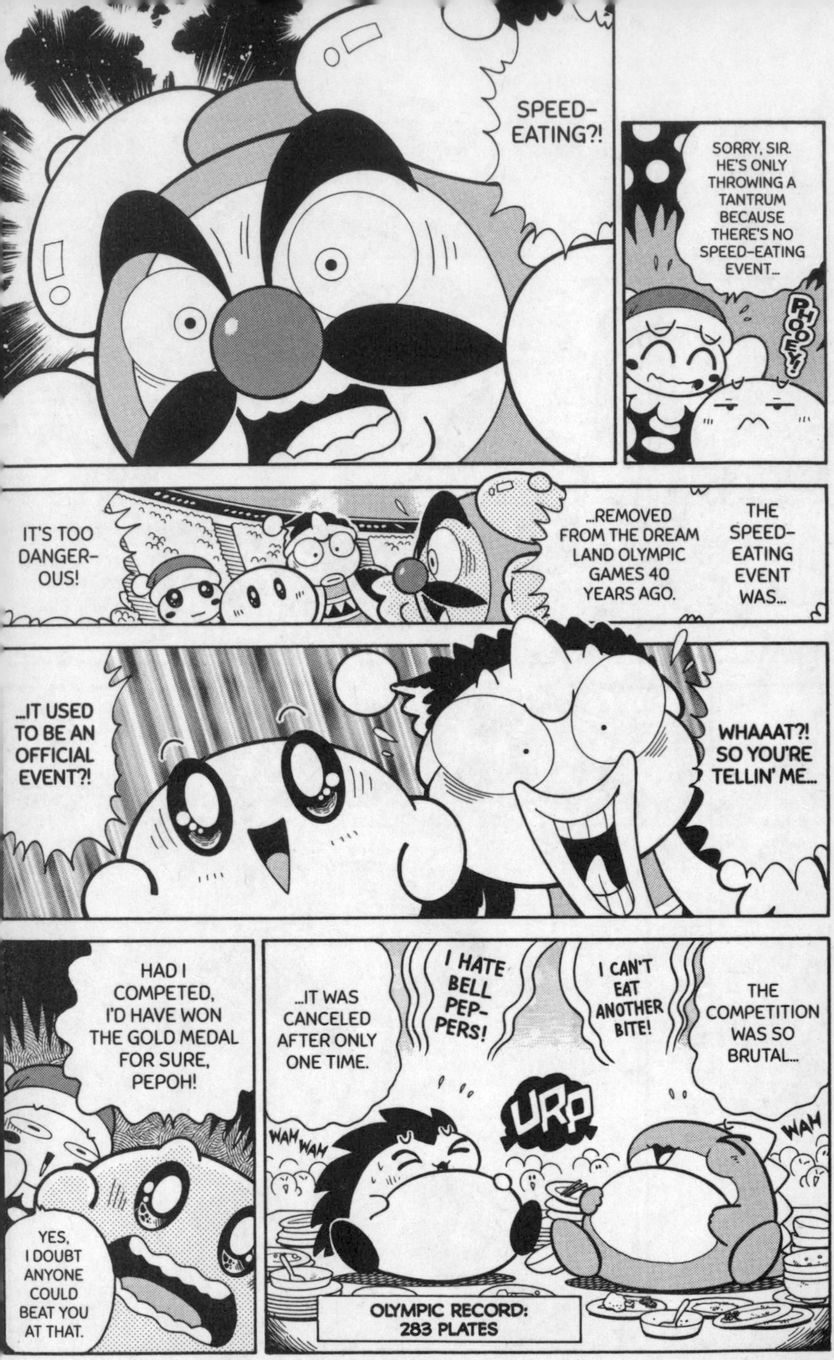
SORRY, SIR. HE'S ONLY THROWING A TANTRUM BECAUSE THERE'S NO SPEED-EATING EVENT...
PHOOEY!
SPEED-EATING?!
THE SPEED-EATING EVENT WAS...
...REMOVED FROM THE DREAM LAND OLYMPIC GAMES 40 YEARS AGO.
IT'S TOO DANGEROUS!
WHAAAT?! SO YOU'RE TELLIN' ME...
...IT USED TO BE AN OFFICIAL EVENT?!
THE COMPETITION WAS SO BRUTAL...
I CAN'T EAT ANOTHER BITE!
I HATE BELL PEPPERS!
...IT WAS CANCELED AFTER ONLY ONE TIME.
WAH
URP
WAH WAH
OLYMPIC RECORD: 283 PLATES
HAD I COMPETED, I'D HAVE WON THE GOLD MEDAL FOR SURE, PEPOH!
YES, I DOUBT ANYONE COULD BEAT YOU AT THAT.

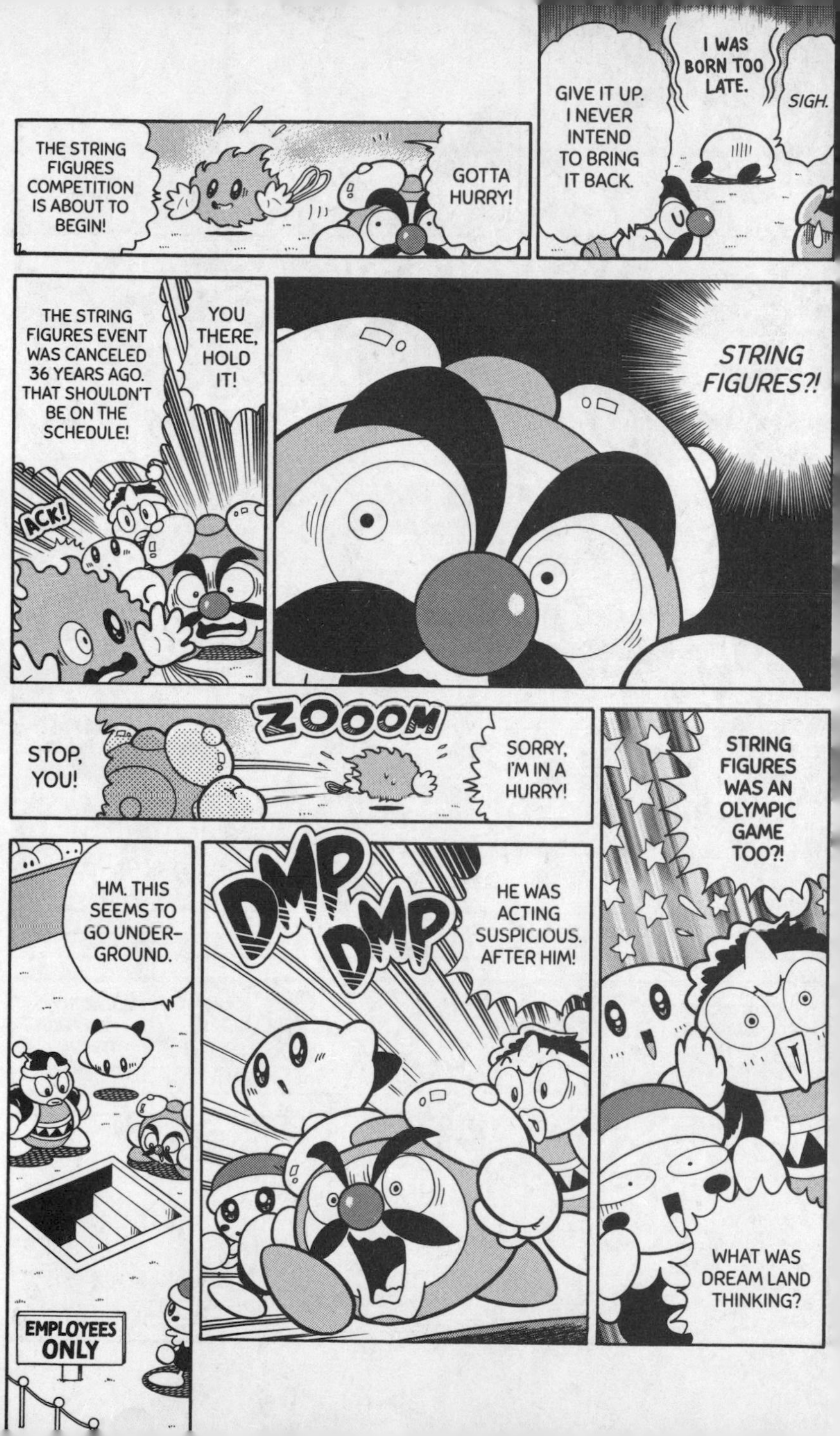
I WAS BORN TOO LATE.
SIGH.
GIVE IT UP. I NEVER INTEND TO BRING IT BACK.
GOTTA HURRY!
THE STRING FIGURES COMPETITION IS ABOUT TO BEGIN!
STRING FIGURES?!
YOU THERE, HOLD IT!
THE STRING FIGURES EVENT WAS CANCELED 36 YEARS AGO. THAT SHOULDN'T BE ON THE SCHEDULE!
ACK!
STRING FIGURES WAS AN OLYMPIC GAME TOO?!
WHAT WAS DREAM LAND THINKING?
SORRY, I'M IN A HURRY!
ZOOOM
STOP, YOU!
HE WAS ACTING SUSPICIOUS. AFTER HIM!
DMP DMP DMP
HM. THIS SEEMS TO GO UNDERGROUND.
EMPLOYEES ONLY

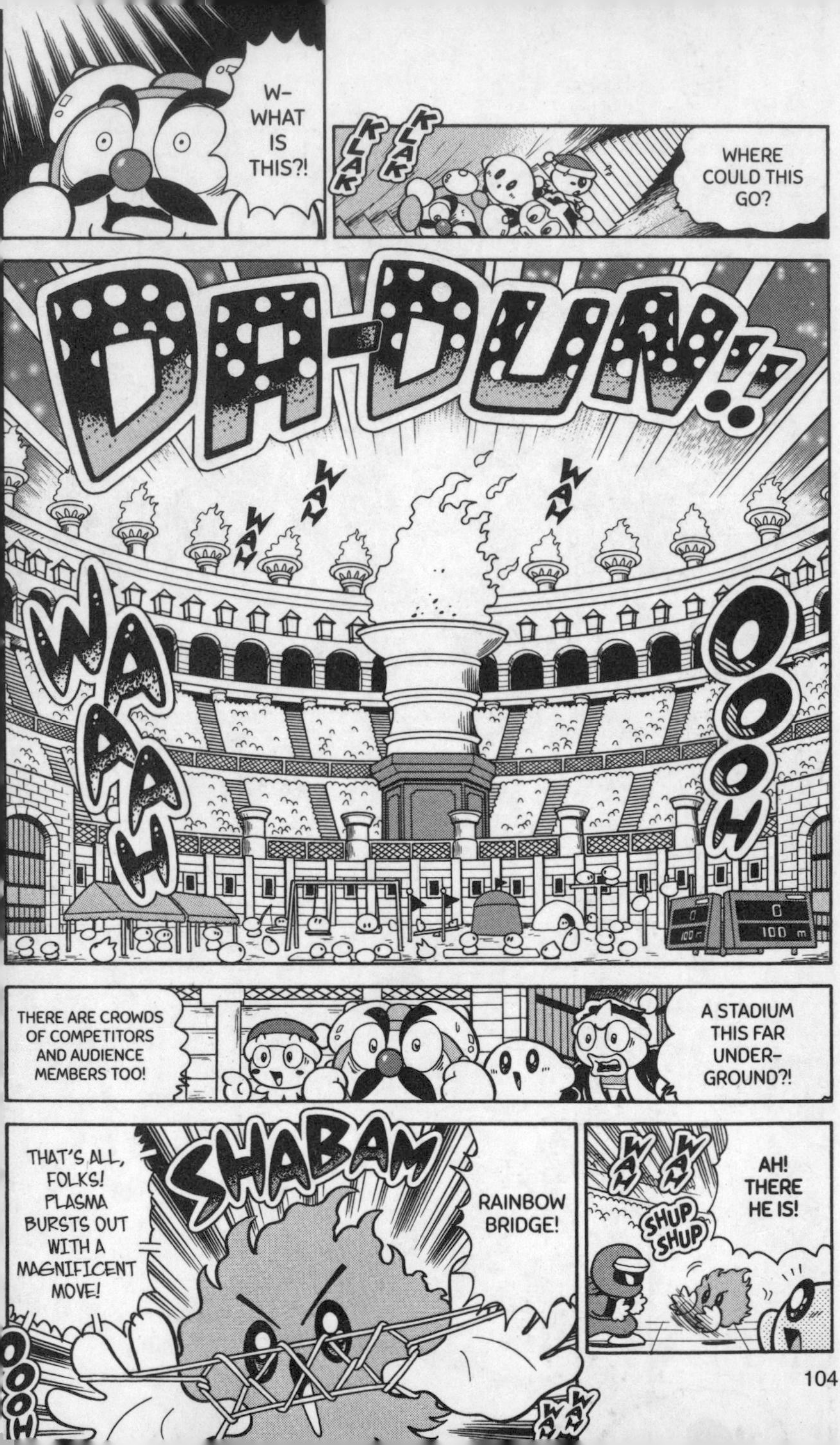
KLAK
KLAK
WHERE COULD THIS GO?
W-WHAT IS THIS?!
DA-DUN!!
WAY
WAY
WAH
OOOOH
WAAAAH
A STADIUM THIS FAR UNDER-GROUND?!
THERE ARE CROWDS OF COMPETITORS AND AUDIENCE MEMBERS TOO!
WAY
WAY
SHUP SHUP
AH! THERE HE IS!
RAINBOW BRIDGE!
SHABAM
THAT'S ALL, FOLKS! PLASMA BURSTS OUT WITH A MAGNIFICENT MOVE!
OOOOH
WAY
WAY

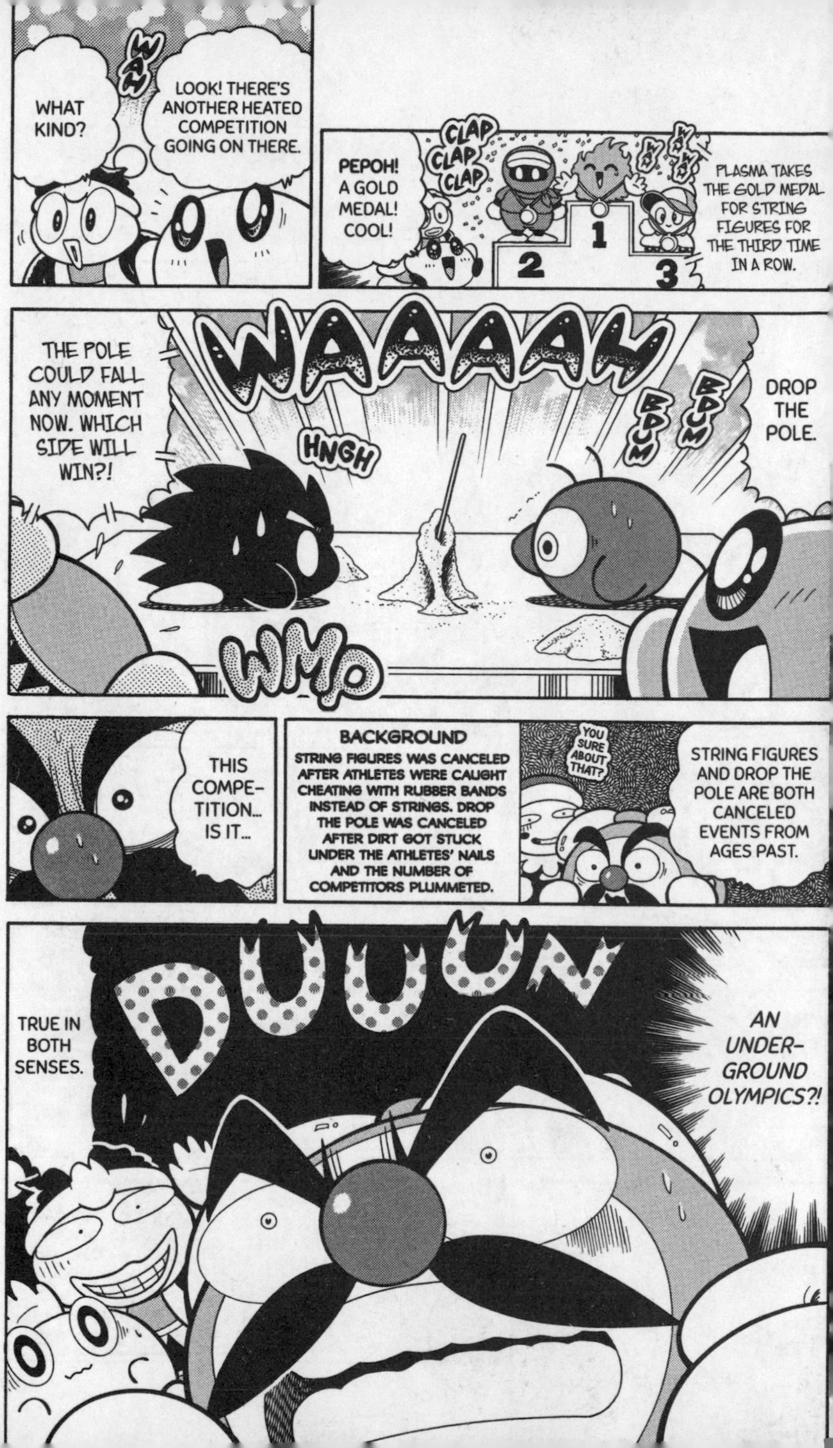
PLASMA TAKES THE GOLD MEDAL FOR STRING FIGURES FOR THE THIRD TIME IN A ROW.
WAH WAH
CLAP CLAP CLAP
PEPOH! A GOLD MEDAL! COOL!
1
2
3
LOOK! THERE'S ANOTHER HEATED COMPETITION GOING ON THERE.
WAH
WHAT KIND?
DROP THE POLE.
BDUM BDUM
WAAAAH
HNGH
THE POLE COULD FALL ANY MOMENT NOW. WHICH SIDE WILL WIN?!
WMP
STRING FIGURES AND DROP THE POLE ARE BOTH CANCELED EVENTS FROM AGES PAST.
YOU SURE ABOUT THAT?
BACKGROUND
STRING FIGURES WAS CANCELED AFTER ATHLETES WERE CAUGHT CHEATING WITH RUBBER BANDS INSTEAD OF STRINGS. DROP THE POLE WAS CANCELED AFTER DIRT GOT STUCK UNDER THE ATHLETES' NAILS AND THE NUMBER OF COMPETITORS PLUMMETED.
THIS COMPE-TITION... IS IT...
AN UNDER-GROUND OLYMPICS?!
DUUUN
TRUE IN BOTH SENSES.

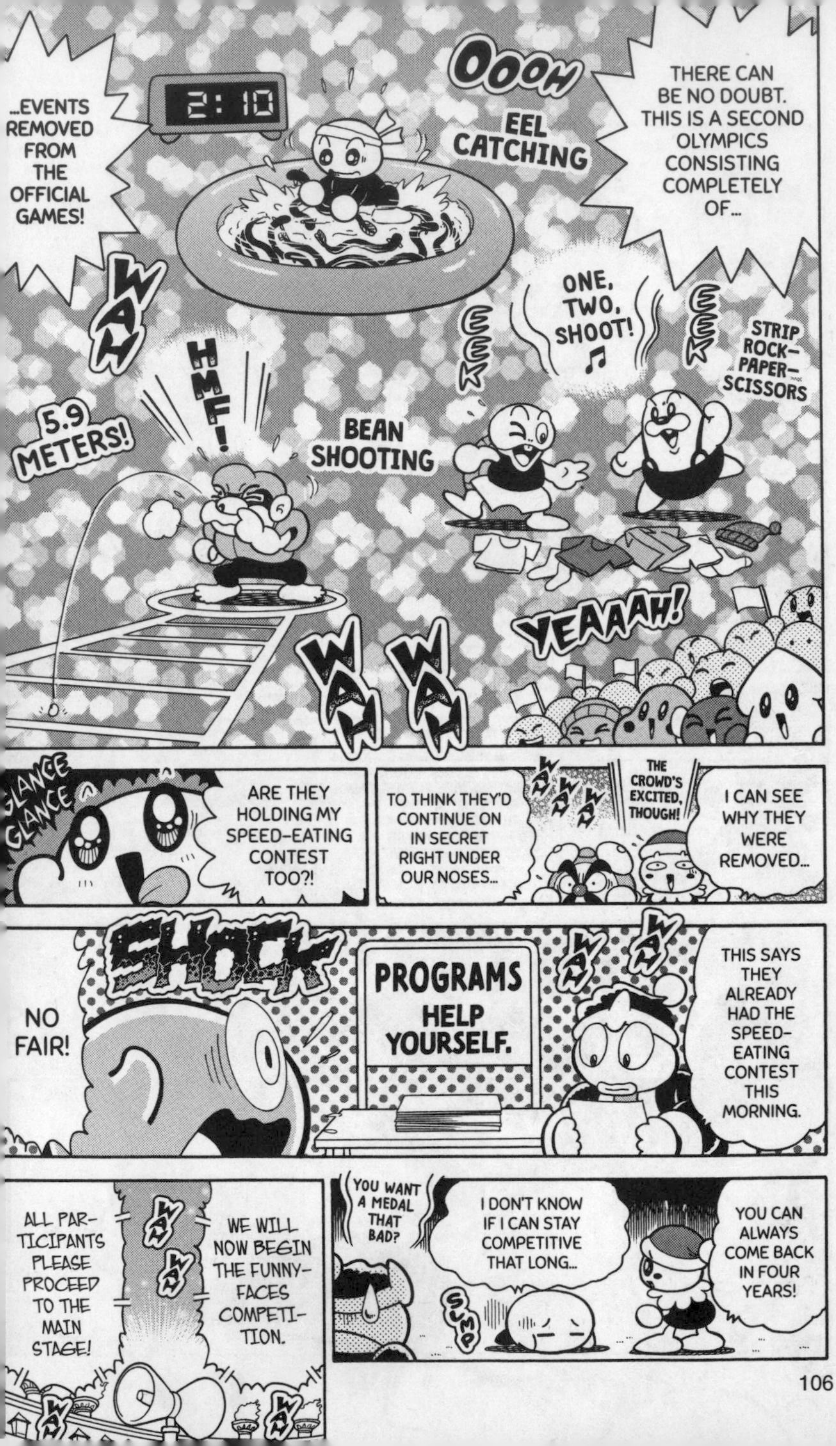
THERE CAN BE NO DOUBT. THIS IS A SECOND OLYMPICS CONSISTING COMPLETELY OF...
OOOH
...EVENTS REMOVED FROM THE OFFICIAL GAMES!
EEL CATCHING
2:10
EEK
ONE, TWO, SHOOT! ♫
EEK
STRIP ROCK-PAPER-SCISSORS
WAH
HMF!
BEAN SHOOTING
5.9 METERS!
YEAAAH!
WAH
WAH
I CAN SEE WHY THEY WERE REMOVED...
THE CROWD'S EXCITED, THOUGH!
WAH WAH WAH
TO THINK THEY'D CONTINUE ON IN SECRET RIGHT UNDER OUR NOSES...
ARE THEY HOLDING MY SPEED-EATING CONTEST TOO?!
GLANCE GLANCE
THIS SAYS THEY ALREADY HAD THE SPEED-EATING CONTEST THIS MORNING.
WAH
WAH
PROGRAMS
HELP YOURSELF.
SHOCK
NO FAIR!
YOU CAN ALWAYS COME BACK IN FOUR YEARS!
I DON'T KNOW IF I CAN STAY COMPETITIVE THAT LONG...
YOU WANT A MEDAL THAT BAD?
SLUMP
WE WILL NOW BEGIN THE FUNNY-FACES COMPETITION.
ALL PARTICIPANTS PLEASE PROCEED TO THE MAIN STAGE!
WAH
WAH
WAH
WAH

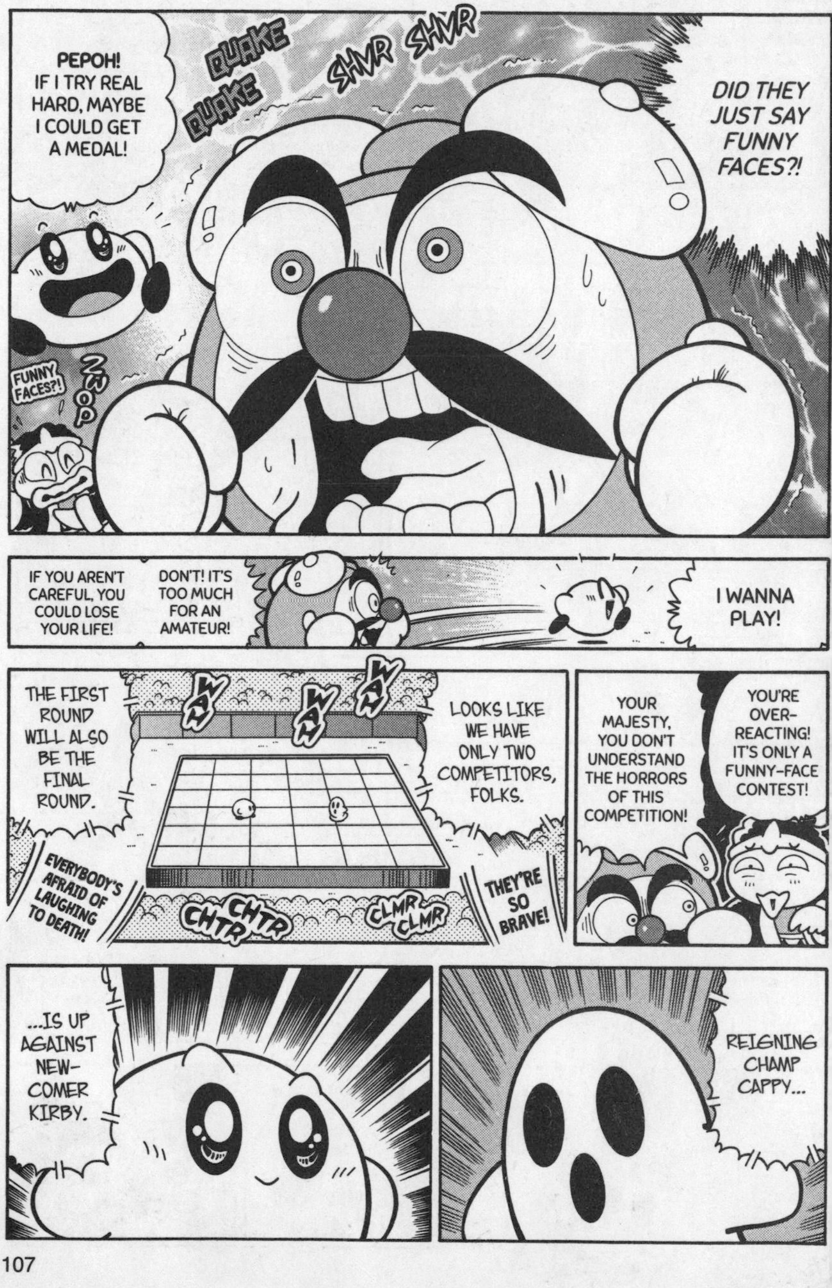
DID THEY JUST SAY FUNNY FACES?!
SHVR SHVR
QUAKE QUAKE
PEPOH! IF I TRY REAL HARD, MAYBE I COULD GET A MEDAL!
FUNNY FACES?!
ZWOOP
I WANNA PLAY!
DON'T! IT'S TOO MUCH FOR AN AMATEUR!
IF YOU AREN'T CAREFUL, YOU COULD LOSE YOUR LIFE!
YOU'RE OVER-REACTING! IT'S ONLY A FUNNY-FACE CONTEST!
YOUR MAJESTY, YOU DON'T UNDERSTAND THE HORRORS OF THIS COMPETITION!
LOOKS LIKE WE HAVE ONLY TWO COMPETITORS, FOLKS.
WAH WAH WAH
THE FIRST ROUND WILL ALSO BE THE FINAL ROUND.
THEY'RE SO BRAVE!
CLMR CLMR
CHTR CHTR
EVERYBODY'S AFRAID OF LAUGHING TO DEATH!
REIGNING CHAMP CAPPY...
...IS UP AGAINST NEW-COMER KIRBY.

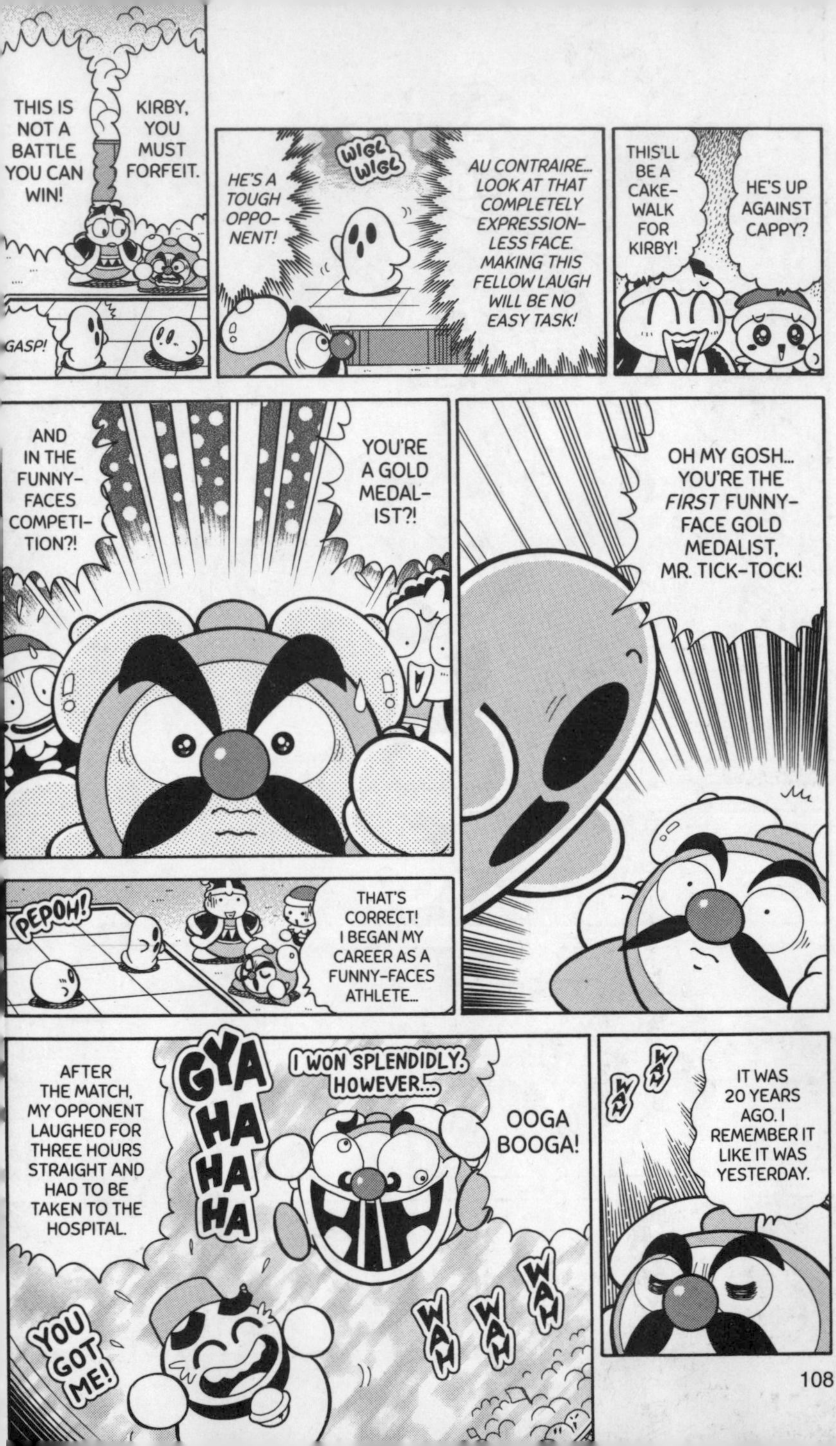
HE'S UP AGAINST CAPPY?
THIS'LL BE A CAKE-WALK FOR KIRBY!
WIGL WIGL
AU CONTRAIRE... LOOK AT THAT COMPLETELY EXPRESSIONLESS FACE. MAKING THIS FELLOW LAUGH WILL BE NO EASY TASK!
HE'S A TOUGH OPPONENT!
KIRBY, YOU MUST FORFEIT.
THIS IS NOT A BATTLE YOU CAN WIN!
GASP!
OH MY GOSH... YOU'RE THE *FIRST* FUNNY-FACE GOLD MEDALIST, MR. TICK-TOCK!
YOU'RE A GOLD MEDALIST?!
AND IN THE FUNNY-FACES COMPETITION?!
THAT'S CORRECT! I BEGAN MY CAREER AS A FUNNY-FACES ATHLETE...
PEPOH!
IT WAS 20 YEARS AGO. I REMEMBER IT LIKE IT WAS YESTERDAY.
WAH WAH
I WON SPLENDIDLY. HOWEVER...
OOGA BOOGA!
GYA HA HA HA HA
AFTER THE MATCH, MY OPPONENT LAUGHED FOR THREE HOURS STRAIGHT AND HAD TO BE TAKEN TO THE HOSPITAL.
WAH WAH WAH
YOU GOT ME!

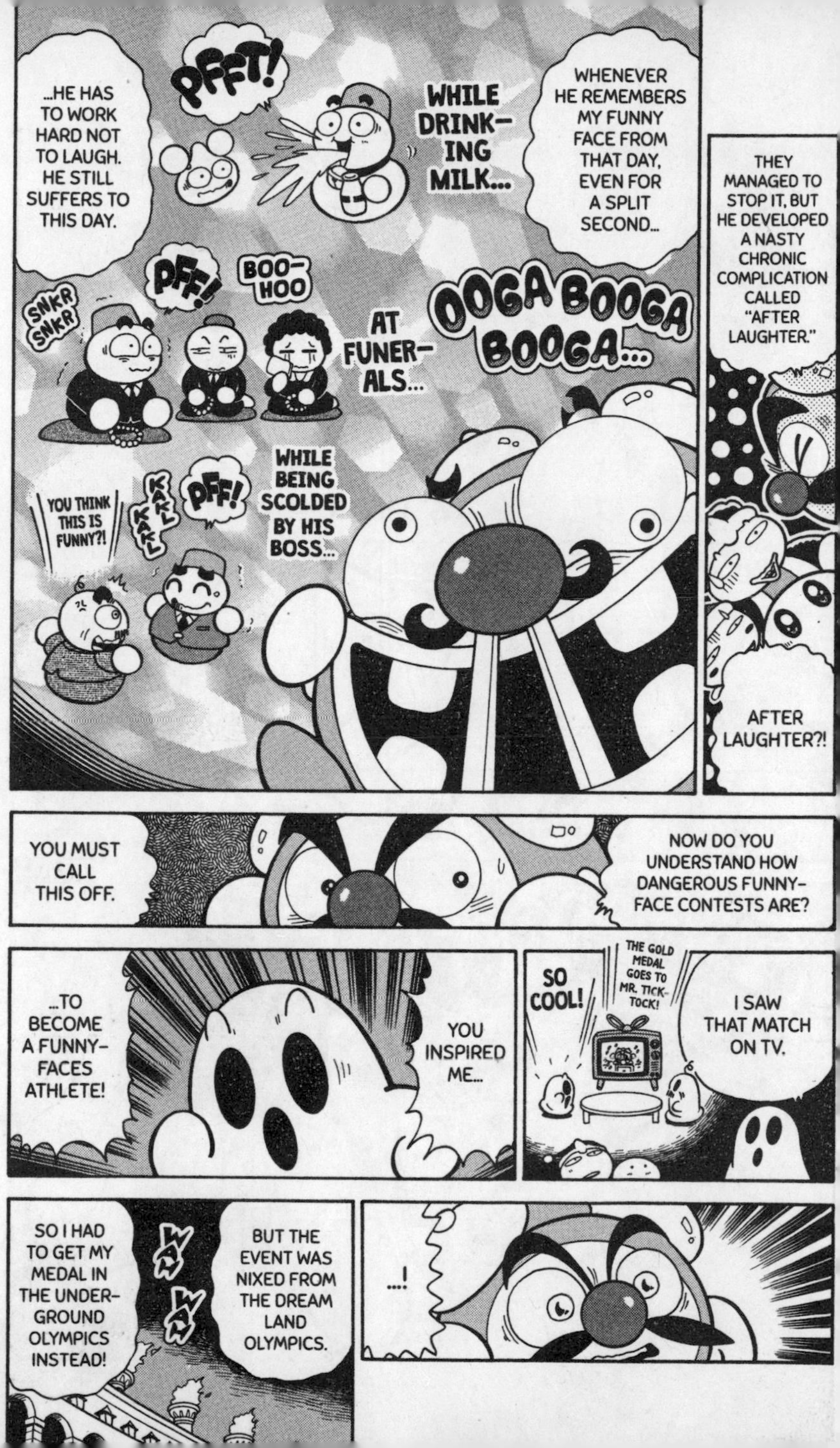
THEY MANAGED TO STOP IT, BUT HE DEVELOPED A NASTY CHRONIC COMPLICATION CALLED "AFTER LAUGHTER."
AFTER LAUGHTER?!
WHENEVER HE REMEMBERS MY FUNNY FACE FROM THAT DAY, EVEN FOR A SPLIT SECOND...
OOGA BOOGA BOOGA...
WHILE DRINK-ING MILK...
PFFT!
...HE HAS TO WORK HARD NOT TO LAUGH. HE STILL SUFFERS TO THIS DAY.
AT FUNER-ALS...
BOO-HOO
PFF!
SNKR SNKR
WHILE BEING SCOLDED BY HIS BOSS...
PFF!
KAKL KAKL
YOU THINK THIS IS FUNNY?!
NOW DO YOU UNDERSTAND HOW DANGEROUS FUNNY-FACE CONTESTS ARE?
YOU MUST CALL THIS OFF.
I SAW THAT MATCH ON TV.
THE GOLD MEDAL GOES TO MR. TICK-TOCK!
SO COOL!
YOU INSPIRED ME...
...TO BECOME A FUNNY-FACES ATHLETE!
...!
BUT THE EVENT WAS NIXED FROM THE DREAM LAND OLYMPICS.
WAH WAH
SO I HAD TO GET MY MEDAL IN THE UNDER-GROUND OLYMPICS INSTEAD!

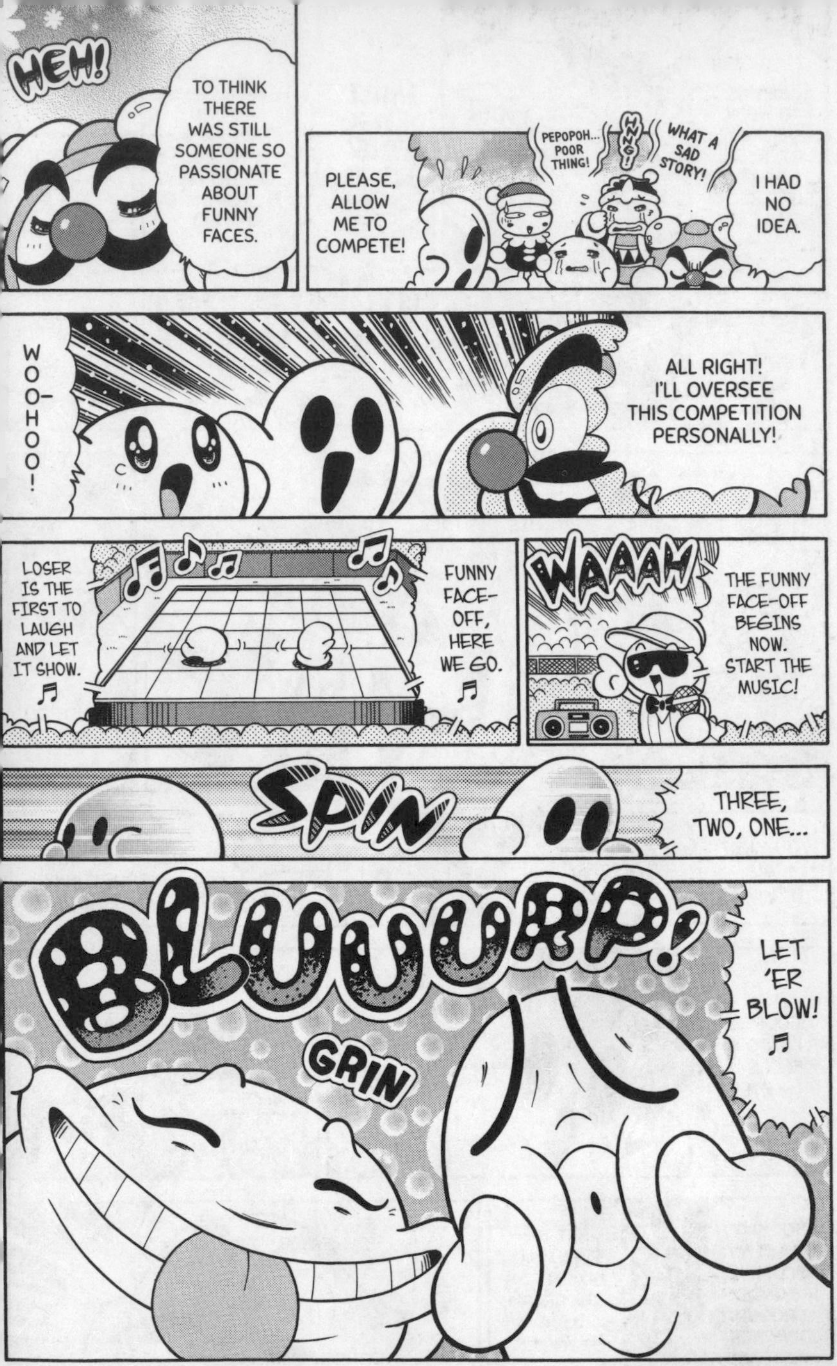
I HAD NO IDEA.
WHAT A SAD STORY!
HNNG!
PEPOPOH... POOR THING!
PLEASE, ALLOW ME TO COMPETE!
HEH!
TO THINK THERE WAS STILL SOMEONE SO PASSIONATE ABOUT FUNNY FACES.
ALL RIGHT! I'LL OVERSEE THIS COMPETITION PERSONALLY!
WOOHOO!
WAAAH
THE FUNNY FACE-OFF BEGINS NOW. START THE MUSIC!
FUNNY FACE-OFF, HERE WE GO. ♪
LOSER IS THE FIRST TO LAUGH AND LET IT SHOW. ♪
THREE, TWO, ONE...
SPIN
LET 'ER BLOW! ♪
BLUUURP!
GRIN

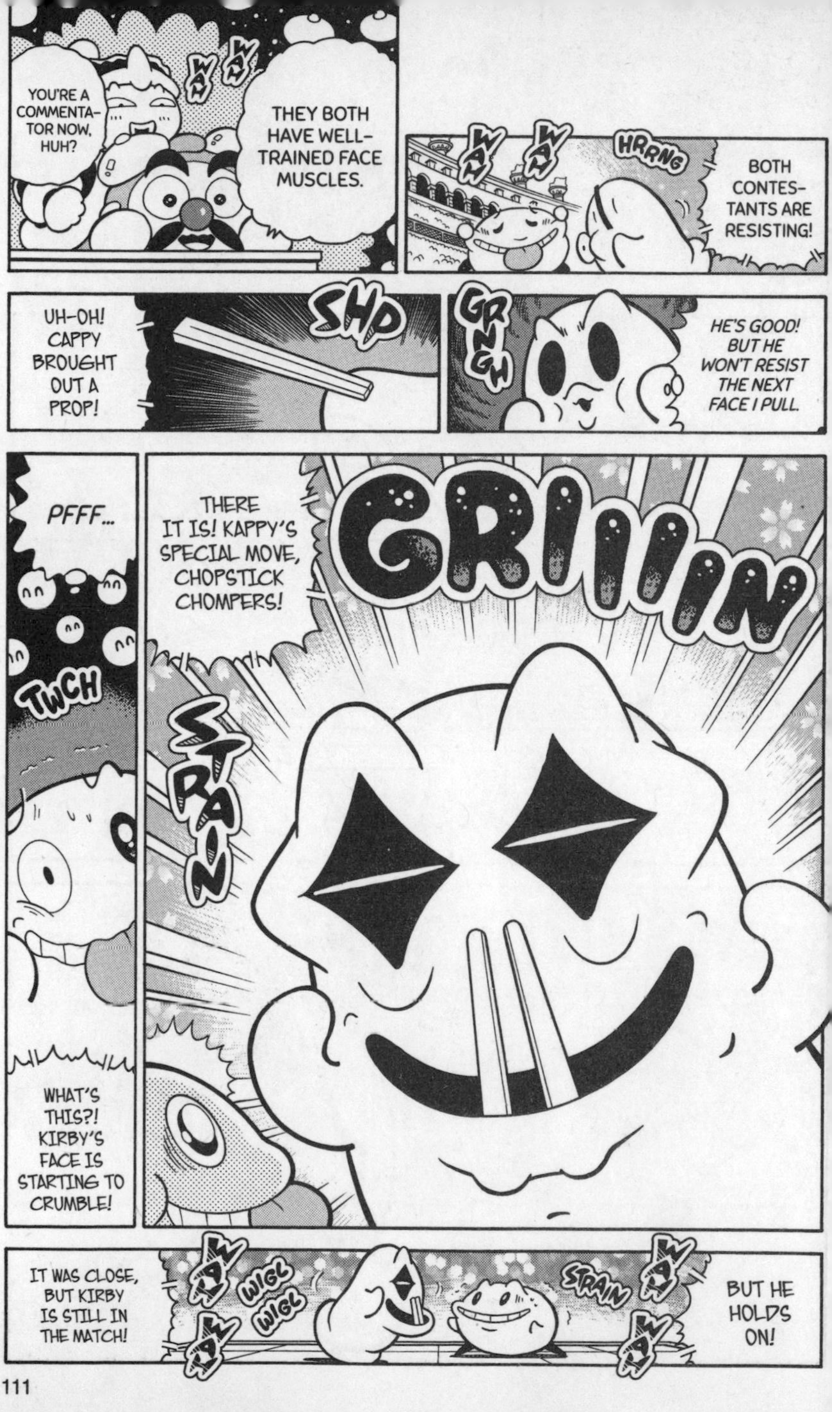
HRRNG
WAH WAH
BOTH CONTESTANTS ARE RESISTING!
WAH WAH
THEY BOTH HAVE WELL-TRAINED FACE MUSCLES.
YOU'RE A COMMENTATOR NOW, HUH?
GRNGH
HE'S GOOD! BUT HE WON'T RESIST THE NEXT FACE I PULL.
SHP
UH-OH! CAPPY BROUGHT OUT A PROP!
GRIIIIN
THERE IT IS! KAPPY'S SPECIAL MOVE, CHOPSTICK CHOMPERS!
STRAIN
PFFF...
TWCH
WHAT'S THIS?! KIRBY'S FACE IS STARTING TO CRUMBLE!
WAH WAH
BUT HE HOLDS ON!
STRAIN
WIGL WIGL
WAH WAH
IT WAS CLOSE, BUT KIRBY IS STILL IN THE MATCH!

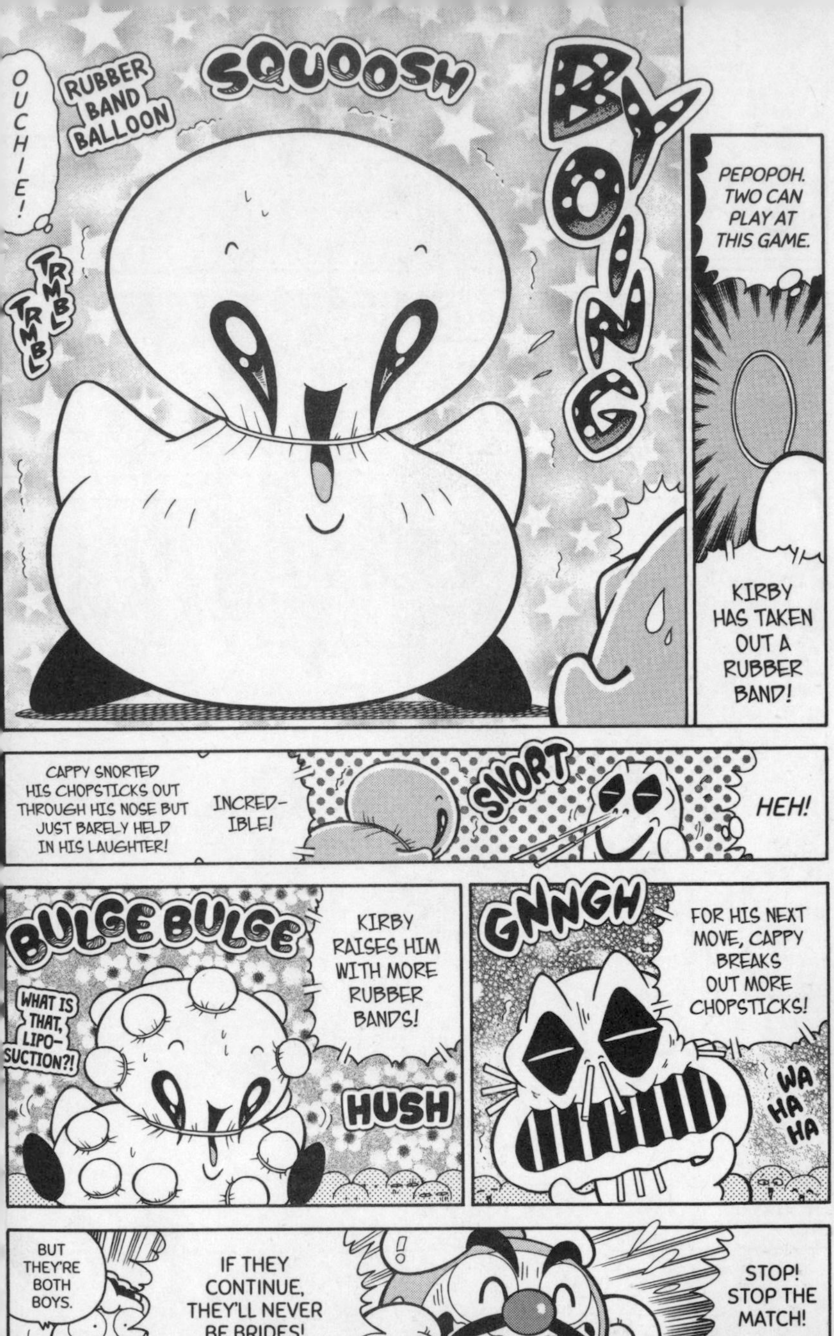
PEPOPOH. TWO CAN PLAY AT THIS GAME.
KIRBY HAS TAKEN OUT A RUBBER BAND!
BYOING
SQUOOSH
RUBBER BAND BALLOON
OUCHIE!
TRMBL TRMBL
HEH!
SNORT
INCRED-IBLE!
CAPPY SNORTED HIS CHOPSTICKS OUT THROUGH HIS NOSE BUT JUST BARELY HELD IN HIS LAUGHTER!
FOR HIS NEXT MOVE, CAPPY BREAKS OUT MORE CHOPSTICKS!
GNNGH
WA HA HA
KIRBY RAISES HIM WITH MORE RUBBER BANDS!
BULGE BULGE
HUSH
WHAT IS THAT, LIPO-SUCTION?!
STOP! STOP THE MATCH!
!
IF THEY CONTINUE, THEY'LL NEVER BE BRIDES!
BUT THEY'RE BOTH BOYS.

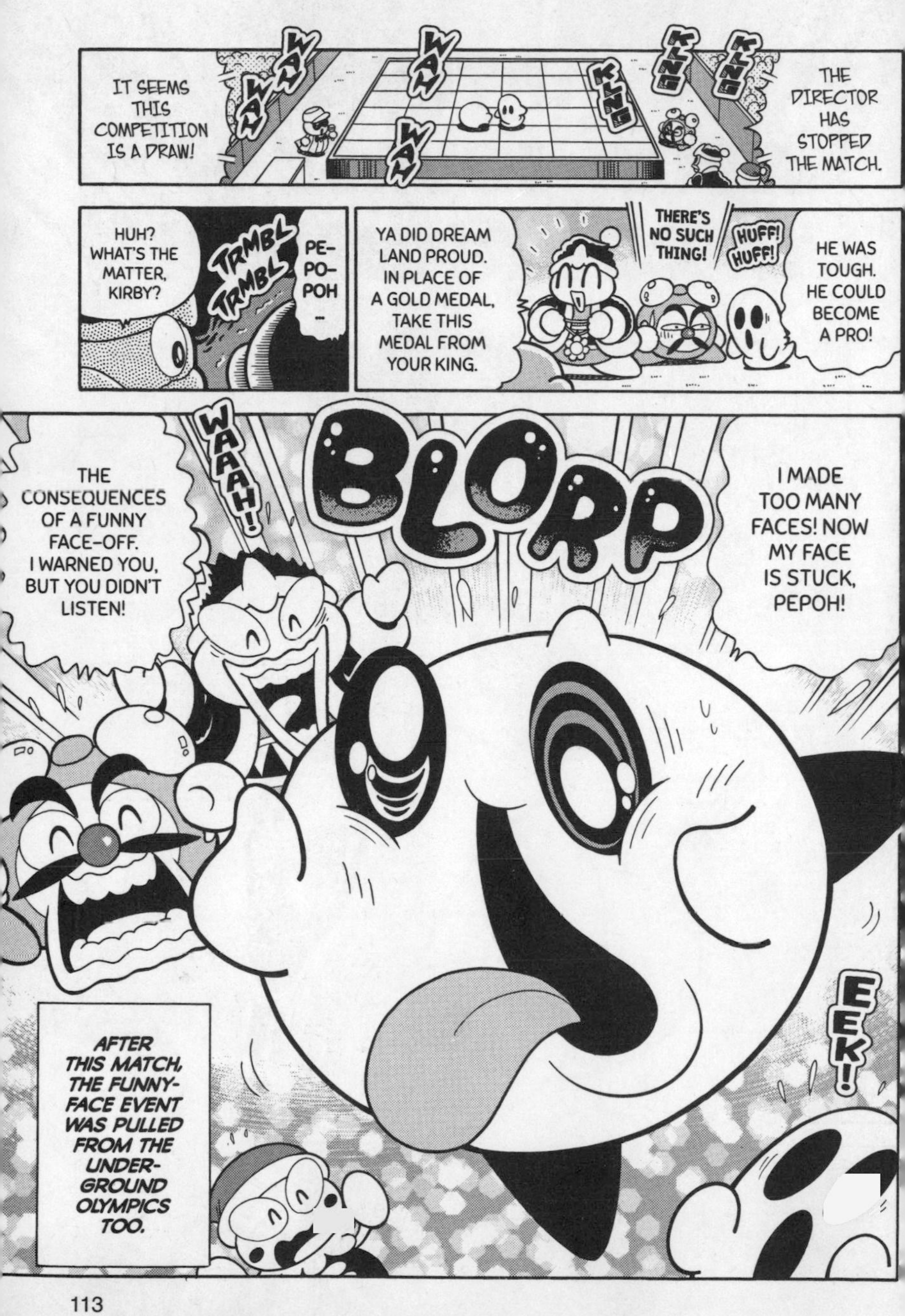
THE DIRECTOR HAS STOPPED THE MATCH.
KLING KLING
KLING
WAH WAH
WAH WAH
WAH
IT SEEMS THIS COMPETITION IS A DRAW!
HE WAS TOUGH. HE COULD BECOME A PRO!
HUFF! HUFF!
THERE'S NO SUCH THING!
YA DID DREAM LAND PROUD. IN PLACE OF A GOLD MEDAL, TAKE THIS MEDAL FROM YOUR KING.
PE-PO-POH...
TRMBL TRMBL
HUH? WHAT'S THE MATTER, KIRBY?
I MADE TOO MANY FACES! NOW MY FACE IS STUCK, PEPOH!
BLORP
WAAAH!
THE CONSEQUENCES OF A FUNNY FACE-OFF. I WARNED YOU, BUT YOU DIDN'T LISTEN!
EEK!
AFTER THIS MATCH, THE FUNNY-FACE EVENT WAS PULLED FROM THE UNDERGROUND OLYMPICS TOO.

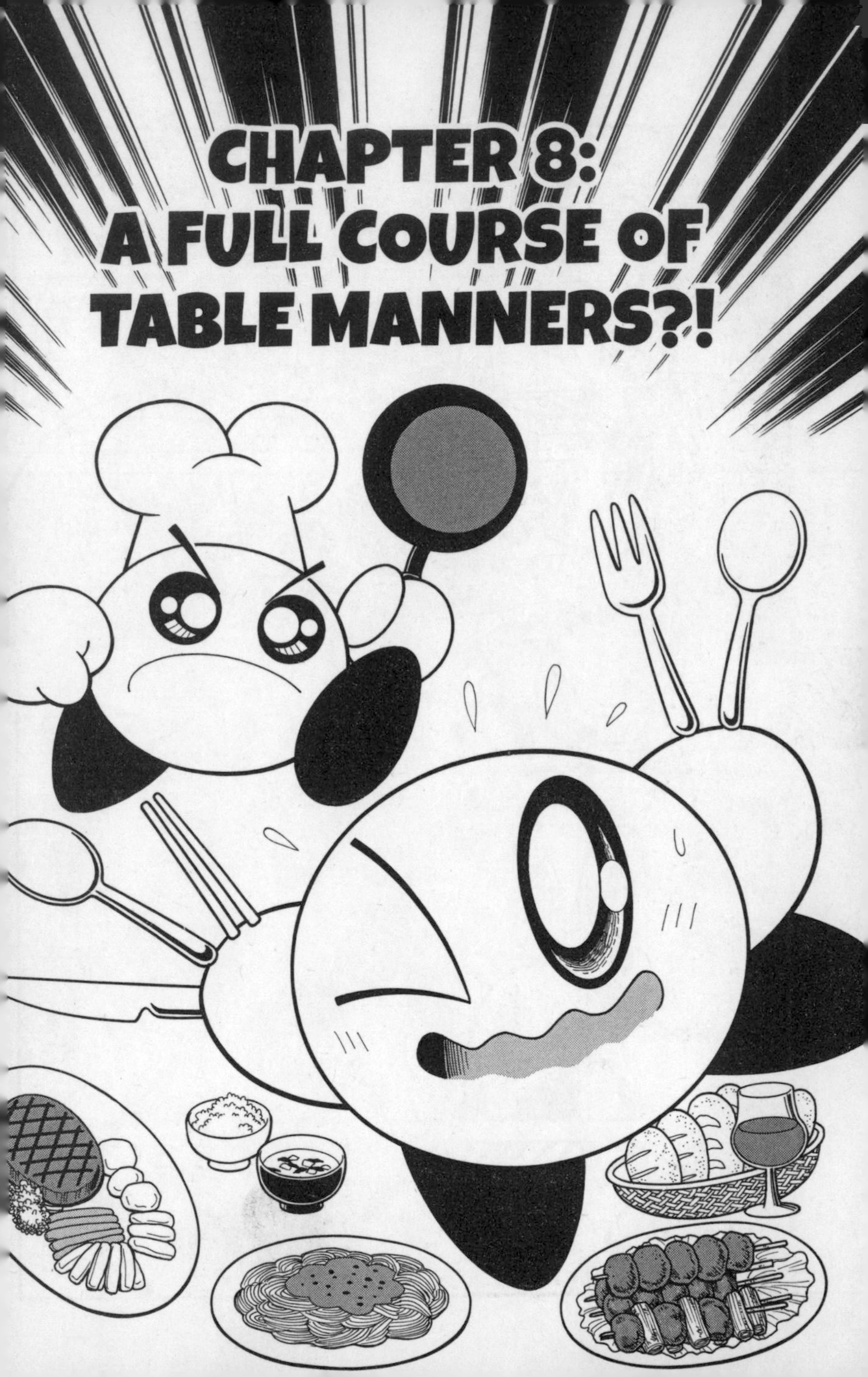
CHAPTER 8:
A FULL COURSE OF
TABLE MANNERS?!

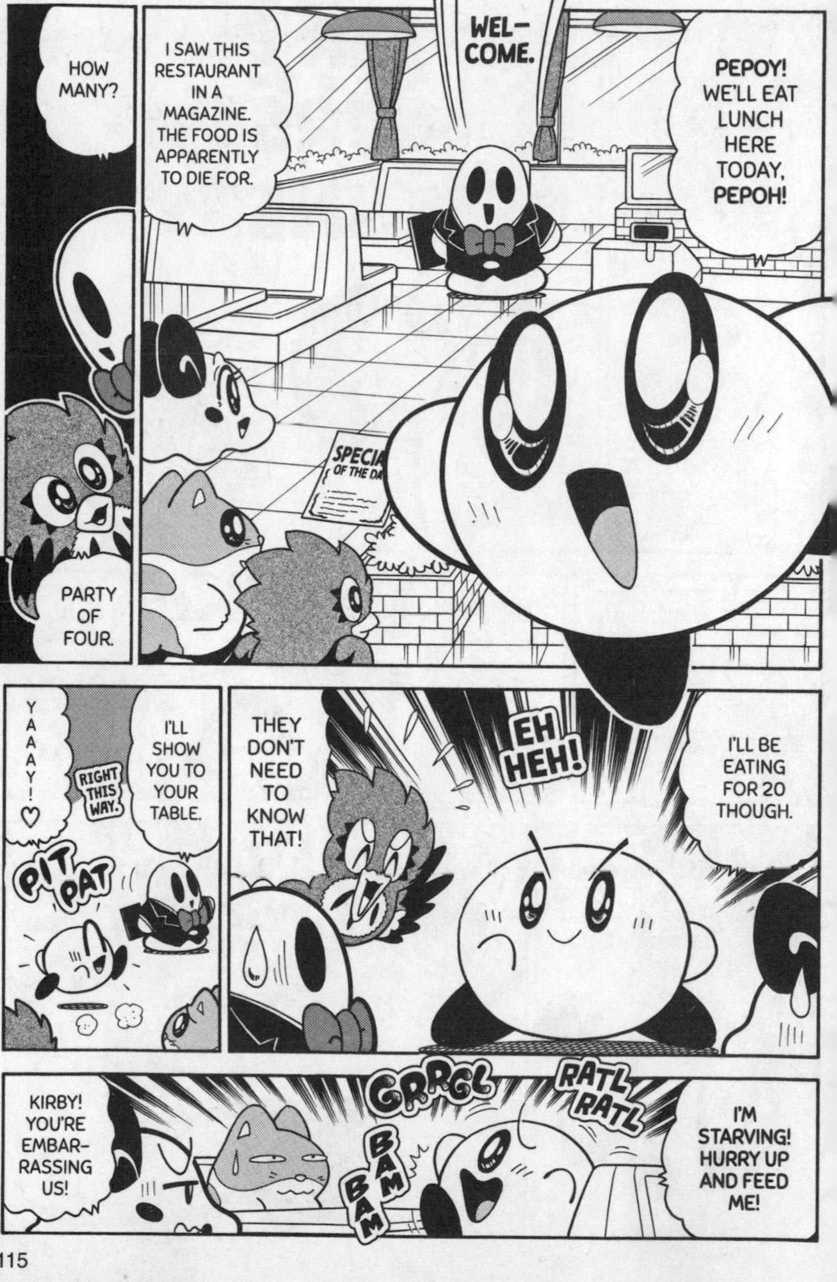
PEPOY! WE'LL EAT LUNCH HERE TODAY, PEPOH!
WEL-COME.
I SAW THIS RESTAURANT IN A MAGAZINE. THE FOOD IS APPARENTLY TO DIE FOR.
HOW MANY?
PARTY OF FOUR.
I'LL BE EATING FOR 20 THOUGH.
EH HEH!
THEY DON'T NEED TO KNOW THAT!
I'LL SHOW YOU TO YOUR TABLE.
RIGHT THIS WAY.
YAAAAY! ♡
PIT PAT
I'M STARVING! HURRY UP AND FEED ME!
RATL RATL
GRRGL
BAM BAM BAM
KIRBY! YOU'RE EMBAR-RASSING US!

AUTHOR'S COMMENT

MANNERS ARE IMPORTANT, AREN'T THEY? MY MENTAL AGE IS STUCK IN FIFTH GRADE, SO MY GROWN-UP MANNERS, ETIQUETTE AND ALL THAT ARE ABYSMAL.

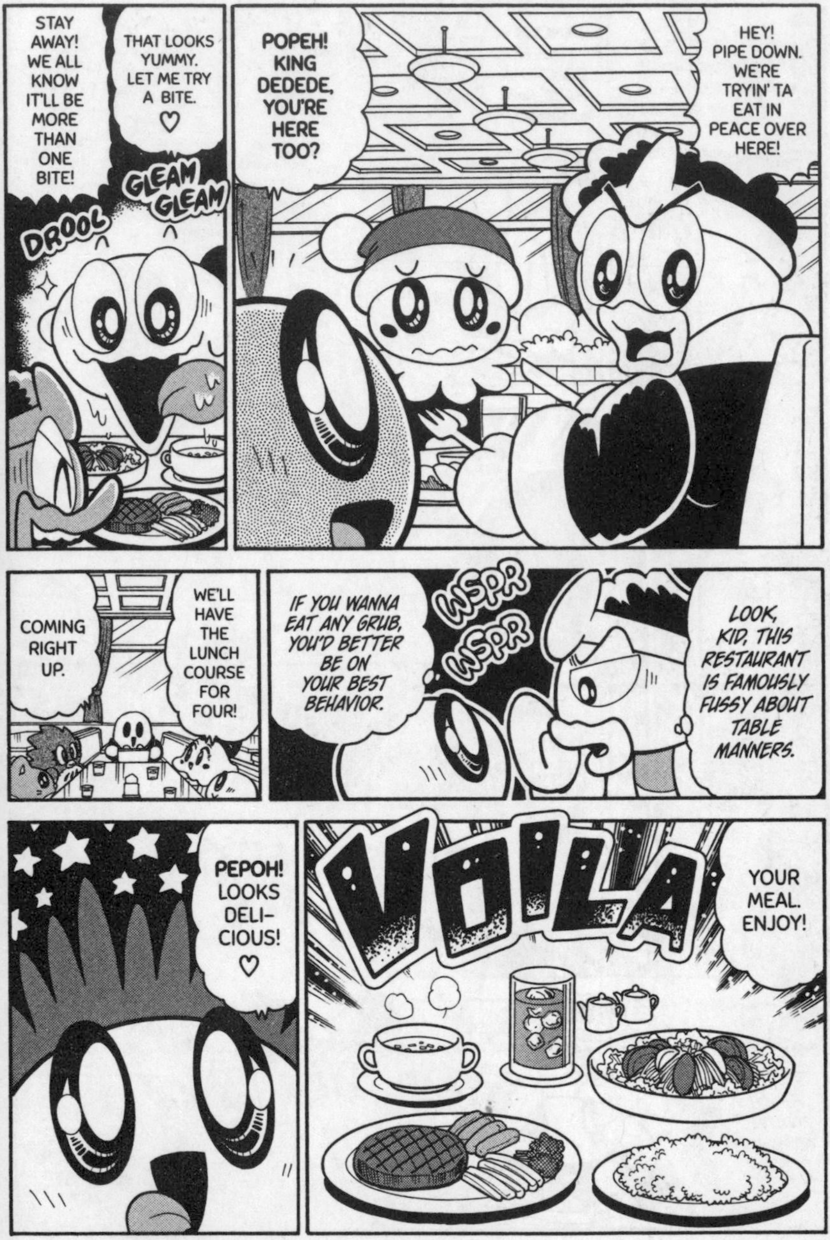
HEY! PIPE DOWN. WE'RE TRYIN' TA EAT IN PEACE OVER HERE!
POPEH! KING DEDEDE, YOU'RE HERE TOO?
THAT LOOKS YUMMY. LET ME TRY A BITE. ♡
STAY AWAY! WE ALL KNOW IT'LL BE MORE THAN ONE BITE!
GLEAM GLEAM
DROOL
LOOK, KID, THIS RESTAURANT IS FAMOUSLY FUSSY ABOUT TABLE MANNERS.
WSPR WSPR
IF YOU WANNA EAT ANY GRUB, YOU'D BETTER BE ON YOUR BEST BEHAVIOR.
WE'LL HAVE THE LUNCH COURSE FOR FOUR!
COMING RIGHT UP.
YOUR MEAL. ENJOY!
VOILA
PEPOH! LOOKS DELI-CIOUS! ♡

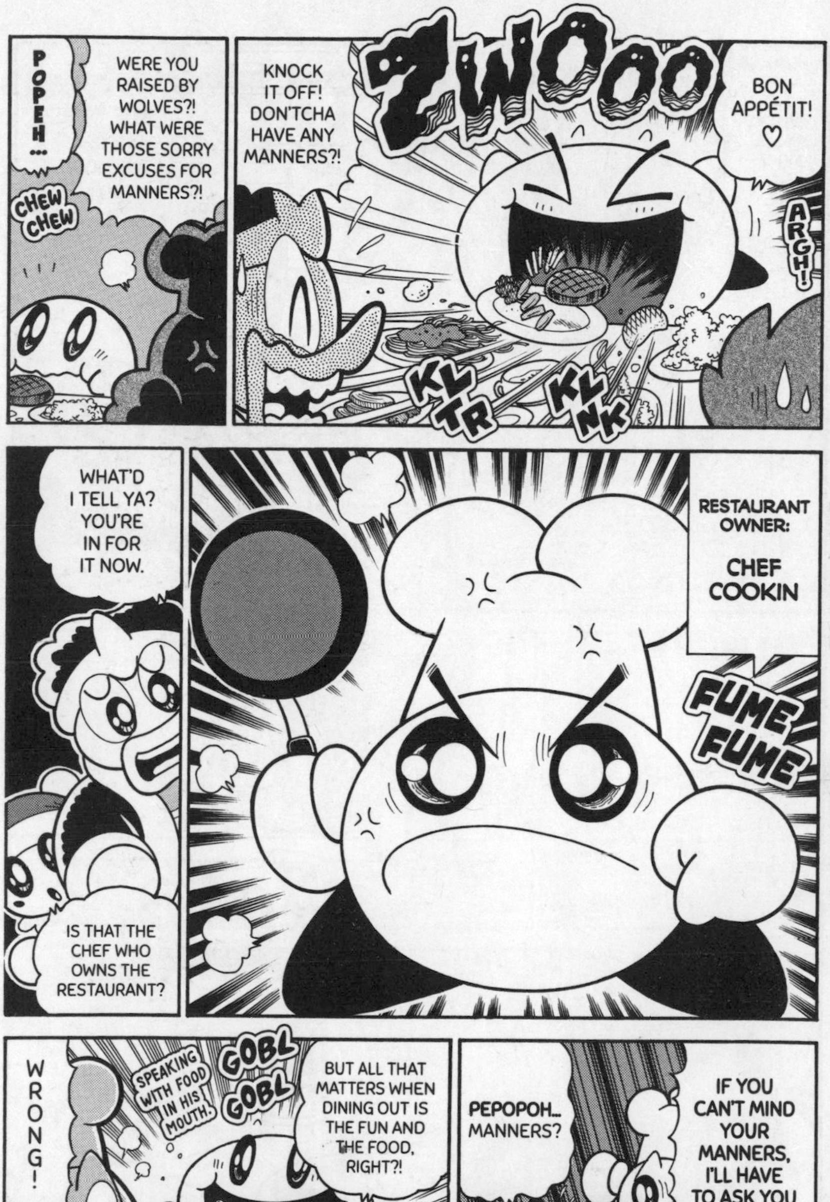
BON APPÉTIT! ♡
ZWOOO
ARGH!
KNOCK IT OFF! DON'TCHA HAVE ANY MANNERS?!
KLTR
KLNK
WERE YOU RAISED BY WOLVES?! WHAT WERE THOSE SORRY EXCUSES FOR MANNERS?!
POPEH...
CHEW CHEW
RESTAURANT OWNER:
CHEF COOKIN
FUME FUME
WHAT'D I TELL YA? YOU'RE IN FOR IT NOW.
IS THAT THE CHEF WHO OWNS THE RESTAURANT?
IF YOU CAN'T MIND YOUR MANNERS, I'LL HAVE TO ASK YOU TO LEAVE!
PEPOPOH... MANNERS?
BUT ALL THAT MATTERS WHEN DINING OUT IS THE FUN AND THE FOOD, RIGHT?!
GOBL GOBL
SPEAKING WITH FOOD IN HIS MOUTH.
WRONG!

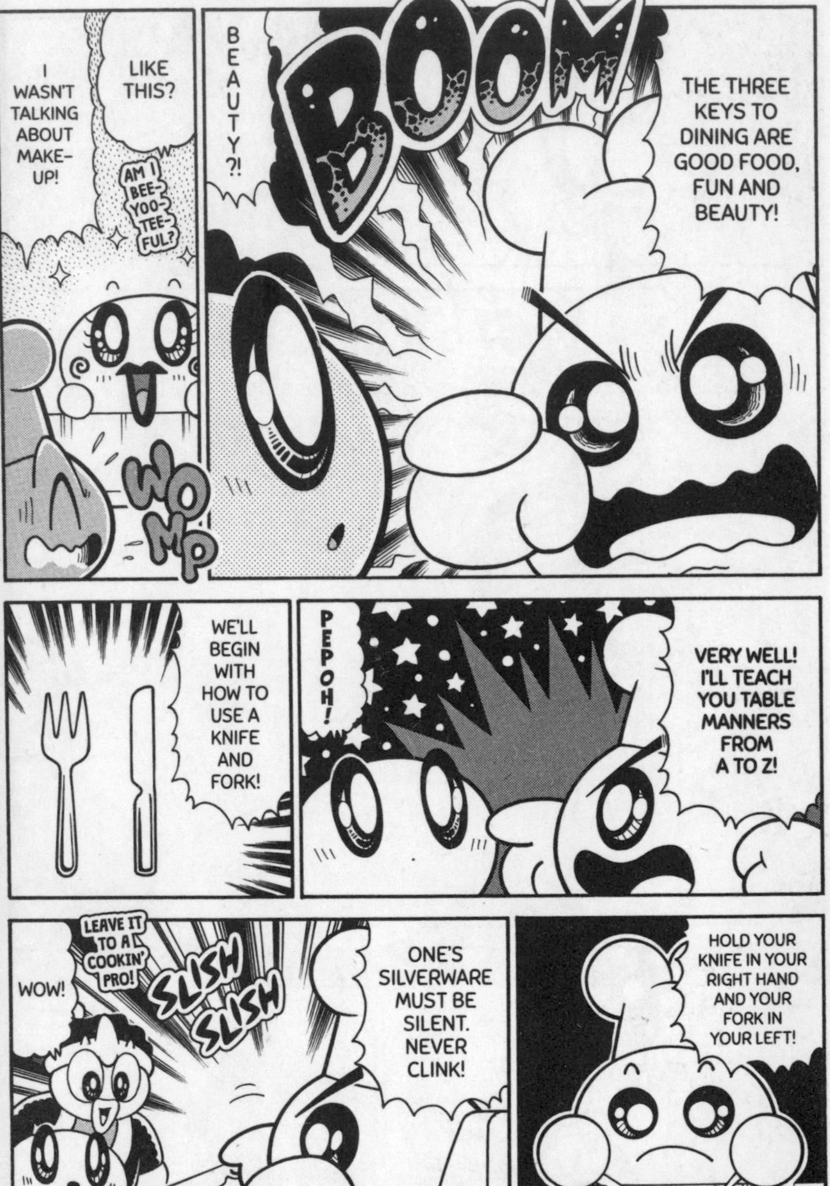
THE THREE KEYS TO DINING ARE GOOD FOOD, FUN AND BEAUTY!
BOOM
BEAUTY?!
LIKE THIS?
AM I BEE-YOO-TEE-FUL?
I WASN'T TALKING ABOUT MAKE-UP!
WOMP
VERY WELL! I'LL TEACH YOU TABLE MANNERS FROM A TO Z!
PEPOH!
WE'LL BEGIN WITH HOW TO USE A KNIFE AND FORK!
HOLD YOUR KNIFE IN YOUR RIGHT HAND AND YOUR FORK IN YOUR LEFT!
ONE'S SILVERWARE MUST BE SILENT. NEVER CLINK!
SLISH SLISH
LEAVE IT TO A COOKIN' PRO!
WOW!

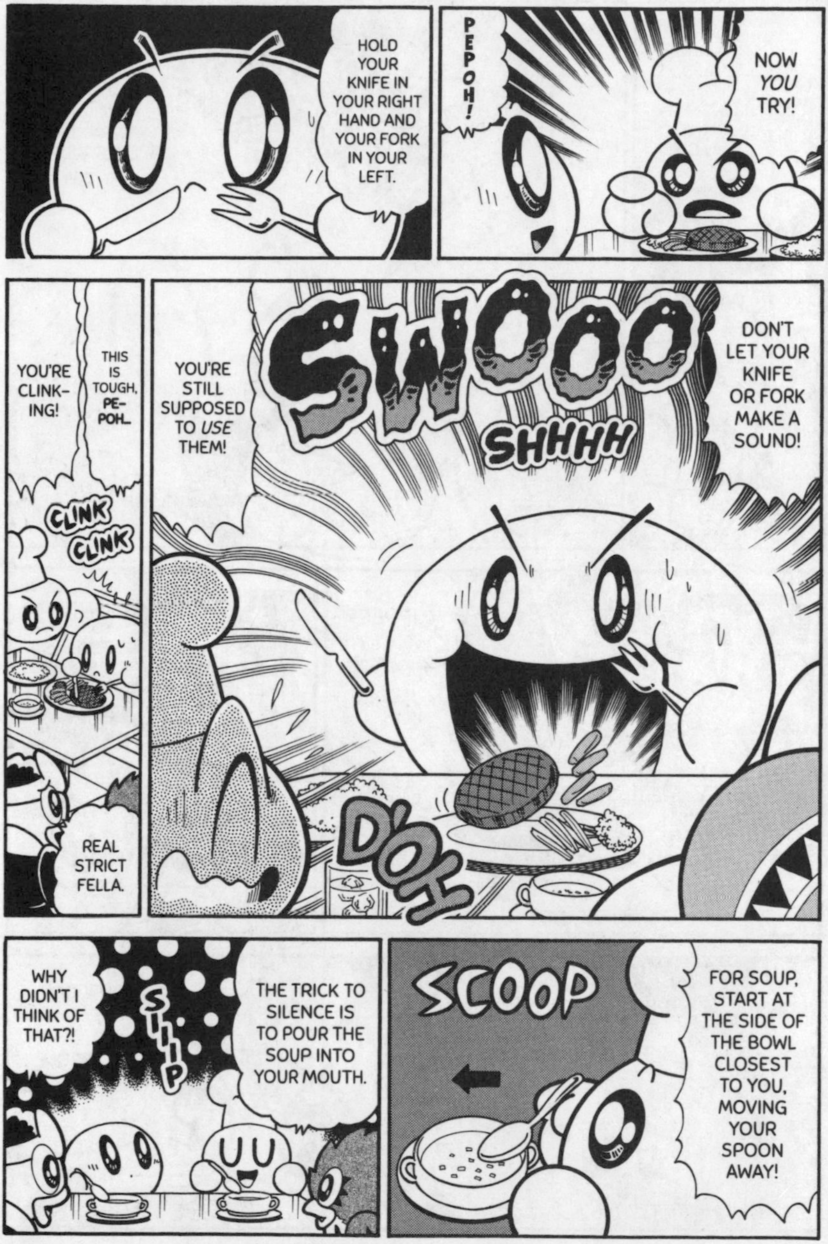
NOW *YOU* TRY!
PEPOH!
HOLD YOUR KNIFE IN YOUR RIGHT HAND AND YOUR FORK IN YOUR LEFT.
DON'T LET YOUR KNIFE OR FORK MAKE A SOUND!
SWOOO
SHHHH
YOU'RE STILL SUPPOSED TO *USE* THEM!
D'OH
THIS IS TOUGH, PEPOH..
YOU'RE CLINKING!
CLINK CLINK
REAL STRICT FELLA.
SCOOP
FOR SOUP, START AT THE SIDE OF THE BOWL CLOSEST TO YOU, MOVING YOUR SPOON AWAY!
THE TRICK TO SILENCE IS TO POUR THE SOUP INTO YOUR MOUTH.
SHIIIP
WHY DIDN'T I THINK OF THAT?!

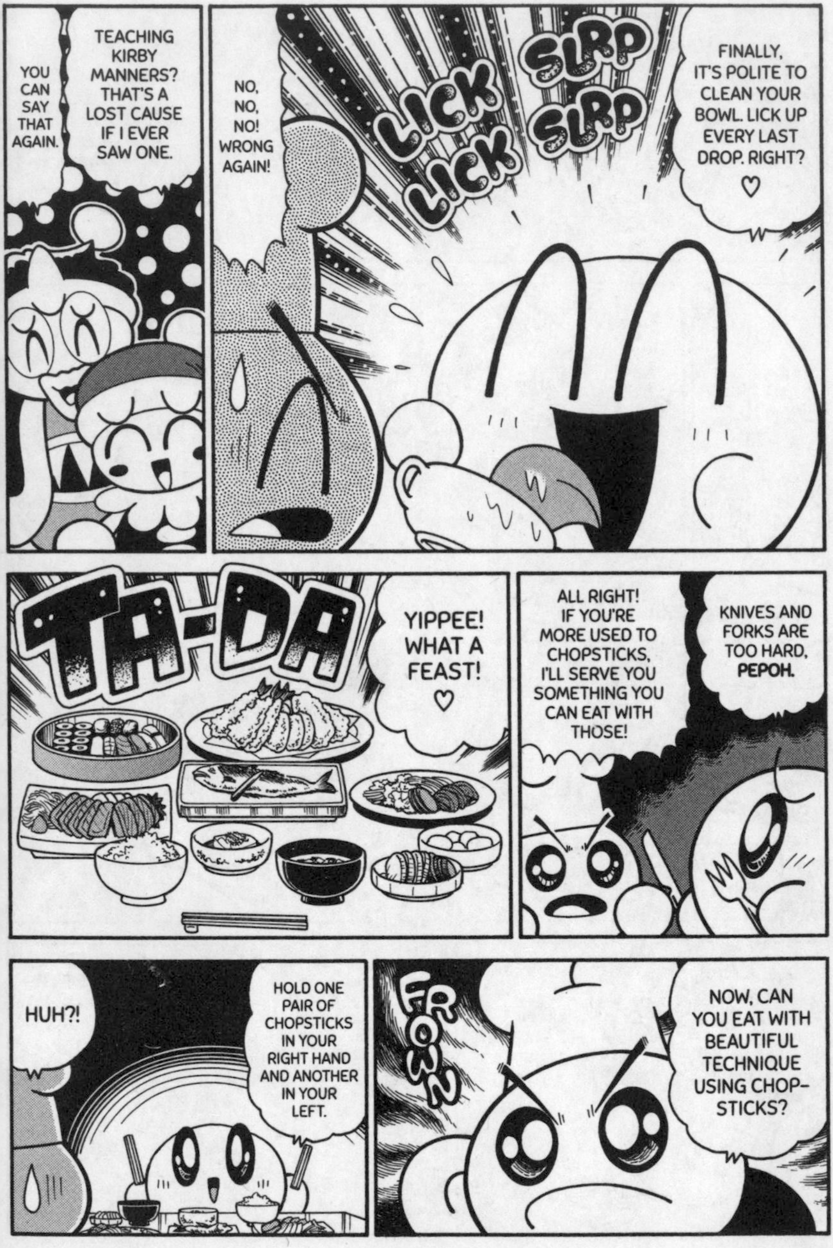
FINALLY, IT'S POLITE TO CLEAN YOUR BOWL. LICK UP EVERY LAST DROP. RIGHT? ♡
SLRP SLRP
LICK LICK
NO, NO, NO! WRONG AGAIN!
TEACHING KIRBY MANNERS? THAT'S A LOST CAUSE IF I EVER SAW ONE.
YOU CAN SAY THAT AGAIN.
KNIVES AND FORKS ARE TOO HARD, **PEPOH.**
ALL RIGHT! IF YOU'RE MORE USED TO CHOPSTICKS, I'LL SERVE YOU SOMETHING YOU CAN EAT WITH THOSE!
TA-DA
YIPPEE! WHAT A FEAST! ♡
NOW, CAN YOU EAT WITH BEAUTIFUL TECHNIQUE USING CHOP-STICKS?
FROWN
HOLD ONE PAIR OF CHOPSTICKS IN YOUR RIGHT HAND AND ANOTHER IN YOUR LEFT.
HUH?!

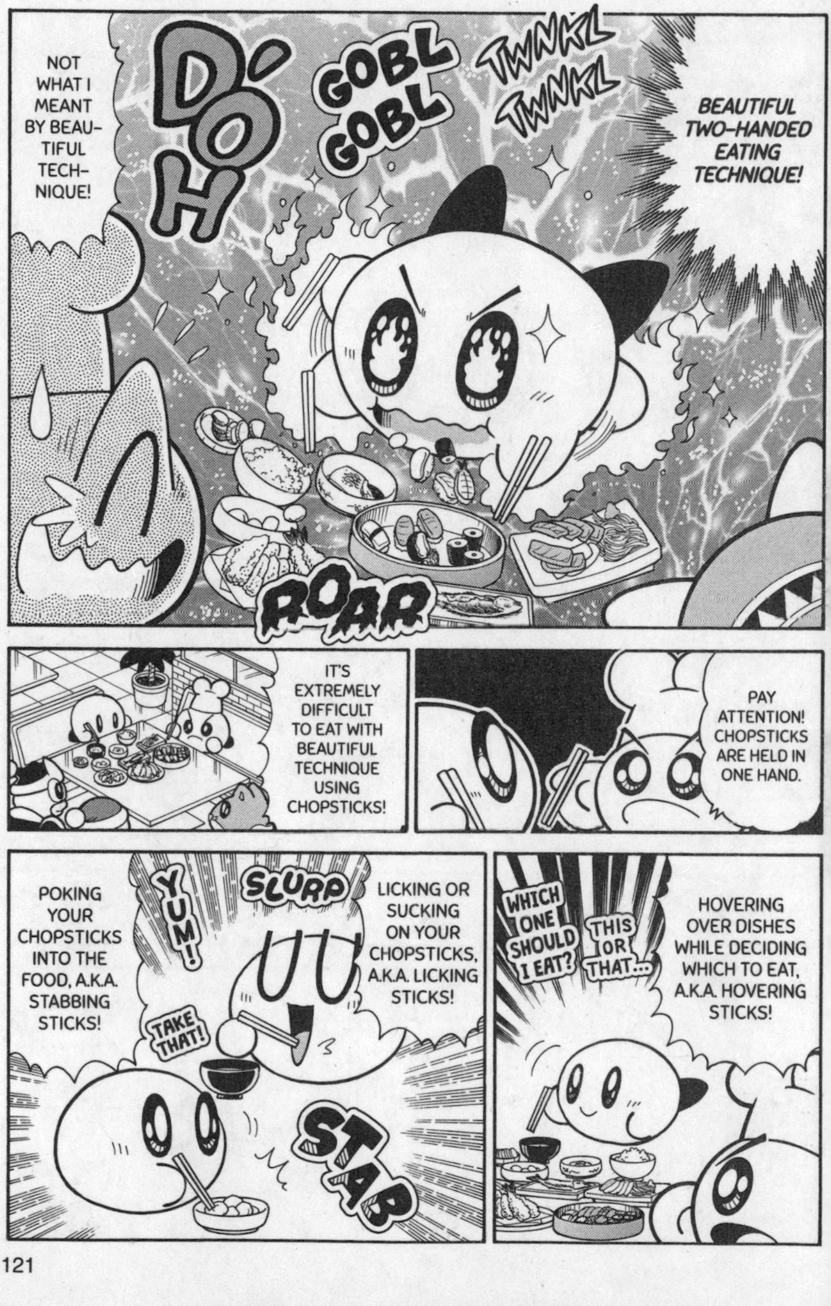
TWNKL TWNKL
BEAUTIFUL TWO-HANDED EATING TECHNIQUE!
GOBL GOBL
D'OH
NOT WHAT I MEANT BY BEAUTIFUL TECHNIQUE!
ROAR
PAY ATTENTION! CHOPSTICKS ARE HELD IN ONE HAND.
IT'S EXTREMELY DIFFICULT TO EAT WITH BEAUTIFUL TECHNIQUE USING CHOPSTICKS!
HOVERING OVER DISHES WHILE DECIDING WHICH TO EAT, A.K.A. HOVERING STICKS!
THIS OR THAT...
WHICH ONE SHOULD I EAT?
LICKING OR SUCKING ON YOUR CHOPSTICKS, A.K.A. LICKING STICKS!
SLURP
YUM!
POKING YOUR CHOPSTICKS INTO THE FOOD, A.K.A. STABBING STICKS!
TAKE THAT!
STAB

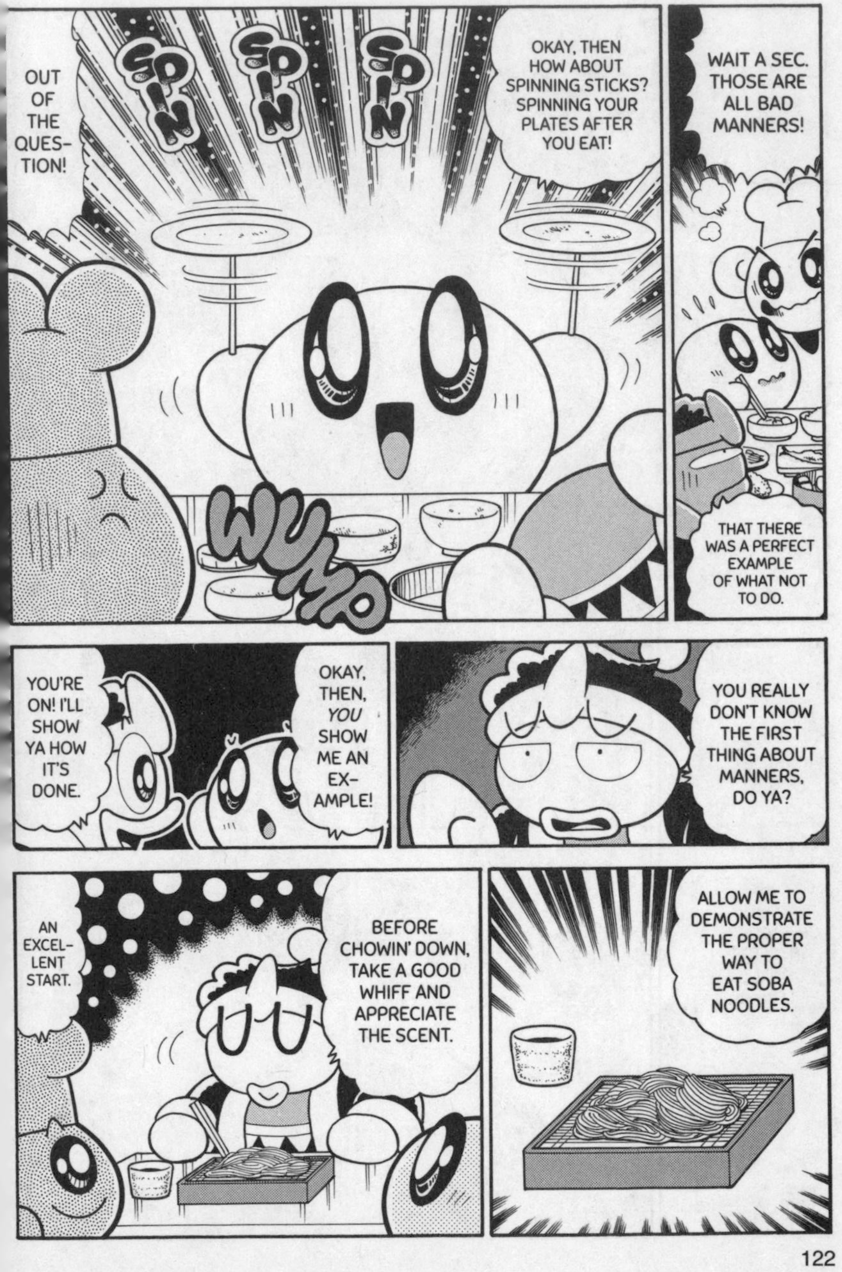
WAIT A SEC. THOSE ARE ALL BAD MANNERS!
THAT THERE WAS A PERFECT EXAMPLE OF WHAT NOT TO DO.
OKAY, THEN HOW ABOUT SPINNING STICKS? SPINNING YOUR PLATES AFTER YOU EAT!
SPIN SPIN SPIN
OUT OF THE QUES-TION!
WUMP
YOU REALLY DON'T KNOW THE FIRST THING ABOUT MANNERS, DO YA?
OKAY, THEN, *YOU* SHOW ME AN EX-AMPLE!
YOU'RE ON! I'LL SHOW YA HOW IT'S DONE.
ALLOW ME TO DEMONSTRATE THE PROPER WAY TO EAT SOBA NOODLES.
BEFORE CHOWIN' DOWN, TAKE A GOOD WHIFF AND APPRECIATE THE SCENT.
AN EXCEL-LENT START.

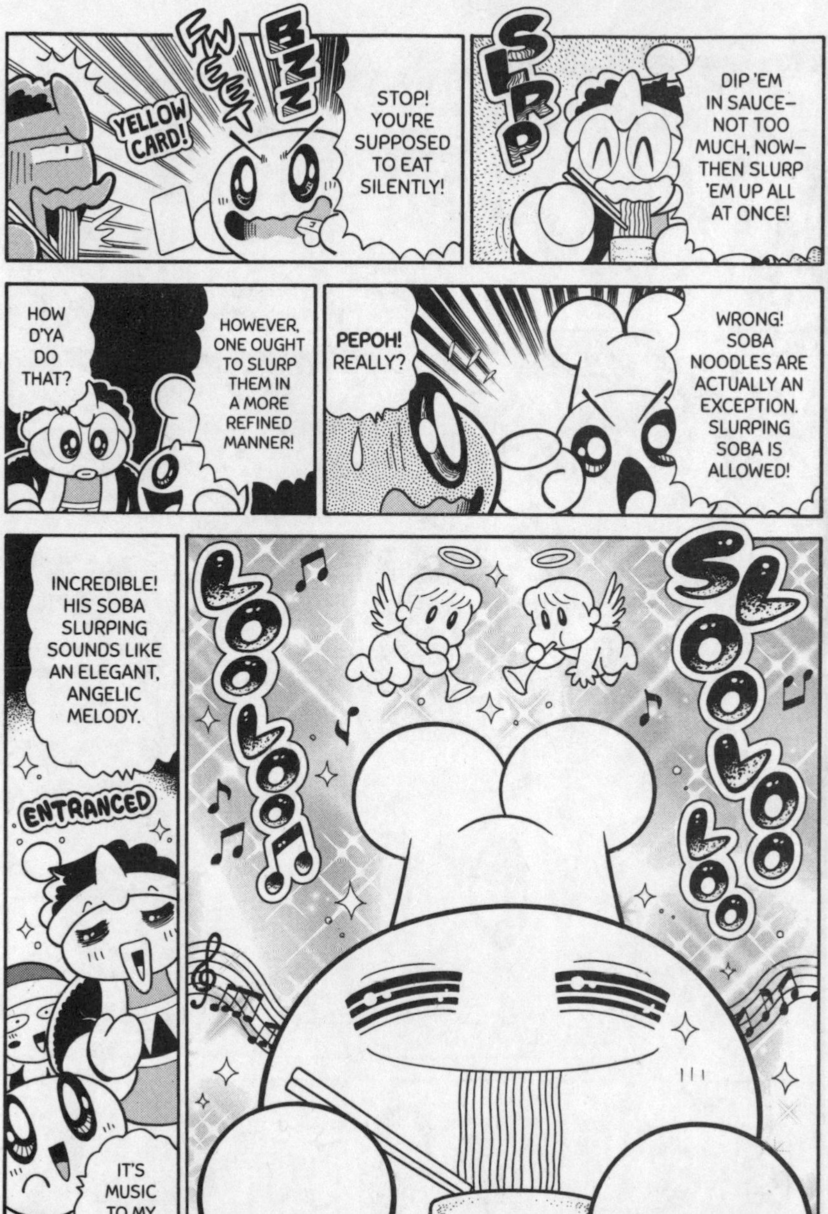
SLRP
DIP 'EM IN SAUCE—NOT TOO MUCH, NOW—THEN SLURP 'EM UP ALL AT ONCE!
BZZ
FWEET
STOP! YOU'RE SUPPOSED TO EAT SILENTLY!
YELLOW CARD!
WRONG! SOBA NOODLES ARE ACTUALLY AN EXCEPTION. SLURPING SOBA IS ALLOWED!
PEPOH! REALLY?
HOWEVER, ONE OUGHT TO SLURP THEM IN A MORE REFINED MANNER!
HOW D'YA DO THAT?
SLOOOLOOLOO
LOOOLOOO
INCREDIBLE! HIS SOBA SLURPING SOUNDS LIKE AN ELEGANT, ANGELIC MELODY.
ENTRANCED
IT'S MUSIC TO MY EARS!

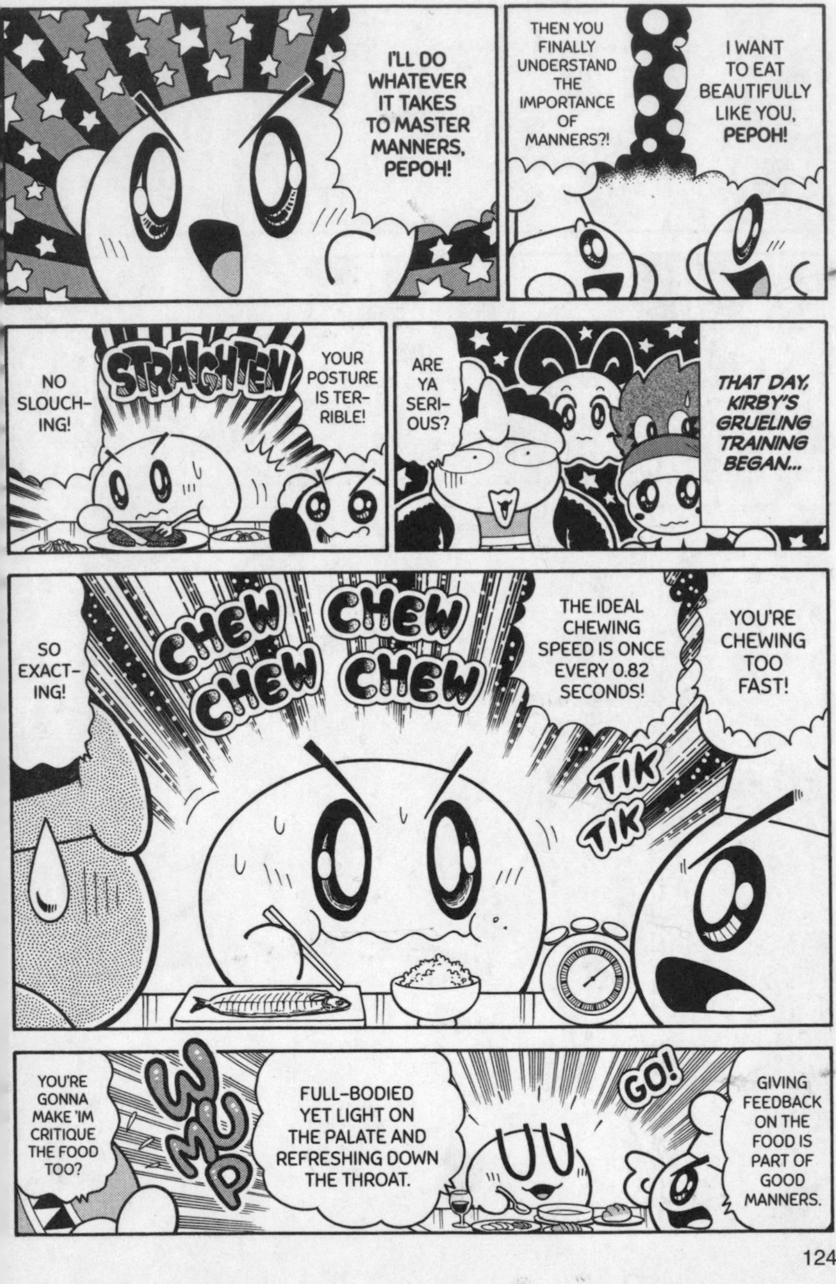

I WANT TO EAT BEAUTIFULLY LIKE YOU, PEPOH!
THEN YOU FINALLY UNDERSTAND THE IMPORTANCE OF MANNERS?!
I'LL DO WHATEVER IT TAKES TO MASTER MANNERS, PEPOH!
THAT DAY, KIRBY'S GRUELING TRAINING BEGAN...
ARE YA SERIOUS?
YOUR POSTURE IS TERRIBLE!
STRAIGHTEN
NO SLOUCHING!
YOU'RE CHEWING TOO FAST!
THE IDEAL CHEWING SPEED IS ONCE EVERY 0.82 SECONDS!
TIK TIK
CHEW CHEW CHEW CHEW
SO EXACTING!
GIVING FEEDBACK ON THE FOOD IS PART OF GOOD MANNERS.
GO!
FULL-BODIED YET LIGHT ON THE PALATE AND REFRESHING DOWN THE THROAT.
YOU'RE GONNA MAKE 'IM CRITIQUE THE FOOD TOO?

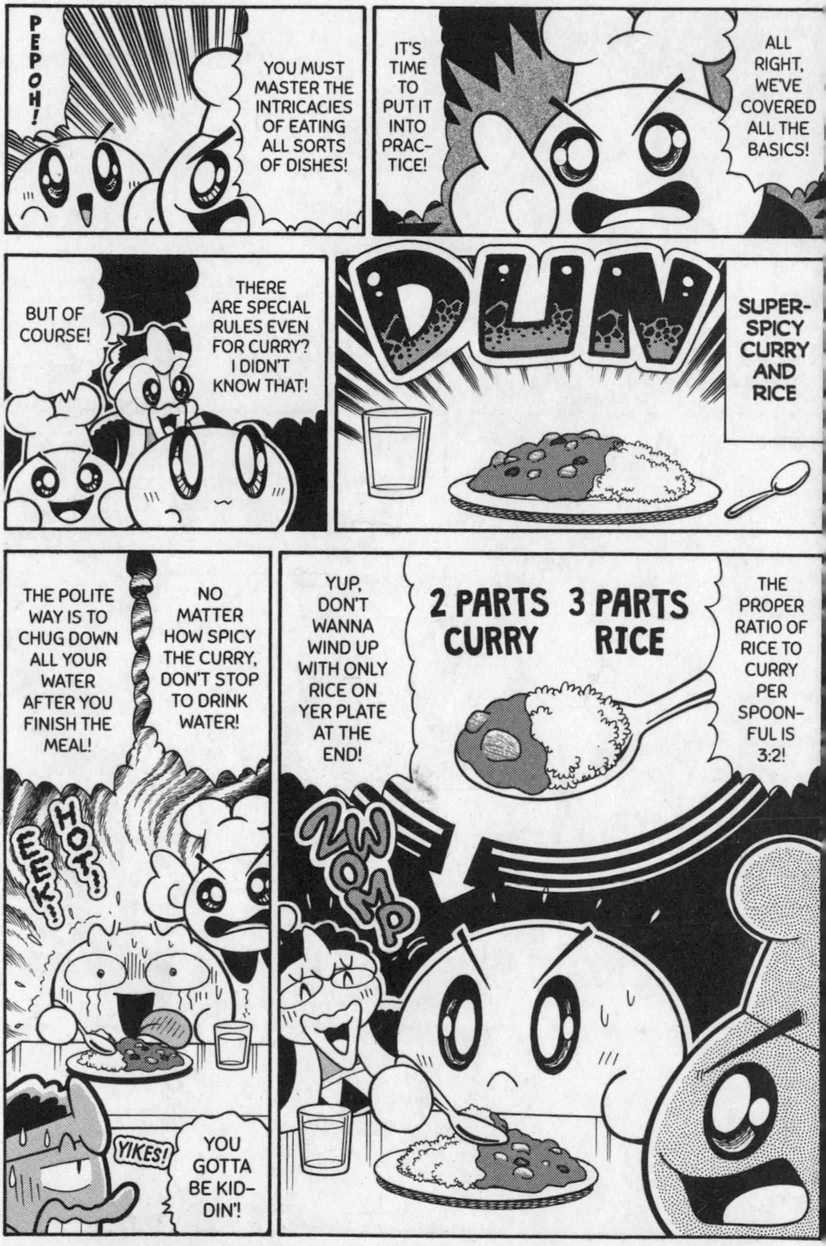
ALL RIGHT, WE'VE COVERED ALL THE BASICS!
IT'S TIME TO PUT IT INTO PRAC-TICE!
YOU MUST MASTER THE INTRICACIES OF EATING ALL SORTS OF DISHES!
PEPOH!
SUPER-SPICY CURRY AND RICE
DUN
THERE ARE SPECIAL RULES EVEN FOR CURRY? I DIDN'T KNOW THAT!
BUT OF COURSE!
THE PROPER RATIO OF RICE TO CURRY PER SPOON-FUL IS 3:2!
3 PARTS RICE
2 PARTS CURRY
YUP, DON'T WANNA WIND UP WITH ONLY RICE ON YER PLATE AT THE END!
ZWOMP
NO MATTER HOW SPICY THE CURRY, DON'T STOP TO DRINK WATER!
THE POLITE WAY IS TO CHUG DOWN ALL YOUR WATER AFTER YOU FINISH THE MEAL!
HOT...
EEK...
YIKES!
YOU GOTTA BE KID-DIN'!

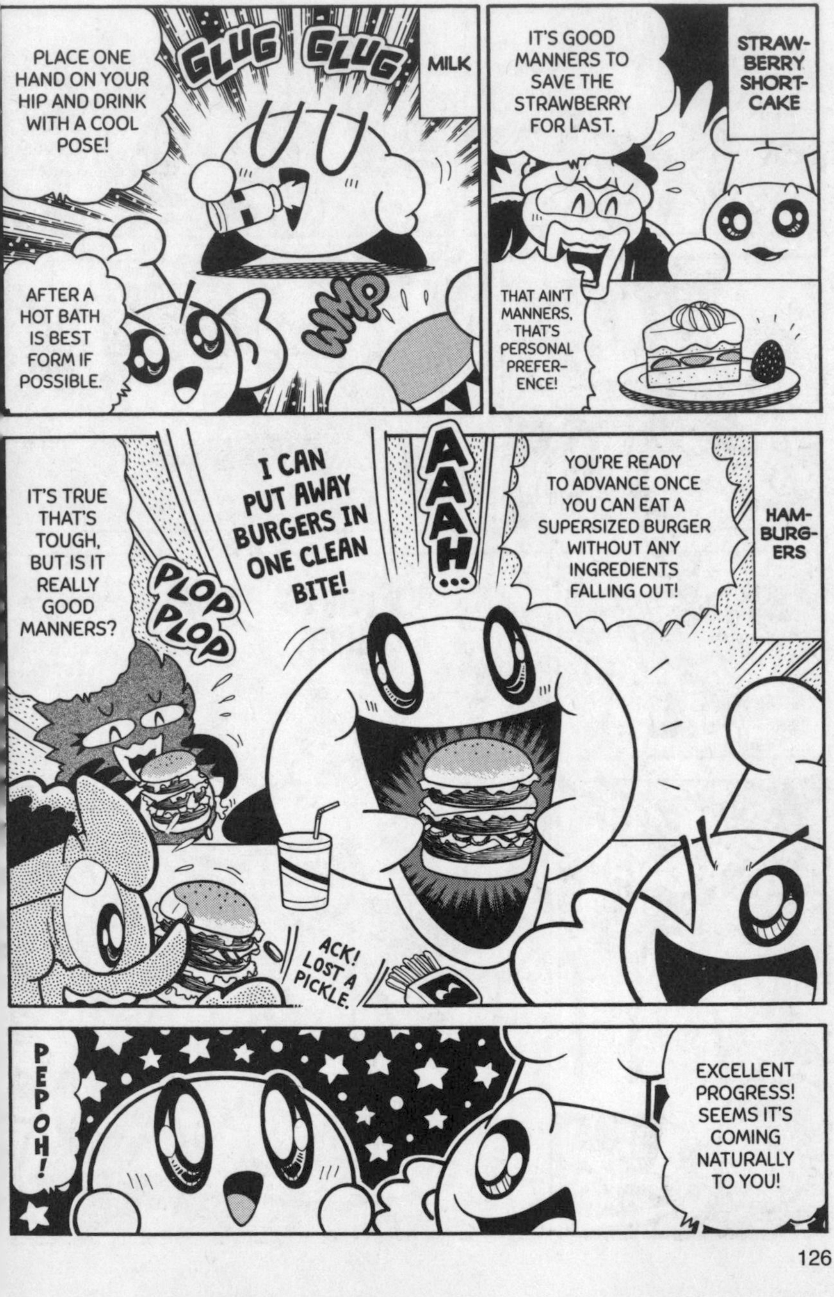
STRAWBERRY SHORTCAKE
IT'S GOOD MANNERS TO SAVE THE STRAWBERRY FOR LAST.
THAT AIN'T MANNERS, THAT'S PERSONAL PREFERENCE!
MILK
GLUG GLUG
PLACE ONE HAND ON YOUR HIP AND DRINK WITH A COOL POSE!
WMP
AFTER A HOT BATH IS BEST FORM IF POSSIBLE.
HAMBURGERS
YOU'RE READY TO ADVANCE ONCE YOU CAN EAT A SUPERSIZED BURGER WITHOUT ANY INGREDIENTS FALLING OUT!
AAAH...
I CAN PUT AWAY BURGERS IN ONE CLEAN BITE!
IT'S TRUE THAT'S TOUGH, BUT IS IT REALLY GOOD MANNERS?
PLOP PLOP
ACK! LOST A PICKLE.
EXCELLENT PROGRESS! SEEMS IT'S COMING NATURALLY TO YOU!
PEPOH!

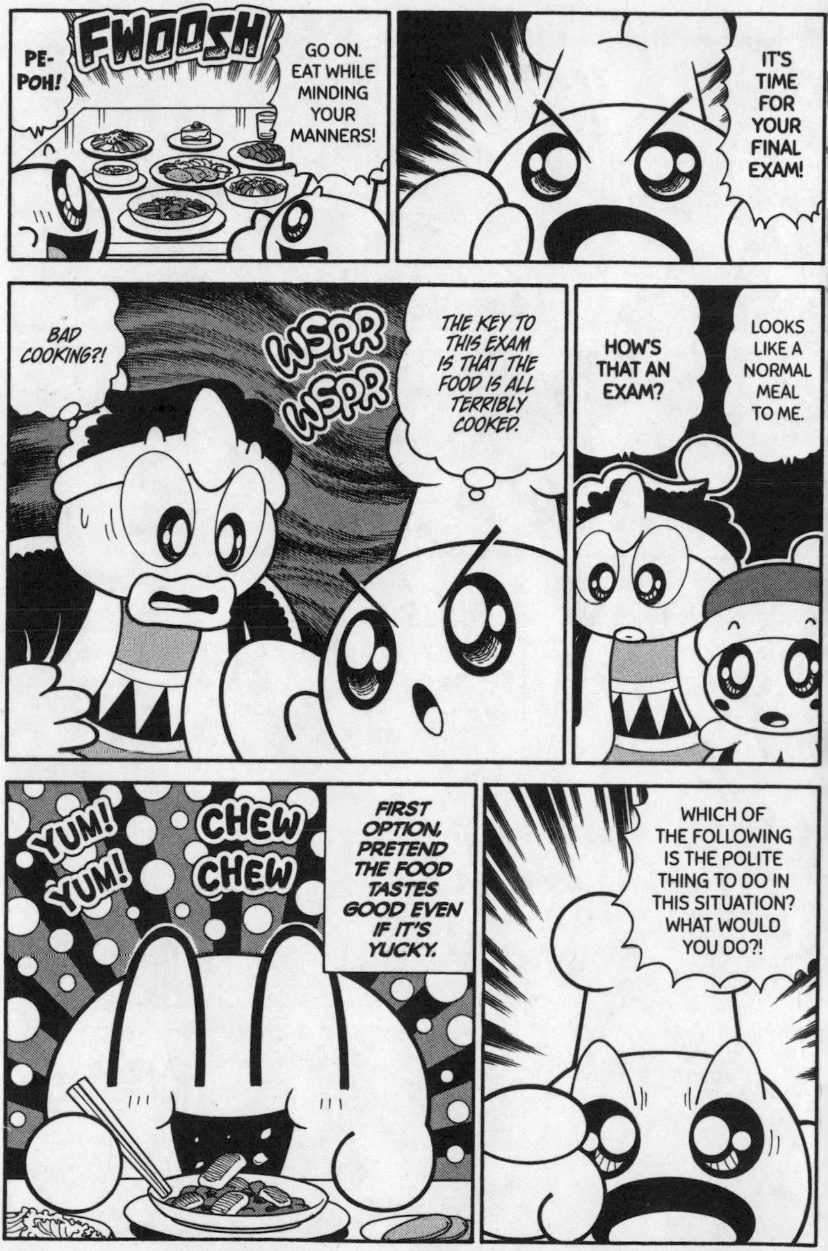
IT'S TIME FOR YOUR FINAL EXAM!
GO ON. EAT WHILE MINDING YOUR MANNERS!
FWOOSH
PE-POH!
LOOKS LIKE A NORMAL MEAL TO ME.
HOW'S THAT AN EXAM?
THE KEY TO THIS EXAM IS THAT THE FOOD IS ALL TERRIBLY COOKED.
WSPR WSPR
BAD COOKING?!
WHICH OF THE FOLLOWING IS THE POLITE THING TO DO IN THIS SITUATION? WHAT WOULD YOU DO?!
FIRST OPTION, PRETEND THE FOOD TASTES GOOD EVEN IF IT'S YUCKY.
CHEW CHEW
YUM! YUM!

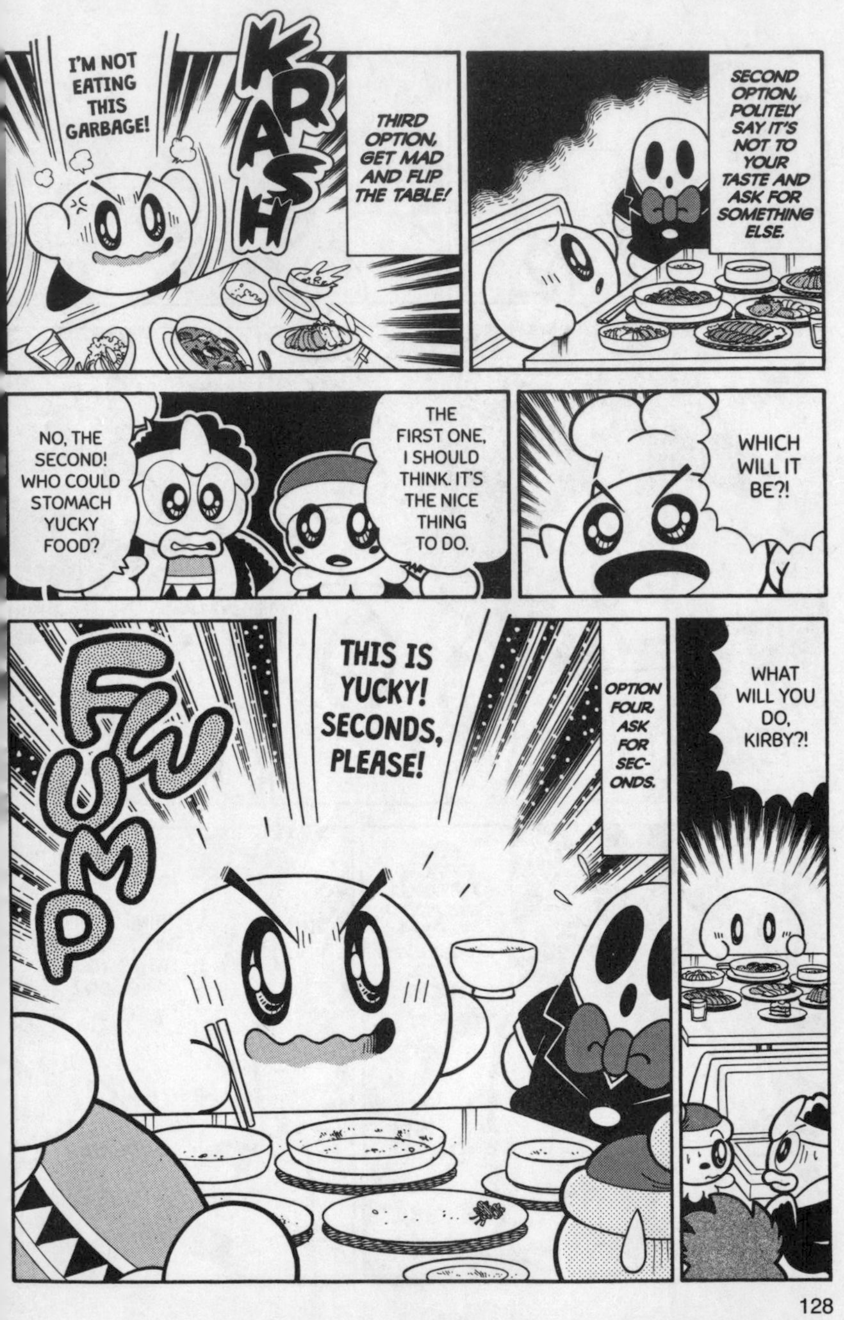
SECOND OPTION, POLITELY SAY IT'S NOT TO YOUR TASTE AND ASK FOR SOMETHING ELSE.
THIRD OPTION, GET MAD AND FLIP THE TABLE!
KRASH
I'M NOT EATING THIS GARBAGE!
WHICH WILL IT BE?!
THE FIRST ONE, I SHOULD THINK. IT'S THE NICE THING TO DO.
NO, THE SECOND! WHO COULD STOMACH YUCKY FOOD?
WHAT WILL YOU DO, KIRBY?!
OPTION FOUR, ASK FOR SEC-ONDS.
THIS IS YUCKY! SECONDS, PLEASE!
FWUMP

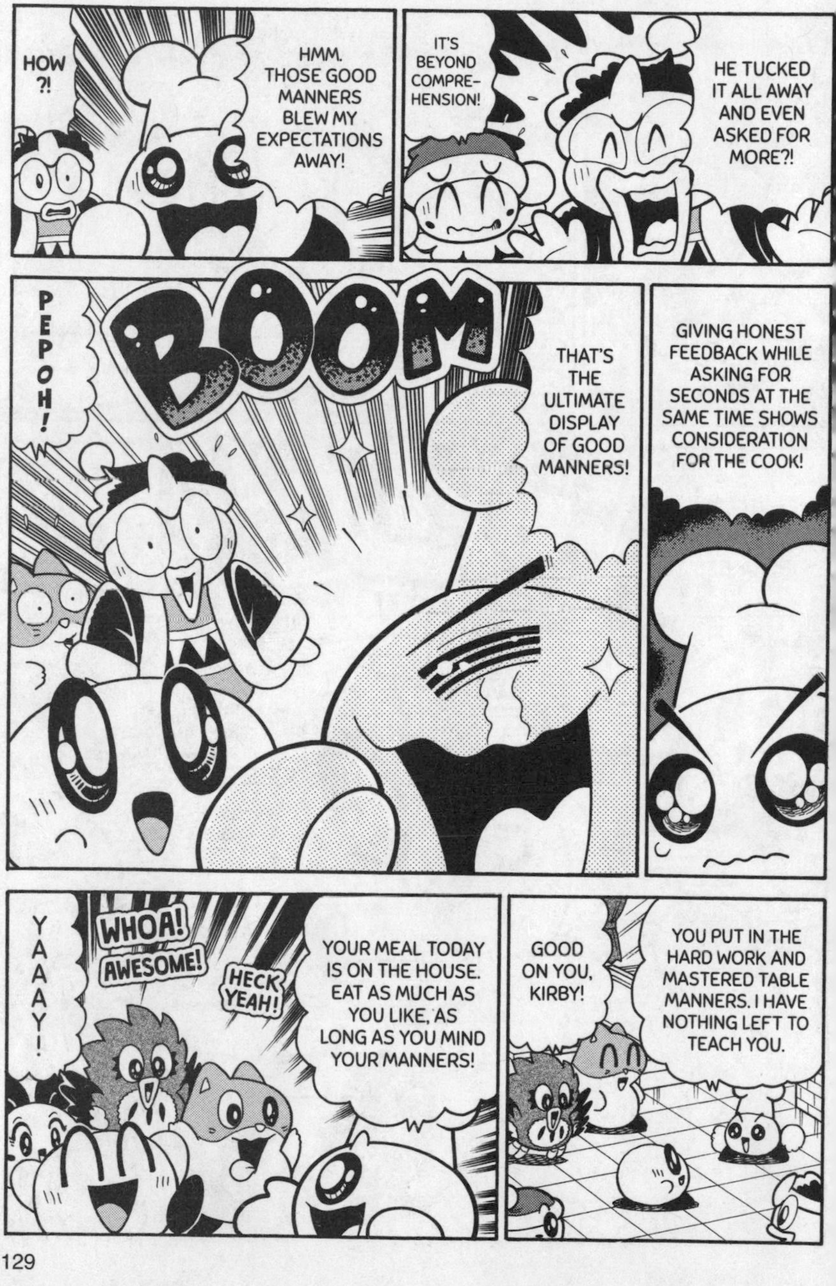

HE TUCKED IT ALL AWAY AND EVEN ASKED FOR MORE?!
IT'S BEYOND COMPRE-HENSION!
HMM. THOSE GOOD MANNERS BLEW MY EXPECTATIONS AWAY!
HOW?!
GIVING HONEST FEEDBACK WHILE ASKING FOR SECONDS AT THE SAME TIME SHOWS CONSIDERATION FOR THE COOK!
THAT'S THE ULTIMATE DISPLAY OF GOOD MANNERS!
BOOM
PEPOH!
YOU PUT IN THE HARD WORK AND MASTERED TABLE MANNERS. I HAVE NOTHING LEFT TO TEACH YOU.
GOOD ON YOU, KIRBY!
YOUR MEAL TODAY IS ON THE HOUSE. EAT AS MUCH AS YOU LIKE, AS LONG AS YOU MIND YOUR MANNERS!
HECK YEAH!
WHOA! AWESOME!
YAAAY!

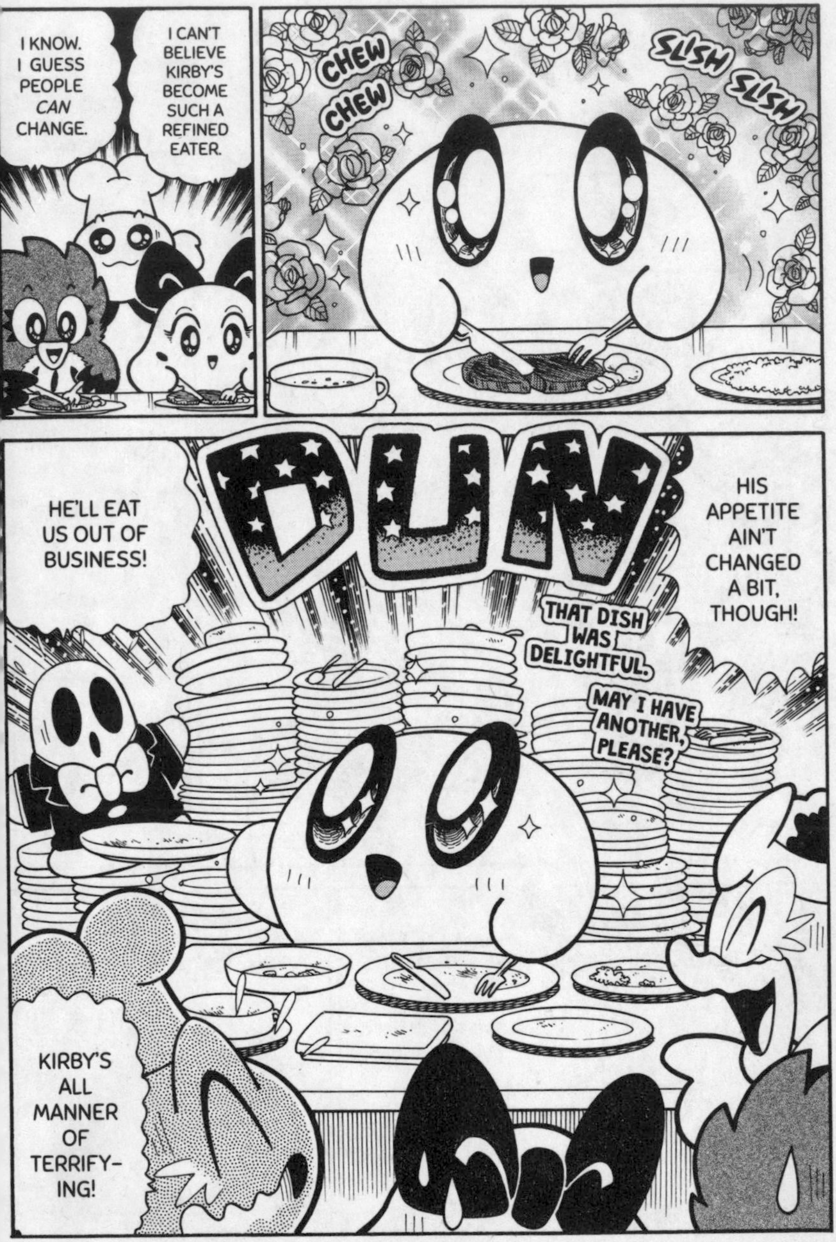
CHEW CHEW
SLISH SLISH
I CAN'T BELIEVE KIRBY'S BECOME SUCH A REFINED EATER.
I KNOW. I GUESS PEOPLE *CAN* CHANGE.
DUN
HIS APPETITE AIN'T CHANGED A BIT, THOUGH!
THAT DISH WAS DELIGHTFUL.
MAY I HAVE ANOTHER, PLEASE?
HE'LL EAT US OUT OF BUSINESS!
KIRBY'S ALL MANNER OF TERRIFY-ING!

CENSORSHIP

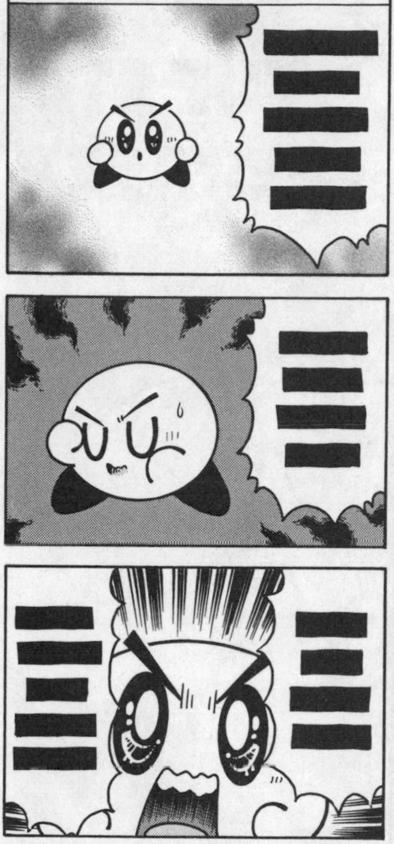
[redacted]
[redacted]
[redacted]
[redacted]

KIRBY'S CONVICTIONS

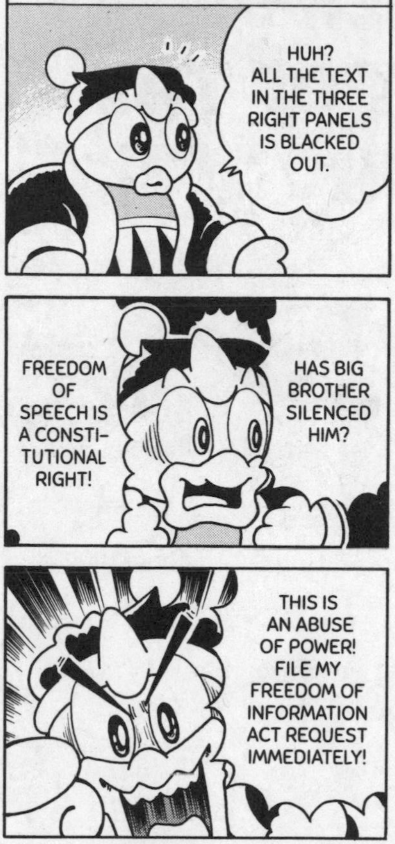
HUH? ALL THE TEXT IN THE THREE RIGHT PANELS IS BLACKED OUT.
HAS BIG BROTHER SILENCED HIM?
FREEDOM OF SPEECH IS A CONSTI-TUTIONAL RIGHT!
THIS IS AN ABUSE OF POWER! FILE MY FREEDOM OF INFORMATION ACT REQUEST IMMEDIATELY!

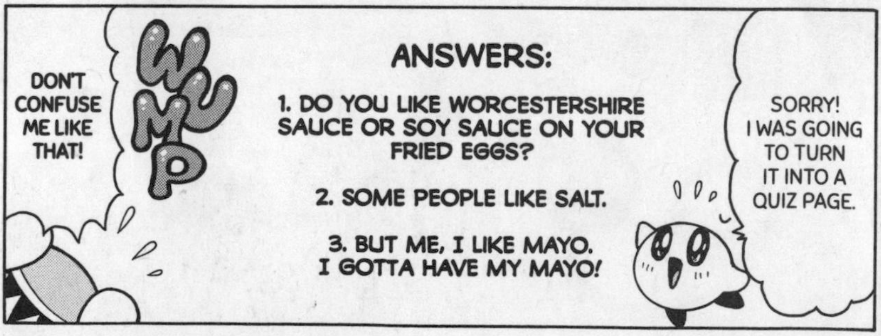
SORRY! I WAS GOING TO TURN IT INTO A QUIZ PAGE.
ANSWERS:
1. DO YOU LIKE WORCESTERSHIRE SAUCE OR SOY SAUCE ON YOUR FRIED EGGS?
2. SOME PEOPLE LIKE SALT.
3. BUT ME, I LIKE MAYO. I GOTTA HAVE MY MAYO!
WHUMP
DON'T CONFUSE ME LIKE THAT!

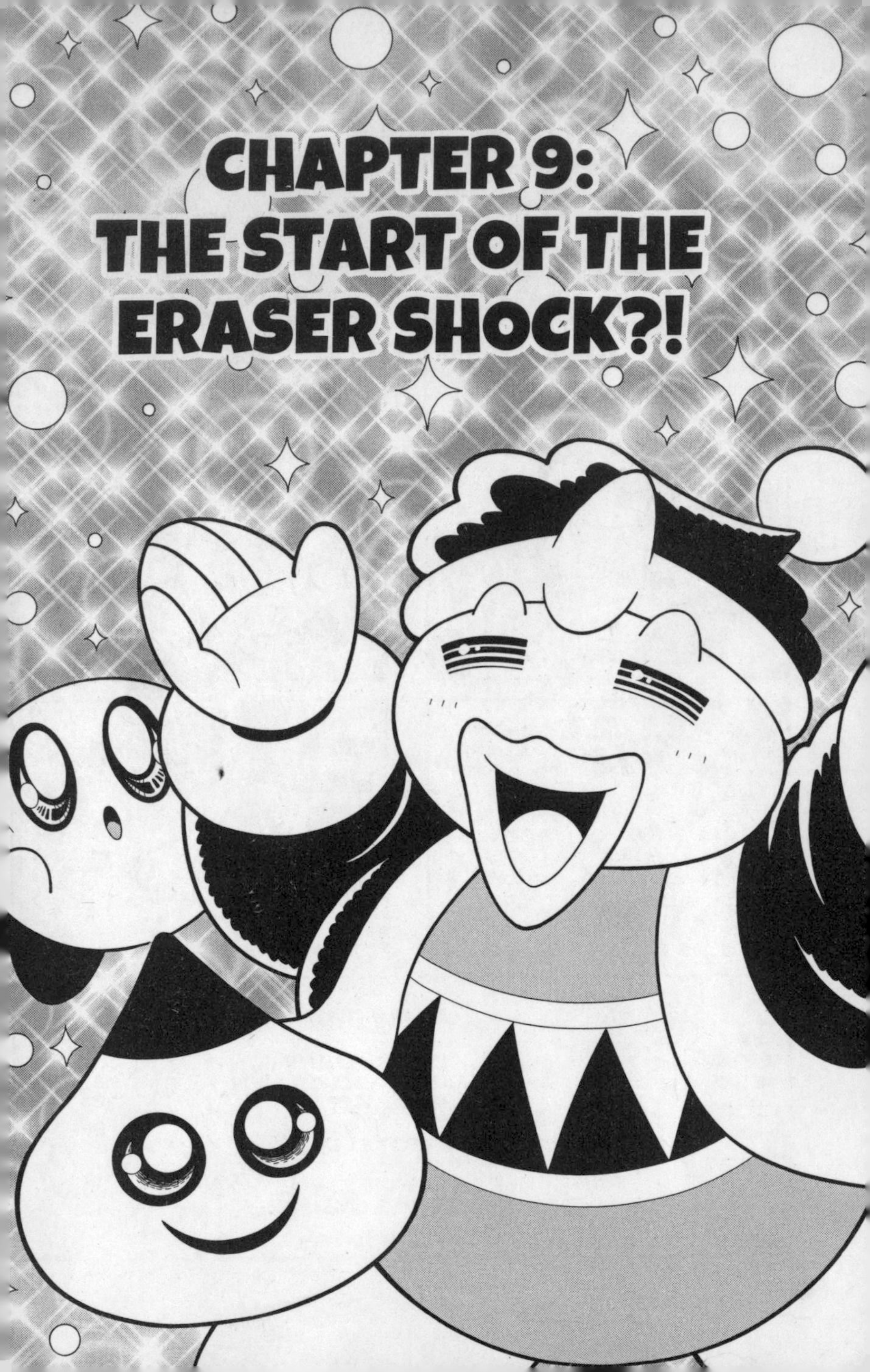
CHAPTER 9:
THE START OF THE
ERASER SHOCK?!

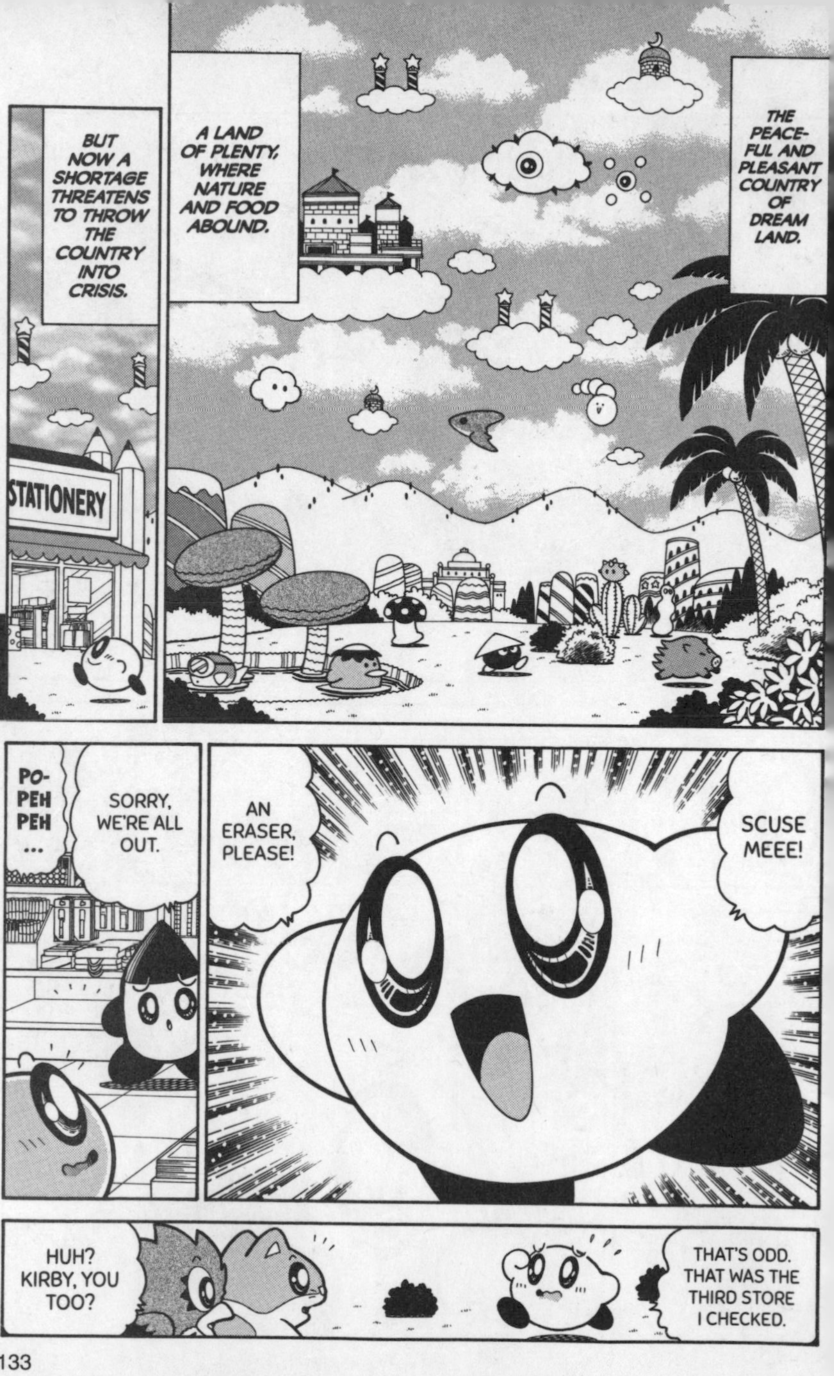
THE PEACEFUL AND PLEASANT COUNTRY OF DREAM LAND.
A LAND OF PLENTY, WHERE NATURE AND FOOD ABOUND.
BUT NOW A SHORTAGE THREATENS TO THROW THE COUNTRY INTO CRISIS.
STATIONERY
SCUSE MEEE!
AN ERASER, PLEASE!
SORRY, WE'RE ALL OUT.
PO-PEH PEH...
THAT'S ODD. THAT WAS THE THIRD STORE I CHECKED.
HUH? KIRBY, YOU TOO?

AUTHOR'S COMMENT

THIS STORY MIXED BUSINESS WITH PLEASURE(?). I MOBILIZED ALL MY STOCK MARKET KNOWLEDGE AND ANECDOTES. PERHAPS THE SINGULAR MASTERPIECE FROM THE *KIRBY* MANGA'S LATTER HALF?

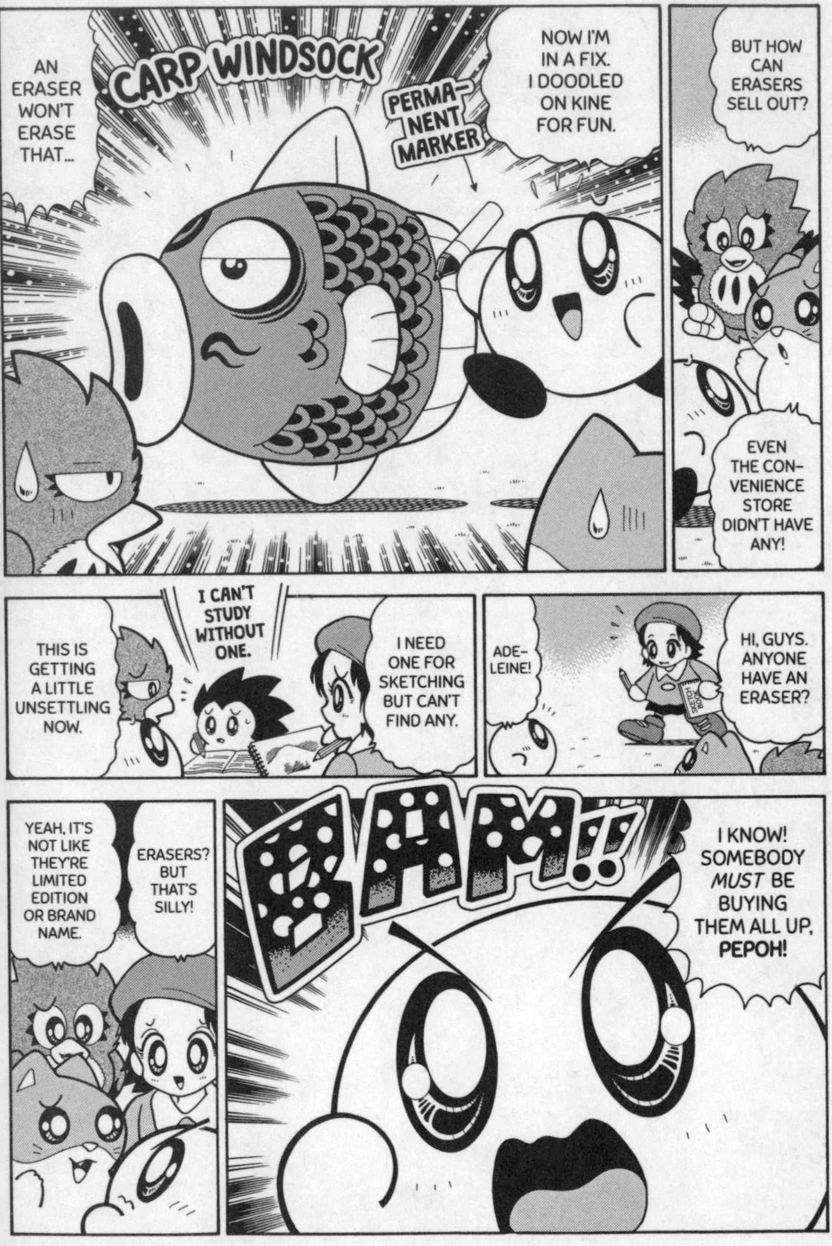

BUT HOW CAN ERASERS SELL OUT?
EVEN THE CONVENIENCE STORE DIDN'T HAVE ANY!
NOW I'M IN A FIX. I DOODLED ON KINE FOR FUN.
PERMANENT MARKER
CARP WINDSOCK
AN ERASER WON'T ERASE THAT...
HI, GUYS. ANYONE HAVE AN ERASER?
SKETCH BOOK
ADELEINE!
I NEED ONE FOR SKETCHING BUT CAN'T FIND ANY.
I CAN'T STUDY WITHOUT ONE.
THIS IS GETTING A LITTLE UNSETTLING NOW.
BAM!!
I KNOW! SOMEBODY *MUST* BE BUYING THEM ALL UP, **PEPOH!**
ERASERS? BUT THAT'S SILLY!
YEAH, IT'S NOT LIKE THEY'RE LIMITED EDITION OR BRAND NAME.

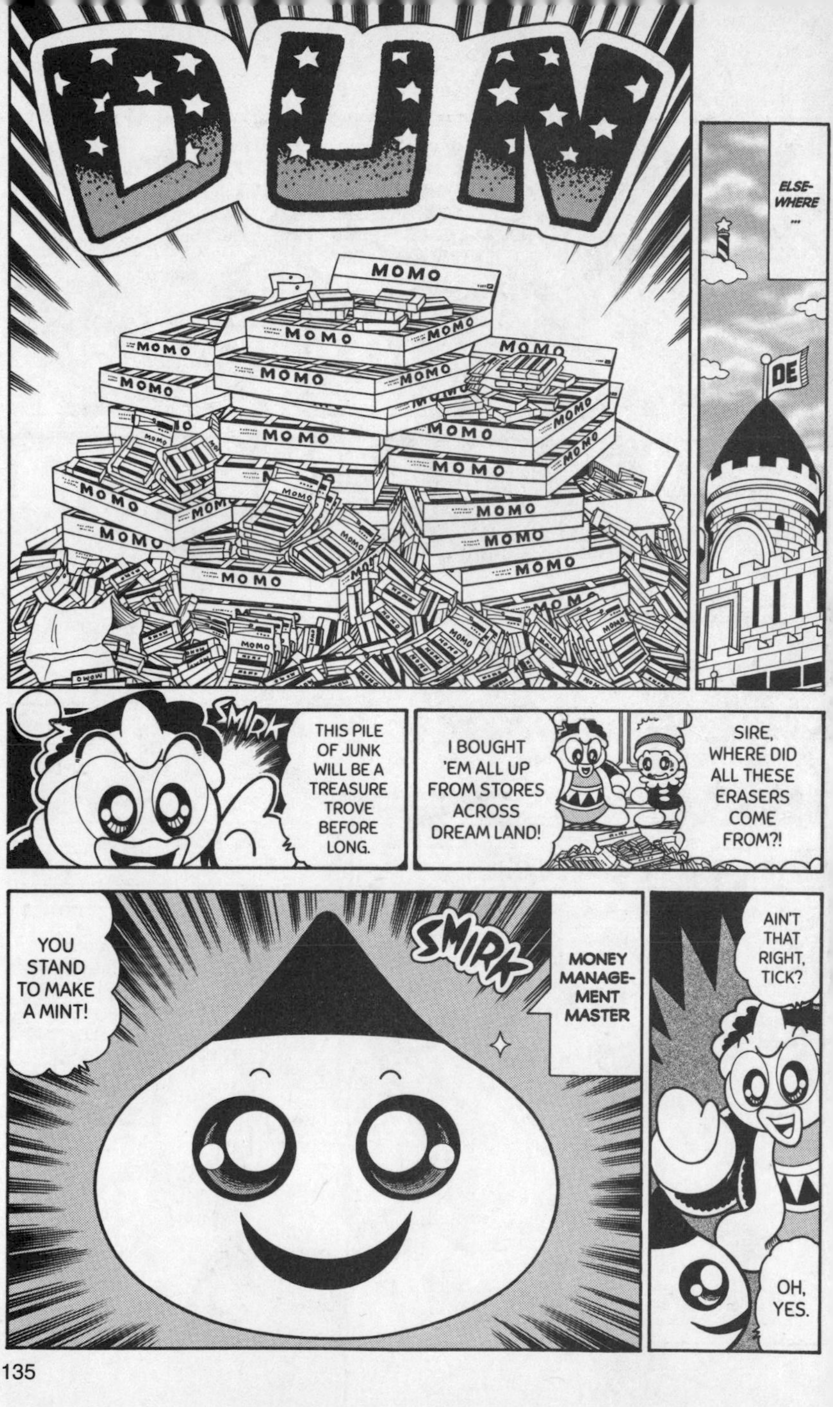
ELSE-WHERE...
DE
DUN
MOMO
SIRE, WHERE DID ALL THESE ERASERS COME FROM?!
I BOUGHT 'EM ALL UP FROM STORES ACROSS DREAM LAND!
SMIRK
THIS PILE OF JUNK WILL BE A TREASURE TROVE BEFORE LONG.
AIN'T THAT RIGHT, TICK?
OH, YES.
MONEY MANAGEMENT MASTER
SMIRK
YOU STAND TO MAKE A MINT!

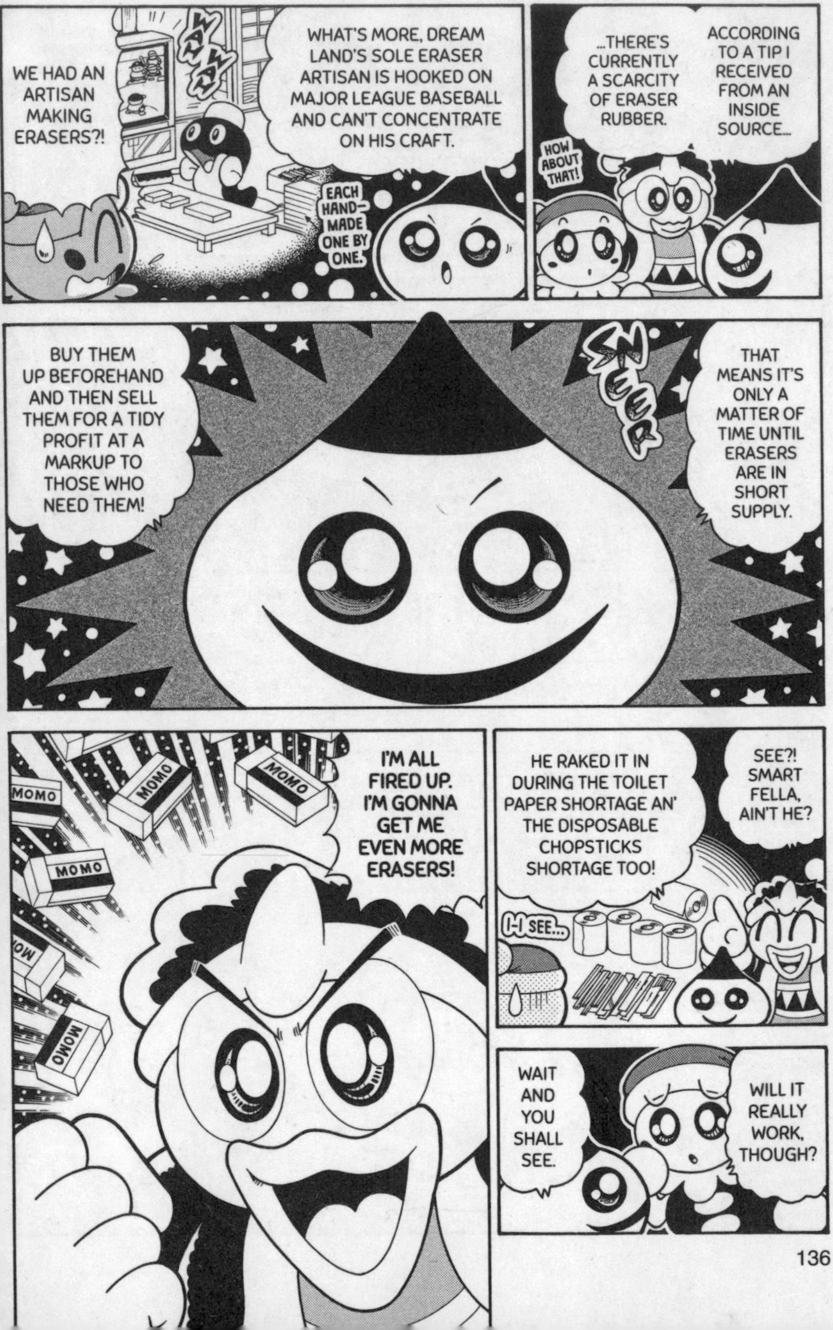
ACCORDING TO A TIP I RECEIVED FROM AN INSIDE SOURCE...
...THERE'S CURRENTLY A SCARCITY OF ERASER RUBBER.
HOW ABOUT THAT!
WHAT'S MORE, DREAM LAND'S SOLE ERASER ARTISAN IS HOOKED ON MAJOR LEAGUE BASEBALL AND CAN'T CONCENTRATE ON HIS CRAFT.
EACH HAND-MADE ONE BY ONE.
WE HAD AN ARTISAN MAKING ERASERS?!
THAT MEANS IT'S ONLY A MATTER OF TIME UNTIL ERASERS ARE IN SHORT SUPPLY.
SNEER
BUY THEM UP BEFOREHAND AND THEN SELL THEM FOR A TIDY PROFIT AT A MARKUP TO THOSE WHO NEED THEM!
SEE?! SMART FELLA, AIN'T HE?
HE RAKED IT IN DURING THE TOILET PAPER SHORTAGE AN' THE DISPOSABLE CHOPSTICKS SHORTAGE TOO!
I-I SEE...
WILL IT REALLY WORK, THOUGH?
WAIT AND YOU SHALL SEE.
I'M ALL FIRED UP. I'M GONNA GET ME EVEN MORE ERASERS!
MOMO
MOMO
MOMO
MOMO
MOMO
MOMO

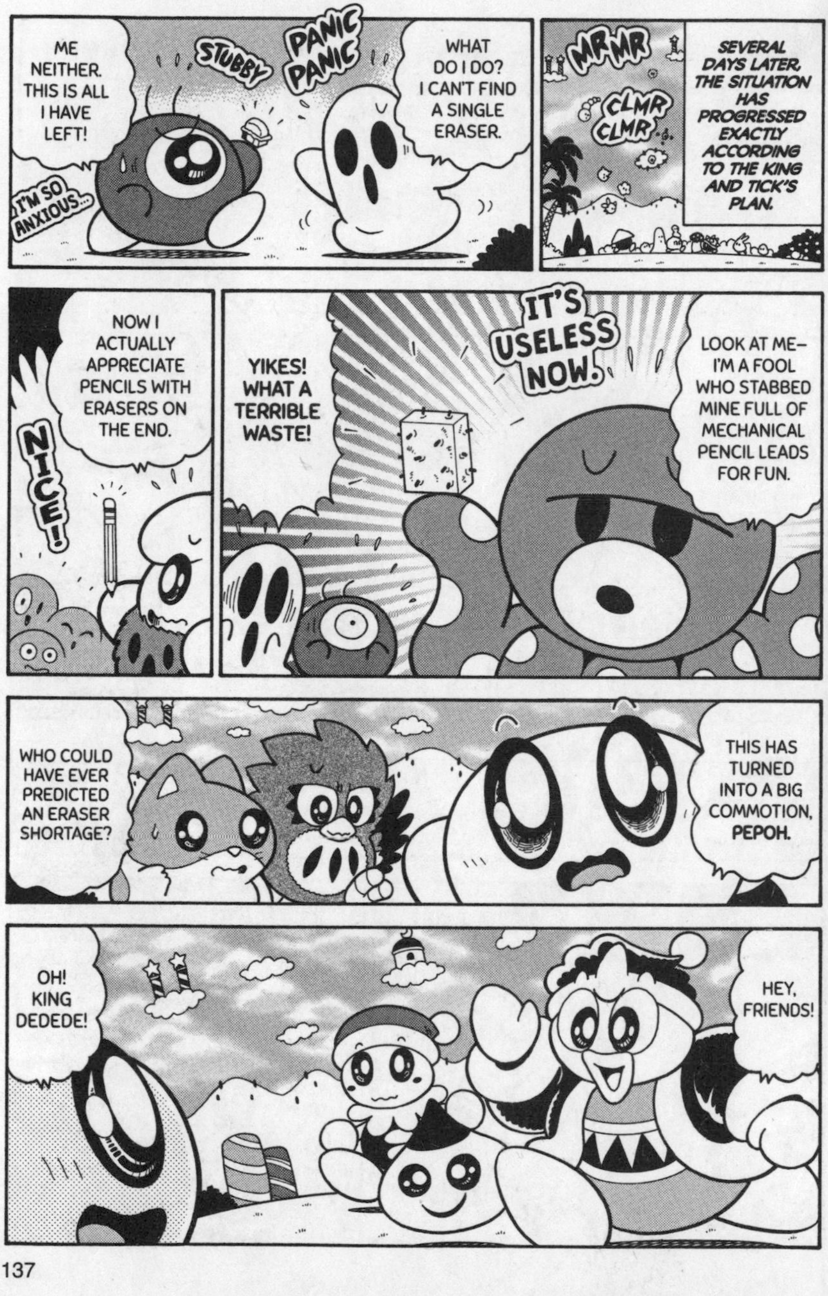

SEVERAL DAYS LATER, THE SITUATION HAS PROGRESSED EXACTLY ACCORDING TO THE KING AND TICK'S PLAN.
MRMR
CLMR CLMR
WHAT DO I DO? I CAN'T FIND A SINGLE ERASER.
PANIC PANIC
STUBBY
ME NEITHER. THIS IS ALL I HAVE LEFT!
I'M SO ANXIOUS...
LOOK AT ME—I'M A FOOL WHO STABBED MINE FULL OF MECHANICAL PENCIL LEADS FOR FUN.
IT'S USELESS NOW.
YIKES! WHAT A TERRIBLE WASTE!
NOW I ACTUALLY APPRECIATE PENCILS WITH ERASERS ON THE END.
NICE!
THIS HAS TURNED INTO A BIG COMMOTION, **PEPOH.**
WHO COULD HAVE EVER PREDICTED AN ERASER SHORTAGE?
HEY, FRIENDS!
OH! KING DEDEDE!

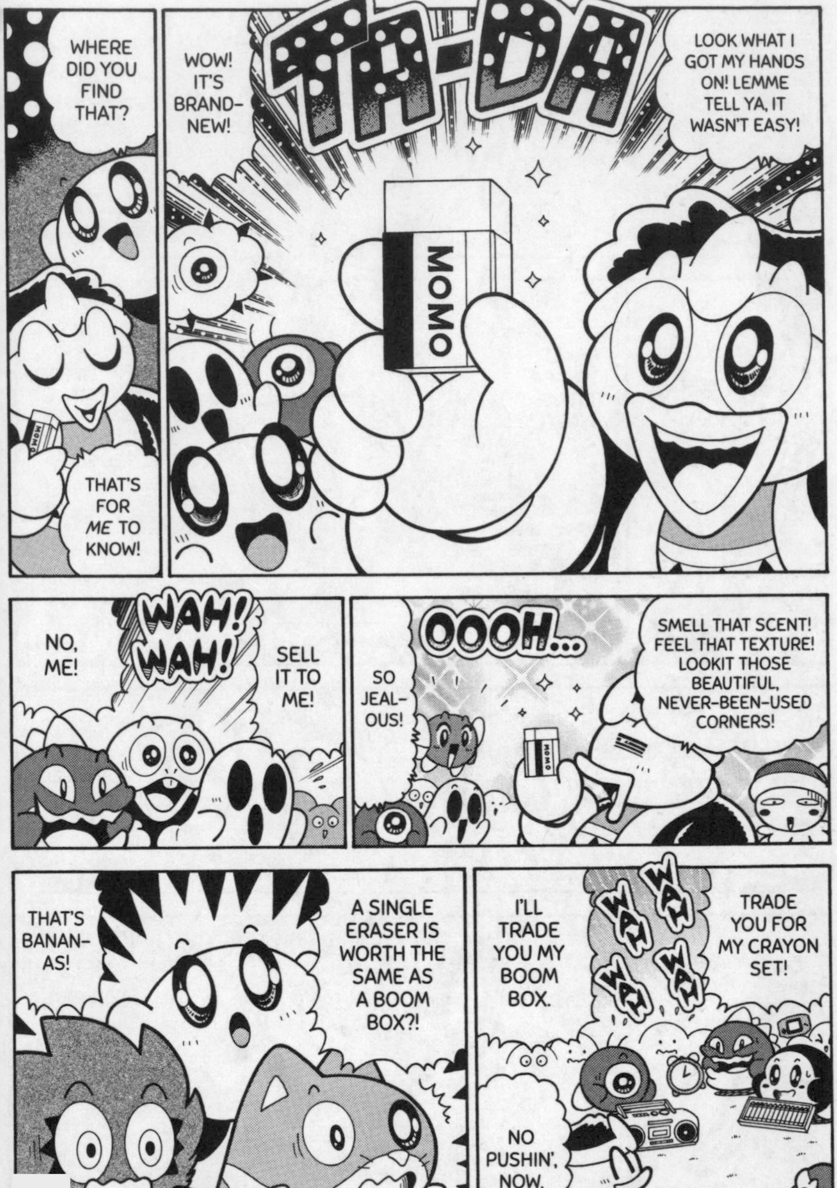
TA-DA
LOOK WHAT I GOT MY HANDS ON! LEMME TELL YA, IT WASN'T EASY!
MOMO
WOW! IT'S BRAND-NEW!
WHERE DID YOU FIND THAT?
THAT'S FOR *ME* TO KNOW!
SMELL THAT SCENT! FEEL THAT TEXTURE! LOOKIT THOSE BEAUTIFUL, NEVER-BEEN-USED CORNERS!
OOOH...
SO JEAL-OUS!
SELL IT TO ME!
WAH! WAH!
NO, ME!
TRADE YOU FOR MY CRAYON SET!
WAH WAH WAH WAH
I'LL TRADE YOU MY BOOM BOX.
NO PUSHIN', NOW.
A SINGLE ERASER IS WORTH THE SAME AS A BOOM BOX?!
THAT'S BANAN-AS!

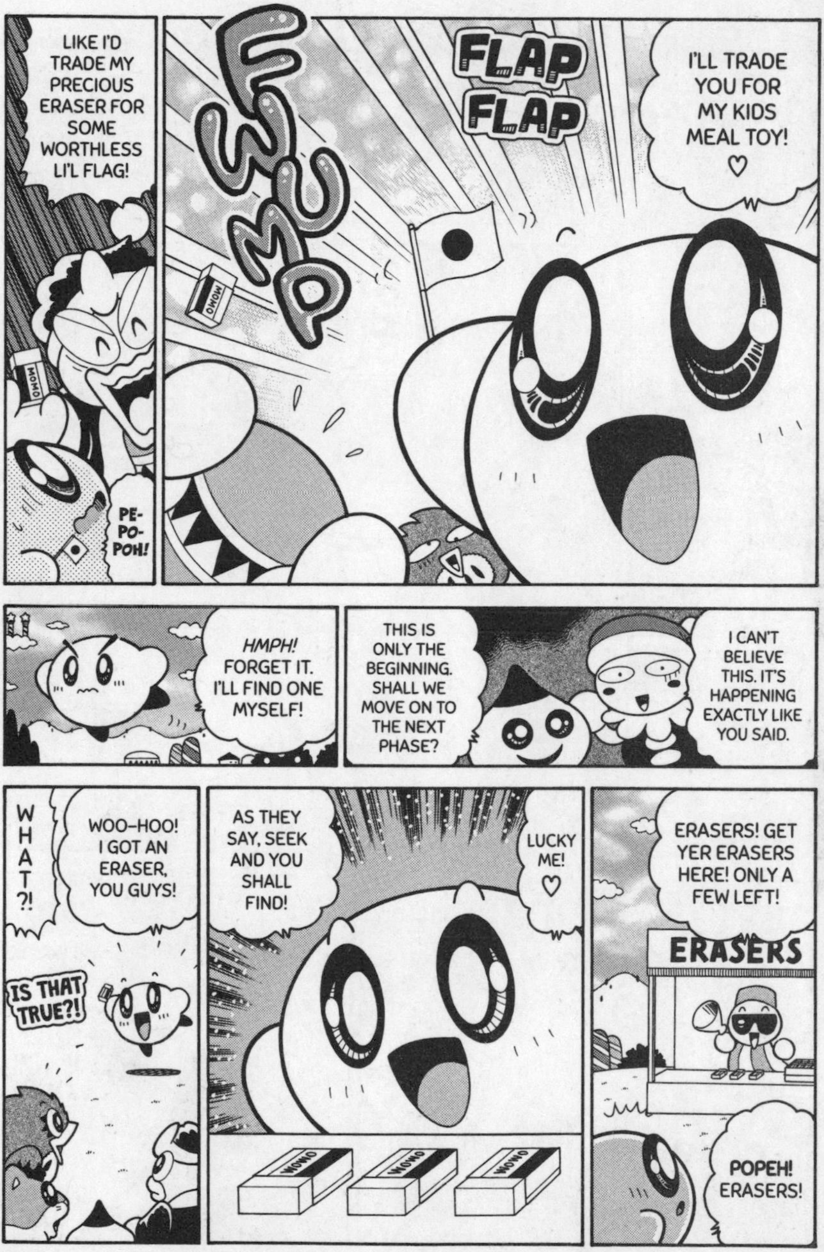
I'LL TRADE YOU FOR MY KIDS MEAL TOY! ♡
FLAP FLAP
FWUMP
LIKE I'D TRADE MY PRECIOUS ERASER FOR SOME WORTHLESS LI'L FLAG!
PE-PO-POH!
I CAN'T BELIEVE THIS. IT'S HAPPENING EXACTLY LIKE YOU SAID.
THIS IS ONLY THE BEGINNING. SHALL WE MOVE ON TO THE NEXT PHASE?
HMPH! FORGET IT. I'LL FIND ONE MYSELF!
ERASERS! GET YER ERASERS HERE! ONLY A FEW LEFT!
ERASERS
POPEH! ERASERS!
LUCKY ME! ♡
AS THEY SAY, SEEK AND YOU SHALL FIND!
WOO-HOO! I GOT AN ERASER, YOU GUYS!
WHAT?!
IS THAT TRUE?!

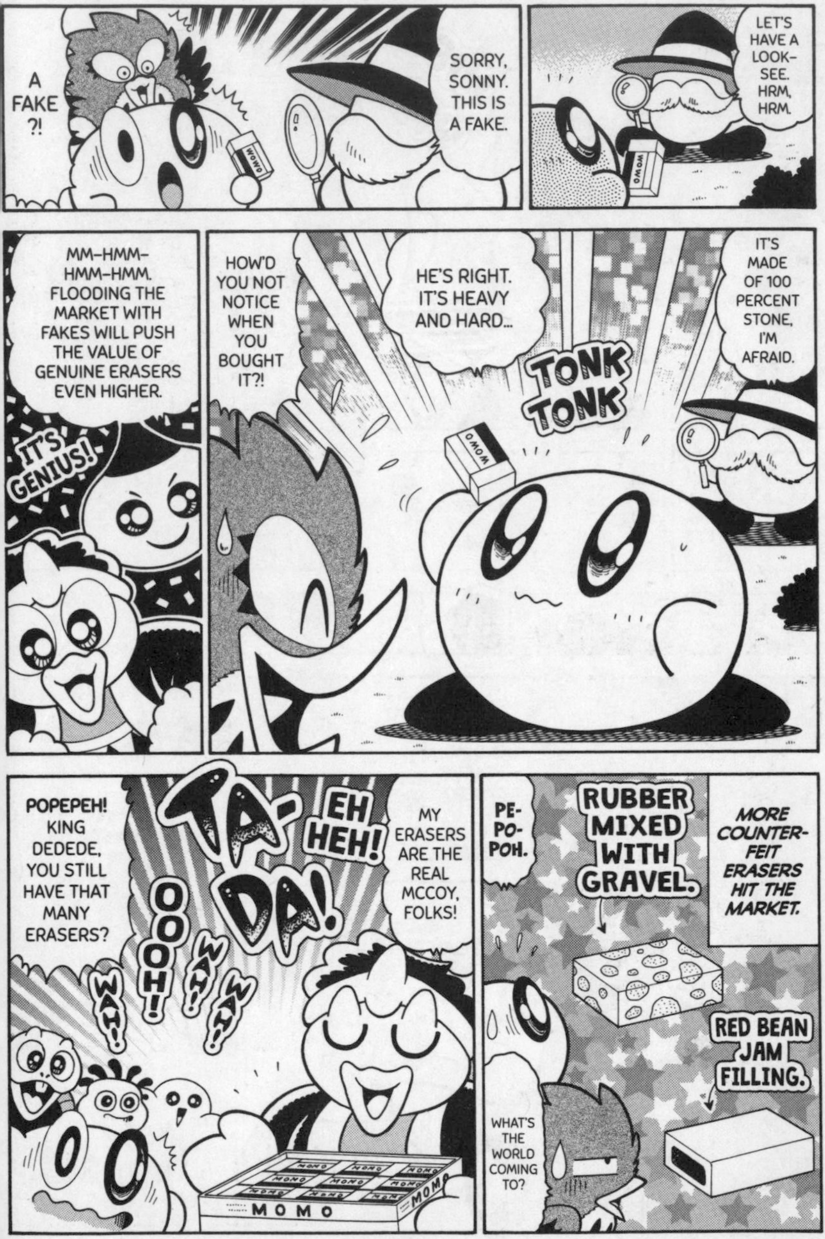
LET'S HAVE A LOOK-SEE. HRM, HRM.
WOWO
SORRY, SONNY. THIS IS A FAKE.
A FAKE ?!
IT'S MADE OF 100 PERCENT STONE, I'M AFRAID.
TONK TONK
HE'S RIGHT. IT'S HEAVY AND HARD...
HOW'D YOU NOT NOTICE WHEN YOU BOUGHT IT?!
MM-HMM-HMM-HMM. FLOODING THE MARKET WITH FAKES WILL PUSH THE VALUE OF GENUINE ERASERS EVEN HIGHER.
IT'S GENIUS!
MORE COUNTERFEIT ERASERS HIT THE MARKET.
RUBBER MIXED WITH GRAVEL.
PE-PO-POH.
RED BEAN JAM FILLING.
WHAT'S THE WORLD COMING TO?
MY ERASERS ARE THE REAL MCCOY, FOLKS!
EH HEH!
TA-DA!
POPEPEH! KING DEDEDE, YOU STILL HAVE THAT MANY ERASERS?
OOOOH!
WAH! WAH! WAH!
MOMO

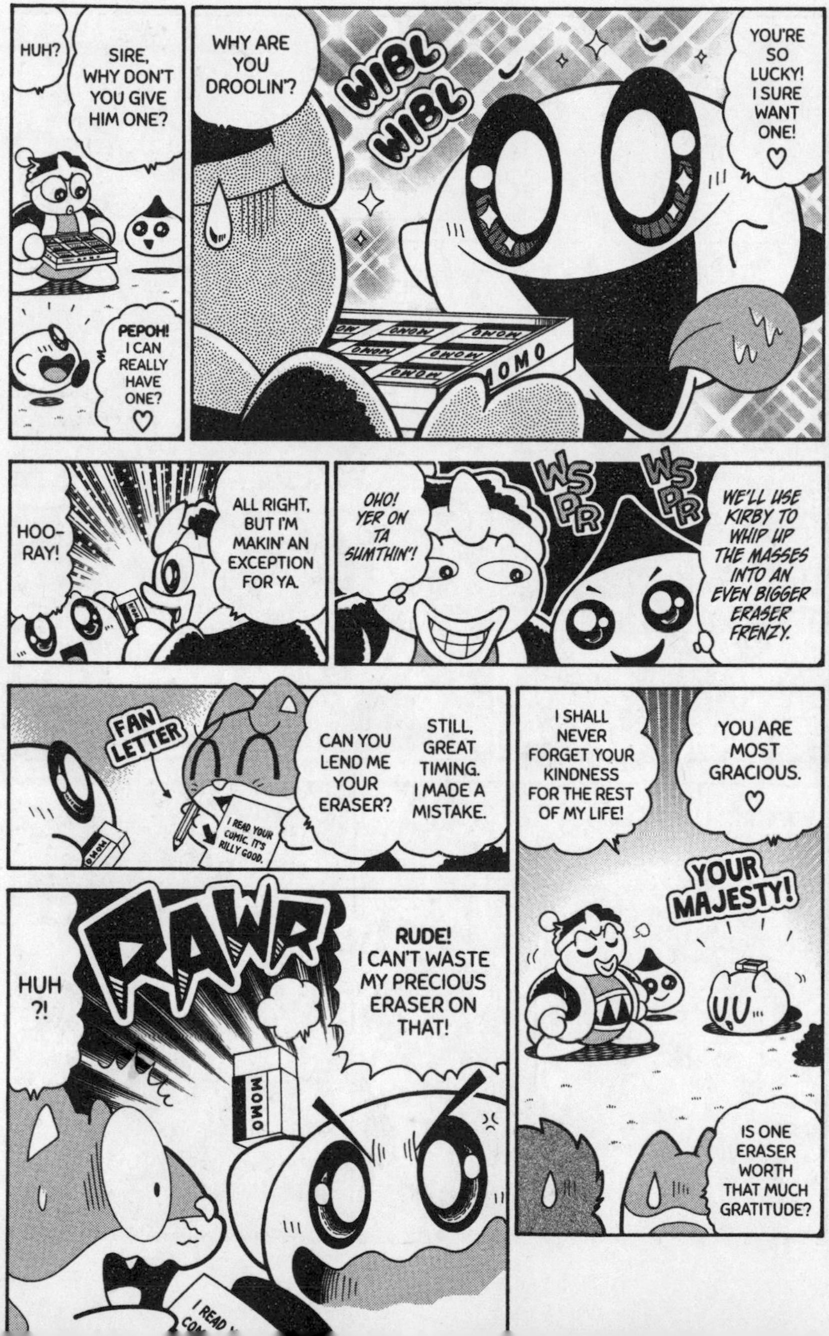
YOU'RE SO LUCKY! I SURE WANT ONE! ♡
WIBL WIBL
WHY ARE YOU DROOLIN'?
MOMO
SIRE, WHY DON'T YOU GIVE HIM ONE?
HUH?
PEPOH! I CAN REALLY HAVE ONE? ♡
WE'LL USE KIRBY TO WHIP UP THE MASSES INTO AN EVEN BIGGER ERASER FRENZY.
WSPR
WSPR
OHO! YER ON TA SUMTHIN'!
ALL RIGHT, BUT I'M MAKIN' AN EXCEPTION FOR YA.
HOO-RAY!
YOU ARE MOST GRACIOUS. ♡
I SHALL NEVER FORGET YOUR KINDNESS FOR THE REST OF MY LIFE!
YOUR MAJESTY!
IS ONE ERASER WORTH THAT MUCH GRATITUDE?
STILL, GREAT TIMING. I MADE A MISTAKE.
CAN YOU LEND ME YOUR ERASER?
FAN LETTER
I READ YOUR COMIC. IT'S RILLY GOOD.
RUDE! I CAN'T WASTE MY PRECIOUS ERASER ON THAT!
RAWR
HUH ?!
MOMO

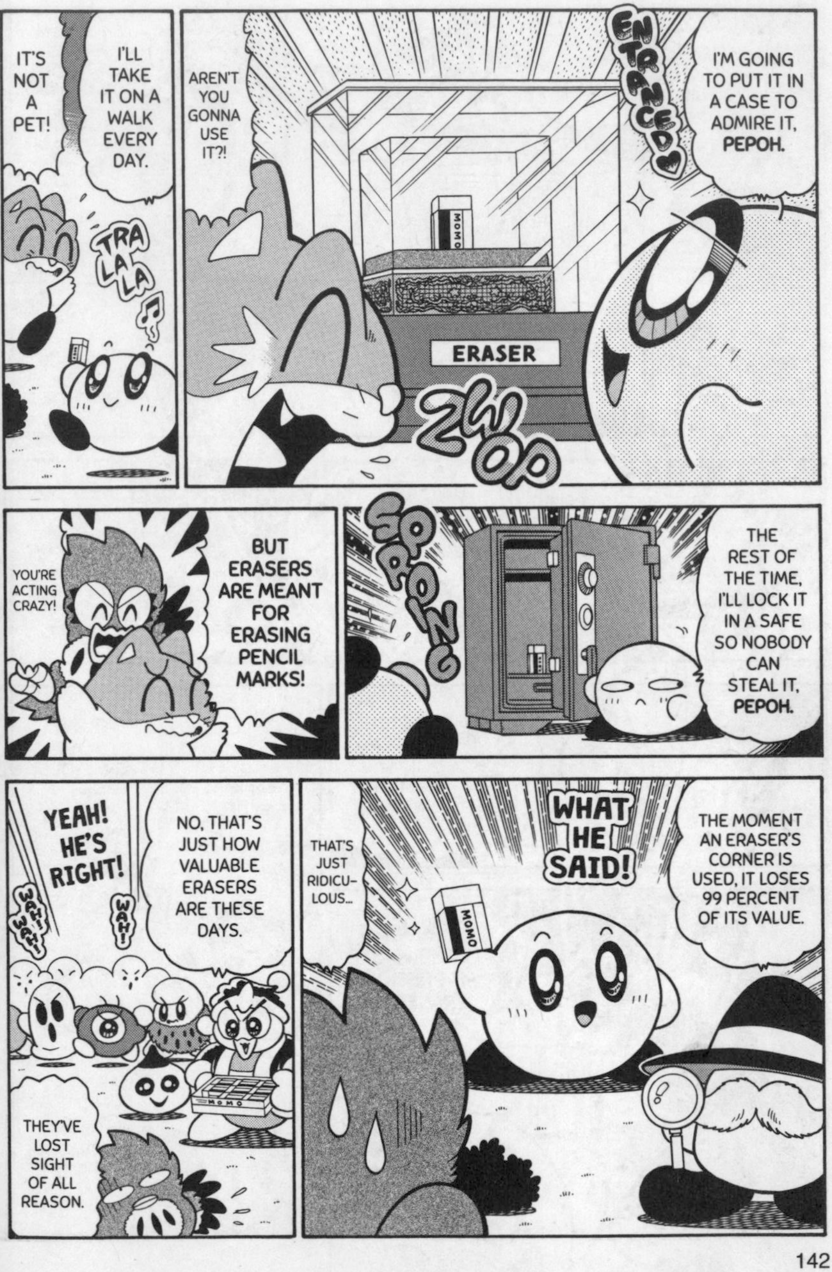
ENTRANCED♥
I'M GOING TO PUT IT IN A CASE TO ADMIRE IT, PEPOH.
AREN'T YOU GONNA USE IT?!
MOMO
ERASER
ZWOOP
I'LL TAKE IT ON A WALK EVERY DAY.
IT'S NOT A PET!
TRA LA LA ♪
THE REST OF THE TIME, I'LL LOCK IT IN A SAFE SO NOBODY CAN STEAL IT, PEPOH.
SPROING
BUT ERASERS ARE MEANT FOR ERASING PENCIL MARKS!
YOU'RE ACTING CRAZY!
THE MOMENT AN ERASER'S CORNER IS USED, IT LOSES 99 PERCENT OF ITS VALUE.
WHAT HE SAID!
THAT'S JUST RIDICU-LOUS...
MOMO
NO, THAT'S JUST HOW VALUABLE ERASERS ARE THESE DAYS.
YEAH! HE'S RIGHT!
WAH!
WAH! WAH!
MOMO
THEY'VE LOST SIGHT OF ALL REASON.

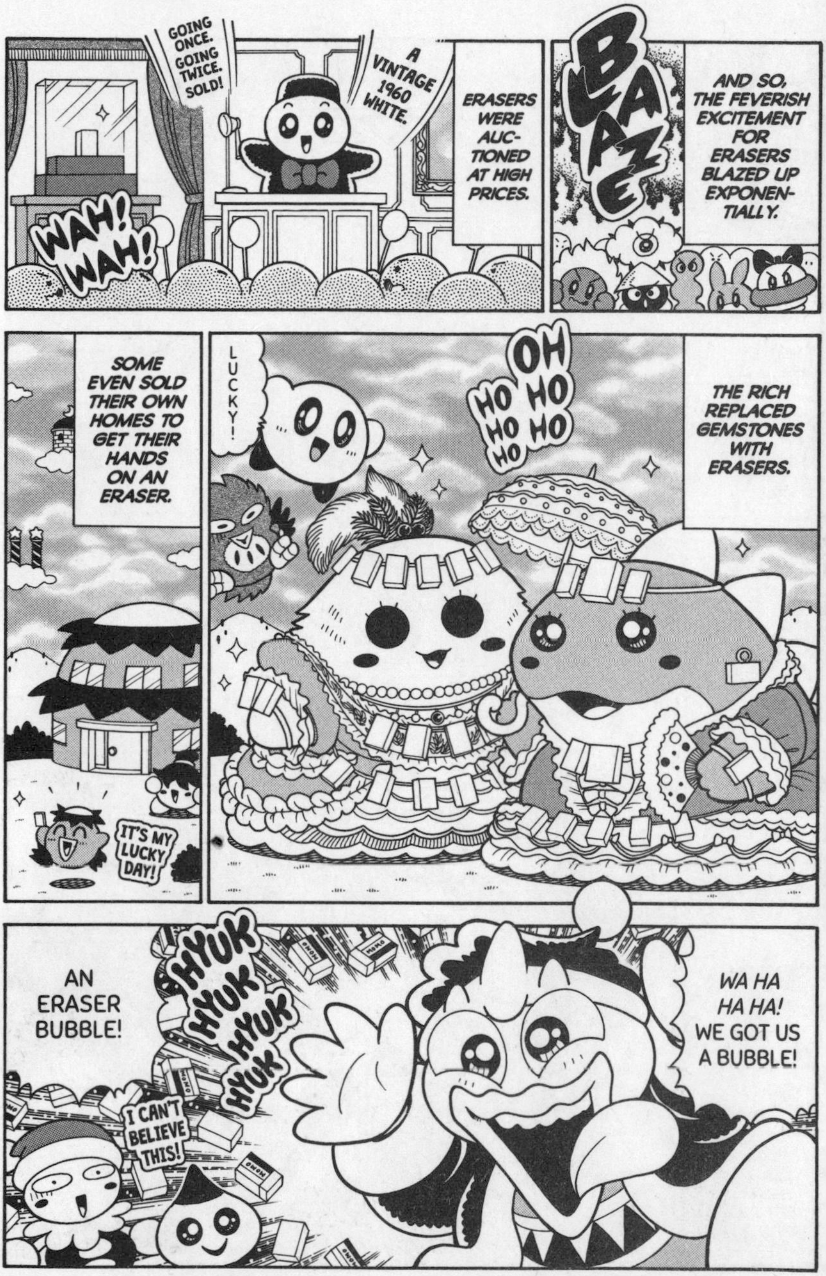
BLAZE
AND SO, THE FEVERISH EXCITEMENT FOR ERASERS BLAZED UP EXPONENTIALLY.
ERASERS WERE AUCTIONED AT HIGH PRICES.
A VINTAGE 1960 WHITE.
GOING ONCE. GOING TWICE. SOLD!
WAH! WAH!
THE RICH REPLACED GEMSTONES WITH ERASERS.
OH HO HO HO HO HO
LUCKY!
SOME EVEN SOLD THEIR OWN HOMES TO GET THEIR HANDS ON AN ERASER.
IT'S MY LUCKY DAY!
WA HA HA HA! WE GOT US A BUBBLE!
HYUK HYUK HYUK HYUK
I CAN'T BELIEVE THIS!
AN ERASER BUBBLE!

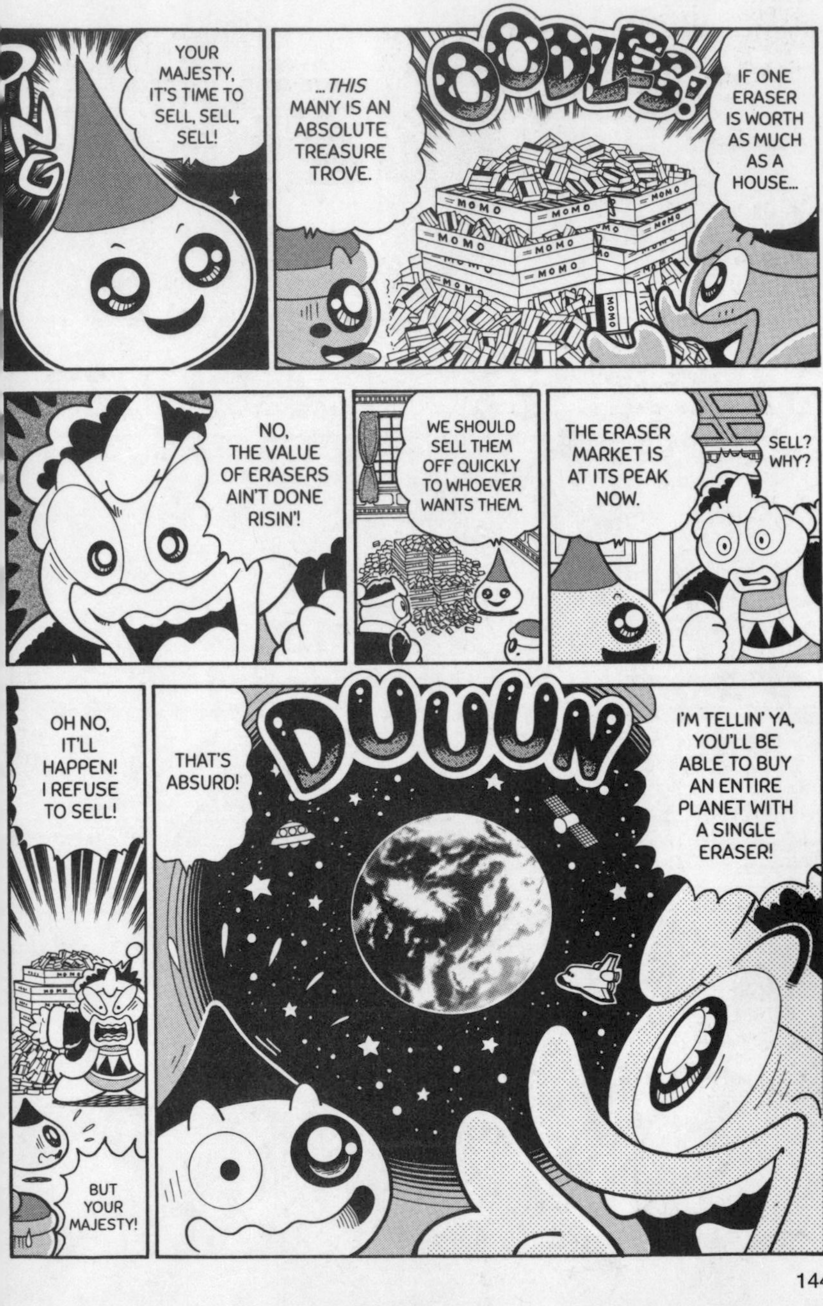
OODLES!
IF ONE ERASER IS WORTH AS MUCH AS A HOUSE...
...*THIS* MANY IS AN ABSOLUTE TREASURE TROVE.
MOMO
YOUR MAJESTY, IT'S TIME TO SELL, SELL, SELL!
SELL? WHY?
THE ERASER MARKET IS AT ITS PEAK NOW.
WE SHOULD SELL THEM OFF QUICKLY TO WHOEVER WANTS THEM.
NO, THE VALUE OF ERASERS AIN'T DONE RISIN'!
I'M TELLIN' YA, YOU'LL BE ABLE TO BUY AN ENTIRE PLANET WITH A SINGLE ERASER!
DUUUN
THAT'S ABSURD!
OH NO, IT'LL HAPPEN! I REFUSE TO SELL!
BUT YOUR MAJESTY!

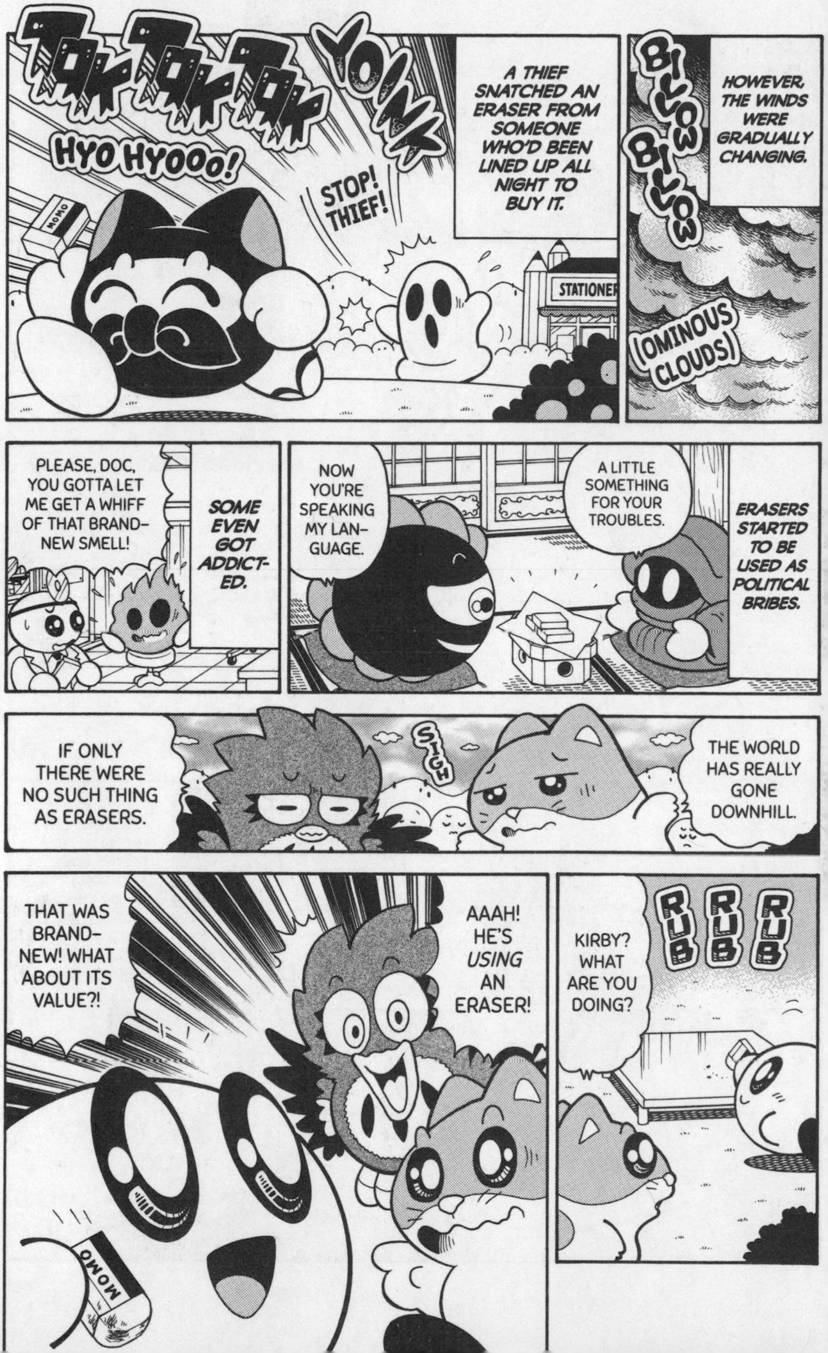
HOWEVER, THE WINDS WERE GRADUALLY CHANGING.
BIYOW BIYOW
(OMINOUS CLOUDS)
A THIEF SNATCHED AN ERASER FROM SOMEONE WHO'D BEEN LINED UP ALL NIGHT TO BUY IT.
YOINK
STOP! THIEF!
TOK TOK TOK
HYO HYOOO!
STATIONER
MOMO
ERASERS STARTED TO BE USED AS POLITICAL BRIBES.
A LITTLE SOMETHING FOR YOUR TROUBLES.
NOW YOU'RE SPEAKING MY LAN-GUAGE.
SOME EVEN GOT ADDICT-ED.
PLEASE, DOC, YOU GOTTA LET ME GET A WHIFF OF THAT BRAND-NEW SMELL!
THE WORLD HAS REALLY GONE DOWNHILL.
SIGH
IF ONLY THERE WERE NO SUCH THING AS ERASERS.
RUB RUB RUB
KIRBY? WHAT ARE YOU DOING?
AAAH! HE'S *USING* AN ERASER!
THAT WAS BRAND-NEW! WHAT ABOUT ITS VALUE?!
MOMO

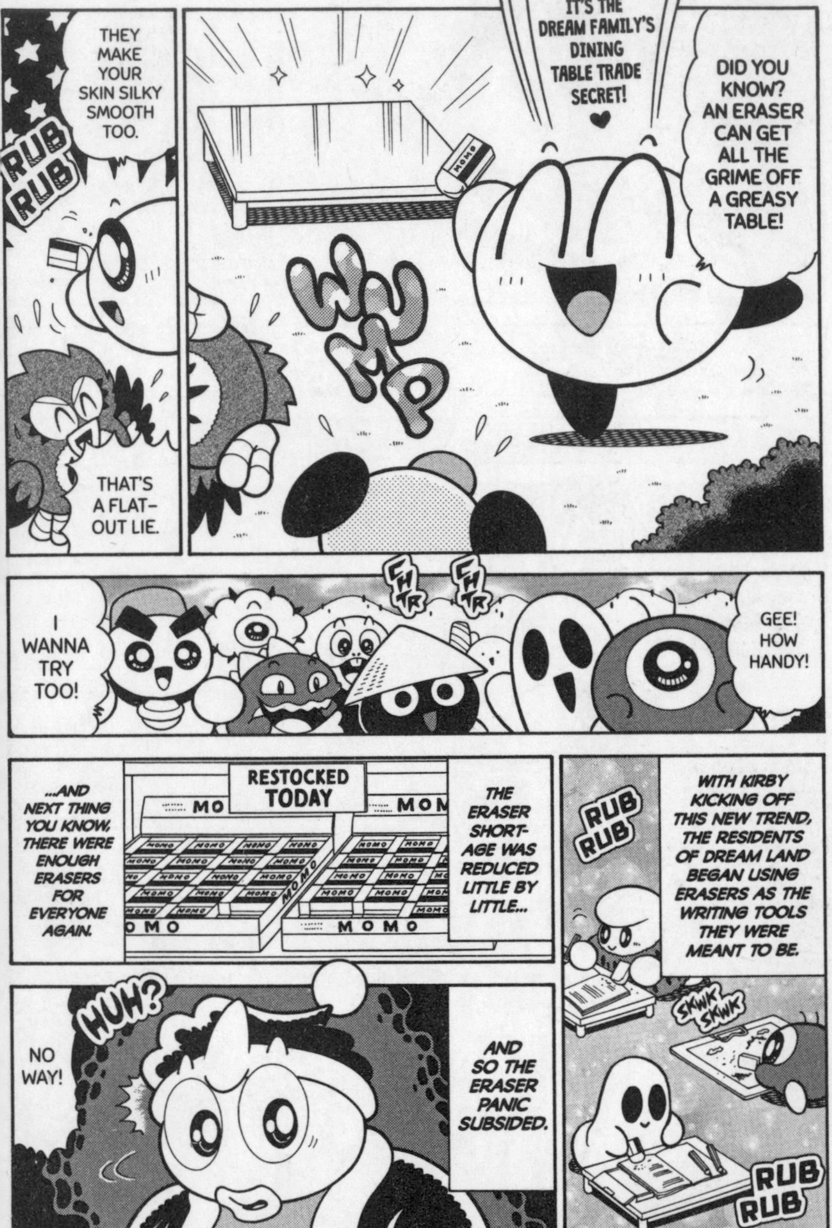
DID YOU KNOW? AN ERASER CAN GET ALL THE GRIME OFF A GREASY TABLE!
IT'S THE DREAM FAMILY'S DINING TABLE TRADE SECRET! ♥
WHUMP
RUB RUB
THEY MAKE YOUR SKIN SILKY SMOOTH TOO.
THAT'S A FLAT-OUT LIE.
GEE! HOW HANDY!
CHTR
CHTR
I WANNA TRY TOO!
WITH KIRBY KICKING OFF THIS NEW TREND, THE RESIDENTS OF DREAM LAND BEGAN USING ERASERS AS THE WRITING TOOLS THEY WERE MEANT TO BE.
RUB RUB
SKWIK SKWIK
RUB RUB
THE ERASER SHORTAGE WAS REDUCED LITTLE BY LITTLE...
RESTOCKED TODAY
...AND NEXT THING YOU KNOW, THERE WERE ENOUGH ERASERS FOR EVERYONE AGAIN.
AND SO THE ERASER PANIC SUBSIDED.
HUH?
NO WAY!

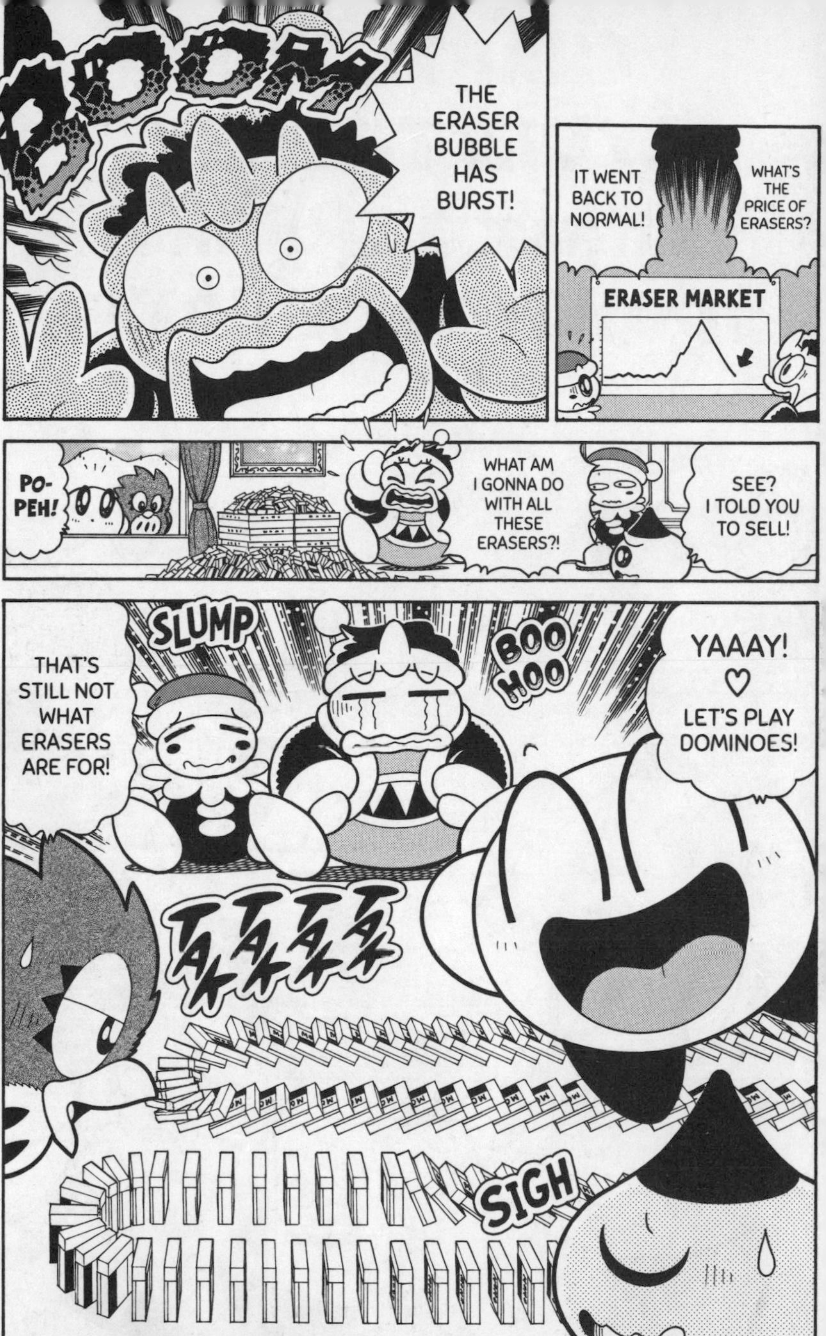
WHAT'S THE PRICE OF ERASERS?
IT WENT BACK TO NORMAL!
ERASER MARKET
THE ERASER BUBBLE HAS BURST!
BOOM
SEE? I TOLD YOU TO SELL!
WHAT AM I GONNA DO WITH ALL THESE ERASERS?!
PO-PEH!
YAAAY! ♡ LET'S PLAY DOMINOES!
BOO HOO
SLUMP
THAT'S STILL NOT WHAT ERASERS ARE FOR!
TAK TAK TAK TAK
SIGH

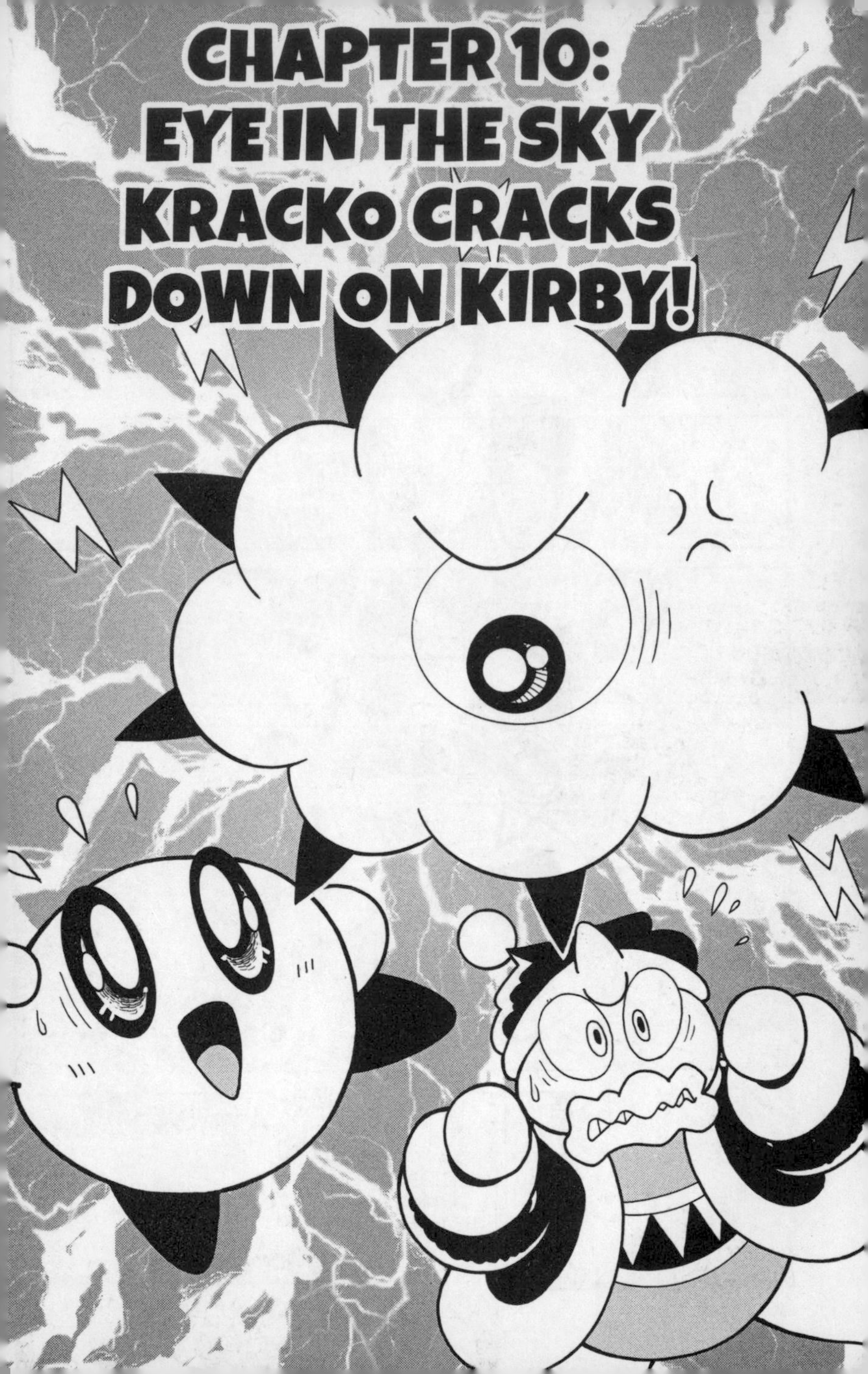
CHAPTER 10:
EYE IN THE SKY
KRACKO CRACKS
DOWN ON KIRBY!

AUTHOR'S COMMENT

THE FIRST DRAFT OF THIS STORY WAS ACTUALLY THE FIRST THING I CAME UP WITH WHEN WE FLOATED THE IDEA OF A *CORO CORO ANIKI* MAGAZINE *KIRBY* COMEBACK COMIC. IT'S A TRIAL-AND-ERROR PROCESS AS I DESPERATELY TRY TO REMEMBER HOW I USED TO DO IT.

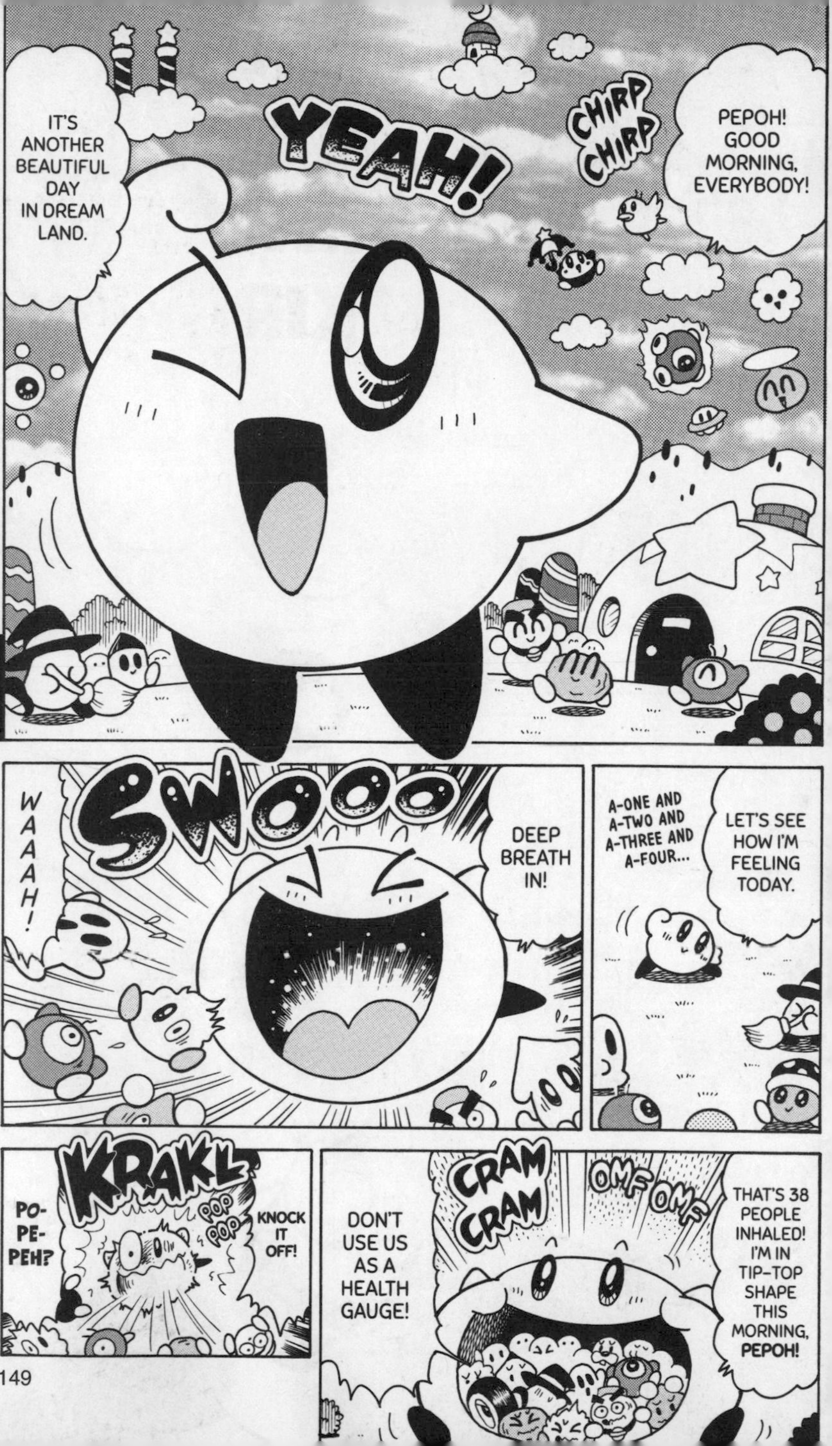
PEPOH! GOOD MORNING, EVERYBODY!
CHIRP CHIRP
YEAH!
IT'S ANOTHER BEAUTIFUL DAY IN DREAM LAND.
LET'S SEE HOW I'M FEELING TODAY.
A-ONE AND A-TWO AND A-THREE AND A-FOUR...
DEEP BREATH IN!
SWOOO
WAAAAH!
THAT'S 38 PEOPLE INHALED! I'M IN TIP-TOP SHAPE THIS MORNING, **PEPOH!**
OMF OMF
CRAM CRAM
DON'T USE US AS A HEALTH GAUGE!
KNOCK IT OFF!
POP POP
KRAKL
PO-PE-PEH?

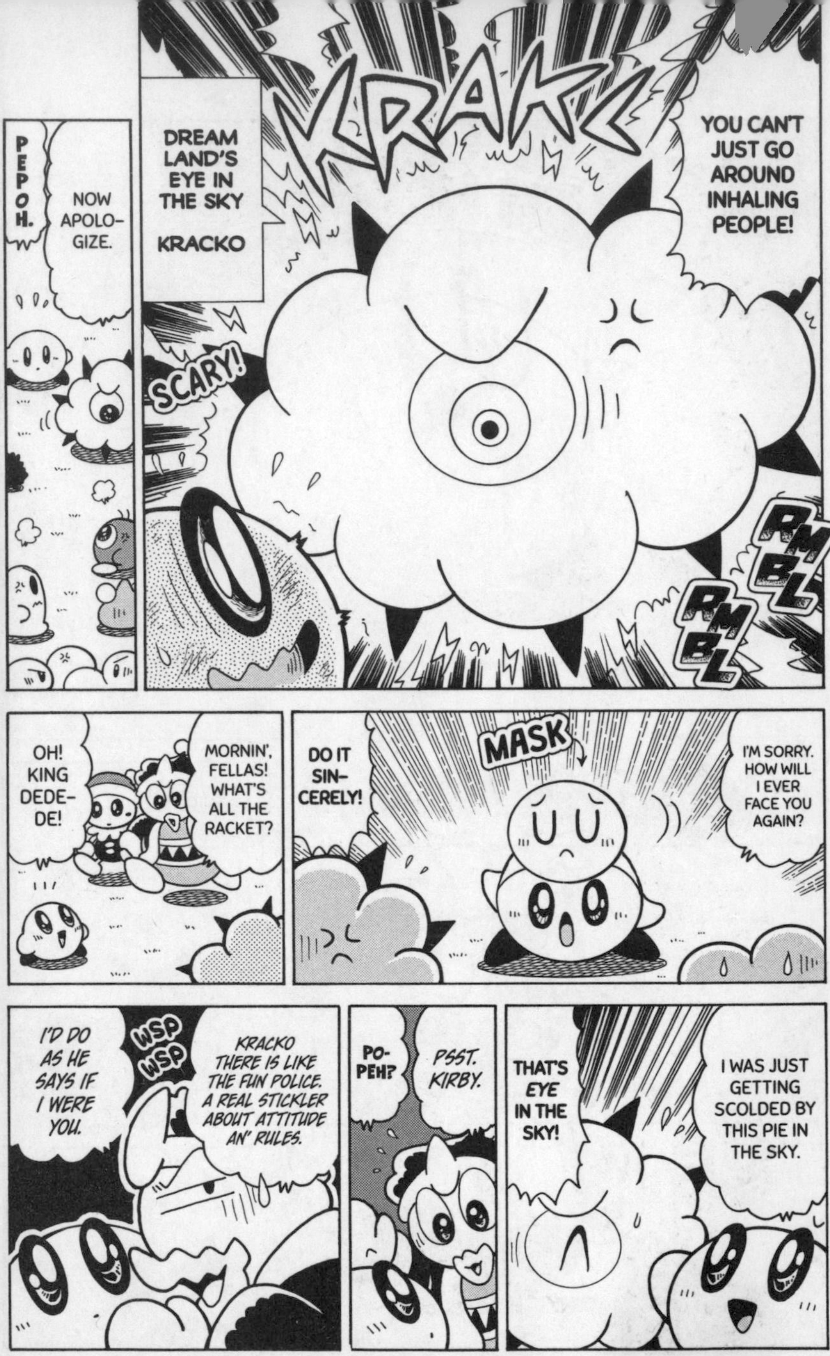
KRAK!
YOU CAN'T JUST GO AROUND INHALING PEOPLE!
DREAM LAND'S EYE IN THE SKY
KRACKO
SCARY!
RMBL
RMBL
NOW APOLO-GIZE.
PEPOH.
MASK
I'M SORRY. HOW WILL I EVER FACE YOU AGAIN?
DO IT SIN-CERELY!
MORNIN', FELLAS! WHAT'S ALL THE RACKET?
OH! KING DEDE-DE!
I WAS JUST GETTING SCOLDED BY THIS PIE IN THE SKY.
THAT'S EYE IN THE SKY!
PSST. KIRBY.
PO-PEH?
KRACKO THERE IS LIKE THE FUN POLICE. A REAL STICKLER ABOUT ATTITUDE AN' RULES.
WSP WSP
I'D DO AS HE SAYS IF I WERE YOU.

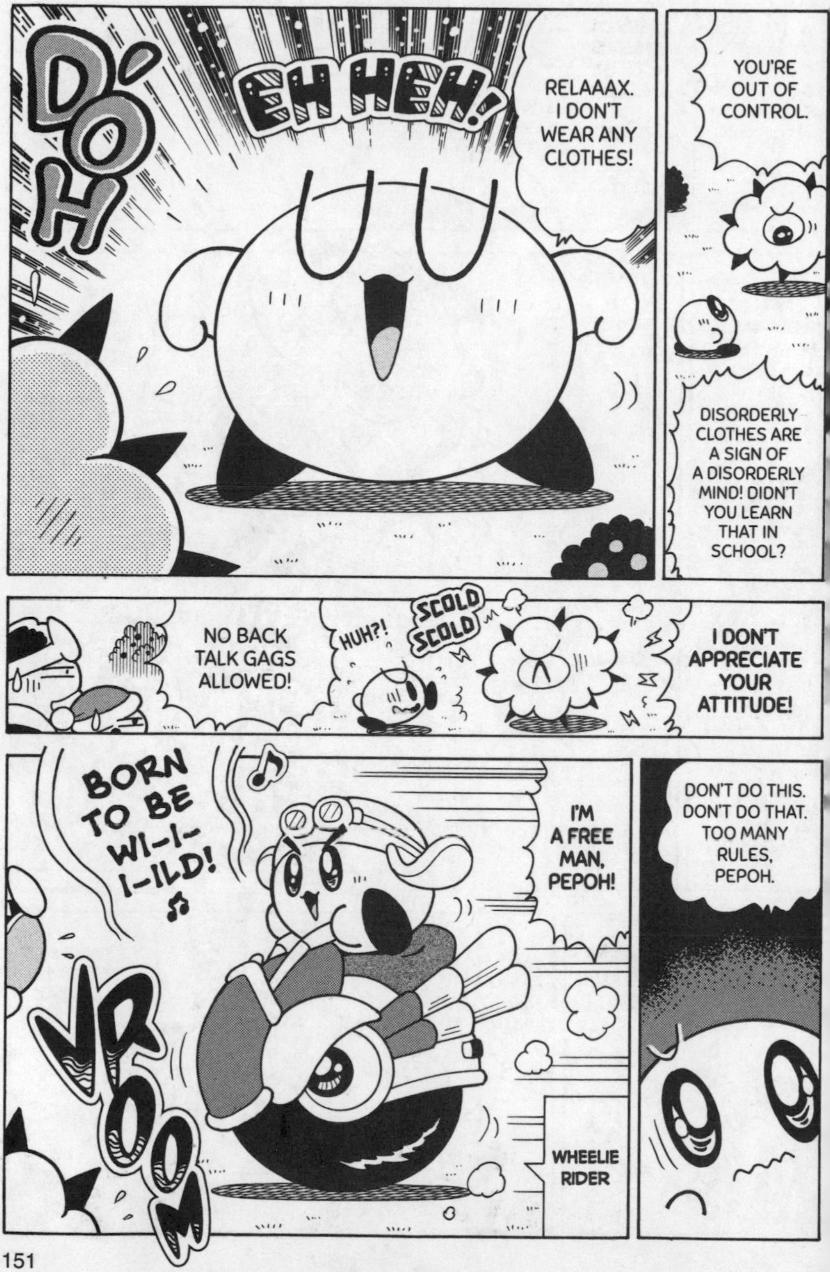
YOU'RE OUT OF CONTROL.
DISORDERLY CLOTHES ARE A SIGN OF A DISORDERLY MIND! DIDN'T YOU LEARN THAT IN SCHOOL?
RELAAAX. I DON'T WEAR ANY CLOTHES!
EH HEH!
D'OH
I DON'T APPRECIATE YOUR ATTITUDE!
SCOLD SCOLD
HUH?!
NO BACK TALK GAGS ALLOWED!
DON'T DO THIS. DON'T DO THAT. TOO MANY RULES, PEPOH.
I'M A FREE MAN, PEPOH!
BORN TO BE WI-I-I-ILD! ♫
WHEELIE RIDER
VROOOM

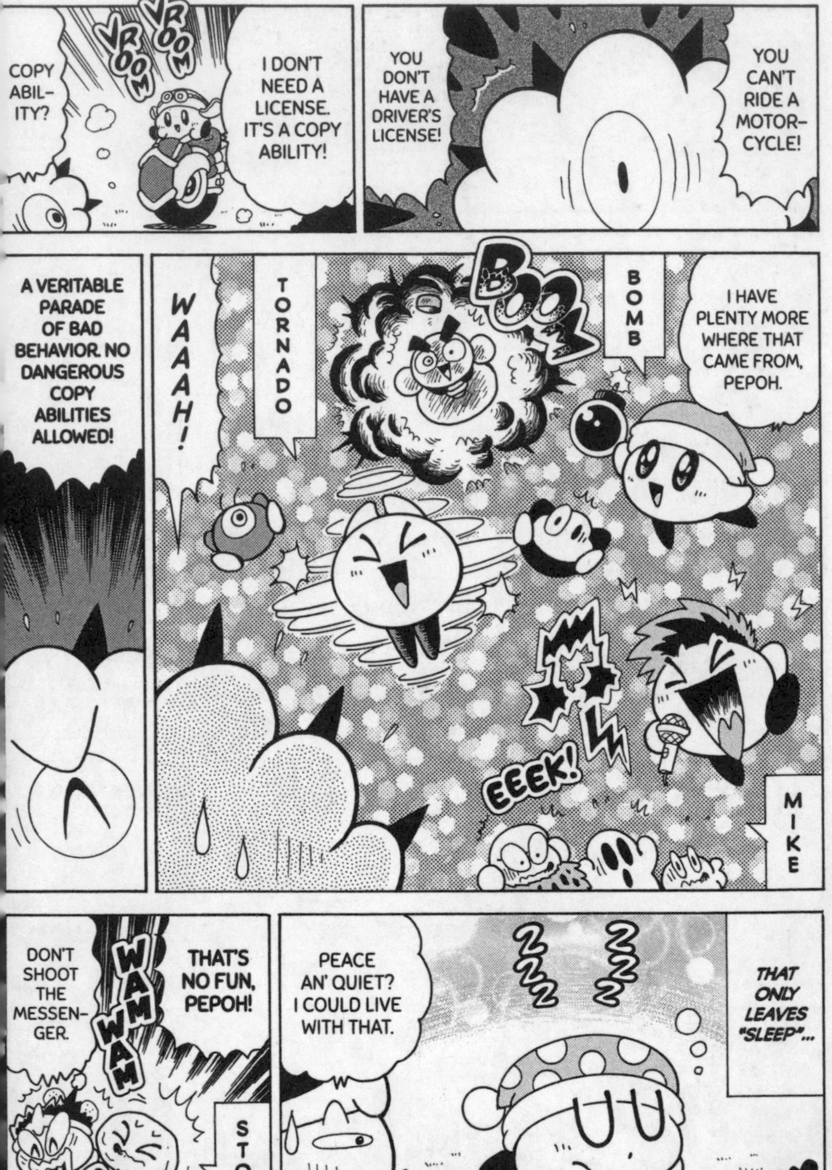
YOU CAN'T RIDE A MOTOR-CYCLE!
YOU DON'T HAVE A DRIVER'S LICENSE!
VROOM VROOM
I DON'T NEED A LICENSE. IT'S A COPY ABILITY!
COPY ABIL-ITY?
I HAVE PLENTY MORE WHERE THAT CAME FROM, PEPOH.
BOMB
BOOM
TORNADO
WAAAAH!
EEEK!
MIKE
A VERITABLE PARADE OF BAD BEHAVIOR. NO DANGEROUS COPY ABILITIES ALLOWED!
THAT ONLY LEAVES "SLEEP"...
ZZZ
ZZZ
PEACE AN' QUIET? I COULD LIVE WITH THAT.
THAT'S NO FUN, PEPOH!
WAM WAM
DON'T SHOOT THE MESSEN-GER.
STONE

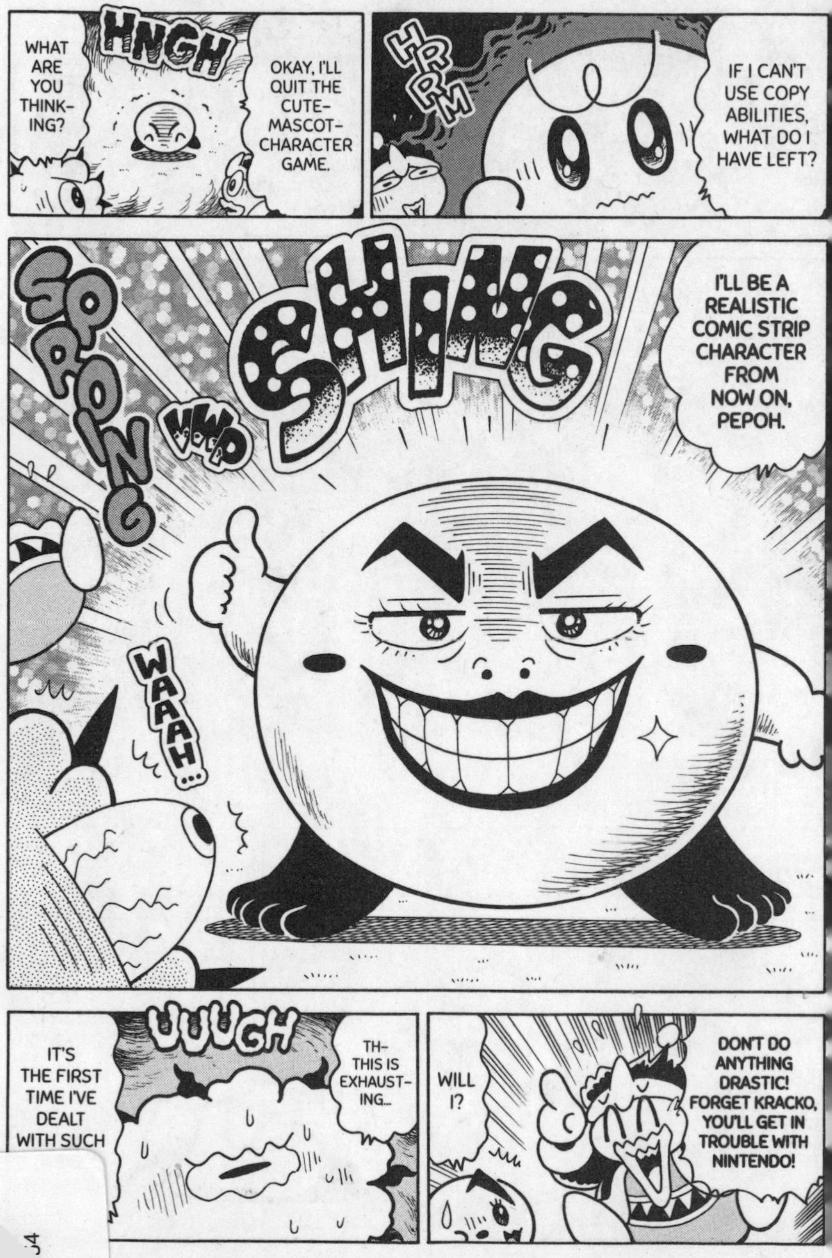
IF I CAN'T USE COPY ABILITIES, WHAT DO I HAVE LEFT?
HRRM
OKAY, I'LL QUIT THE CUTE-MASCOT-CHARACTER GAME.
HNGH
WHAT ARE YOU THINKING?
I'LL BE A REALISTIC COMIC STRIP CHARACTER FROM NOW ON, PEPOH.
SHING
SPROING
WAAAH...
DON'T DO ANYTHING DRASTIC! FORGET KRACKO, YOU'LL GET IN TROUBLE WITH NINTENDO!
WILL I?
TH- THIS IS EXHAUSTING...
UUUGH
IT'S THE FIRST TIME I'VE DEALT WITH SUCH

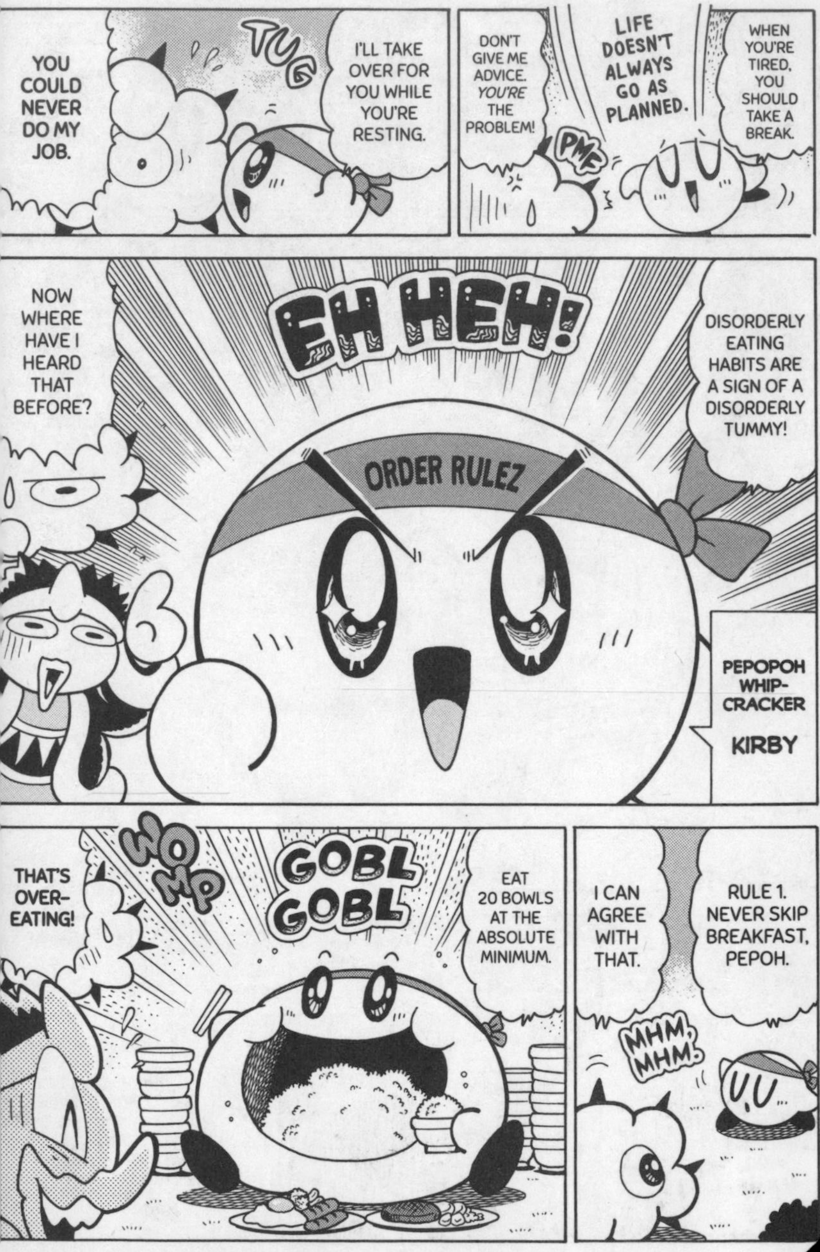
WHEN YOU'RE TIRED, YOU SHOULD TAKE A BREAK.
LIFE DOESN'T ALWAYS GO AS PLANNED.
DON'T GIVE ME ADVICE. *YOU'RE* THE PROBLEM!
PMF
TUG
I'LL TAKE OVER FOR YOU WHILE YOU'RE RESTING.
YOU COULD NEVER DO MY JOB.
EH HEH!
DISORDERLY EATING HABITS ARE A SIGN OF A DISORDERLY TUMMY!
ORDER RULEZ
PEPOPOH WHIP-CRACKER
KIRBY
NOW WHERE HAVE I HEARD THAT BEFORE?
RULE 1. NEVER SKIP BREAKFAST, PEPOH.
I CAN AGREE WITH THAT.
MHM, MHM.
EAT 20 BOWLS AT THE ABSOLUTE MINIMUM.
GOBL GOBL
WOMP
THAT'S OVER-EATING!

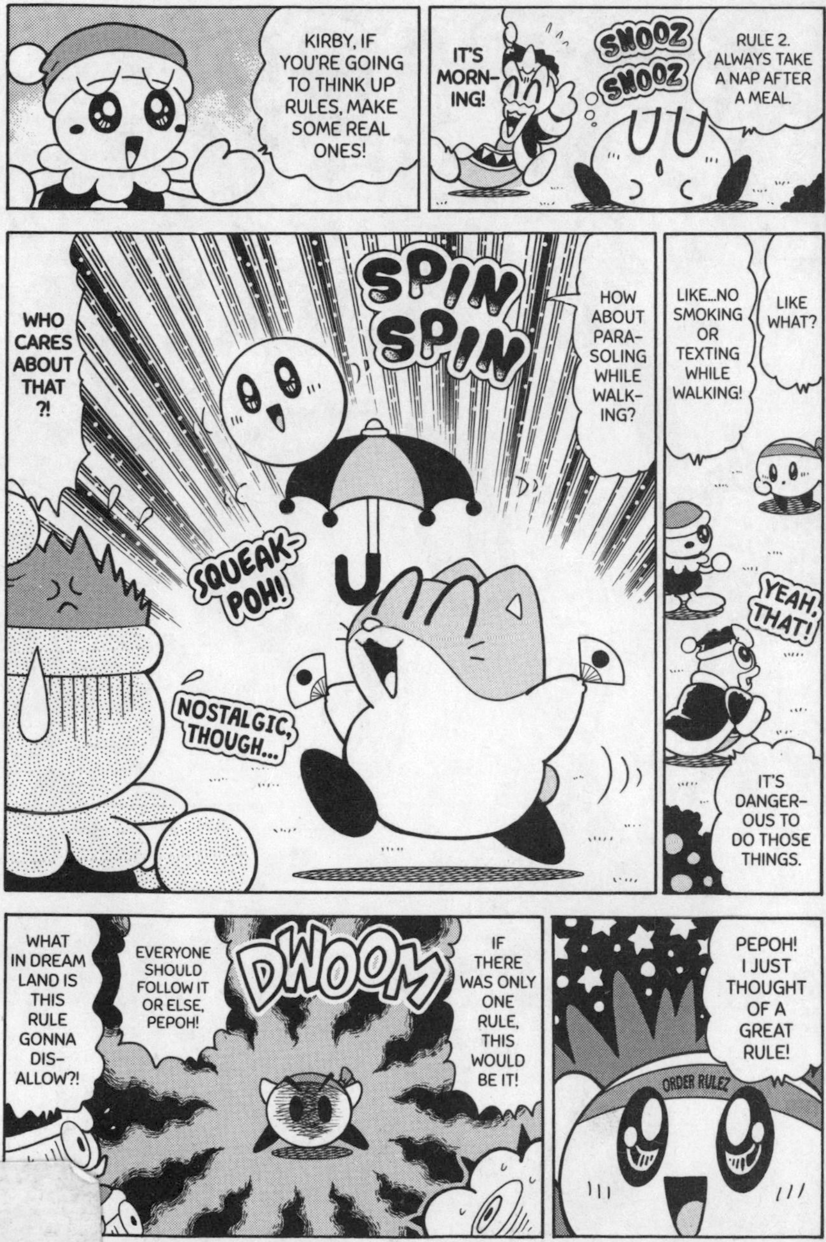
RULE 2. ALWAYS TAKE A NAP AFTER A MEAL.
SNOOZ SNOOZ
IT'S MORNING!
KIRBY, IF YOU'RE GOING TO THINK UP RULES, MAKE SOME REAL ONES!
LIKE WHAT?
LIKE...NO SMOKING OR TEXTING WHILE WALKING!
YEAH, THAT!
IT'S DANGEROUS TO DO THOSE THINGS.
HOW ABOUT PARASOLING WHILE WALKING?
SPIN SPIN
WHO CARES ABOUT THAT?!
SQUEAK-POH!
NOSTALGIC, THOUGH...
PEPOH! I JUST THOUGHT OF A GREAT RULE!
ORDER RULEZ
IF THERE WAS ONLY ONE RULE, THIS WOULD BE IT!
DWOOM
EVERYONE SHOULD FOLLOW IT OR ELSE, PEPOH!
WHAT IN DREAM LAND IS THIS RULE GONNA DISALLOW?!

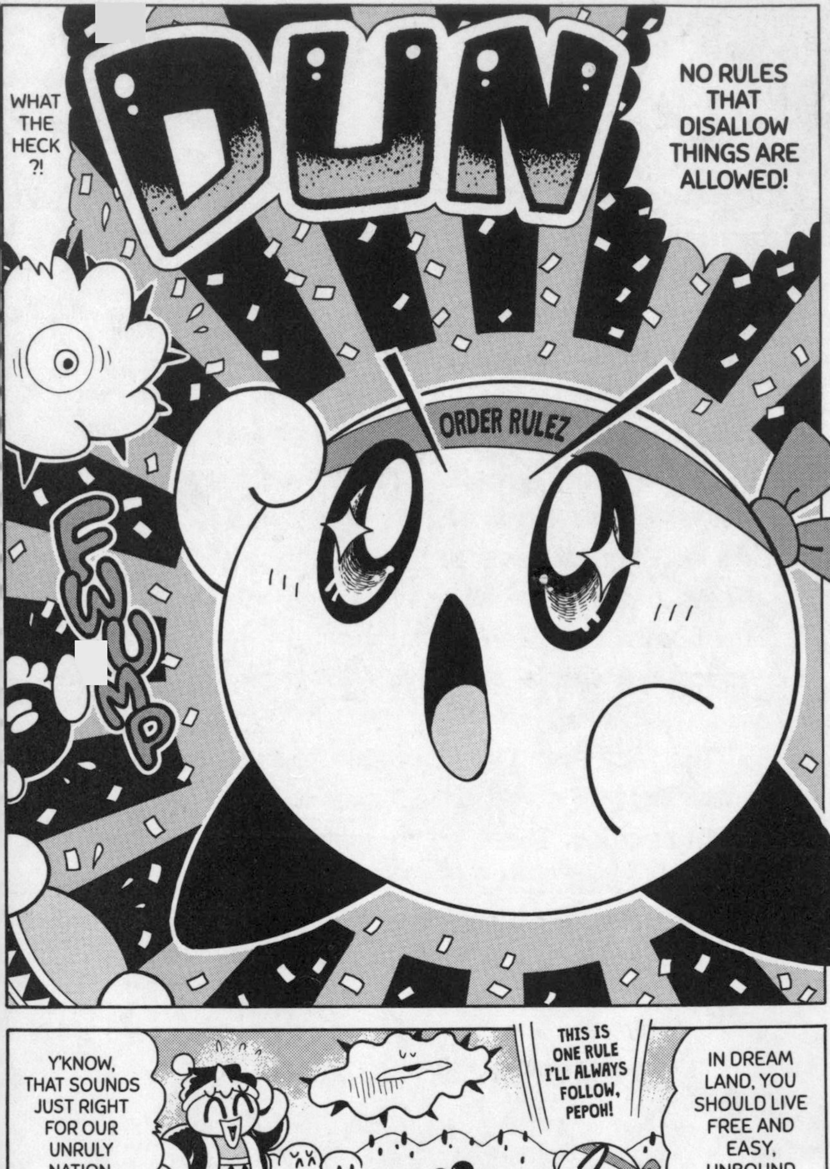
NO RULES THAT DISALLOW THINGS ARE ALLOWED!
DUN
WHAT THE HECK ?!
ORDER RULEZ
FWUMP
IN DREAM LAND, YOU SHOULD LIVE FREE AND EASY, UNBOUND BY RULES!
THIS IS ONE RULE I'LL ALWAYS FOLLOW, PEPOH!
Y'KNOW, THAT SOUNDS JUST RIGHT FOR OUR UNRULY NATION.

KIRBY MANGA MANIA 2: THE END!

Thank you for reading
Kirby Manga Mania vol. 2.

I still can't believe a talentless person
like me made it as a manga artist.
There are so many reasons for my success.

Credit goes to the folks in editorial who took
me under their wing and taught me; manga
master Shinbo Nomura, to whom I owe a ton;
my exceptional assistants; a character called
Kirby; and most of all, every reader who buys
my books. I've been helped along by so many
people. A special thank you to all of them.

The fact that I've been able to put out
two best-of comic collections now fills me
with emotion. These are all comics I put my
whole heart into back then, and they all
have some real sidesplitters. I hope you'll
enjoy reading them again and again!

HIROKAZU HIKAWA

Kirby Manga Mania Vol. 3 Coming Soon!

My favorite
copy ability
is sleep.

Did you enjoy volume 1? Volume 2 is presented with
another heaping serving of the spice of laughter.
Reading these old stories again fills me with
nostalgia as well as the sadness of knowing I
can no longer draw with that level of energy.

HIROKAZU HIKAWA

•••••••••••••••••••••••••••••••••••

Hirokazu Hikawa was born July 4, 1967,
in Aichi Prefecture. He is best known
for his manga adaptations of *Bonk* and
Kirby. In 1987, he won an honorable
mention for *Kaisei!! Aozora Kyoushitsu*
(Beautiful Day! Outdoor Classroom)
at the 14th Fujiko Fujio Awards.

Volume 2
VIZ Media Edition

Story and Art
HIROKAZU HIKAWA

TRANSLATION Amanda Haley
ENGLISH ADAPTATION Jennifer LeBlanc
TOUCH-UP ART + LETTERING Jeannie Lee
DESIGN Shawn Carrico
EDITOR Jennifer LeBlanc

©Nintendo / HAL Laboratory, Inc.

HOSHINO KIRBY - DEDEDE DE PUPUPU NA MONOGATARI - KESSAKUSEN PUPUPU HEN
by Hirokazu HIKAWA
© 2018 Hirokazu HIKAWA
All rights reserved.
Original Japanese edition published by SHOGAKUKAN.
English translation rights in the United States of America,
Canada, the United Kingdom, Ireland, Australia
and New Zealand arranged with SHOGAKUKAN.

ORIGINAL COVER DESIGN SEIKO TSUCHIHASHI [HIVE & CO., LTD.]

Printed in the U.S.A.

Published by VIZ Media, LLC
P.O. Box 77010
San Francisco, CA 94107

10 9 8 7 6 5 4 3 2 1
First printing, September 2021

viz.com

THIS IS THE LAST PAGE!

Kirby Manga Mania reads from right to left, starting in the upper-right corner. Japanese is read from right to left, meaning that action, sound effects and word-balloon order are completely reversed from English order.